A PLACE
CALLED
FAIRHAVENS

Paul Krebill

This is a work of fiction. Names, characters, places and incidents either are the product of the author's imagination or are used fictitiously, and any resemblance to any actual persons, living or dead, events, or locales is entirely coincidental.

This book was printed in the United States of America.

To order additional copies of this book, contact:
Xlibris Corporation
1-888-7-XLIBRIS
www.Xlibris.com
Orders@Xlibris.com

PART I

CHAPTER 1

There was a touch of fall in the air. In fact it felt quite crisp to those assembled at the cemetery on the outskirts of Tipton, Montana. The sun shone brilliantly under a vivid blue sky, almost totally cloudless, on the afternoon of Oral Sundquists' burial. "Beautiful day," the local mortician whispered to the bronze faced rancher standing next to him, one of the pall-bearers who had carried the casket and placed it over the open grave.

"It's gonna be a bad one though," the Tipton native replied, referring to the winter soon to come.

"Like '49, they say," the mortician responded under his breath as the preacher began the brief interment ritual.

Located in the northern edge of the Gallatin valley not far from the headwaters of the Missouri, Tipton is surrounded by mountain ranges. The Bridgers to the East; the Gallatin range in the south, and farther toward the horizon in the west are the Tobacco Roots. The grass lands of the broad valley floor had by this time of the year turned golden. Most of the recently harvested wheat strips were now stubble, alternating with strips of black fallow soil. The trees in the cemetery, mostly cotton-woods, had some of their leaves already showing yellow. The grass under foot was dry and dusty, as were the gravel lanes between blocks of burial plots. Stone monuments of various sizes, shapes and conditions were everywhere. Fortunately on this particular day in October the wind was not blowing.

A small group of people, mostly in their sixties and seventies, stood in solemn attention at a newly opened grave. The men wearing cowboy boots, stood stiffly in freshly washed Levis and denim jackets, a few in western-cut suit jackets. They held their broad-brimmed western hats nervously while the preacher intoned the words of the funeral service. Most of the women, were dressed in pant suits, as elderly rural women frequently wear. However, a few were in cotton dresses. Ill-fitting polyester car coats seemed to be the order of the day. The folks thus assembled bowed their heads during the final prayer offered by the town's only preacher:

"... until the shadows lengthen and the evening comes,
and the busy world is hushed, and the fever of life is over,
and our work is done, then in Thy great mercy grant us a
safe lodging, and a holy rest, and peace at the last ..."

As the young minister read the concluding phrases of the traditional prayer for the grave side, his mind turned over the words he'd just read, "safe lodging ... rest ... peace ..." How those words bore in upon his mind on this October morning as he stood facing the tiny group of mourners with bowed heads. His duties had often brought him to this tiny country cemetery at the base of the Bridger Mountains of Montana. Before him was the open grave prepared for Oral Sundquist. Oral had been the young minister's only true supporter. In fact at the Session meeting a week before, Oral had been the only member to speak in favor of the preacher's ideas throughout the meeting. If that church board meeting had not signaled the end of Max Ritter's ministry at Tipton, certainly now Oral's untimely death foreshadowed Max's defeat as a young pastor in his first parish. Only two years after seminary graduation and he was feeling like a failure. He should have stayed in the hotel business, he thought.

Max and Gwen Ritter had moved to Montana from Chicago. If you were to ask most members of the congregation in Tipton to describe their minister they would probably have mentioned first that he was from Chicago. That was seen as the first strike against him. They would say that he was a serious sort of young man. He approached his work quite responsibly, obviously working long hours on the preparation of each Sunday service and sermon. Some said he studied too much, for his sermons were "hard to follow," they said. He was friendly but seemed just a bit reserved. "Big city ways," some said. Gwendolyn, the preacher's wife, was on the shy side. This was seen by not a few as "stand-offishness." The fact that the minister and his wife took Mondays off and spent most of them away from Tipton did not escape the notice of the congregation. They knew that most of those days found their preacher and his wife in the university town of Bozeman, less than twenty-five miles away. Or when the weather was good and roads were open they were known often to be in Butte, an hour and half to the west, or in Billings three hours east. Oral Sundquist had often said when the subject came up, "Let 'em get away. They're in a fish-bowl around here. Besides, if going to Butte keeps them from missing Chicago, they'll stay here longer." While this reasoning made a lot of sense to Oral, he seldom found much agreement. The last time the subject had come up was when a group of church members had been visiting with one another during the noon lunch at a local farm auction. One of the women responded to Oral's defense, "If they like Butte so much, they oughta move there. They don't fit here."

"Yeah, like the last one!" her husband retorted.

At this Oral took up the defense again: "Why don't you look at the good things?"

"What things?" someone in the group challenged.

"Lots of things—been a while since we've had a preacher give such good funerals as Max does." To this evaluation there was some reluctant agreement voiced, especially by the widows in the group.

"Safe lodging . . . rest . . . and above all . . . peace!" These conditions Max craved as he surveyed the little clutch of his detractors. So many of the people opposed him. Like Delbert Owen standing there with an angry face. Always negative, especially toward any ideas Max presented. In fact at the last Session meeting Max had suggested: "I'd like to start a Sunday morning adult class."

"On what?" Owen had snapped.

"On current problems. "Answers for Today," Max said he would call it.

"That's meddling, preacher. Stick to the Bible." An unfriendly sort—Delbert Owen. His wife, Mona, appeared friendly and co-operative on the surface; but she would never cross her husband; and so she too gave little support to the preacher.

At the conclusion of the grave-side committal, the tiny con-gregation stood around engaging in comfortable conversation, mostly about the weather, the crops, or the price of cattle. They all knew each other quite well. Most had lived in Tipton all their lives. Since Oral Sundquist had been a bachelor, there were no bereaved family members to console.

The Rev. Maxwell Ritter waited at the head of the grave while the funeral director from Bozeman busied himself with the floral pieces. After a respectable interval he and his assistant cranked down the straps, lowering the casket into the grave until it rested on the base of the metal vault.

Eventually the little crowd ambled toward their dusty cars and pick-ups. When the first of the vehicles started its engine the mortician signaled to the two cemetery workers who had been lurking in the background, "O K, boys," he said in a suitably subdued voice. They came forward and lifted the metal vault which had been placed ten or so feet away, and lowered it into the grave. As one of the workers brought over a tractor with a blade to fill in the grave, the funeral director ushered Max Ritter into the passen-ger door of the polished black Cadillac funeral coach to be driven by the mortician's assistant.

During the fifteen minutes it had taken for the crowd to dis-perse, no one had said anything to Max. At such occasions in the past Oral Sundquist had often stepped over to Max and said, "Good job!" But he was gone now.

There were other things to think about as the Rev. Mr. Max Ritter rode home in the stately funeral coach. Fortunately the mortician's assistant wasn't very talkative. This gave Max time to think about the wedding he was to perform in three and a half hours. The couple were not members of his congregation, not at all unusual, he reflected. Beyond that, the two didn't seem well suited for each other. Also not unusual, he thought.

When seven o'clock came, the church was packed. Many more seats were filled than on Sundays, Max thought. Most of the afternoon's grave-side mourners were now present for the wedding. The candles were flickering: the bridesmaids in pale green were excited; and the groomsmen looked uncomfortably dressed up. They had on black levis, blue formal shirts, black tuxedo jackets and large black cowboy hats to match. Max had asked them to remove their "ten gallon" hats at the signal when he said "Let us pray!" The attendants had reluctantly agreed.

During the wedding ceremony Max's mind wandered once again, as it had done earlier during the funeral. This time as he prayed:

> "Guide them together, we beseech Thee, in the way of righteousness and peace, that loving and serving Thee, with one heart and mind, all the days of their life, they may be abundantly enriched with the tokens of thine everlasting favor . . ."

Still ringing in his ear were the final words of the vows: "As long as we both shall live."

Max was reminded of a popular revision: "as long as we both shall love," and wondered if such a version might be more honest; though he was repelled by the idea of changing the wedding service in so radical a way to accommodate the modern weakened view of marriage. One letter changed and the entire vow is corrupted by the changeable whims and foibles of human selfishness. An "o" for an "i"! But who was he to say? What about his own marriage? A vague nameless anger surged through his consciousness. He determined in that moment to by-pass the reception to be held at the local lodge hall. Oh how he hated wedding receptions, especially the wedding parties of those whose entire family and circle of friends could care less about the church or about him as its current minister. If the truth were told, Max had a deeply imbedded shy streak.

After waiting around until the last well-wisher was out of the church door, Max shut off the lights in the small sanctuary, made sure the candles had been snuffed out, locked the little frame building and walked across the weedy lawn to the dilapidated manse. When he came up to the house he was surprised to find it dark. That was strange. Gwendolyn had not gone to the wedding. She never did. So far as he knew she had not gone out on any errands. She should by all accounts be home. It was too early for her to be in bed.

As he opened the door, he felt an uneasy quiet within the ancient parsonage. He turned on a lamp and called, "Gwen, I'm home!" There was no answer. She was not in the living room or kitchen. He climbed the steep narrow stairway to the second floor where they had their bedroom. He did not find her there. But to his shock he found her clothes closet emptied and her suitcase gone from its place in the closet. Next he checked the garage and found their vintage Subaru missing. Stunned by her absence and apparent departure he needed time to think. He fixed himself a cup of instant coffee and sat down at the old wooden kitchen table—dazed. No note. But he could imagine what the note would have said. Something on this order: "I can't take it any longer. Don't follow me. I need time with my own kind." So this is the way! He'd always wondered how it would come, especially lately as a sense of foreboding had intensified. Last night he had finally told her about the recent Session meeting and how everyone except Oral had opposed him. He told her that some of the elders had been downright mean about it, like Delbert Owen. Yes, nasty! And then he and Gwen had reminded themselves of the subtle ways many of the women had been cruel to Gwendolyn. Never really accepting her as part of the community, they had made it clear how they felt about her. She had not been invited to many gatherings. But now as Max thought about it, when she had been invited to an extension club meeting in their first few months, she

had turned down the invitation. Oh, there was more, but why go
all over that again.

Hers had been a fairly upper-class background at home and in
her college and sorority experience. The "come down" to Tipton,
Montana had been a jolt to say the least, he'd have to admit. She
had not been happy here. A feeling of sorrowful compassion over-
came him as he thought about what he had done to Gwen in
bringing her here. When they had first met she had assumed he
was headed for a career in the hotel business. Then, without much
warning, he had dragged her along as he attended the required
three years of theological seminary; and then to Tipton. He was
overcome with a feeling of sadness for Gwen. She had been lonely;
and he told himself that he had done little to help her adjust to
the rigors of being a pastor's wife in a tiny Montana town.

Long after the dregs of his coffee cup had gone cold Max had
to rouse himself, for there was tomorrow morning's 10:30 service.
Why did tough things always seem to happen on Saturdays! Added
to his normal Sunday duties, he would have to peddle some sort of
story in answer to the many not so well intentioned questions:
"Where is Mrs. Ritter, this morning, Reverend?" Fortunately, this
would be a shortened Sunday morning; for he had a scheduled
trip to Denver immediately after the sermon. He was to fly out of
the local airport at 12:30 for a denominational conference. That
brought up another problem. With the car gone, how would he
get to the airport twenty miles away? He didn't want to admit the
disappearance of his car to anyone in the congregation.

He decided to call Dale Kober who ran the local Conoco station. A good feeling filled him temporarily as he thought about
Dale. He had been the only person in town Max had been able to
call a friend; and ironically Dale was not a church attender. Dale
and his wife, Maude, had come to Tipton from North Dakota
some years back to take over the only oil company in town. Well
liked by the community they had easily fit into the life of Tipton.
"Nice people—runs a good station and bulk plant," everyone said.
Max had traded at the Conoco ever since moving to Tipton. A

friendship had developed between the two men as Max had begun to depend more and more upon Dale for his car repair and maintenance needs; and, strange to say-for personal friendship as well. Since Dale had the bulk plant in addition to the service station, he had contact with many of the Tipton area farmers and ranchers who were members of Max's congregation. Max guessed that Dale had a fairly good idea of how people felt about him. He respected Dale for not letting any of that rub off. In fact, if the truth were known, Dale increasingly reached out in friendship to Max as his ratings in the congregation sank. All this had made Max question sometimes who the real Christians in the community were! Dale was the sort of man among men who did not allow his soft side to be seen, but Max could feel it. Many times after a particularly difficult meeting or before making an awkward call, Max's gasoline stop at Dale's had given him the boost he needed.

Without hesitation Max dialed Dale's number:

"Hulo, Tipton Conoco—Dale speaking."

"Dale, this is Max. I've got a problem.

"What's that?"

"My wife's got the car and I have to get to the airport tomorrow morning by 11:45 right after my service—really right after the sermon. Any chance for a lift?"

"Sure, buddy—no problem."

"Thanks, Dale."

"Any time! I'll be there—outside I mean!"

"Outside's fine—that's where I need you! I figure that about 11:15 would do it. Thanks, Dale. I'll see you then."

The next morning with the sermon over, admittedly a bit shorter on this particular Sunday, the Rev. Max Ritter dashed over to his study in the manse, grabbed his suitcase, and made a last check of his desk and file for things to include in his briefcase. Flipping through the file drawers just on a curious whim, he took out his passport and put it in his briefcase. Then he was out of the manse and ran to the curb where Dale Kober was waiting with the motor running in his new Chevy 4x4 pick-up. As Max ran the

short distance from the house to the Chevy he heard the final
hymn, which the Tipton congregation always sang at the end of
every service:

"God be with you 'till we meet again,
By his counsels guide uphold you,
With his sheep securely fold you."

"What you goin' to Denver for?" Dale asked as they sped off.

"Got a church meeting there through Wednesday." Max felt a
rush of personal warmth for this big burly mechanic who had
befriended him as no-one in the congregation had. The way he felt
at this point, he needed Dale for more than a lift to airport. And so
he told him, "Dale, nobody knows this, but it'll come out. My wife
left me yesterday. That's why I didn't have a car to take to the airport."

"Oh, man, I'm sorry. That's a bad deal."

"Yeah, and I don't know where she went or how. My only
hope is that it is temporary."

"If there's anything Maude and I can do, Reverend, let us
know, you've got our number! And we'll keep mum about it."

"Thanks, Dale. That means a lot."

They remained quiet until they got into the airport terminal
area and drove by the long-term parking lot, when Dale said, "Look,
there's your Sub!"

"So, she's flown somewhere," Max said, as if to himself. "Probably home to her family in Illinois." And then turning to his friend,
"Dale, here's my car key. Would you mind having somebody pick
up the car and bring it back to my garage?"

"Sure! My kid, Sonny. He's always wantin' to drive—anywhere."

Dale drove up to the terminal entry and Max got out, "So
long, Dale. Thanks a lot for the lift! . . . and for everything . . ."

"That's ok—anytime."

With that the young minister disappeared into the terminal;
and the Conoco dealer drove off thinking about what had been
told to him by this new friend.

The 737 lifted off, flying west away from the Bridger mountains, over Tipton, before veering sharply to the south and then on a straight line to Salt Lake City. Max could see the entire town of Tipton below him from his window seat. The plane cast a small cross-shaped shadow which raced across the town as it disappeared to the South.

The 737 shadow swung over Mona Owen's house as she stood at her electric range frying chicken for Delbert's Sunday Dinner. As the frying pan sizzled, she heard a jet overhead; and said to her husband, "There goes the Reverend's plane, Delbert!"

"Yeah, glad he's gone. Good riddance!"

"Delbert, where was his Missus this morning? Hear anything about it?"

"No, but I got my suspicions."

"What do you mean?"

"Why did he have Dale take him to the airport. He could have driven that Jap car of his."

Mona confessed, "I had a look in his garage window after church. It was gone!"

Delbert didn't reply. That's how he often treated his wife's interesting information.

"What do you think that means, Delbert?"

"I don't know, but are you thinkin' what I am?" he intimated.

"Well, if you really want to know, Phyllis Hollier told me that she saw the Reverend's missus driving toward the airport yesterday afternoon during the wedding! I think she's left him!"

"Could have been a trip back to her people . . . wherever it is she came from," Delbert offered without much conviction.

"I don't think so. I just have a feeling. The way the Reverend answered, when we asked about her this morning. It just gave me the idea she may have flown the coop!"

"That boy's a dud every way you look at it."

High above and miles away Max rested back in his window seat to immerse himself in deep thought. So much had needed to be done since discovering his wife's absence the evening before. It wasn't until now that he could ponder what had occurred. His attempt to phone Gwen's parents the night before had met with a constant busy signal. Hopefully there would be time to try again from the air terminal. If not in Salt Lake City, then from Denver. His thoughts formed a heavy shroud around him until he was interrupted finally by the flight attendant announcing:

"We have begun our descent into Salt Lake City. Please fasten your seat belts and place your seat backs in the upright position."

As Max prepared for the landing in Salt Lake City he felt overwhelmed by a sense of profound loss, the double loss of his wife and of his desire to be in Tipton anymore.

He was to change planes in Salt Lake for a flight to Denver. But as the plane was landing another announcement came over the cabin loud speaker:

"Passengers scheduled for flight number 1047 for Denver please check at the Delta information desk. Your Denver flight has been canceled due to bad weather over the Colorado Rockies." Max realized that 1047 was his flight.

After waiting the usual interminable few minutes until the cabin doors were opened he walked out onto Concourse D and hurried to Delta Information. At the Delta Information Desk the agent said: "The earliest flight we can get you on will be 6:30 tomorrow morning. May I put you on that flight?"

"Please do, if that's the best you can give me."

Max located the nearest pay-phone. With a certain amount of trepidation he dialed Gwen's parents number. After six or seven rings he was about to hang up when there was an answer. He recognized her father. "Hello"

"Hello, this is Max, may I . . ."

He heard the receiver quietly replaced, and the line went dead. So that's how it is, he thought. I'll have to write; but not much hope for that either.

He slowly walked along the concourse and spotted the City Deli. He stopped for a snack and a cup of coffee and some time to decide what to do next. He found a seat at the only empty table.

As he took a bite from his corned beef sandwich a distinguished looking man in his fifties, balancing a cup of coffee and a doughnut, came up to Max's table and asked: "May I join you? There doesn't seem to be any seats left."

"Certainly." Max replied.

The stranger was wearing a neatly pressed western style suit, powder gray in color. A silver bolo tie adorned a striped western shirt. He was not wearing a hat to cover his balding head.

"Where have you come from?" Max asked after the man was seated.

"I just got off the flight from Billings. Got a little time before my Chicago flight. How about you?"

"I've come from Bozeman. I'm trying to get to Denver, but that flight's been canceled. Nothing until morning."

"That's too bad. I'd have been on your flight since I'm really from Park County. But the only seat I could get was on a flight out of Billings, so I drove over to Billings."

"Park County—Livingston?"

"No, actually up Paradise Valley where I manage a resort. You live in Bozeman?"

"I'm from Tipton." Max replied guardedly. He did not feel inclined to tell about his clergy status. "I don't think I know where Paradise Valley is."

"South of Livingston along the Yellowstone River"

"On the way to the Park?"

"That's right," the man said, finishing the subject. "Family in Denver?"

"No, I'm going there for a conference," Max replied and quickly asked, "What takes you to Chicago?"

"It's a business trip."

After a few more minutes of small talk the stranger looked at his watch, finished his coffee and said, "I'd better get over to my gate now. Quite a ways to Concourse B. Thanks for the seat."

"You're welcome. Good talking to you."

Max was left to figure out what he would do until morning.

By this time it was three o'clock. He made his way to one of the Delta gate lounges and took a seat some distance from where passengers were waiting for their flight. His immediate obligation was the Denver conference; but his more important concern was Gwen. On that he was totally frustrated. Maybe time would help. Luckily he had given her his phone number at the conference. All the more urgent was it for him to get there—in case she was trying to reach him. Although, he thought, she may not want to talk to him at this point.

Tipton was another matter. He'd just as soon not see those people again—except, maybe, Dale. But the conference was scheduled to adjourn Wednesday noon, and by late that night he was scheduled to arrive back home. Home alone. Then what? But that was Wednesday. He needed to make some arrangements for himself until his flight in the morning.

CHAPTER 2

After leaving the crowded City Deli Dr. Conrad Schneider hurried along the concourse as rapidly as possible, weaving in and out of the crowd in order to reach his Chicago flight at the end of Concourse D. When he arrived at his gate he joined the line of passengers already boarding. He arrived in his window seat only minutes before the cabin door was shut. Soon he was in the air looking down upon Salt Lake City, as the pilot circled east toward the Wasatch range.

Finally catching his breath he began thinking about his Chicago destination and what would follow. With a mixture of urgency and apprehension he contemplated the appointment in downtown Chicago. He'd not seen Craig Warren since college, but they had exchanged Christmas correspondence most years since college. Twenty-five years out of law school and Craig was a partner in a prestigious Chicago law firm. Besides, Con Schneider thought—and this might prove to be even more significant—he's an elder in his church out in the suburbs. Hopefully, that, plus what Conrad remembered of Craig's interest in social causes during college should make him look positively at the project.

Looking down on the Wasatch, Conrad continued his line of thought: So, I'll hope for a good hearing. Can't really expect more at this stage. I'll just do my best to get Craig interested in Fairhavens. Then maybe he'll give me some funding ideas. And perhaps some names of people I can talk to.

As the 727 droned on eastward over the pristine golden plains of Wyoming, Conrad could not help but prepare himself for the upcoming interview. This trip was one of extreme urgency as far as Conrad Schneider was concerned. While he pondered business matters he could see the ground far down below. There were no clouds to keep him from noticing the tiny strands of I-80 as it stretched across the dry grass of the Great Plains. It would be some time before he would see anything resembling a city. Perhaps Cheyenne later; and in an hour and a half, not long before landing, he'd see the Mississippi cutting the continent in two, unless the usual overcast of the Midwest obscured the view. And then Chicago, most likely covered with gray clouds, as so often he'd known it to be.

The previous Monday afternoon Conrad Schneider had attended a gathering of locals at the Yellowstone Inn in Livingston. What he had heard there had threatened to undermine the most important thing in his life—Fairhavens.

"A Place Called Fairhavens:

A Center for Retreat, Recreation, and Renewal in Paradise Valley

Pray, Montana—59065

Dr. Conrad Schneider, Director."

So stated the Fairhavens letterhead at the top. Across the bottom of the stationery the mountains along the upper Yellowstone River were depicted. Fairhavens was situated in the lush grasslands of Paradise Valley at the foot of the Absaroka mountains facing the broad and placid Yellowstone flowing nearby to the west. Untouched by modern commercial development, Paradise Valley is a sparsely populated area of Montana ranches adjoining the northern border of Yellowstone National Park.

The founder-director of Fairhavens had joined many of his neighbors in responding to an invitation, which had boasted: "Come to a special presentation by Mr. Cody Vermillian of Las Vegas, Nevada, who is offering a very unique opportunity for landowners and residents in the Paradise Valley. Come and learn how you can get in on the ground floor of the most exciting development in the history of Park County. Refreshments at 2 PM, Presentation at 3 PM. At the Best Western Yellowstone Inn and Convention Center, Livingston, Montana on September thirteenth"

Arriving a few minutes before three Conrad went to the designated conference room and picked up a cup of punch and a few fancy cookies from the lavish buffet table. He found that many of his friends and neighbors from up the Yellowstone were there. Circulating among the crowd of locals was a man in a flashy western-cut suit. He sported a large jade bolo tie, and was wearing brand new cowboy boots. The thing that spoiled his carefully planned image was the fact that his western pants were tucked inside his boot tops, something one never sees among authentic westerners. With him was an attractive young woman in a tightly clinging black dress with a very short mini-skirt. When not listening to the man with the tucked-in boots she busied herself with stacks of brochures at the head-table. Conrad also noticed a couple of other men in suits, whom he did not recognize. They were less conspicuously dressed in ordinary, but expensive business suits, but still out of place in a room where no other suits were to be seen. Conrad had worn a cardigan with an open sport shirt.

It was almost three when the man with the jade bolo came up to Conrad and introduced himself, "Hello, my name is Cody Vermillian, and I'm very glad that you have come. You are?"

"Yes, Hello, I'm Conrad Schneider from Fairhavens,"

When Vermillian heard "Fairhavens" his eyes seemed to enlarge and he said. "Fairhavens! I really want a chance to talk with you in private. Would you mind staying afterward? I've got something very special to offer you."

"Why, yes, I guess I could stick around."

"Good, I've got to get this show on the road now; so I'll talk to you later," Vermillian said as he strode up to the table in the front of the room.

At three o'clock the crowd took their seats. Cody Vermillian and the other two strangers in suits took their places at the cloth covered banquet table in front. On another table to the side there appeared to be a display of some kind, also covered with a green table cloth. Nearby stood an easel with presentation boards reversed so that they could not be seen at this point.

One of the men stood up, went to the lectern and began:

"Good afternoon, friends, I'm Worth Benson of the Benson & Anderson law firm in Billings. On my left is Todd Brown of the B.J.T. Architectural firm in Billings. And on my right is the man who has called us together this afternoon! Mr. Cody Vermillian, formerly of Las Vegas, Nevada, and now of Emigrant, Montana. I'm pleased to present to you Mr. Vermillian!"

Cody Vermillian stood up and began: "Thank you, Worth! And Howdy Neighbors!" He seemed to wait a moment for some response, but hearing none he began again: "Thank you for coming up to Livingston today."

Conrad remarked to himself that he should have said "down" not "up" to Livingston. For that's the way the Yellowstone River flowed–down from Yellowstone Park to Livingston.

Cody Vermillian continued, "and before we're done I believe you'll be thanking us! Because what we have to show you this afternoon will be the most exciting thing ever to have come to the Paradise Valley—except, of course, the gold itself! We plan to turn 'our valley' into one of the most visited tourist Meccas in Montana or Wyoming—except, of course, Yellowstone itself! What you are going to see this afternoon is the architectural rendering of the proposed PARADISE PLAYTIME RESORT AND RENDEZ-VOUS. Todd, show the folks our plans!"

At this point Todd Brown stepped up and unveiled an architects' model of an extensive resort development, designed in nineteenth century frontier style and decor. He then turned the presentation boards so that they faced the audience. He prepared to flip the boards to coordinate with items in Cody's presentation.

Cody continued: "Folks, what you see here in this model is a super five star resort which our organization plans to put in at Emigrant Gulch. It will include the following: An 1870's Western Mining town with a main street complete with gift shops, restaurants, old time bars, and three casinos; Main Street will continue up Emigrant Gulch with typical 1870's buildings on both sides of a picturesque winding street. Each building will be one of the typical mining town buildings—assay office, newspaper office, mens clothing, drug store, etc. You get the idea! Each of these in actuality is to be a guest cabin related to the main hotel. There'll be horse barns for guest riding, an old fashioned casino-bordello style cocktail lounge. And more. An 18 hole golf course. An Olympic sized swimming pool which will be covered with a plexi-glass dome for winter use—for you know what 'our' winters are! Right?" He waited a moment for laughter. But the crowd was silent. Vermillian continued, undismayed, "Of course the pool will have removable panels for summer use. The pool will be shielded from view by a 'mountain' installed so that the modern pool doesn't clash with the 1870's decor; A three story 1870's vintage hotel will be the center-piece. We plan an underground parking garage so as not to spoil the western mining town look.

And finally we plan to sub-divide all the adjoining land into parcels in order to provide 170 half-acre homesites. This, of course, will mean tearing down the present shacks along the gulch as well as the removal of the present lodge building at—what's it called? Ah—ah—ah, Fairway, I think it is."

Conrad Schneider had been listening with increasing agitation. When he heard the casual, misnamed reference to Fairhavens and its destruction, he could barely stay in the room. But Cody continued unaware that Conrad and most of the locals had become acutely disturbed by the whole scheme. "We plan to build re-created mines and ore processing plants. In every way we want to give the public a view of how it was in the gold-mining era. In fact—get this!—we even plan to put in an authentic-appearing period cemetery!

"What I've listed so far will be Phase I. We also plan phase II which will include a private air strip for small jets, a chalet for cross-country skiers, and an Olympic size ice skating rink!"

At the conclusion of this stunning list Cody paused, as if to anticipate applause. The only audible reaction of the crowd was a nervous shuffling. Undaunted, Cody sought to enlist further interest and curiosity: "Now I know you will have questions, so I want to open the floor for questions. We have five minutes remain-

ing for questions. I promised to get you out of here by 3:30."
There were questions, lots of them concerning how the project
would be financed; and about water: where would enough be found
to support such a large development? And about the necessary
employee work-force, where would it come from and where would
there be sufficient housing for them? How did Vermillian propose
to obtain the amount of property needed? Where would all this be
located, in addition to the Gulch itself? Isn't this development to
be located at or near the present location of Fairhavens? What about
county land-use restrictions and the E.P.A. standards?

Instead of giving any clear answers to these questions the developer assured the audience that he has a team of "experts" from
his company in Las Vegas working out answers to everything, which
has been brought up. "All very good questions, by the way! Now
before we close, Todd, do you have anything to add?" The architect wanted folks to be sure to look at the model site plan on the
table and to have another look at any of the presentation boards on
the easel.

"Worth, anything from our attorneys?"

As if on cue the attorney stated: "Just want all of you to know
that this will be done in the most proper manner possible. We will
be meeting with the county planning people tomorrow; and in
the next week or two representatives of our firm will be contacting
any of you who are property owners in the targeted area. I think
you'll find our offers quite attractive. Thank you."

Cody, obviously impressed with his presentation concluded
with a note of victory in his voice, "Well, folks, that's it for now.
My secretary will give you a descriptive project proposal brochure
on your way out; and before you leave come up and have a look at
this beautiful model of our project! That's it, neighbors, I look
forward to seeing you at all the community functions from here
on!" The young woman in the tight dress with the mini skirt gathered up a stack of brochures and walked through the crowd to the
door where she stood waiting to distribute them as people filed
out of the conference room.

The crowd arose. Most of the local ranchers and residents of Paradise Valley left quietly without saying much, and without looking at the graphic displays in the front of the room. Conrad noticed that the only people to gather to see the displays and to talk with the development group seemed to be residents from town. In fact, the only hint of enthusiasm that Conrad could see was on the part of Clyde Blackwood, the director of Park County Chamber of Commerce. He had buttonholed Cody and appeared to be deep in conversation with him. This troubled Con because Clyde Blackwood, among his many local connections, served on the Fairhavens Board of Directors.

Conrad hated the thought of having to meet with Vermillian and his men; but on the other hand, he was curious to know what they wanted. It probably had to do with the Fairhavens property. After the crowd dispersed Cody Vermillian, accompanied by Worth Benson, led Conrad to a table in the empty restaurant of the Inn. While waitresses were preparing the tables for the evening meal, Cody started immediately into the matter at hand. "Now, Dr. Schneider, you, no doubt, picked up on my reference to Fairway."

"It's Fairhavens, Mr. Vermillian."

"Oh yes, Fairhavens. Now, if you observed carefully our site plan. you will have seen that the major center of our development is slated for the very site of Fairhavens Lodge. Since you are merely renters, we have taken steps to purchase that property from its absentee owners. We thought it only fair to let you know that. Worth, why don't you explain where we are on this."

"Well, we have consulted with the owners and they are eager to sell to us as soon as the way be clear. And that, you probably know involves removing the first option to buy, which was given to the Fairhavens Board when your project was begun some years ago. Our understanding is that the $175,000 selling price for the property is prohibitive to your people; and so we think it is just a matter of form for the owner—after a rejection of the first option— to go ahead and accept our own purchase offer. And to be perfectly honest, the lodge and the other buildings on the property will need to be razed. That reduces the value of the property to us to $125,000, which is the price we will offer the owners. Any questions, Dr. Schneider?"

"No, what you say is quite clear, although I find it most unacceptable."

"I don't understand what you mean, Sir." Cody cut in.

"What I mean is that, the loss of the lodge and this location would amount to the end of our project; and you can't expect me to accept that with a smile and a pat on the back. As a non-profit organization we are not in a position to compete with commercial developments.

"What do you mean, non-profit? I thought you were a small resort hotel." Cody replied.

"Fairhavens is a non-profit corporation under the laws of the state of Montana dedicated to providing people therapeutic retreat and restoration on a sliding fee scale. Those who come only for recreation pay the going rate, but that revenue is what makes our sliding fees possible. Furthermore, we believe that our location near Yellowstone in a semi-isolated environment is critical to our mission."

After a brief private conversation with his attorney Cody offered, "Dr. Schneider, in light of what you have told us just now, we are prepared to sell to the Fairhavens Board, at a somewhat reduced price, one of our half-acre homesites, provided your improvements conform to our style and standards."

Conrad, preparing to leave, said, "Gentlemen, I need to return to my duties. How much time do we have?"

"You mean to purchase a homesite?" Cody said.

"No, to take up our option to buy the Fairhavens property."

"Oh? Worth, can you answer that?"

"Yes, It isn't very long. It is by the original agreement one month from the firm offer, which means that you have two weeks remaining."

"Thank you, our attorney will be contacting the owners shortly. Now, Good evening to you." With that Conrad hurried out to his car, confronted with the dire urgency of obtaining the $175,000.

And sickened by the appalling spectacle of what Vermillian planned to do to Fairhavens and with Paradise Valley.

For the duration of his flight to Chicago, Conrad's mind raced over and over the problem facing Fairhavens; until the plane was on the ground at O'Hare, the seat belt signs were turned off, and he was standing up waiting for the cabin door to open. Once in the terminal he put in a call to a nearby motel for a room for the night. He would not be able to see Craig until the morning.

CHAPTER 3

After a night of fitful sleep Con awakened anticipating his crucial meeting with Craig Warren. His appointment was for 9:15 in the morning. He checked out and took the motel courtesy van back to O'Hare. Rain was coming down in torrents. Under a cloud darkened sky headlights reflected on the wet pavement of the busy free-ways leading into and out of the world's busiest airport. He was deposited on the departure level from which it was an easy walk through the terminal to public transportation. Soon he was on the crowded "El" careening toward the Loop with the rain pelting the grimy windows of the commuter train.

Again his mind began mulling the Fairhavens problem. The really scary thing about this Las Vegas developer's plan was that he had already made a firm offer to buy the Lodge property from the family who owned it. Technically the property had been on the market for $175,000 for the last couple of years; but everybody thought that it would not sell and that the Fairhavens board would probably be able to continue leasing it for the forseeable future. Such had been the assumption until Cody Vermillian appeared in the valley, he thought as he watched the city speed by.

Chicago was familiar to Con Schneider. He'd grown up on the far south side—Morgan Park to be exact. Soon the sound of the moving train changed pitch and the windows went black; no longer rain-soaked as the rapid transit entered the subway. Now at each stop when the doors opened he smelled the familiar dank odor and heard the hollow echos in the underground tube. It would not be many more stops before he would recognize the one nearest Craig's office, Randolph, in the Loop.

Once up on the street with the rain still coming down, he very quickly entered the revolving doors of the office building in which Craig's law firm was located. He walked across the marble lobby with high vaulted ceiling, he pressed the button, and almost immediately he stepped into the express elevator compartment and was surrounded with its mirrored walls. His mind couldn't stop, as the elevator shot upward to the twenty-third floor. Cody Vermillian, a new and dangerous player had entered the field. Conrad feared that, given enough pressure from Vermillian, the family would sell. That would be the end of the Fairhavens project—just when it was beginning to fly! If he could just beat the hotshot developer to the buy-sell! $175,000 would pull it off, but how in the world could he come up with that kind of money? That's why he had come to Chicago.

He stepped off the elevator onto the 23rd floor and entered directly into the lavishly appointed reception lounge of Craig's law offices. The firm occupies the entire floor, he surmised, as he stepped up to the mahogany desk from which a young and attractive receptionist greeted him: "Good morning, sir. May I help you?"

"I'm Dr. Conrad Schneider to see Craig Warren."

"Do you have an appointment to see Mr. Warren, Sir?"

"Yes, at 9:30."

"Thank you," she said as she reviewed her appointment book. "Yes, I see. Please have a seat. It will be just a few minutes. Mr. Warren is seeing someone just now. May I get you a cup of coffee, Sir?"

"No, thank you." Conrad replied as he took a seat. He picked up a "Fortune" magazine to fill the time. Conrad was further impressed as he heard the receptionist frequently answer the low unobtrusive ring of the phone: "Good morning! Law Offices: Collins, Engstrom and Warren! How may I direct your call?"

After about ten minutes the receptionist addressed him, "Mr. Warren will see you now. Come this way."

"May I leave my carry-on bag with you while I see Mr. Warren?"

"Certainly, sir," and she led him down a long mahogany paneled corridor lined with offices on both sides. Along the walls hanging between the office doors, were artists renderings of well-known Chicago buildings, most of which were representative of what is known as the Chicago school of architecture. Before they reached the far end of the hall, Craig Warren came out of his office dressed in expensive navy blue cuffed trousers and a starched white shirt. He wore a red and blue striped bow tie, framed by dark blue suspenders. He exuberantly extended his hand to Conrad, "Con! So good to see you—after all these years!"

"And great to see you, Craig! Not since college."

"A lot has gone under the bridge since then."

"Yes, it has," Con replied, "We'll have to catch up."

"You're right; and as a matter of fact Lynn and I would like to have you in for dinner this evening. what do you say?"

"I'd like that. I know we can't take up your office time on the memory thing!"

"We have a condo out in Oak Park. Before we're through I'll give you directions. About 6:30, OK?" Warren said cordially, "Now, tell me what really brings you here, Con," the attorney asked in a professional tone.

Con nervously thought: this is my chance. I better make it good! He began "Well, you know what our Fairhavens project is all about, I'm sure. It's been written up in the Alumni Bulletin; and you've heard more than you want to know from my Christmas letters, I'm sure." He paused while Craig nodded. Anyway, at this point in time the project's survival is severely threatened, and I must find the funds to avert its demise."

"How much are we talking about?" Craig inquired.

"$175,000—and, by the way, I'm not asking you for the funds. But let me explain what has happened." For the next thirty minutes Conrad shared the story of the Nevada developer, the proposed development, and the impending purchase of the property out from under the Fairhavens project.

Craig took notes on his yellow legal pad and from time to time interrupted with a question of clarification.

When Con finished his account he addressed Craig: "What I have come to you for, is for advice. I know you are acquainted with various private funding sources; and you must be aware of how and where cultural and human services agencies obtain major contributions and grants. Fairhavens needs some of those contacts. In our isolated location we just don't have ready access to such resources. What comes to mind, Craig? Or am I out in left field?"

"Oh no, 175 isn't all that much; but I'm going to need to do a little research." At this point Craig got his law clerk on the intercom and asked, "Michael, will you get me the list of contributors to the capital campaign we helped with last year for The Evanston Home?"

He turned to Con and said,"I'm on the board for a Presbyterian Retirement Home up in Evanston. In that connection I helped on a major gifts campaign conducted last year for a new wing."

There was a quiet knock on the door and the law clerk brought in a file folder. Craig found the page and began running his pen down the list of donors. Con watched and saw him stop about half way down the page.

"Now, here is a real possibility, Con: Mrs. Huntley Baxter, a widow with ample resources, who has a special interest in social service agencies. In her earlier years she had been a social worker. Her late husband had owned a string of shopping malls throughout the Midwest. She is a Presbyterian elder in the River Forest church. You might enlist her interest. That would be a start. I tell you what: I'll phone her and give her a thumb-nail on Fairhavens. I'll try to set up an appointment for you. By tonight when you are out at the house, I should have an answer."

"That would be great!"

"Well, we'll see if it is. Let's get a few more names here," The lawyer continued as if to himself. Conrad Schneider looked out the tall windows of Craig Warren's office. In the distance through the gray, rain-spattered atmosphere he identified the Sears Tower and the Standard Oil building. Good to be back home in Chicago, Con thought to himself while he waited for Craig to complete his review of contributors.

Craig took down a few more names, closed the file, and said, "I see a few more possibilities, but none as good as Leona Baxter. I'll get in touch with her and see what I can arrange."

Con could see that his time was up and that he had better prepare to leave. "Well, Craig, you're going the extra mile—when all I was coming for was advice!"

"The least I can do."

"I'll look forward to seeing you and Lynn this evening."

"Good, here's how to get to our home. Take the Eisenhower to Harlem and go up past Lake Street one block; turn right and our building is on your right. Here's my card with address and phone. Look for you at 6:30!"

As Conrad descended to the street in the mirrored elevator he continued to feel the excitement of his interview. He realized he needed two things immediately: a room for the night, and a car rental. Down on the street, the rain had almost completely stopped. He found himself in front of the Palmer House.—Expensive, but handy, oh well, let's go for it, he thought. He entered and walked through the street-level arcade of upscale shops and found an elevator up to the lobby. He stepped over to Reservations and got himself a room.

He spent the rest of the morning back on the downtown streets renewing his acquaintance with the city of his youth. Toward noon he walked through the first floor of Marshall Fields with its fine merchandise displayed amid exquisite decorations. He remembered the Walnut Room. He took the elevator up to the elegant old restaurant, and treated himself to a gourmet lunch of spinach salad with raspberry vinaigrette dressing. He topped it off with a french silk chocolate cream pie. Sort of a celebration, he thought, even though a bit pre-mature.

After leaving Fields he returned to his room at the Palmer House and spent the afternoon relaxing. On the table near the phone he picked up a card which urged him to call Enterprise and promised that they would bring a car to his hotel. After a shower and dressing he phoned for a car. By 5:30 he was in heavy traffic on the Eisenhower expressway making his way out to Oak Park.

As Conrad drove westward, creeping along in the heavy flow of cars leaving the loop for the suburbs he thought: Might it possibly be that I could obtain from Mrs. Baxter enough for a substantial earnest payment. That would show that we are in with both feet. . . .then, with a little more time . . . But what if she isn't interested . . . or does not want to see me, he warned himself.

Taking the Harlem Avenue exit, he drove north a mile or so and located the Warren's building, found a parking place within the block, and took the elevator to Craig and Lynn's fourth floor condo. He was greeted by Craig who brought him into the living room, who had taken off his bow tie, but otherwise had remained dressed. While they waited a few minutes for dinner he announced, "Con, I have an appointment with Leona Baxter for you for tomorrow afternoon!"

"Great!"

"However, I couldn't tell what, if any, interest she may have; but at least she's willing to hear your story."

Con breathed a short sigh of relief and said, "Well, that gives me a chance, at any rate!"

"Yes, I think it may be a start for you." At that point Craig's wife, Lynn, entered the living room. Her blonde hair of college days was now slightly shaded with gray. She wore a white cashmere sweater and a straight dusty pink skirt, still a very beautiful woman appearing so at ease with life. Con felt a surge of envy and then the familiar lonely pang. After introductions she announced that dinner was on the table. It was a pleasant meal with lots of talk of old times in college. Lynn had been three years behind Craig. Con remembered many of the same people she had known. Whenever there was a lull in the conversation Con's mind raced ahead to his appointment the next day.

Before Con left later in the evening Craig asked: "Con, be sure and phone me after you have seen Mrs.Baxter. I may have some further leads; also I'll want to know how you lucked out with Leona."

"That I'll do," and Con turned include both Warrens, "Thanks so much for a really delightful evening! It's been so good to catch up." Con said, taking his leave from Craig and Lynn Warren.

The Eisenhower had become filled with its nighttime traffic with streams of headlights on Con's left and streaks of red tail lights in front of him tracing the hurried travels of hundreds of hundreds of Chicagoans out for the night. Having lived in Montana for over thirty years, Con simply could not comprehend the never-ending surge of nameless drivers passing him in both directions.

The next afternoon he found himself in yet another stream of cars, again on the Eisenhower, traveling out to the western suburbs. Once again he took the Harlem exit, but this time turned west on Lake Street to enter River Forest, just west of Warren's home in Oak Park. River Forest was even more well-to-do than what he had seen of Oak Park. After the continuous rush and roar of the freeway Con was struck with the peacefulness of the streets in this suburb as he located the Baxter residence. The house was set quite far back from the quiet street, with a lush tree-shaded lawn in front. The broad rectangular lines of the house with its large porch across the front reminded Con of the Frank Lloyd Wright residences he'd seen years ago in Oak Park, where the famed architect had once lived and worked. He parked the car in the long drive leading to the Baxter house, took the curving brick walk way to the house and mounted the steps to the front door. He rang the bell apprehensively. He heard chimes ring inside. Soon the door opened.

"Hello, I'm Leona Baxter; and you are Dr. Schneider?" She said warmly as she held out her hand.

"Yes, hello, Mrs. Baxter; I'm Conrad Schneider," he said as he took her hand. It was warm to the touch.

"Come in, won't you?"

The picture of Mrs. Baxter Con had developed in his imagination did not in the least match the person whom he was now meeting. He had imagined her as elderly, dignified, blue-haired, and remote. Perhaps haughty. But Leona Baxter appeared much younger, than he had expected, looking quite trim in a teal Land's

End sort of sweat suit, embossed with a wild life scene, featuring a pair of mallards. Con thought her attractive in a calm and casual sort of way. In her early fifties, he thought, with graying hair loosely arranged. Her voice was soft and musical, without the slightest affectation. Her expression was relaxed and friendly. Anything but haughty. She led him across the waxed flag stones of the center foyer into a large and inviting living room on the right. The room, as the foyer, was done in deep earth tones, oak paneling half way up the walls, light brown subtly patterned wall-paper above. Light fixtures with ivory and amber stained glass shades gave the room a warm subdued feel. They took winged-back chairs facing each other arranged at right angles to a glass encased fireplace. The overall impression which the Baxter home gave to Con Schneider was that of comfortable wealth, not in the least ostentatious. A home furnished in good taste, and yet obviously lived in, with a number of magazines and books lying on occasional tables throughout the room.

"Mr. Warren tells me you are from Montana and that you direct a very unique retreat and renewal center in the mountains."

"That's right, but I grew up in this area, down in Morgan Park," he replied in an unconscious effort to fit in. She acknowledged this revelation with interest and seemed to invite him to go on.

"We are a non-profit organization committed to the restorative care of persons in a community environment amid the grandeur of one of Montana's better known mountain valleys—the Yellowstone."

"Sounds impressive, but a bit like a canned ad, dare I say?"

"I guess you're right—I'm on my soap box."

"I'm sorry. I didn't mean to be rude, but I want to hear your story, and yes, your need, in a down-to-earth, person to person way. I'm that sort, you know, even though this monstrosity of a house looks otherwise!" She had a warm way of putting Con at ease.

For the next hour Con Schneider shared the Fairhavens story with Leona Baxter, not hesitating to reveal his own emotional commitment to Fairhavens. He then went on to explain the present crisis. His listener was attentive and interested, asking some very penetrating questions along the way.

When he had concluded, there was a seemingly long period of silence while Leona Baxter rested back in her chair deep in thought. She then leaned forward and said very earnestly, "Con—may I call you that?"

"Yes, of course."

"I think I see very clearly what you are about at Fairhavens—and what you are up against. My heart goes out to your group. I really want to help; but at this point I can't make a commitment until I've a chance to talk with the people who help me manage my finances. What I'd like to do is make some phone calls tomorrow morning; and then by mid-afternoon tomorrow I'll phone Craig, and he can relay my response to you. Does that sound OK to you?"

"It certainly does, Mrs. Baxter. I really appreciate your interest."

"I am interested," she assured him, "But please don't assume anything at this point."

"Thank you so much for your time, Mrs. Baxter."

He got up to prepare to leave when Leona put her hand on his arm to restrain him, "Won't you stay for a bit of supper. I get tired eating alone and surely you must be ready for a bite!"

Quite taken back by this overture of friendliness, Con sputtered, "Well, I guess I could—if you're sure it's no trouble—Mrs. Baxter."

"No, no. And by the way, do call me Lee. My friends all do! Now, if you'll excuse me, I'll put something on the table for us. There's some magazines on the coffee table, or you can switch on the TV. Just make yourself at home. There is a guest bathroom in the hallway to your right."

Too keyed up to get much out of the magazines, Con turned on the television and in a distracted sort of way watched some local area news. All he could really think about was about what amount of funding he could expect, if any.

After twenty minutes or so Leona appeared wearing an apron

and said,"Supper's ready! Do you mind if we eat in the breakfast
room? What I have isn't extensive enough for a formal dining room.
And besides, I want to get acquainted with you on an informal
basis. No Fairhavens talk now!" she said with a impish grin. Con
was taken with the alluring warmth with which Lee Baxter spoke
to him. Her breakfast room had floor to ceiling windows on two of
its outer walls. It looked out into a wooded area of her side yard.

She had laid a very ample table of cold meats and cheeses,
tossed salad and dinner rolls. She served ice cream for desert. During the meal the conversation was limited to comments on the
weather, tid-bits of current news, and about her house. "It's Frank
Lloyd Wright influence, but done by a River Forest architect some
years later."

After they finished their ice cream, Lee said, "Let's take our
coffee in the den." They went into a family room adjoining the
kitchen. Con saw that it was furnished with over-stuffed chairs
and couches. "Real leather," he thought. He could smell the faint
aroma of leather. And just a faint lingering trace of cigar. What
followed was a relaxed sharing of their life stories with each other.
Seldom in Con's life had he been with someone so easy to talk
with. And they had just met!

Leona told of her childhood in a small central Iowa town and
her college years at Buena Vista in Iowa. After graduating in business she had come to Chicago and gotten a job with a mall development company."And eventually I married the boss," she said,
"We had two children, and before long the nest was empty," she
paused to breathe more deeply before continuing. "And then the
shocker for me! Huntley died suddenly of a massive heart attack."

Con expressed his sympathy. She explained how she was left
alone but very amply cared for financially. Over the years Huntley
Baxter had acquired a number of retail department stores located
in malls in the Chicago and Indianapolis areas, and eventually
some of the Malls themselves.

"It was during an Indianapolis business trip that he had died
in his motel room." Lee obviously wanted to relate this more fully.

"The bellman discovered his body after the desk clerk had been unable to get an answer from his room. His last cigar had burned itself out in the ash tray next to his bed. Sort of a victor and the vanquished scene!" she added sadly.

Widowed for seven years Leona was once again beginning to enjoy life. "That's my life story—not too exciting especially since Hunt's been gone. Now tell me about you!"

"Well, not too much excitement for me either, excepting the present Fairhavens crisis. But enough of that. I grew up on the far south side in Morgan Park. My father was an attorney in a downtown firm and my mother did not work outside the home, but she did a lot at the Morgan Park Presbyterian Church where we were members. After high school I went to Lake Forest College and graduated after the normal four years. It was a liberal arts degree with social work as my particular option. Lake Forest is where Craig Warren and I met and became friends. Next Fall, by the way, will be our thirtieth college class reunion."

Lee broke in at this point to say, "My Buena Vista class celebrated its twenty-fifth a few years ago, but I couldn't attend. That was too soon after I had lost my husband—but go on, Con."

"After college I got a job with Erie Neighborhood house in Chicago as a group worker, sort of a social work job, but since I did not have a masters in social work I couldn't really work in that capacity. And so after a couple of years I went back to school for my masters; and then a doctorate in social work from the University of Chicago. That was a two year program. I returned to Erie House as a full-fledged social worker.

"While at Erie House I became restless and lost interest and concentration in my work. I needed to get away into a new setting. That was when I moved to Montana to take a social work job for Deaconess Medical Center in Billings. It was during those years that the idea for the Fairhavens project developed.

"After getting some grants we started Fairhavens in the Paradise Valley between Livingston, Montana and Yellowstone Park. That was five years ago and you know the rest." At this point Con looked at his watch and said, "My sakes, it's 9:30. I'm staying much too long; but it has been so enjoyable, Lee."

"It has been delightful for me as well. But there's one unanswered question!"

"What's that?"

"You didn't mention anything about marriage or family?" Lee asked somewhat hesitantly.

"Oh, that. No—to both."

Lee could see that there would be no more self-disclosure along this line, and so she reluctantly concluded the evening: "I'm so glad you could stay for supper with me. How long do you plan to be in Chicago?"

"I have a late afternoon flight out on Thursday. I need to get back."

"Well, why don't you give me a jingle sometime before you leave."

"I'll do that! Thanks so much for your consideration and for a good meal and especially for our conversation."

As he got to the door Lee held out her hand to say goodbye. It seemed to Con that she held his hand a bit longer than custom required!

On the drive downtown to the Palmer House, once again amid a steady of stream of headlights and tail lights Con's mind was filled with thoughts of his afternoon and evening with Leona Baxter. Wondering what the financial outcome would be . . . . but more than that . . . . thinking about Lee. In a way, quite unusual for him; he had felt drawn to her; he couldn't help but think that it had been mutual. And about this he wondered as well. He hoped the financial question would be answered the next day when he was to phone Craig. There was nothing more he could do until he heard from Craig about Lee Baxter's decision. The more intriguing personal question might be longer to wonder about.

CHAPTER 4

Leaving his place of refuge in the Delta lounge, Max walked out among the people who were hurriedly moving along the concourse. He was struck by the fact that everyone was intent on going to their destinations one direction or the other, while he had no particular place to go at this point. Without a flight until morning, and no plan for the night he walked along aimlessly while scores of other travelers passed him by. When he thought about it, he wasn't very set on his Denver destination either. Now that he was away from Tipton, Max had lost his interest in the conference he was to attend. It was a Small Church Conference, and so far as he was concerned at this point he'd had enough of the small church!

However, he was obligated to attend. The synod was paying his way. But that was tomorrow. What about today and tonight? Here I am in Salt Lake City—who do I know in Salt Lake City, he wondered?

Max remembered Duane Rustin, a former friend from back home who had moved to Salt Lake. He thought he remembered that Duane was teaching at the University of Utah. I wonder if he's in the phone book. Finding the number he phoned, "Hello, Duke! . . . This is Max Ritter . . . Right! I'm here at the airport with some time to kill. Just thought I'd give you a ring and see how you're doing . . . I can't get out until 6:30 tomorrow morning . . . Are you sure? I wouldn't want to impose . . . Positive you haven't got plans?"

"No, I'd love to see you, Max. In fact, if you can't get out until in the morning, why don't you plan to stay overnight here at my place?"

"Really?"

"No problem, I'll come by the terminal in about twenty minutes. What airline? . . . OK be outside Delta."

"Great, Duane—I'll be outside Delta in twenty minutes . . . What'll I look for? . . . ok—got it. See you then."

Soon he saw Duane's blue Chevy Blazer coming. When it pulled up to him, Duane Rustin jumped out, "Max! Good to see you! Let me grab your bag, and you get in."

When Max was seated on the passenger side and Duane took the wheel he asked, "You haven't had supper yet, have you? If not, why don't we stop somewhere?"

"That would be fine. I haven't eaten much today."

Duane pulled into a Dennys and they ordered dinners. While they ate there was a flood of talk as the two brought each other up to date on their lives since leaving home. Duane was on the Sociology faculty at the University of Utah; and had never married, "Married to my work" he said. "How about you?"

"I've been married three years. Gwen and I were married before I went to seminary. I was working in a hotel at the time." Max answered guardedly, then he quickly went on, "How long did you say you have been in Salt Lake City?"

"It's been four years."

After leaving the restaurant, Duane drove into down-town Salt Lake to his apartment in a new high-rise. After he put his bag in the guest bedroom Max came out into the living room.

"What have you been up to besides work, Duane?"

"Well, the big thing for me lately was spending last summer in New Zealand. I fell in love with the place and would go back anytime anybody would pay my way again!"

"What took you to New Zealand?"

"I went over on an exchange teaching assignment. I taught at Otago University in Dunedin for a semester, while one of their people taught in my place here. It was great!"

"Tell me about it. Sounds good to me at this point!" Max offered.

"Instead of telling you in so many words, would you like to

see my slides? I've put them together in sort of a program so that I wouldn't bore people with endless rambling. You know how that is?" Duane said.

"I'm interested—show me!" Max replied, really quite eager to get his mind off his own problems.

For the next hour and a half Max was transported heart and mind to the "beautiful isles down under." After Duane put the lights back on, Max said, "That was one of the most delightful travelogues I've ever seen. You've given me someplace to dream of visiting."

"Good! I hope you do one of these days, Max."

By the time the two had "returned from New Zealand" it was time to turn in. Through the night vague and misty images of New Zealand filled Max's mind as he slept somewhat lightly. He was up at five. His friend delivered him back to the Delta ticket desk by a quarter to six.

An hour later Max Ritter was in the air, bound for Denver and the Small Church Conference. The conference, held at the Denver Stapleton, a motel out by the Denver air terminal, was attended mostly by ministers and church officers from Colorado and Wyoming. Max didn't know anyone at the meeting. He found the meeting to be something of a drag, he had to admit to himself, mainly because of his own personal problems, which kept surfacing in his mind, no matter what else was going on. He was tempted to drop out and return home. But then—return to what?—he thought!

The afternoon session finally ended and Max ate a quick supper alone in the motel cafe before returning to his room. He hadn't wanted to stand around and talk with people between sessions. He knew what that would be—everyone telling their own church stories—some bragging—most complaining. Ordinarily such informal times had been enjoyable to him, but not on this occasion. Before going to his room he stopped by the desk to check for messages. He had been hoping that Gwen would call.

The desk clerk handed him a notice of a phone call. Looking

at the number to call, a chill swept through his body. His Clerk of Session, Wilbur Mason had called and asked for Max to phone him at his home that evening. What could this mean? Not good! Max thought, with a strong sense of foreboding.

As soon as he got to his room he phoned. No use waiting. Get it over with, he thought. Wilbur answered: "Yeah, this is Wilbur. You at the conference?

"Yes, it has just started"

"Well, I just wanted to let you know that the Session met last night and voted unanimously for you to resign."

This struck like a sharp icicle into his chest. Max was speechless. He regained some control and asked in measured words: "Who moderated the meeting in my absence? That couldn't have been a legal meeting without me, Wilbur."

Wilbur quickly came back, "We made sure we were legal, and got Dr. Dixon, the Committee on Ministry chairman, to come over from Bozeman."

Now Max was angry, "I'll talk to him then." And he hung up.

He immediately phoned Dixon, "That meeting couldn't have been legal." he said sharply.

Dixon was apologetic and agreed, "I suppose not, but when a thing has gone this far, I've always said, the minister might just as well leave."

"Is that what your committee is recommending to me?"

"The committee hasn't met, but that's my recommendation!"

"Thanks for your free advice. While you're at it, tell me what reason the Session gave you for asking me to resign."

"They said you just aren't 'spiritual enough'."

"I see. Sounds just like them."

"Will you be resigning then?"

"I'll wait to hear what your committee says." With that Max hung up.

He was devastated. He'd been standing while phoning and now it felt as though the floor was shifting back and forth and the room was turning. He sat down on the bed—stunned. Later on he tried to sleep, but spent the night tossing and turning.

When he awakened the one thing he knew was, that he was not going to the conference that morning; nor did he want to see anyone from the conference just yet. He needed to get some of this worked through. Max was the sort of person who didn't want anyone else trying to help him solve his problems. But for the moment he was too bruised in spirit to think about much. So he took the motel limousine to the air terminal where he got himself some breakfast. Then he caught a bus for downtown Denver where he spent the morning browsing through book stores and other small shops, just to distract himself. Nothing much interested him as he sauntered up and down the streets. He was about ready to catch the return bus when he came to the display window of a travel agency. In it he saw posters advertising New Zealand.

New Zealand! The picture on the poster was a scene Duke had photographed he thought. He looked more closely and read the description: "Mitre Peak on Milford Sound." The poster caught his eye because of the enthusiasm Duke had shared for the "beautiful isles down under." On impulse Max went in and asked the first agent who wasn't busy, "Just for information, what would it cost to fly to New Zealand?"

"When do you plan to go and to what city in New Zealand?" she asked.

"Oh, I don't have any specific plans. Just give me a ball-park figure."

She pulled up on her computer relevant information and replied, "Well, if you were going, say this Thursday: Los Angeles to Auckland would be $1,289 plus boarding fees. Christchurch would be $1,328."

"How about reservations? Are they hard to get? How long ahead do you need to make them?"

"Let me see—I could get you on the 9:50 PM flight out of LAX on Thursday!"

"That would be great, but I can't do that so quickly—if at all. but you sure entice me!"

"Let me know, sir, if you change your mind. Here. Take my card—just in case!"

When he returned to the motel after lunch, intending to return to the afternoon session, he was given another telephone message. Hurriedly Max dialed the familiar number. "Hello, this is Max!"

Gwen's mother answered in a business-like tone: "I'll call Gwendolyn to the phone."

The next voice was Gwen's; but not at all reassuring. "Max: I am not returning to Montana. I've decided to stay here. I intend to go back and get a graduate degree."

Max cut in at that point, "I'm through at Tipton. I can move back and find something."

"No, Max. I need my own space—alone, for a while!"

"You mean . . . ?"

"I'm seeing a counselor and she advises complete separation at this time and at a later date she says that I should decide what to do.

"Where is my input in all this, Gwen?"

"My counselor told me that you have had long enough for your input. Now, it is my turn." Gwen answered diffidently.

"Oh Gwen, let me come and see you and talk this out. I'll get a flight and be there in the morning. Don't let it be like this! Give me a chance!"

"No, I've made up my mind. You take care of your life for now and I'll take care of me."

"How long?"

"I have no idea." Gwen protested.

"Gwen, can't we agree on a time when we can consider a new start?"

"Like when?" she asked, seeming to relent.

"A month, maybe."

There was a silence, broken finally by Gwen: "After the first of the year, Maxwell. After my first semester in graduate school. I'll write you then."

"How about between now and then? I still love, you, Gwen"

"Don't call me. Daddy said that it would be much better if you didn't phone. And he and mother don't want to discuss this with you either." With that she hung up, and their three years of marriage came to a complete stand-off—if not an end.

Dazed, Max could think of nothing except to get out of Denver and away from the conference—far beyond any human contact. All he could hear was the final click of the receiver. He wanted no more phone calls, no more talk. Maybe it was a weakness of his; some said it was; but when difficulty confronted him his first reaction was to run. This time he wanted to go as far away as he possibly could. Not just Salt Lake City; not just Bozeman! But to the ends of the earth, he thought.

Ends of the earth! That reminded him of something Duke had said when he showed him his New Zealand slides. One particular slide came to mind. It was a view of the Pacific from—where was that? Stewart Island, he remembered. Duke had said, "One of the intriguing things to me about the south shore of the South Island, and even more so—Stewart Island, was that when you look toward the sea, there is nothing between you and Antarctica—the South Pole! You're literally at the end of the earth—the very bottom of it—about as far away as you can get!"

With that thought in mind, a plan began to form in Max's troubled mind: Could I possibly get to New Zealand? Three things needed: Flight reservation, money, time. Time! Looks like I've got all the time in the world! Reservations—available! Money? There was that nest egg he'd been given. His grandmother had said, before she died, "Max, I want you to have this for a rainy day." She had then handed him a check for $10,000, which he had banked with his banker friend back home seven years ago. Well, wasn't this a rainy day? That's it! I'll go for it!"

Max phoned his banker friend: "Fred, this is Max Ritter . . . yeah, pretty good, but I need some funds in my account. Could you by any chance convert that CD I have to cash and transfer the full amount to my account at Security Bank, Bozeman, Montana?

"If I have your request in writing. A FAX would be ok."

"How soon?

"If you FAX me right away, I can electronically have it in Bozeman within the hour. I'll need your Montana account number."

Max gave him his account number and got Fred's FAX number and signed off, "Fred, you're an angel! I hope I see you sometime when I get back home. I'll send the FAX immediately."

Max wrote out the order to the bank on motel stationary, went down to the office and FAXED it on its way. Returning to his room he took out the card from the woman at the travel agency, phoned her and made his reservations for the Thursday flight from L.A. to Christchurch; and obtained a flight from Denver to L.A. by way of Salt Lake on the next flight out at 4:30 pm.

Quickly packing, he checked out, and taking the motel van to the air terminal he boarded a downtown bus to pick up his ticket at the travel agency. He found a bookstore and bought a travel guide for New Zealand. Then to the terminal and to the boarding area. He was soon bound for Los Angeles.

When he arrived, he checked into a downtown hotel so that the next day he could conveniently shop for some additional clothes for a longer stay in New Zealand.

Nine-fifty Thursday evening finally came and Max Ritter stepped onto the Air New Zealand 747 which would take him out of the country and into the Southern Hemisphere thousands of miles away from his former life.

He settled into his seat and forced his troubled thoughts into the back of his mind. When the cabin became completely full and the cabin doors were secured shut the mellow voice of the cabin attendant from New Zealand brought to him audible proof that he was on his way. Her accent was intoxicating: "On behalf of Air New Zealand, welcome. We shall be departing shortly for our non-stop flight to Christchurch, New Zealand. If at anytime during our flight you should have particular needs, please contact one of your flight attendants, and we shall honored to assist you. Thank you."

When the giant Boeing 747 lifted off into the night and was airborne, Max was fascinated by the graphic map on the screen in the cabin showing the progress of the plane as it left the west coast flying south-westward over the Pacific. Away from his troubled life in Montana and into a whole new universe, it seemed.

In his imagination he could see Tipton off to the right of the screen. He saw the church packed as it had been four years ago on the night of his installation as its pastor. He and Gwen had been elated, filled with anticipation of this his first call after seminary. The moderator of Presbytery had conducted the service of installation. She was an elder from the Butte church. The pastor of the Bozeman church, an older man, had issued the Charge to the Congregation. In the charge he had advised the Tipton congregation: "Love your new pastor and his wife. Take them into your homes, and help them to become a full fledged part of your community. Let them know of your appreciation of their efforts on behalf of your congregation. Surround and support them with your love and prayers, your hugs and your gifts." Well, in four years none of that had ever happened. Just the opposite, it turned out. Some of the words of the Charge to the Pastor had stuck in his memory. The pastor in Deer Lodge had read from the Book of Common Worship: "You are an overseer of Christ's flock, as such you will have a watchful regard for your people. You will be their guide and leader, and they will follow you as they see you follow Christ." Those words had not come true either. A disturbing question jabbed his consciousness: "They didn't follow me because they did not see me follow Christ? And maybe I haven't . . . ?" A disquieting thought. "Not spiritual enough." Maybe they were right.

The stewards were wheeling the dinner cart up the aisle and soon he had before him an excellent New Zealand dinner. Lamb chops, mashed potatoes and some orange colored turnips, which the steward referred to as swedes. After dinner, chocolate bon bons and coffee were served. When the trays had been removed, pillows and blankets were distributed, and the lights were turned out. It was time to try to sleep so that a new day in a new world could be faced with a refreshed body and mind, but with a troubled spirit, he thought.

But before such a respite could come, he had more hard thoughts to mull. Thoughts of Gwendolyn, their wedding, and of the five years following that day in hot and humid Chicago in July when each had vowed "In plenty and in want, In joy and in sorrow; In sickness and in health; As long as we both shall live." Why hadn't those words come true? Certain other words came back to him, words which he had said: "to be thy loving and faithful husband;" Had he been? Faithful—yes. Loving—I wonder? I let Gwen down, I guess. There she was, miles from home and separated from friends, plunked down into a group of people she didn't know, and who were in so many ways different from the people she had grown up with. Especially at first I was all she had; and now I wonder if I was there for her. Or was I too busy and excited about my work? These were not easy thoughts for Max. He wanted to put them away. He took out the air line magazine to get his mind onto something else. And then, out of sheer exhaustion he fell asleep, while the huge and heavy airliner droned on south-westward over the dark Pacific to a new day.

Max awakened once during the night and noticed the plane's location on the graphic map on the screen. He watched as the plane crossed the international date line. Thinking about that as he drifted back to sleep he repeated to himself, "today is tomorrow! . . . yesterday's gone, tomorrow's here . . . today never was . . . yesterday's tomorrow . . . tomorrow's today . . . " Southward and westward the plane moved across the screen, while most of the three hundred forty or so travelers slept—some returning home, others being carried further and further from home. He awakened a few minutes later to see the plane symbol cross the Equator and enter the Southern Hemisphere. Now he was indeed a very long way from his former life. He slept again, this time more soundly than he had for days.

CHAPTER 5

On the morning of the second day after Conrad's interview and his evening with Leona Baxter he was awakened by the ringing of the phone in his hotel room.

"Hello, Conrad, this is Lee Baxter. I hope I didn't get you up, but I didn't want to miss you. Why don't you turn your car in to the Enterprise people in Oak Park and let me drive you out to O'Hare. It's such a hassle out there. I'd like to see you again anyway. In fact, come out early enough so that we can have lunch somewhere on the way. And don't mention the money again! Your phone call last night was sweet—and that was thanks enough.!"

Con replied, "If you really want to do that, I'd be delighted."

"Yes, that's exactly what I want to do, so what time shall I meet you at Enterprise in Oak Park? Remember I suggested lunch!"

"Why don't I drop the car off at 12 and meet you 12 to 12:30?"

"I'll be there."

Leona Baxter picked a quiet tea room in Arlington Heights, estimating that they had a couple of hours before needing to be at O'Hare. Over a delicious luncheon of Caesar salad with broiled chicken accompanied by gourmet coffee and chocolate mousse, Lee and Con resumed their easy conversation, which had begun so pleasurably on Tuesday evening. Con found it much more comfortable to talk about Fairhavens now that the money question had been resolved.

His enthusiasm for the project was infectious, prompting Lee to say, "You know I'd really like to see Fairhavens and to get the feel of it first hand, but I don't especially want to go as a basket case needing a remodel job!"

Con laughed, "No you don't need the works. Remember the 3

R's! "Retreat, Recreation, Renewal. It's not all 'repair.' We have guests who check in for their own R. & R. and these folks really don't enter into the more serious program. But often they get caught up in some of the lighter social aspects. You could come on that basis. Or better yet, you could come as my own invited guest—as a friend!"

"Con, I'd like that."

Conrad was delighted. "Give me time to work through some of this legal real estate stuff, and then come when I'm a bit more relaxed. A couple of months ought to do it. Why don't you fly out then?. I'd love to show you, not only Fairhavens but much of the greater Yellowstone area! How about it, Lee?"

"You're certain I wouldn't be in the way?"

"Absolutely not!"

"OK, then I'll come, but not a word about who the donor is!"

"I'll give you the word when the coast is clear, so to speak." Con assured. "Let me know when you fly and I'll be at the airport. By the way, have your travel agent book you into Bozeman. Now, I hate to end this. It's been fun. But I really should get out to O'Hare."

Con persuaded Lee to let him off on the curb on the departure circle. After a warm hand-shake and an almost emotional "good-bye" he was in the terminal checking in at the Delta counter.

As the plane climbed up through the smog which covered the city like an umbrella, Con rested back in his seat, with his mind filled with thoughts of Lee Baxter. Soon the plane broke out of the smog and cloud cover and soared into the bright sunlit blue sky, giving Con a feeling of exhilaration he had seldom experienced in his life. Fairhavens would be saved. And on a personal level he felt himself slipping into a new and enticing dimension. He was returning to Montana not only with the needed funds but with a new lease on life—as a different person.

The Fairhavens board was made up of six members representing various interests. Don Hunter from Billings represented the Montana Mental Health Association; Audrey O'Connor, the Executive

Director of the Montana Association of Churches (MAC), also from Billings; Clyde Blackwood of the Chamber of Commerce of Park County; Howard Eldridge, a resort owner in Gardiner; Patty Sherman and Barb Muir, ranchers in Paradise Valley and close friends with each other.

As soon as Conrad Schneider had gotten back he had contacted each board member asking for a special meeting of the board for the following Friday noon. He had explained that the purpose of the meeting was to decide on making an offer to buy the Fairhavens property immediately. Miraculously each of the six had indicated willingness to attend.

The board members began arriving a few minutes before noon on Friday, the day after Conrad's return from Chicago. Patty and Barb arrived first in Patty's Jeep Cherokee. Patty had picked up Barb Muir at her ranch at the foot of Emigrant Peak on her way down from Gardiner. She and her husband had a couple hundred head of Hereford cattle on a ranch out of Gardiner. In her thirties, Patty had on jeans and a sweatshirt with her blond hair in a pony tail. The Muirs also were cattle ranchers. In their case—Angus. Barb was in her early sixties and came dressed in a denim skirt with a western-style blouse. Next Clyde Blackwood drove up in his new black Olds 98. He was dressed to match with a dark gray suit with a white shirt and dark tone tie. Clyde was in his prime years as a businessman, around fifty. He had numerous interests and holdings in Livingston and throughout Park county. His time was spent principally in managing the Yellowstone Best Western Inn, which he and his wife owned. Clyde was followed by Howard Eldridge who drove up in his Ford Explorer with his resort logo on the front door announcing "Elk Lodge Resort." Neatly pressed Levis, cowboy boots, western shirt, bolo tie and a western cut corduroy sport jacket advertised Howard as a local resort owner. The last car to arrive was a Toyota with county "3" plates indicating Billings. Don was dressed in his usual turtle-neck and cords. The bearded Don Hunter, psychotherapist, age-35, had brought Audrey O'Connor dressed in a dark green sweater and a tartan skirt. Ms O'Connor at

33 was the first Roman Catholic to serve as the M.A.C. executive. Highly thought-of she had earned respect from both clergy and lay, Protestant and Catholic participants in the state-wide church federation.

During lunch while the board members were involved in their own conversations Con was savoring in his mind his recent memory of the climax of his Chicago trip. On Wednesday Con had driven up to Lake Forest for old time's sake, just to see his Alma Mater again. It had been years, but he noticed very few changes on the tree shaded campus. And then he had headed south on Lake Shore Drive to his old neighborhood of Morgan Park. It was always an energizing thrill to Con when he followed the shore of Lake Michigan, watching the breakers coming in to the shoreline park with its assortment of Chicago's humanity enjoying bikeways, grassy parkland and the shoreline as it stretched southward for miles. Further south he had swung by his boyhood home, a large graceful frame house on 110th Street.

After a most enjoyable journey into his personal past he had returned to his hotel room to make his call to Craig. "Hello, Craig, do you have any news for me?" The news he heard from Craig was quite overwhelming!

"Con," he said, "I have a cashier's check for $75,000, which you can pick up now. Come up to the office as soon as you can. What's more, I have a letter of intent from Mrs. Baxter's attorneys indicating that an additional $100,000 would be made available to the Fairhavens board upon completion and approval of legal papers pertaining to the sale and purchase of the property by the Fairhavens board!" How vivid and exciting all this was in Con's reverie as he awaited the business meeting of the board.

After a luncheon served by the Dining Room staff, Howard Eldridge, president, called the meeting to order and turned the floor over to Con.

"As you know, Cody Vermillian's group has placed a firm offer with the family, to buy the entire Fairhavens property. And you know also that we now have a week and half to take up our first option to buy. I have been on a trip to Chicago to seek advice on fund raising. My trip was most successful!" He paused to let this sink in, and then continued, " I have here an anonymous gift of $75,000 which we can use as earnest money. Furthermore, from this same donor the remaining $100,000 of the purchase price will be made available on completion of the paperwork and approval by the donor's attorney."

The board members were struck dumb-founded by this news. There was a reverential quiet in the room after Con made his announcement. Barb Muir wanted to know what were the next steps. Clyde Blackwood asked, "What are the strings attached to this gift?" Audrey O'Connor asked: "Can you tell us anything about the donor. That's too much of a gift to go unacknowledged."

Con tried to answer the flood of questions: "To begin with, I can't say anything more about the donor, except that she has been thanked personally. About strings: none except that we keep on doing what we are doing here at Fairhavens. It was our mission and approach which won this generous response. Now about next steps. First of all, Board action is needed to make the offer. That's the purpose of our meeting. Then our attorney needs to contact the attorney for the family to work up a buy/sell. After that the paperwork needs to be FAXED to Chicago for the approval of the donor's lawyers. Upon completion of such approval, the balance of the funds should be available, after which we are home free!"

Patty Sherman initiated the action: "I move that the Fairhavens board make a firm offer of $175,000 to the family for purchase of the property, and that earnest money of $75,000 accompany our offer."

"Second" said Don Hunter.

"Any discussion?" offered Eldridge. "Yes, Clyde."

"I don't think we should act so fast. We may have the purchase funds, or most of it, but what about the costs that ownership will incur immediately and over the years. Can we really afford this property with these old buildings? I think we might be better off taking the funds and accepting Cody's offer of a homesite on a half acre and building something to meet our needs there."

Audrey replied, "You can't be serious! Without this location, and this amount of property we would have to revise our program radically."

"And then, as Con has intimated, the funds might not be ours to use." Hunter added.

"Well, I guess that's what I meant by strings, isn't it?" retorted Blackwood.

At this point there was a lull in the discussion and Barb Muir called for the question.

Eldridge responded with, "All those in favor of voting on the question signify with an 'Aye'." A general response of ayes was given. "All those opposed signify with a 'No'." "No!" shouted Clyde Blackwood. "The ayes have it and now we are ready for the vote on the question of making a $175,000 offer on the property. All those in favor, signify with an aye . . ."

"Wait a minute, I call for a show of hands." Clyde demanded.

"OK, all in favor raise your right hand . . . Those opposed raise your hand." Five voted in favor. Clyde Blackwood opposed. "The motion has passed, five to one." Eldridge continued, "As President of the Board I direct Conrad to meet with our attorney and carry out the necessary actions subsequent to this action."

The meeting adjourned and everyone left the room in animated discussion of this fortuitous development for Fairhavens. Excepting Blackwood, who left quite quickly making some sort of statement that he had appointments in town.

After the board members had dispersed and Con was sitting in his office alone, he pondered Clyde's negative reactions. He remembered the way in which the Livingston Chamber people had shown so much interest in Vermillian's project during the presentation the week previous. This would not be the last of Clyde's attempted obstruction, he feared.

Con phoned the Fairhavens attorney and made an appointment for Monday morning to work out the details which would lead to the buy/sell and finally to the purchase of the property. Con felt a surge of relief. The rest was paper-work. Lee Baxter had saved the day! He was tempted to phone her, but thought better of it. No, we had better get this thing sewed up before I do any celebrating!

Monday morning came and Con Schneider was sitting in the Livingston law office of Mark Engle. They were waiting for a scheduled conference phone call. The phone rang, Mark immediately answered, and the operator spoke:" Mr. Engle, I'm ready with your conference call."

"Good."

"Hello, Mr. Holloway, are you on the line?"

"Yes." Quentin Holloway, Chicago, representing Leona Baxter, had been notified by Mrs. Baxter, of the anticipated gift for the purchase of Fairhavens in Montana.

"Mr. Nordstrom, are you on?"

"Yes, I am." Sherman Nordstrom of Corvalis, Oregon, the attorney for the family who owned the Fairhavens property, had been apprized of the offer pending.

"All right, you may go ahead with your conference call."

"Mark Engle, here: I represent the Fairhavens board and I have asked for this conference meeting to work out final arrangements in regard to Board action yesterday to make a firm offer of $175,000 to purchase the Fairhavens property from the present owners. Said offer is hereby made. I have been instructed to accompany this offer with a payment of $75,000 earnest money. It is our understanding that the Fairhavens board had been given first right of refusal."

"Sherman Nordstrom speaking: I have informed the owners of the property of this offer and its terms, as I had been apprized last evening. I am prepared to accept this offer on behalf of the owners pending the full issuance of all the proper papers."

"Yes, I am Quentin Holloway of Chicago. My part in this is to receive the proper papers, and on approval of these, the balance of $100,000 will be forwarded to the Fairhavens Board for full and final payment to the sellers."

"Engle, here, I am delighted; and I shall fax the papers to your office, Mr. Nordstrom, in the morning; I will prepare an electronic transfer of funds also in the morning. I will fax copies to you, Mr. Holloway, at the same time.

"Holloway speaking: We shall review them immediately so that upon approval we can transfer funds to your office for Fairhavens payment of the balance."

"Nordstrom speaking: We will be very happy for the speed with which you are working through the paperwork, for you may not be aware, but we have in hand another offer, which of course, we will have to refuse as soon as the sale is completed and filed with Park County."

"Mark Engle, here: We believe that if all goes well, this could be filed within four days. Thank you, gentlemen. I believe that concludes our business at this point. Good bye."

"Good bye."

"Good bye."

Mark hung up and turned to Con and said: "It's a done deal! This should be totally concluded in a week's time at the outside."

"I can hardly believe it. I really was afraid we were going to lose it."

"I'll need your Board president and two other members in my office at eleven tomorrow morning for official signatures. Can you arrange that?"

"I'm sure I can. And I'll be here to cheer them on!"

"I've got to get cracking, so we'll look for you tomorrow."

"Thanks, Mark." Con said as he left the office to return to Fairhavens.

PART II

CHAPTER 6

As the sun crept above the north-eastern horizon its beams reached inside the cabin of the aircraft. Awakening travelers began to stir. A few lifted their shades allowing the morning light to spread throughout the plane as it droned southward toward its destination. Max opened his eyes to watch the graphics on the large screen. During his sleeping hours the outline of the eastern shore line of New Zealand had begun to appear. The data on the screen indicated 537 miles remaining as the airplane shaped symbol moved ever closer to land. About an hour more, he thought.

Attendants were coming down the aisles with hot towels, using silver tongs to give one to each passenger. Max rubbed the sleep out of his eyes and tried to focus on the new day ahead. A breakfast of guava juice, omelets and English muffins was served, followed by coffee or tea poured from silver servers brought by the attendants.

On the screen, the numbers appeared again. This time 145 miles remaining. What was in store for him? He had no idea. All he knew was that Tipton, and Gwendolyn, and every other familiar part of his life had been left far far behind—in a world far away—another life! Anticipation, yes; but no visual images. A clean slate, a blank screen!

His reverie was interrupted by a marked change in the drone of the engines, a slowing down perhaps? He felt the beginning of the descent of the huge aircraft. He looked out his window and observed the gray-green of land becoming dimly visible. New Zealand! As the ground grew more distinct he thought he could see rivers coursing across fields of vegetation into deltas at the sea coast.

The slight crackling sound from the loud speaker brought the voice of one of the attendants: "Kia Ora! Welcome to New Zealand. Aotearoa—land of the long white cloud! We have begun our descent into Christchurch. Please fasten your seat belts. Return your tray tables and your seat backs to the upright position. We estimate our arrival time into the terminal at Christchurch to be twenty minutes. Please remain in your seats until we have reached the gate and the aircraft has come to a complete stop."

The Boeing 747 was descending more rapidly now. Before long Max spotted the tower and terminal building as the airliner swung around to position itself for landing. He heard the abrupt sound of the landing gears being deployed; and then in a few minutes the double thump of touch down—the sudden engine reversal for the forced slow-down—taxiing to the waiting walkway. Then the slow approach and an almost imperceptible stop. A sudden unclicking of seat belts throughout the cabin, scurrying to open the luggage compartments overhead, and people beginning to fill the aisles. There followed the usual long wait for the cabin door to be opened and finally the deplaning process.

Max felt as if he had sea legs as he followed the stream of passengers into the Customs Hall, so strangely quiet as people retrieved their luggage from the swishing carousals. Most had obtained wheeled luggage carts with which they formed lines before the customs desks. When he got to the customs officer, he was asked to present his passport, and to show his return ticket. Then with a polite smile, "Enjoy your visit to New Zealand, sir."

Finally on his own in the terminal, he set his watch to the current time as posted: 11:28 AM. Saturday. At the Air New Zealand domestic ticket counter he secured a reservation and a ticket for Invercargill. His flight would leave at 2:30 PM. He checked his bags with the attendant.

On the advice of the woman at the ticket counter he took a city bus down-town to Cathedral Square, a pedestrian plaza with imposing buildings on each side. The Anglican Cathedral dominated the east side of the Square. Max entered through the great door and slipped into the hushed stillness of the majestic gray stone neo-Gothic cathedral. He went into a pew toward the rear and sat down for a few moments to pray.

After he left the Cathedral he crossed the square and walked along Worcester Street with its bridge over the stately willow-lined Avon River. A few blocks further west he came to the Canterbury Museum. His brief visit to the museum provided him an introduction to New Zealand. He was especially taken with the Hall of Antarctica Discovery with its displays of scenes and artifacts of the arduous and danger-filled Antarctic explorations. Most of the exploration parties had set out over the southern sea from Christchurch. Literally to the end of the earth, he mused. Such expeditions were metaphors for what Max himself was doing: searching to find a place as far to the South as possible—a far off place where he might somehow find himself again. He stopped in at a small cafe on the lower level of the museum, which he would later learn was called a "take-away." He selected a meat sandwich from the glass case and ordered a pot of tea—without milk he hastened to reply. After his modest lunch he noted that it was time to board a bus bound for the airport.

As Max returned to the air terminal he felt a deep loneliness; and an uncomfortable sense of being out of place. He felt this as a gnawing sensation in the pit of his stomach. Maybe jet lag, he thought. No, he realized. He had never been so alone. There was absolutely no one with whom he had even a passing acquaintance anywhere at all in the entire country—the hemisphere, for that matter. The thought overwhelmed Max. No face in the crowd would be familiar. He had never felt so much on his own in all his life as he sat in the midst of a small group of travelers conversing among themselves as they waited for the flight to Invercargill.

Soon the flight was called and once again Max was on board an Air New Zealand aircraft, a Boeing 737 flying still further toward the bottom of the world, to South Island's, Invercargill.

As the 737 flew ever southward, Max learned from his guide book that this city of 52,000 to which he was being carried, was

the southernmost city of any size in the world. It had been settled
by the Scottish in the mid to late 1800's. It was its Scottish heri-
tage which accounts for the fact that so many of its streets bear
names of rivers in Scotland. And that most of the parishes in the
surrounding towns were Presbyterian, he would discover. As the
737 flew above the pasture lands surrounding Invercargill, Max
could see why the guide book had proclaimed that this area of
Southland was one of the richest areas for sheep production in the
country.

The travel agent in Denver had advised him to use Budget
Rental; and so after landing he entered the small terminal and
immediately went to the Budget counter. He obtained a Toyota
Corrola. Right-hand drive, of course! Awkward at first, especially
on the busy streets of a city totally unknown to him. The clerk at
Budget had recommended the Tower Lodge on Queens Drive,
"Take Dee Street north to Gala and go five blocks east to Queens.
It will be on your right."

"Dee Street?"

"Yes, Dee is the first major street you come to as you leave the
Airport going east."

Max found the lodge after a somewhat nerve-wracking drive
through traffic, on the "wrong side of the street!" Located just
south of Invercargill's large and impressive Queens Park, Tower
Lodge gave Max a comfortable and much needed resting place, a
sort of staging area from which to begin his "new life" on this
island so very far away, in which he was so alone.

The next morning, Sunday, impelled by some inner compass to go
as far south as he could, Max went south on Dee Street and drove
16 miles on highway 6 and then on No. 1 to Bluff, the port town
at the very southern tip of the South Island. At Land's End overlooking the sea he was fascinated by the yellow "AA" New Zealand
mile marker post with its multiple signs pointing to cities in all
directions. One of the markers read: "15008 km NEW YORK"
Another: "LONDON 18958 km." While at Land's End he met a

man who told him about Stewart Island—still further south. Max remembered that Duane also had mentioned Stewart Island.

"But," the stranger said, "I wouldn't take the ferry. The Foveaux Strait is too rough. Take South Seas Air from the airport in Invercargill. Much quicker. And you won't get sick!"

Max thanked the stranger. After having some oysters and chips at a take-away near the docks, by noon he had returned to Invercargill and to his room at the Tower Inn. He phoned for reservations on the next scheduled flight to Stewart Island. Max, once again turned to his guide book, and found the description of Stewart Island.

"Stewart Island lies south of Bluff across Foveaux Strait. This small island gives one the impression of what New Zealand must have been before human habitation. It is heavily forested with walking tracks instead of roads. The only bit of civilization is the tiny town of Oban on the shores of Halfmoon Bay on the northeast portion of the Island. The Maori name for Stewart Island is "Rakiura," meaning "heavenly glow," named for the frequent sightings of the Aurora Australis (Southern Lights).

By 3:30 Max had checked out and found himself in a tiny eight passenger prop plane flying low over the strait making its way to a landing strip on Stewart Island. The noisy aircraft roared and vibrated for a twenty minute ride until it put down on a dirt strip in the bush. There were no buildings at the air strip. A van from the town of Oban was waiting to take the passengers into Halfmoon Bay.

Situated on the bay was the South Seas Hotel, in which Max obtained a room. The clerk handed him his room key, an old fashioned long key attached to a large leather paddle with "NUMBER 4" embossed on it. "Your room, sir, is on the second floor, up the stairs over there. Your room faces the bay. You will find the water closet and bathroom at the end of your hall. Tea will be ready in a quarter of an hour in the dining room on our left. I do hope that you will enjoy your stay here with us at the South Seas."

"Thank you very much." Max took his two bags and went

upstairs to Number 4. A quaint high ceilinged room looking like something from the turn-of-the century. A good bed, though. He found that "faces the bay" merely indicated that it was a room on the bay side of the building. A third of the way down the hall was a door which led to the veranda, which indeed overlooked Halfmoon Bay.

After dinner—"tea" that is!—he set out on foot to explore the tiny community of Oban. Nearby on a hill sparsely covered with modest residences he came to the Parish Church. A fairly large building for so small a town, it was not entirely in good repair. The door to the sanctuary was open and he entered. The dominant color tone of this quiet place of worship was mahogany—not only the ancient pews, pulpit and communion table, but the ceiling rafters as well. Rather than a gloomy cast, which one might expect from such dark wood, the sacred space imparted to Max a feeling of peace. Upon leaving the sanctuary he read more carefully the sign outside making a note of the fact that Sunday services were at 8:00 pm. This evening, he thought. Just enough time to go back to his room and get ready for worship. He put on a white sweater—"jersey" as he would learn to say, and walked back to the church. By this time a number of folk had arrived. The women typically wore straight woolen skirts and sweaters also of wool. The men wore woolen suits, some appearing to be quite tight and out-dated by Max's standards. He was greeted at the door by a man in his fifties who gave him a warm and genuine welcome. Max took a seat toward the back while a prelude made up of a series of hymns was being played on an upright piano. Most of the hymns were unfamiliar, but one caught his attention. He remembered it from Wednesday evening prayer services in his home church as a small boy. He didn't remember its name but the words of the refrain came back to him, "I am bound for the Promised Land." This nostalgic remembrance put Max in a mellow and receptive mood for the service which followed.

The text of the sermon was from Psalm 42:

> As the hart panteth after the water brooks,
> so panteth my soul after thee, O God.

> My soul thirsteth for God, the living God:
> when shall I come and appear before God?

Max mused that in some ways he had arrived at a "promised land," at least in the sense that Duane Rustin predicted it to be a desirable place to which to flee.

The preacher began: "The subject of today's sermon is *Spirituality*." This triggered immediately in Max's memory Tipton's dissatisfaction—"Not spiritual enough!" In the course of the sermon the preacher, an older man, referred to a recent meeting: "This past week at a meeting of Southland Presbytery some of the younger clergy proposed a day of fasting for all the churches—'to bring about a revival of spirituality in all our congregations,' they asserted. In the discussion they charged the rest of us for having lost our faith! I say they are unfair. Faith is a gift of God, and God is still blessing all of us each day with Grace, by which faith is engendered. It is just that all of us do not express our faith—our spirituality— in the same manner that these young clergy do. They believe theirs to be the only way. I have been reading some of the sermons of Jonathan Edwards the early preacher in seventeenth century America. He said something very helpful, I believe. In the midst of a revival in New England called The Great Awakening, he warned against people who 'make their own experience the rule, and reject such and such things as are now professed and experienced, because they never felt them themselves.'"

After Max heard this quote from Edwards he heard little else. These words brought comforting relief and freedom to him. When the Tipton people had said "Not spiritual enough" quite possibly they meant not spiritual by their definition!

After the service the worshipers in the pews near Max lingered in order to greet him and to urge him to come to the home of one of the elders where the minister's retirement was to be celebrated in a reception. The invitation was so sincere that Max found himself accepting. He joined the procession up the hill to the elder's home. During the reception he did not feel in the least out of place. He was included in the conversations as everyone ate "finger food" as they called it. When it was his turn to speak to the minister he said, "I appreciated your words this evening, especially in connection with that Edwards quote."

"I'm glad you did. Some of us in the meeting were severely criticized for what we believed to be our own form of Christianity. This is a problem these days in New Zealand. It's the influence of what I'd call some irresponsible overseas evangelists coming here to create revivals. Creating havoc would be more to the point!"

This struck a chord in Max's mind as he replied: "We are having this kind of controversy in America as well; and what you said helps me as I think about my own church experience. Anyway, I wish you well in your retirement, sir"

"Thank you very much. I'm glad you could join us this evening."

By the time Max left to walk down the hill to his hotel room he had been welcomed by almost everyone at the reception. He felt almost as if the celebration had been held in his honor. He had been quite moved by the warmth he felt in the congregation. They had gone out of their way to wish him a good experience on Stewart Island and a good stay in New Zealand. He did not feel so alone when he returned to his room and as he prepared for bed. He slept very well and awoke fresh and ready for Stewart Island on a Monday morning.

Before breakfast in the hotel dining room Max slipped out to the veranda and found a deck chair from which he viewed the most beautiful sunrise he had ever experienced. Blood red streaks in the sky above the shimmering cherry-wood red surface of the placid bay. A few boats gently bobbed up and down, while nothing else was yet stirring.

Breakfast was oatmeal—"porridge"—and toast with marmalade. The coffee, he concluded had been made with instant or perhaps freeze-dried. Maybe that's why they go for tea, he quipped to himself. His first feeling of light-heartedness since before Oral's funeral! Only two other tables in the dining room were occupied, allowing the waitress time to chat with the guests, he noticed.

When she came to pour him some more coffee he asked: "What would you recommend for a stranger to do here on Stewart Island today?"

"Ah, you're an American!"

"Yes, I am."

"I'd say you ought to get out into the bush a bit. If you have time, there are two main walks: the Rakiura Track and the North-West Circuit. To complete either one, would take you more than one day, however."

"I'm afraid I don't want that extensive a walk."

"Then you can start out through the virgin bush on the Rakiura and get to some very scenic and isolated beaches on the other side of the island—and be back here by evening tea."

It was nine o'clock when he finished breakfast.

His waitress and informal tour guide packed him a box lunch, loaned him a day pack and asked him, "What track did you decide to take, sir?"

"I think I'll take the Rakiura as far as you suggested"

"Good! You will find it worthwhile. It begins just behind the hotel. There is a sign." She bid him, "Cheerio!" as he left the dining room.

He set out with a day pack on his back and a flush of boyish excitement in his soul. He felt a freedom that had not been his since childhood trips to forest preserves near his home. The first big difference struck him immediately. Here he was completely alone in the woods—"bush!" Under a canopy of a variety of evergreen trees unfamiliar to him. The underbrush was dense and moist. In among the thicket were lush green ferns of many varieties. The most outstanding of which he learned later were the tree ferns, with tree-like trunks topped with a broad circle of plumes of fern fronds. The quiet of the woodland path was pierced and speckled with bird calls, shrill and musical. Calls he'd never heard before. As he walked along, some of these exotic birds flew close by and perched in tree limbs over his head. These were large birds; some looked like parrots, and others like sleek blackbirds with white decorations. The further into the bush he walked the more enveloped with flora and fauna he became.

The morning's walk took him from Halfmoon Bay to the south shore of the island. He emerged from the dense growth onto a ridge overlooking the sea. Beneath him was a small isolated beach formed by the action of the sea in a miniature bay. Dropping down onto the white sand he came to a sun-dried log, a good spot for his lunch break. The hotel had fixed corned beef sandwiches and included a cucumber as garnish. For the beverage there was a can of mixed tropical fruit juice. Desert consisted of four English tea biscuits. He wished he had something hot to go with them.

Just as he was ready to devour the cookies—"biscuits" as his waitress had called them, a young man and woman walking hand in hand came out of the woods and were coming toward the water. They stopped to greet Max: "G'day, Mate!" the man said, while the woman chimed in with, "Hello, there."

"Good afternoon."

"You are an American! Not many of you folks get this far south, do they?" said the woman.

"How could you tell from only two words?"

The man hardly knew how to answer: "Don't really know— but one just does, doesn't he!"

"And you are newly-weds!" ventured Max

"Why—yes, we are. We were married Saturday in Riverton! Now, you tell me how you knew that?"

"Your brand new shiny wedding bands!"

They both looked down sheepishly at their rings.

Apparently wanting to change the subject, the woman wanted to know what brought Max here.

"Well, I've had some tragedies recently, and I needed to get as far away from home as I could—this is it!"

"Ah,—Yes." responded the man. "Do you plan to stay long"

"Not here on Stewart Island, but I'd like to find a modest

cabin somewhere overlooking the southern coast. Know any such place?

"We surely do! We spent our first two nights at a little Inn a few kilometers west of Riverton. It is located across the road from the shore."

The woman offered further information, "It is called Colac Bay Inn." You will find Colac bay on the map. It is such a small place that when you get there you will see the Inn as soon as you are at the shore. Hardly anyone there, but the owner is a good sort. Still a bit early in the season, it seems."

"Will I need reservations?"

"No, not at all. Just go to the little take-away at the center door and she'll book you in." said the woman.

"We must keep going, Sweet," said the man, and to Max they both said, "Cheerio," and they continued their walk along the shore line.

Thus, as a result of this chance meeting, Max Ritter's New Zealand odyssey would develop in some surprising ways. It would change his life.

CHAPTER 7

When South Seas Air flight 18 from Stewart Island flew low over the coastal plain near Invercargill, Max felt a tingling excitement, not a little like the feeling associated with a homecoming. Soon he was on the tarmac walking toward the terminal. In the airport car park he picked up his rental car and took Dee Street to Highway 6 north to number 99, which veered off to the west and out from town.

Max was beginning to get the feel of the right hand drive, and so picked up speed. Heading west toward Riverton and Colac Bay he began to feel a scary sense of expectancy. After Riverton his anxious feelings intensified, not knowing what he would find. The honeymooners hadn't given him much information, but it was their romantic enthusiasm which had taken hold of him. His wouldn't be a honeymoon, but it would be a new beginning!

He could see the ocean about a quarter of a mile on his left. He soon came to a sign pointing to Colac Bay where he turned left toward the sea. He came to a narrow deserted road running along the sandy shoreline. No other cars were in sight. He saw no signs of life as he drove slowly along the shore. Stopping the car, he cranked down the window, turned off the motor, and sat listening to the sound of the waves lapping up onto the sand. There were repeating ridges of turbulence in the water a short distance out. Beyond those the sea seemed to be calm. A bright sun in the north spread a glistening of silver-gold on the lapping surface of the water. He felt drawn to the ocean as if into a wilderness. Max had come to his destination, his point farthest away. He found a place to park his car and walked down to the water line in the sand and was mesmerized as he watched the glittering rolls of water come sliding up the slanting sand, each one receding again into the lapping waves; sometimes coming up to him, and other times not swishing up nearly as close. He found a water-worn log lodged in the sand far enough back to be dry and sat on it looking as far south as he could. A wondrous peace seemed to wash over him with each of the incoming waves. The further he looked beyond the bay the more relaxed he became. Each curving froth seemed to sweep away from his mind more and more of the debris which had filled his life during the past few weeks. With his mind thus cleansed he became able again to dip back in his memory to the good times.

Max remembered what it had felt like when he and Gwen had been on their way out to Montana the very first time. It had been a few weeks after the festive parties and farewells of seminary commencement. And just a week after graduation there was the deeply moving ordination service in his home church. Both sets of his grandparents had been there with his parents; and Gwen's mother and father as well. The organ music, the hymn singing, the charge to the pastor given by Max's pastor in which the words, "Preach the *whole* Gospel, Max!" still sounded in his mind. The final Ordination Question hung in his memory:

"Will you seek to serve the people with energy, intelligence, and love?"

He had solemnly answered: "I will."

A formal reception had followed in which he and Gwendolyn were greeted by countless numbers of well-wishers, many of whom he had known since childhood.

He didn't remember very much detail of the fourteen hundred mile drive to Tipton, except something of one of their overnight stops on the way. After a long day's drive they had climbed into bed in a motel in Jamestown, North Dakota. Tired, but they were both so excited that sleep seemed reluctant to intrude. He and Gwen had held each other in their arms in pleasant anticipation of arriving in Tipton the very next day.

He remembered waking the next morning with renewed energy. In his imagination he was racing to "see" Tipton and its people—the people whom they were now committed to love. At breakfast at a small cafe near the motel, he and Gwen shared their intense anticipation. "I can't wait to get there," Max said as he drained a second cup of coffee.

"I feel the excitement too, but I'm scared,' Gwen added.

"I guess I'm more curious than afraid; but a bit apprehensive, though," Max confessed. "But not exactly scared—sort of a first day at school feeling."

"I know," Gwen said.

Max could see that she really was worried. He reached across the table and took her hand in his, "I'm dragging you to an unknown place a long way from home, Gwen. I know it won't be easy for you. I'm the one who has been preparing for this day at least for the three years of seminary. But you're along for the ride. The 'better or worse' part of the marriage vow, Right?"

"Right! I wish now you would have asked for an interview trip instead of settling things by conference phone call. That way, we'd at least have some idea of what we are getting into," Gwen complained.

"Yeah, now it looks that way. At the time I was trying to save the church's money. I knew it was where I felt called by God to go. If they could feel the same about me from a phone call, then I thought we could go for it."

"Well, they are in pretty poor shape if all they could spend on us was a phone call!"

Max detected an edge of bitterness, which he hoped would be dispelled as soon as they got to Tipton. "Let's get started. The sooner we get there the better you'll feel about the whole thing, Gwen."

They checked out, got in their car again, and followed the seemingly endless ribbon of I-90 as it hastened to the Montana State Line! And what deeply moving excitement it was for both of them as they sped past the sign on the border bearing the words, "Welcome to Montana—the Big Sky Country!"

He could feel the June sun bathing the plains all around them in its brightness. Under a cloudless morning sky, bluer than they had ever seen, they were almost the only car on the road as they sped westward. The call of God impelling him, the Rev. Maxwell Ritter, to Tipton, Montana to become pastor of First Church! Max experienced a tingly feeling as hour by hour he came closer and closer to the new life ready to open and envelope him—but ultimately to reject them both, he reminded himself now as he thought about it.

That was two years ago. Now, here he was alone in a wilderness at the very bottom of the world, the southernmost edge of the South Island of New Zealand, he thought. He got up, and walking along the shore, he found a rocky ledge on which he could sit facing south. He learned later that this spot was known by locals as "Point of Rocks". Here he could look out over the unobstructed sea to the southern horizon of the earth. Beyond this was lonely and awesome Antarctica. The air was warm with a breeze stirring. The sea was calm. He sat entranced for a very long time. The sun arching behind him warmed first his left shoulder and then, as the day moved on, it shone on his right side. He thought, and he meditated. He rested his body on this portion of land's end while his mind floated above the earth, sometimes here in New Zealand, then back to his child hood, and again to Montana. He sensed that this isolated place along the southern shore of the world would be his place of healing, a sort of field hospital in which he would be restored. He determined to remain here at Colac Bay for as long as it would take to live—and love again. This would be his Gilead, he thought, as the words of the spiritual came to him over and over:
There is a balm in Gilead to make the wounded whole.

> There is a balm in Gilead to heal the sinsick soul.
> Sometimes I feel discouraged, and think my work's in vain,
> But then the Holy Spirit revives my soul again.
> There is a balm in Gilead to make the wounded whole.

By the time the sun was beginning to set in the northwest, it was casting copper plates across the waters. Max reluctantly left his shoreline retreat to arrange for his lodging. Down the road from where he had parked his car he found what looked like a small motel with a sign which read: "Colac Bay Inn—Bed and Breakfast" This was the place which had been recommended by the honeymoon couple on Stewart Island. It seemed to have about six units with windows and doors facing the sea: three on each side of a center unit which appeared to be the office and a small take-away café.

When he entered there didn't seem to be anyone around. He tapped the bell on the counter. From the rear there came a young woman dressed in a full denim skirt and a pink sweat shirt. Her shoulder-length light brown hair rested gently upon her shoulders. Her face, free of make-up, was relaxed and natural. Max felt a freshness and a warmth about her when she addressed him: "Hello—welcome to Colac Bay, I'm Bronwyn MacKenzie; may I help you?"

"Yes, I'm Max Ritter. Do you have a room and perhaps some supper?"

"Oh yes! I have a room for you. In fact I have no other guests in the Inn just now. And I think I can find something for your tea this evening."

"I'll be glad for that."

At that she picked a key off a board behind the counter and said, "Would you like to see your room?

"No, I'm sure it will be fine."

She then reached into a small refrigerator, took out a small bottle of milk and gave it to Max, saying, "Come with me. I'll show you to your room." She led him to the unit on the far west end. "While you are getting settled, I'll fix tea. Come back to the take-away when you are ready."

When he returned to the office and eating area he found that she had prepared a place at a small table by the window. She invited him to sit down, while she brought a pot of tea, some cold beef, a dish of hot cooked peas, and two slices of bread. Then she brought a registration card for him to sign as she sat at the table opposite him while he signed up. He paid her some advance money for three nights. He noticed an engagement ring on her finger.

"Breakfast comes with the room, Mr. Ritter, and for your other meals I have a few things here at the take-away which you can eat here or in your room. You are also welcome to fix things in your room. There's a small fridge there and an electric kettle, a hot plate and everything you'll be needing for light meals."

"Thank you very much, Ms. MacKenzie. Just what I need. I'm really lucky to have found you open. This is still your off-season, isn't it?"

"Yes, but I stay open all year just in case there is someone like you who might need a place. A week or two and I'll be full."

He then said, "If I decide to stay longer than three days, will that be possible?"

"Ah—Yes, that would be fine."

"Good! I guess I'll be turning in now. What time is breakfast?"

"Anytime after eight o'clock. Just come in here and ring the bell. If there is anything else you need, please let me know," she waited for any requests, and then added, "So goodnight now."

Back in his room he thought about Bronwyn MacKenzie and how she seemed to project a certain sadness about her, along with her obvious cordiality. That fits, he thought. I most likely do too!

He unpacked his bag and carry-on, hanging up what little he had brought. Before turning in for the night he stepped outside his room.

It was very dark. Only a few lights on the front of the building to illuminate the sign. A dim light remained on in the office area. He noticed an older Victorian style house behind the motel, almost adjoining, in which there was a light. He guessed that to be where Miss MacKenzie lived. There was a rocking chair outside his unit in which he sat for a while watching the glistening black/silver water in the bay and listening to its lapping in the darkness.

The steady sound of it had a hypnotic effect upon him, sending him to bed with a good feeling.

The next morning after breakfast Max sat looking out the window of the small café absent-mindedly watching the waves as they swept up onto the sand rank after rank, each washing part way up the flattened sand glistening with sea water.. Occasionally he stretched his eyes as far south across the rolling sea as he could look. The map he had bought at the air terminal in Christchurch told him that beyond this southern sea-coast from where he was now looking there was nothing but sea until it washed up onto the frozen shores of Antarctica at the very bottom of the world. He had reached his destination, the ultimate point of his running. Lost in reverie, his coffee had gotten too cold to drink. But little did he know that, when a mellow alto voice brought him back to land:

"Excuse me, Mr. Ritter, but you'll need your coffee warmed a bit, won't you?"

Reluctantly he turned his eyes away from the sea and took in the interior of the Colac Bay Café bringing his attention to its proprietor, Bronwyn MacKenzie. He nodded agreement, and she poured him a fresh steaming cup."Thank you, Ms. MacKenzie." he said as he watched her return to her work behind the counter.

She was medium in height, and seemed to be in her late twenties. He observed that she was what is called a dishwater blond. This morning she had her hair tied into a pony tail which bobbed from side to side as she worked. Her ears were uncovered fully exposing a tiny pearl in each lobe. Some strands had come loose and fell down the sides of her face in way that made her look girlish and innocent. She wore a short sleeved white blouse lightly starched and a plain khaki skirt just above her knees. Her arms were tanned, and her hands a bit ruddy from her work at the sink. Her blond hair was also found in her eye brows and lightly on her forearms. As Max studied her he concluded that there were two very outstanding things about her appearance. Her captivating blue-gray eyes, and her ready and unrestrained smile which brought appealing dimples to her cheeks, and tiny wrinkles to the corners of her eyes. Without make-up her few wrinkles as well as the normal imperfections of her complexion seemed to enhance her appearance rather than to spoil it. Her face too was tanned from the sun; she seemingly made no attempt to alter her normal appearance with cosmetics. So different from other women he had known.

There was something very refreshing about her, as he thought about it. Unsophisticated and naively friendly, he thought. Somewhat slender, but not really delicate or fine boned. Max Ritter found himself fascinated as he watched Bronwyn busy at her morning work. He was unabashedly taken by this woman so obviously confident and cheerful, unassuming and warm, yet strangely sad.

The entrancing and relaxing expanse of southern sea seemed to find expression in the calm and easy-going manner of Bronwyn MacKenzie. He had been on the run, away from human contact, wanting only to be by himself as he took himself as far away as any land could carry him. He'd gotten to the very bottom of the world thousands and thousands of miles from Tipton, Montana. Now here on the brink of an almost limitless expanse of rolling sea, was a person, another human being, whose presence somehow affected him in ways he could not, or would not, understand. He had expected the sea to be therapeutic; and it was. He would continue to let it wash over his consciousness in the coming days. But Bronwyn MacKenzie's infectious smile and soft alto voice also seemed to have healing qualities, he mused, as he got up and prepared to go out.

"Ah, Mr. Ritter, I hope this will be a good day for you! Do you plan to be back for a noon meal?"

"Er—yes, I guess so."

"Good,' I'll have a wee bit of something ready for you."

He momentarily thought he should decline this offer which he understood to be more than the normal provision for a bed and breakfast, but he was drawn to her hospitality. "Thank you very much. I'll plan on returning around one o'clock."

"I'll see you then. Cheerio!"

Max left to go back to his room before taking off for a spot along the coast line and the anticipated and much needed therapy of the salt sea.

A routine began to fix itself for Max with his meals at the take-away served by Bronwyn MacKenzie and his mornings and afternoons exploring the surrounding area. He always made sure to spend some extended time at the coastal look-out he had found. A small-home made sign labeled it "Point of Rocks" marked the place along the shore he had found. It was so situated that when one rested there, only the sea was visible in any direction except to one's back. It was isolated. The rocks themselves shielded one from view. The only sound was that of the wind and the waves—usually. However, on one particular morning not long after Max had discovered Point of Rocks, he thought he heard music as he sat facing the gray-blue sea. Musical notes, wistfully sad, were interspersed with the sound of the gusting wind. Thus, what melody may have become apparent was interrupted. But the sound itself was something like a flute. Even though he looked all around him, his location was such that no source of such mysterious music was visible. He wondered if it was some sort of audible apparition. In succeeding visits to the point the musical sound was to be heard only once or twice more.

After his first week at Colac Bay, Max drove in to Invercargill to extend his rental car lease. While in Invercargill he decided to make contact with Dale back in Tipton, to let him know that he'd not be returning for a while and that Dale should hang on to his car for him. He would not reveal his whereabouts, however. When he reached Dale by phone, before he could talk about the car, Dale said:

"You've heard the news haven't you?"

"No, what news?"

"Oh, I'm sorry to have to be the one to tell you, Max . . ."

"What is it, Dale? Tell me."

"Well, it is very sad news. Last Saturday night, we heard, that

Gwendolyn was in a serious car accident. Max, I'm sorry—but she was killed instantly!"

This news hit like a frigid shaft of steel penetrating Max to his heart. After a long silence he asked, "Dale! When did this happen? and where?"

"Right near her home, I guess. It was last Wednesday. "

"Has there been a funeral service, do you know?"

"The church people here wondered that too. I guess somebody called and found out that it was held last Sunday in her home town church."

"Oh, dear Lord, God!"

"Hey, where are you, man, Maude and I want to help you!"

"I'm too far away—but thanks, Dale. I gotta run!"

"Hey, wait!"

But Max hung up and left the phone booth, stunned and weak. What could he do? The shock was overwhelming. He could not think straight. He knew he needed human contact, or else he might go to pieces. So he turned back to Colac Bay. About half way he came to a tiny church at a town along the road called Waimatuka. He felt compelled to stop and to go in.

He went up near the front of the quiet sanctuary and kneeled to pray. "Hold me together, Dear God, or I'll fall apart." He thought of Gwen, and almost as if in prayer to her he uttered aloud. "Gwen, I'll always love you! I wanted to make it right with you. There's so much more I should have done for you. . . ." No other thoughts took shape in words. Suddenly an image formed in his mind's eye. It was the familiar painting of Jesus—the Good Shepherd with a staff in one hand and holding a lamb in the other. The gentle loving look in the eyes of Jesus made Christ come alive to Max in that moment! But the strange thing in that moment was that the eyes of Christ were blue-gray. Then he heard an inner voice singing, "There is a balm in Gilead to make the wounded whole." Fortunately no-one was anywhere around. He was unaware of how long he had been on his knees in that little church, but now Max wanted and needed to get back to "his Gilead" as quickly as possible.

Once back in Colac Bay Max went to his room, but found that he needed someone to be near him. So he went to the office and rang for Bronwyn. She came and greeted him with her gentle smile. Then seeing his distraught face, she said, "Mr. Ritter, you're not well, are you? What can I do to help you?"

"Ms. MacKenzie, I've just gotten some terrible news, and I'm heartsick. Could you bring me some hot tea and maybe a scone or two? But mainly I need you to talk to 'til I get my feet under me again, if you don't mind and have the time."

"Certainly! Sit down, Max, and I'll bring some right away. I have a pot ready. Will you be all right until I get it?"

"Yes, I'm sure."——-There is a balm in Gilead to make the wounded whole. There is a balm . . . Max sang in silence.

Bronwyn returned very quickly with a tray with a pot of tea, two cups and saucers and some scones, which she immediately administered to her wounded guest. "Can you tell me, what has been your news? Perhaps a private matter, is it?" she paused waiting a word from Max. But he was as yet silent, and she continued, "Or too difficult for you to talk about, is it?"

"No, I think I can tell you. When I was in Invercargill, I called a friend in my town in the US, and he told me the tragic news that my wife, who had left me two weeks ago, was killed in a car accident last Wednesday. And, Oh, I am just sick about it. Even though she refused to see me or have me phone her, I was hoping that by the time I returned home it might be different somehow. And now she's gone forever!"

At this point Bronwyn put her hand over Max's to comfort him and looked deeply into his eyes and said, "I am so very very sorry."

Max felt the strength and compassion of this other human being, through her voice, her eyes and her hand.—the balm, he thought, "to make the wounded whole" She didn't ask anymore questions; nor did she have any platitudes to mouth. Just the firm, warmth of her hand and the quiet peace of her own presence seemed to draw out of his own body and soul the shivering cold and clammy weight of misery. They continued to take their tea in silence, but it was a silence filled with compassion. Finally Bronwyn broke the spell: "Ah, Mr. Ritter, are you all right now to be by yourself?"

"Yes, Ms. MacKenzie, I'll be ok. You've begun to take some of my pain from me!"

"It's good you have felt some relief. I have not known such grief as yours; but I do know some sadness, and what that feels like, Mr. Ritter."

CHAPTER 8

News of Gwendolyn's death continued to be unsettling for Max, despite his prayerful vision at Waimatuku, and the "balm" Bronwyn had applied to his wounded soul. Waking in the night after his call to Dale, Max was experiencing mixed emotions. Shock and genuine sadness as well as sympathy for Gwen's family. He felt a pervasive guilt, which he could not shake. But, these feelings were also mixed with a sense of—difficult to admit to himself—relief! If he tried to put this in a rational framework, it was to tell himself that he was spared the pain and utter frustration of separation without recourse. His recognition of relief was very close to a new and unfamiliar feeling of freedom. Free from what? He had to admit that ever since the Saturday of her departure her overbearing presence had lurked always in the back of his mind, never allowing him to be completely joyful; or content, for that matter. Now that her awesome presence had been brutally taken away she was already receding from his unconscious mind.

At the same time he felt the need to do something. He surely should make some attempt to express sorrow to Gwen's family. He hadn't been able to attend her memorial service. They had made it plain that they did not want to talk with him. They no doubt were blaming him for Gwen's unhappiness: perhaps even for her death, irrational as that might be. If her mother wondered why he had not made any contact, she could not have discovered why not. And yet, he couldn't bring himself to talk directly to Gwendoyln's family. A letter would be too slow. But a telegram! Not from New Zealand, he didn't want to be traced. The idea of having someone in the US send a telegram began to take shape.

After breakfast the next morning he was on his way into

Invercargill to pick up some items of clothing he had been needing. He would phone Dale from there, and give him word for
word the telegram to send! And besides, he had forgotten to ask
Dale to hang on to his car, in the midst of the shocking news in
yesterday's call.

After "wiring" his condolences through Dale, Max felt a burden
had been lifted. He decided on taking the long way home. He felt
a reticence about seeing Bronwyn MacKenzie quite so soon after
having bared his innermost feelings in her presence. He took this
opportunity for a diversion—to do some sight-seeing in the region
north of Colac Bay. Instead of turning onto 99 he continued on
No. 6 northward to Winton, where he turned west on 96 through
Otautau and Tuatapere. It was good to see some new scenery and
to drive through a number of small New Zealand towns untouched
by modern tourism. Driving through the countryside underscored
for Max how far from home he was.

Nevertheless, tragic thoughts of Gwen kept coming back upon
him. From Tuatapere, he drove to the southern coastline at Waihoaka
and then back to Colac Bay. He parked at the Inn and went
immediately out to Point of Rocks. It was a dark overcast sky laden
with moisture which threatened to drop torrents any minute.
Memories of Gwen crowded to the surface of his mind as he looked
out over the gray Pacific.

His wedding day had been similar, with rain holding off until they
had gotten to the hotel for the reception. The smell of moisture in the
air reminded him of walking into the church with his best man just
before the marriage service was to begin. He had been nervous, and
excited all at the same time. Later, when Gwen came down the aisle
on her father's arm he was overcome with feelings of love and anticipation. She too was nervous, he had observed, when he saw her tight,
almost forced smile. However, the ceremony went off without a hitch.
The reception had been fun, he thought. Amid the loud shouts and
the cheering of relatives and friends, they had left for their first night
in a nearby motel. They had been off the next morning to a whirl-

wind honeymoon on Macinac Island at the Grand Hotel! Costly, yes! But her father had made it possible. After the week in Michigan they had returned for a few days before beginning their long drive to Montana.

The rain over the sea and on the rocks was beginning, forcing Max to draw his reverie to a close and to leave his favorite spot at midday. When he returned to the Inn take-away he found that Bronwyn had a cozy fire going in the fireplace. She greeted him when he came in: "Oh, come in and warm up by the fire. You've been in that rain, haven't you now?"

"Yes, a bit. Fire's inviting!"

"Sit down and I'll bring you a wee lunch."

Max sat at a small table near the fire, warming himself.

Bronwyn brought him some pumpkin soup with bread and cheese. She said, "This ought to warm you. Mind if I take some soup with you?"

"No, be my guest!"

They both took their soup in silence; and then she offered to get some tea. She brought a tea pot and poured two cups. The clouds were becoming blacker. By this time the rain was coming down in torrents beating against the front window. Responding to the coziness of the fire and the warmth of the tea, and wanting to avoid further talk of his sadness, Max ventured,

"Ms MacKenzie, tell me a bit about yourself, if I may ask? You live alone, I believe. Have you been here long?"

The question took her by surprise. She showed her embarrassment as she formulated an answer. "To begin with, I'd be happy for you to use my given name, Bronwyn. Ms MacKenzie sounds far too formal for this wee place on Colac Bay."

"Thank you, Bronwyn! I'd like that, providing you'll use my first name—Max."

"Yes, I'll do that. Now, to try and answer your question: In the first place this has been my home ever since I was born—not right here, but in the big house just north of here. My brother and I grew up there with our parents. My father had this Inn. He kept some sheep as well. For a number of years my mother worked in the Paua shell factory in Riverton. I went to school in Riverton. After that I began working here, helping father. Both my parents died young and left the motel to my brother and me. He didn't want anything to do with this place. He went to university in Dunedin and now he works in an office in Christchurch. He's married and has two wee ones. I don't see them much, especially after I managed to borrow enough to buy out his half. They rarely come down to Southland. His wife, Elspeth, is from Alexandra. They spend their holidays there. That's about it. Not too exciting, is it? I haven't traveled much. Oh, Queenstown once, and Dunedin some—especially lately."

She put some more chunks of coal on the fire and poured some more tea. The wind continued to swirl and rain was still beating on the front window. "It is a stormy day, isn't it." She commented, changing the subject from her story to something less personal.

However, Max persisted, "But, you've not said anything about yourself now—you know, like married, single, engaged? I guess I'm bold to ask, but I let you in on that part of my story the other day," In the quiet that followed there seemed to be a shared awareness which he acknowledged, "You were such a help to me after the bombshell dropped on me in Invercargill."

"I'm glad I was," she responded warmly, before resuming, "I live in the big house alone except for my cat, Fiona. But, as a matter of fact, I am engaged to Duncan MacKenzie. Before you ask about his name being MacKenzie like mine—he is a distant relative—quite distant. We grew up as childhood friends. His family lived here in Colac Bay until he was ten or eleven. They shifted to Gore then. We got reacquainted at a big MacKenzie clan gathering in Winton when we were both about eighteen. Now he is the Rev. Mr. Duncan MacKenzie, parish pastor in Riverton. But Duncan presently is in the hospital in Dunedin."

"Oh! I'm sorry to hear that. Something serious?"

"I'm thinking it is, considering he had to go to Dunedin. Before that he was in Kew Hospital in Invercargill where I could visit him. But he took a turn for the worse about a fortnight before you came here. He had to go in to Dunedin." Now, I don't get to see him very often.

"May I ask, what his problem is?"

"It's heart related, a murmur or irregularity or something of that sort. They seemed to have it under control at Kew, but then he had a slight stroke, which is why they took him to Dunedin."

"You're worried, aren't you, Bronwyn?"

"Yes, Max . . ." she replied as tears started to come.

"I'm so sorry. I wish there was something I could do."

When she heard this she looked at Max in a questioning sort of way. At first hesitated to answer, but then went ahead: "There might be. It depends upon how long you think you might be here."

"I'm not sure of that. But being here on Colac Bay is doing me a world of good. To tell you the truth, there is nothing calling me back home at this point. As long as my funds don't run out."

She looked at him with a question in her eyes, and then asked, "Have you had some troubles, and that's why you have come here?" She seemed flustered. "Excuse me if I'm being a bit nosey!"

"That's all right. Yes, I have had some troubles. In addition to Gwen leaving me, I lost my job. And so I've been in a state of sadness and confusion."

"I am glad that Colac Bay is helping you, Max." After a moment's hesitation, she continued: "One of the things Duncan did in addition to his work in the parish was to work around this place as a handyman—generally helping me with some of the heavy work, especially when I needed him. Now that he's away there are a lot of little jobs around here simply not getting done. What I wonder is . . ."

"You wonder if I might be able to take his place—as a handyman?"

"Yes, that's right? Could you? For a while anyway?"

"I think I could give you a hand, but I couldn't do it for pay. Immigration wouldn't allow that."

"I hadn't thought of that," she said in surprise.

After some thought she offered: "What I could do would be to give you free room and board in exchange for your help. What would you think of that?"

"Not free! That would hardly be fair to you—reduced rate, perhaps. I tell you what, Bronwyn. Before we settle on some arrangement, why don't you tell me what is needed right now, and I'll see how much I can get done. In fact with this rainy weather I can't sit on my rock. So I might just as well be doing something around here! How about it?"

"Are you sure you want to, Max?"

"I wouldn't have offered if I hadn't been willing. Give me a list and show me where the tools are."

Bronwyn drew up a list and showed Max around the Inn. And then as an afterthought, she suggested, "You needn't continue to pay for a rental car. You can use mine—now that you're on the staff!" she said with a grin.

"I guess, that would be just as well, if you don't mind." Then Max asked a question he'd been thinking about, "I noticed that you use coal in your fireplace. I've never seen that!"

"You haven't? That's what we use all the time. Also wood, of course."

"Where in the world do you find coal. I wouldn't know where to begin in Montana!"

"Ah? We have it just up the road. There's a coal mine at Ohai. Duncan has a wee truck and goes up for it when I need it."

"I drove through Ohai the other day when I took the long way—home." When he heard himself say "home" he felt oddly enticed by the word.

A few days later at breakfast Bronwyn offered Max a fifty per cent reduction in room and board. He agreed to work around the motel on a week to week basis until he should decide to leave, or Duncan should return.

The following Saturday Max drove his rental in to Invercargill to return it and took a bus back to Colac Bay. That evening while

Bronwyn was serving Max tea, he asked, "Who is taking over the services in Riverton while your fiancé is in the hospital."

"Oh, we have been having substitutes from Invercargill; and some of us locals are trying to take his place on Sundays when no one else can help out. A fortnight ago I took the service! Can you imagine?"

"Yes, I can! How did it go?"

"Frankly, it went pretty well, and I have to confess, I enjoyed it! In fact some of the folks teased me and said I ought to go to Theological Hall at Knox and become a pastor!"

"Did you take that idea seriously? What would Duncan say?"

"I really don't know. I think he wouldn't like it; but what entered my mind was, what if he doesn't get well . . ."

" I see what you mean, but don't cross that bridge yet, Bronwyn."

"No, but once in a while I think about what could happen to Duncan," she said pensively. "Tomorrow an assistant pastor from First Church Invercargill is taking the service. Would you like to attend with me?" She suggested hesitantly, and then hurried on to add, "And, Oh yes, I close the Inn on Sundays, and so you'll be needing a few things in your room for meals. I'll help you collect some."

"I think I might take you up on the idea of going in to Riverton for worship."

"'For worship' that's just the way Duncan always says it. He must have picked that up at Knox. All the rest of us say 'go in to church.' That makes you sound like a minister, doesn't it! What do you think of that?" Max didn't answer, but she might have noticed a strange fleeting expression before she said, "I'll be glad to take you in with me. It's at ten o'clock."

Max was tempted to tell her that she had guessed rightly, but decided to wait. Instead he replied: "I'll be ready whenever you want to leave."

"I'd like to leave at nine. I have some responsibilities before the service. I'm a member of the Session, you know."

"No, I didn't know, but I'm impressed. And I will be ready at nine."

"Now, let's get you some things to take to your room for break-fast." She got a small bottle of milk and a carton of corn flakes and gave them to Max saying, "There are packets of coffee and sugar in your room on top of the fridge, I think. Also, here are some slices of bread and some marmalade. You'll find a toaster and an electric kettle in the cupboard."

Max was ready the next morning at nine. He was glad that he had packed a white shirt and tie as well as a suit jacket. The rain which had kept up most of the week had blown north. By Sunday morning it was damp and chilly but sunny. The sky was bright blue as Max walked toward the big house to meet Bronwyn. A different shade of blue than he had seen before. She came out dressed in a light blue long sleeved dress with a full skirt mid calf length. A ruffled top buttoned up to a white laced collar. Her pony tail had been replaced by loosely hanging hair, making her look younger and more feminine. Max found himself drawn to her He must have smiled his approval for she immediately said, "I thought I'd put on something springy. It is such a beautiful day, isn't it?

"Gorgeous, like May in the U.S."

They got in Bronwyn's Subaru. She shared her thoughts with Max as she drove. "I like Sundays, the worship, the singing, and in many ways—best of all—the people. They have meant so much to me during Duncan's illness. This has been my home parish. I was baptized here by my grandfather. He was the pastor then. Even though the members of the congregation realize that I'll one day be the pastor's wife, they still treat me like one of them."

"How do you feel about becoming the pastor's wife?" Max asked, remembering how Gwendolyn had hated her role as wife of the preacher.

"Oh, I look forward to it eagerly. I don't exactly know why. I guess it's because I care so much for the people in this parish that I want to help Duncan make their church experience the best possible."

"That's good that you feel that way. Wouldn't it be too bad if you resented the role, and if the people didn't accept you as one of them?"

"Oh yes, that would be very hard. But I don't know of any place where it's like that, do you?"

"I'm afraid I do." offered Max. He fell silent, reluctant to go further with the subject.

Bronwyn picked up on his hesitancy and said: "I'm sorry to hear that. By the way, would you like for us to get a wee bite of lunch after church, Max?"

"I'd like that. Got a favorite place for that sort of thing?"

"Not really. Duncan and I often went to a place in Riverton, but that is a bit too familiar under the circumstances, if you know my meaning? I think I'd rather find someplace where I'm less known. I'll see if I can think of a place."

They soon entered Riverton and drove along the main street to the parish Church located on the left side of the street in the very center of town. It appeared to be a relatively new building done in the architectural style popular in the U.S. in the fifties, with a high peaked roof over the sanctuary and a low rectangular wing for Sunday School and other activities.

"There is a car-park around back. I hope there's room for us. There should be this early."

After parking they went into the church, and Bronwyn suggested that Max take a seat in the sanctuary. She would join him shortly. He sat toward the back and watched people of a variety of ages trickle in. Almost everyone smiled at him and greeted him warmly.

As he waited for the service to begin he thought about the difference between Gwen and Bronwyn in their feelings about being the pastor's wife. Had Gwen felt as Bronwyn does, she most likely would still be in Tipton, he would not be here in New Zealand—-and Gwen would be alive. The contrast wasn't just a question of their attitudes toward the ministry. In so many ways Bronwyn was very different from Gwen. Bronwyn seemed so self-confident and relaxed. Gwendolyn was so often uptight, worrying over things. Bronwyn seemed to take life in stride, including Duncan's serious illness. Much more at ease with life than Gwen, Bronwyn had helped him to relax and to let go of some of his fears and anxieties. Gwen, on the other hand had a way of intensifying his worries.

A few minutes before the start of the service, Bronwyn joined him smiling at him as she entered the pew and arranged herself beside him. Max thought the young minister from Invercargill did all right, but he could not keep from being a bit critical, thinking that he could have done it better. But when he caught himself thinking this, he remembered how he had been feeling lately— that he would never want to lead a service again—having been a failure.

After the service Bronwyn introduced him to people as they filed out the center aisle. She referred to him as an American tourist staying at the Inn, which seemed to satisfy the curious. But in a strange way it struck Max that Bronwyn thought of this as less than a full explanation.

When they were in the car again Bronwyn announced: "I'd like to drive us into Invercargill. There is a place there which will surprise you. Do you mind if we don't get back home for a while?"

"Home!" he thought. "for her—and in a way for me as well!" he had to admit. "Not at all. As you can guess, I don't have anything going."

As they drove east toward Invercargill Bronwyn talked affectionately about the people she had seen in church, describing many of them individually and offering descriptions of their families. As she told about folks she had seen she wondered out loud about friends whom she had not seen, particularly those who had been missing for a number of weeks. It was obvious to Max how much she cared for people in the congregation and how concerned she was over their absence.

Soon they were in town headed south on Dee Street near the edge of the business district. Suddenly she slowed down and made a right turn into the parking lot of a Pizza Hut! She looked at Max with a grin and said, "I thought you might be lonesome for the US! This should give you a 'back home' feeling!"

"Bronwyn, this is great! I like it! Even though I can't honestly say I'm lonesome for the U.S." *The fact of the matter, he thought, I feel more at home here with Ms MacKenzie and have more of a feeling of comradeship here than I've experienced for a long time.* He realized how socially isolated he had been made to feel in Tipton, where he had not been accepted as 'one of them' as Bronwyn had referred to her relationship to the Riverton church. He certainly hadn't been seen as a man among other men. He had painfully experienced the American rural three gender stereotype: men, women, and ministers! And he had been the sole occupant of the third category in Tipton.

Pizza always is a long wait. Max felt uneasy when the conversation lagged. After turning the matter over in his mind more than once he finally said: "There is something that I haven't told you, that I guess I want to share. It seems appropriate to tell you now on Sunday after attending worship with you."

"What is that, Max?" She looked perplexed.

"Well, the truth of the matter is that I am an ordained Presbyterian minister."

Bronwyn showed signs of surprise, "Is that a fact?" she said approvingly.

"Yes, it is. I recently was pastor of a little congregation in Montana. And there's more. From the way the people responded to my efforts and to me personally, I'd have to say that I was a failure. They treated my wife even worse. To be quite honest, a couple of weeks ago they asked me to resign."

"Oh, I'm so sorry about that! That explains why you are here in New Zealand, doesn't it?"

"Yes it does, Bronwyn. Notice of the Session's request that I resign came to me by phone while I was attending a church conference in Denver, Colorado."

"How cruel!"

"It was very difficult. I decided not to return to Tipton just then. Instead I wanted to get as far away as I possibly could. So, here I am on the very south of the South Island of New Zealand, as far south as Montana is north—the 45th Parallel. Some guys would have sought counseling, but I'm not the type to want that. I'm one to try and solve my problems on my own," he confessed. "That's what's going on inside me while I'm sitting out there on the rocky shore of Colac Bay!"

"Oh, Max! Is it helping you?"

"It is, Bronwyn—and you're helping me also," he confessed, somewhat hesitantly."

"I hadn't known. I find it such a coincidence that you are a pastor. Now that you tell me that, I can see it! Little things like saying 'go to worship' instead of 'go to church.' Remember I commented on that this morning? That you say it like Duncan does?"

The waitress brought their pizzas. Conversation was temporarily delayed while they enjoyed the familiar American dish.

After leaving the pizza parlor Bronwyn announced, "I've another place to show you while we are here in Invercargill." She continued on Dee Street to Herbert and then turned south again on Queens Drive to an entrance to a large city park, where she parked and suggested, "This is Queens Park. Let's get out of the car and walk for a while."

When Max saw where they were he said, "This is very close to the motel I stayed in when I first arrived—the Tower Lodge right over there."

"I know it well. I have a friend who works there. Now that's a coincidence, isn't it?" And then she pressed Max further,"Do you feel like telling me more about your experience in Tipton? I'd be very glad to hear it."

Reluctantly at first, Max replied, "If you really want to hear it, I guess I can fill you in, but stop me if I bore you."

"Oh no, tell me."

As they walked along under the trees now almost fully leafed out, they felt the warmth of the sun as it shone through the partially clad trees. The blue sky formed a magnificent backdrop for the yellow-green of the leaves. Max began by telling of the eager expectation he had felt when the call to Tipton had come to him and then of the disappointments and difficulties he had faced during his four years as pastor. He told of his wife's awkwardness in the role of minister's wife and of the meanness with which she had been treated.

"Weren't there any good experiences?"

"The best times we had were with the youth group we had charge of. Ten or fifteen high schoolers met with us every Sunday evening. We really had a good time. They, at least, appreciated us, I guess."

And then Max told about the evening he had returned to the manse from a wedding to find that Gwendolyn had left him.

There was silence between the two during which Bronwyn in an uncalculated gesture took hold of Max's hand, communicating her deepest sympathy. A healing warmth filled him and he sang in his heart, "There is a balm in Gilead, To make the wounded whole,"

She could sense something of this, and she said, "What is it, Max?"

"Oh, I was singing to myself a song of healing."

"What song?"

He sang quietly,

> There is a balm in Gilead
> To make the wounded whole,
> There is a balm in Gilead
> To heal the sinsick soul.
> Sometimes I feel discouraged,
> And think my work's in vain,
> But then the Holy Spirit
> Revives my soul again.

As he sang he realized that Bronwyn was humming quietly, and that by the end of the stanza she had joined him in the words, "But then the Holy Spirit revives my soul again."

They quietly walked back to the car to begin their return to Colac Bay. Now their conversation was more casual—about the sights they were passing as they left Invercargill. They made their way back through Riverton and home to Colac Bay.

When they arrived at the Inn Bronwyn said, "Let me get you a can of soup and some bread and cheese for your tea in your room. I'll bring it to you there."

"OK, that would be fine."

Max went to his room. After receiving the provisions Bronwyn brought him, he took her hand and said to her, "Bronwyn MacKenzie: You are my Balm in Gilead! Thank you for today."

"I'm glad for that, Good night, Max Ritter."

The lengthening shadows of the Inn extended onto the nearby waters of the Bay as Max sat looking out his window while he ate the simple supper of soup, bread and cheese Bronwyn had given him. Bronwyn MacKenzie! Who is she? He mused. Engaged to become the wife of a pastor. He thought about his feelings for her and sensed that she was more like a sister to him than a woman in whom he might be "interested." He remembered his own sister, Jan, with whom he had lost contact since moving to Montana. In a curious way Bronwyn reminded him of Jan. But he had to admit to himself Bronwyn wasn't just a sister image. He had felt a different sort of warmth when she had taken his hand. But he told himself such feelings must not develop. She is to be Duncan MacKenzie's wife, he said to himself—almost out loud. Bronwyn—with her compassionate blue-gray eyes!

That night as he lay on his bed the music continued in his mind and heart: "To make the wounded whole—-there is a Balm, in Gilead . . ." No longer a tourist, he thought. A wanderer who has found a "home!" Despite what the immigration people ruled, Colac Bay was to be Max Ritter's "permanent" residence. Tipton certainly wasn't. What other home was there for him? And so it would be. Max Ritter of Colac Bay—Southland—New Zealand for the foreseeable future!

CHAPTER 9

Conrad Schneider sat in his office on the second floor of the Lodge at Fairhavens looking out his west windows. His eye followed the mountain range which stretched along the west edge of the valley of the Yellowstone. In this direction with very few trees in view the sunlight made radiant the lush grass lands of Paradise Valley. Con thought about the board meeting earlier that week when the official signing had taken place. He re-lived the luncheon they had shared in the dining room to celebrate the acquisition of the Fairhavens property. Leona Baxter had saved their unique project from the devastating loss which had come so close. Even Clyde Blackwood had joined in the festivities. Con decided that he'd have to draw in a little closer to Clyde, for he knew that Clyde had sympathies for the Cody Vermillian project, and that tended to alienate him. He wondered just what would happen to that project now that the key property would not be taken over. Howard Eldridge had shared with Con the rumor that Cody had failed in a similar project on the West Coast. The conjecture of the two men was that maybe Cody wouldn't complete this one either. Others in the Resort Association were dubious about Vermillian as well, Eldridge had said.

The phone rang."Hello, Conrad, this is Mark Engle. Just wanted you to know that the Fairhavens transaction has just been filed in Park County this afternoon. You're home free."

"Mark, thank you for letting me know. And above all, thank you for all that you have done to make this thing go through."

"I've not done that much. It's what you did on your Chicago trip, that made the difference. You know that."

"Yes, you're right. But the speed your people put this

through has been critical. The Vermillian gang was close on our heels."

"That's so. Well, its closing time. Just wanted you to know. We'll be in touch."

Con looked at his watch. 4:50 PM. That would be 5:50 in Chicago. He dialed the phone.

"Hello, the Baxter residence."

"Yes, this is Con Schneider from Montana. May I speak to Mrs. Baxter, please?"

"This *is* Lee Baxter!—*Con!*"

"I didn't recognize your voice, Lee, sorry to be so formal!"

"That's OK. It's this cold I've got."

"Lee! The sale has gone through! Fairhavens is ours! The deed in the Board's name has just this afternoon been filed in the county court house. We made it, and you are the angel who made this possible. I wanted you to know right away and to tell you how very much all of us appreciate your generosity . . .," to the question Lee cut in, Con hastened, " No, I have not told anyone who the donor is."

"Good," Lee replied, "Considering how recent all this is, will it raise suspicions if I show up at Farihavens sometime?"

"I don't think so. As long as you come as an ordinary guest, coming for R. & R. We can dream up some reason for us to have known each other previously."

"If you're sure. I really am anxious to come out and see Fairhavens—and to see you again, Con."

"I want you to see it." Con assured her, " And, yes, I'm looking forward to seeing you myself."

"Then, I'll call my travel agent on Monday and see when I can get reservations. Where did you say I should fly into?"

"Bozeman. You can fly either Northwest or Delta, whichever gives you the best schedule . . . No need to arrange for ground transportation. I'll be there to meet you and I'll bring you here. On second thought, much as I'd like to, maybe we better send our usual van and driver. We meet planes in Bozeman all the time to bring in guests. I've lost our regular driver, but there will be someone I can send. I'll look for you here at the Lodge then. I'll have the office send you all the introductory information and a request for reservations sheet. That way you come in on a regular basis! . . . Just send it in as soon as you know your date and flight schedule. But also, phone me, so that I can know!"

After saying good-bye, Con resumed his contemplation of the golden grassy foothills in the west—now with the added pleasure of anticipating sharing all the surrounding beauty with Lee. She was someone who was beginning to make a difference in his personal life as well as in the future of Fairhavens.

He was overcome with a sense of thanksgiving, a feeling which needed expression. An idea struck him. He dialed a local number: "Hello, Barbara, this is Con Schneider. Does your church have services on Sunday? . . . What time? . . . Good, I think I'll be there . . . Don't be surprised . . . Oh, I just feel like I ought to show my feelings of thanksgiving for the good things happening! Anyway, I'll most likely see you and Mervin Sunday at nine."

Good things happening! They certainly were, Con thought. Not only saving Fairhavens, but Lee herself. Con had never known anyone quite like her. Or was it rather, that he had never felt about anyone as he was beginning to feel about Lee Baxter. Anyway, we would eagerly await word of her visit!

Cody Vermillian sat at his desk in his office in Livingston—planning. A few minutes before five o'clock his phone rang. He picked it up, "Cody Vermillian speaking."

It was his Billings attorney calling: "Hello, Mr. Vermillian, this is Worth Benson . . ."

"Hello, Worth: What's the good word?"

"I have some news for you, but I'm afraid its not 'the good word' as you say."

"OK, What's the bad news?

"I've just gotten a call from Corvalis, Oregon from the law firm representing the family which owns the Fairhavens property, a Mr. Sherman Nordstrom. He is informing us that the property is now off the market. It has been sold, purchased outright by the Fairhavens board!"

"What? I thought we had that deal practically cinched. No way did they have the money. You sure? Isn't there still a way around them? Some loophole that will hold up the sale. It can't be a done deal."

"No, Cody, there's no way. It has just been filed in your Park County Courthouse—signed, sealed, and settled."

"I can't believe it. That really throws a curve."

"I'm sorry. When we can be of further help, call me,"

Cody didn't reply immediately, saying, "Hold on a minute, Worth."

"What is it?"

"Would you get your people to track down the property owners for all the parcels surrounding the Fairhavens property and get me a list of names and addresses as soon as possible?"

"I think we can do that. We'll need to get a clerk over to Livingston Monday. After an hour's work she should be able to drop that off to you before returning here that night."

"Good, I'll be waiting for that. I'll talk to you after I've seen the list."

"Alright, Goodbye then."

"Right—Goodbye."

Cody hung up and then immediately dialed another Billings number: "Good afternoon, B.J.T. Architecture and Engineering. How can I help you?"

"Yes, Hello, this is Cody Vermillian. Is Todd Brown still in? If so, may I speak to him?"

"I believe he is, Mr. Vermillian. I'll put him on." This was followed by soothing elevator music spilling into Cody's ear while he waited. The music cut off and then, "Cody, Todd Brown speaking. What's up?"

"More than I care to think. We've been beat out of the Fairhavens property. The present renters purchased it, cash on the barrel-head . . . No, I have no idea where they got the money. But

they must have gotten it somewhere. What I want you to do is to
re-draw the site plan without the property, but using all of the
surrounding land . . . that's right. I've got Benson & Anderson
chasing down the current owners of property adjacent to Fairhavens.
We'll begin working on them next week . . . Yes, I'll be in the
office Monday and Tuesday . . . Right, I can consult by phone on
the plan. And as soon as you have something FAX it to me—
Good. Talk to you later.

The next number he dialed was a local number: "Clyde . . . this
is Cody Vermillian . . . no, not fine . . . what happened that you
guys could buy the property? I thought you told me there was no
way you could come up with the money."

"I didn't think there was; and then Schneider made a trip to
Chicago and came back with $75,000 and the promise of 100
more . . . An anonymous donor, is all we were told . . . I know, I
tried to talk them into using it on one of your homesites, and
letting the old shack go, but I was the only one opposed to the
purchase. So, what could I do?"

"Well, it's a nasty set-back; but it won't stop us . . . Yeah, I'm
working on an alternative idea . . . Give me a week and let's have
lunch and I'll tell you what I'm up to."

"OK, phone me."

A couple weeks went by. Con Schneider had been to worship at
Mill Creek twice! That's twice more than he'd been to any church
since his Erie House days! What's coming over me, he wondered.

Now that the Fairhavens Board was the owner of the property
there were implications for both the accounting system and board
responsibilities. Con soon found that it would be necessary for the
Board to increase the frequency of its meetings from quarterly to
one a month. He set up meetings for November and December
before a monthly schedule for the new year was established. Year
end bookkeeping would be complicated by the purchase and a
new method of accounting would be set up for the new year. This
aspect of the work kept Con traveling back and forth to Fairhavens'

accounting firm in Livingston. He found this increased pace exhilarating because of what it meant for the future of Fairhavens.

He was disappointed, however, when a phone call from Lee came a few weeks after the filing of the new ownership. He was in his office late one evening when he heard from Lee: "Con, this is Lee. I have some disconcerting news."

"What's that?" Con asked, fearing what he might hear.

"I was just about to call you this morning to tell you I had my ticket for Montana . . ."

"Yes . . ."

"When my daughter, Corrie, called in tears, wanting me to come to St. Louis, because her husband left her and was filing for a divorce. She has an eight year old boy, and they need me right away. Con, I must go!"

"Of course, Lee. We can put off your trip here."

"I am sorry. I was looking forward to it so."

"Any idea of how long you'll be involved, Lee?"

"No, but my guess is that it will be through Thanksgiving, and maybe even into December." she said reluctantly, "I'll try to phone you, and we can write."

"Don't worry about it, Lee. We want you here when you are most able to enjoy it."

"That's sweet of you. It may have to wait until after the first of the year, with Christmas coming near the time I might be coming home. Now I need to run—so much to do before my flight tomorrow noon."

After exchanging "good-bye's" Con reflected that it really had been too good to be true to think that Lee would be with him any time soon. But then there was so much to do before January 1, that he realized he too might enjoy a visit more in January. Hopefully it will come soon, he thought.

CHAPTER 10

The morning sun was completely obscured by low hanging clouds when Max walked over to the take-away for breakfast with Bronwyn. When she greeted him, she seemed unusually quiet. She brought her regular offering of porridge and coffee to the table and joined Max. The rain had begun pelting against the front window as they sat looking out. Finally Max said, "Bronwyn, you seem so down this morning. Is something wrong?"

"No, no more than usual. Gray days like this often depress me. Often on a dark overcast morning like this I start thinking about things . . ."

"Things like . . . ?"

"Oh, about Duncan. I don't know what's going to happen. It's sad. On days like this I get a premonition that he's not going to get well."

Max did not know what to say. He felt reticent about reaching out to her to comfort her, for fear of acting inappropriately. In this moment he felt close to her, but he respected the boundaries which separated them. So, he asked, "What helps you when it's like this for you?—besides a change in the weather, I mean."

Without hesitation she said, "Music."

Max waited to hear more.

"When I was a little girl—nine, I think, I was often sent to spend my school holidays with my Grandfather and Grandmother. My father had been killed the summer before in a farm accident. His death hit me very hard, and I was having a very difficult time dealing with the loss. My Grandparents lived in Winton. It was from Grandfather that I gained comfort. He was a music teacher

A PLACE
CALLED
FAIRHAVENS

ACKNOWLEDGMENTS

To those many nameless ones who long ago enriched my life experience while I worked for the Oak Park Arms Hotel in the greater Chicago area; and somewhat more recently, when I was on the staff at Zephyr Point Conference Center on Lake Tahoe in Nevada, I am indebted.

For the "cloud of witnesses" whose faithful lives in Wyoming and Montana have led me to a deeper understanding of their world and of our common spirituality I am deeply thankful.

I salute the members of the Oreti Parish on the South Island of New Zealand who introduced me to their particular expression of faith, and who welcomed my wife and me into their community as well as to their uniquely beautiful country. I want especially to extend my appreciation to Sam and Jennifer Woods in Southland, N Z, who helped to refresh my memory of the places, sounds and sights of New Zealand as they reviewed an earlier draft of "Fairhavens".

Finally I want to thank Doris, my wife, whose encouragement along the way has helped me to take the necessary step of crossing over the border into the intriguing realm of imagination and of recording what I found there.

in Central Southland College; and music was his all-consuming love. He was very soft and tender with me.

I remember one very dark and rainy day soon after I had come for my first visit. He found me in the guest room on the bed crying my heart out. He bent over and lifted me up with his very large and sensitive hands. When I was standing he encircled me with his arms. I lay my head against his chest. He let me cry. He said more than once while I was in his arms, 'Weep, my wee lass. 'Tis your weeping that tells God how much you loved your daddy! Weep, wee lass.' It felt so good to be told that I could weep. I had been afraid to cry over father's death at home, for fear of upsetting mum. Now here in Grandpa's arms I could weep." Bronwyn shared this with an emotional trip in her voice.

"After a while Grandfather let go of me. He led me downstairs, and put me in a chair in his music room. He sat down at his piano and began to play. He chose a number of the old hymns of the church—'Abide With Me'—'I Need Thee Every Hour'—'For All the Saints'—and so many more. I can't remember them all. Soon he brought me a hymn book and bid me sing along, 'Sing away your sadness, Lass . . . Sing your sorrow to God, Bronwyn!'

"One hymn I remember especially—a few lines of it, at least:

'Sun of my soul, Thou Saviour dear,
It is not night if Thou be near.'

"I still sing those words sometimes, when the sadness comes, Max."

Max nodded appreciatively as he heard this.

"That day in Grandfather's music room my weeping and his music changed my sorrow into a bittersweet joy!"

Max repeated: "sing away your sadness—weeping tells God how much you loved your daddy. Those words must have been very special to you—I like that!" Max declared.

Bronwyn continued: "In the course of the next few years I spent most of my holidays with my 'grands.' Grandfather taught me to play the piano. He had a harp in his music room, and I was fascinated by it. After I'd made some progress on the piano he gave me harp lessons too. Also, at his suggestion I learned to play the recorder. He had said, 'You can't very well take a piano or a harp out to the sea shore. But if you play the recorder you can take it along and play to the waves of the sea! It's like singing in the grand hall of the universe, Lass!' I have found out since that day, that he was right! Sometimes, when I'm entirely alone by the sea I play to the tides!" At this point Bronwyn paused and seemed embarrassed, and said, "I've never told anyone about my playing out there."

When Max heard this, he thought of the music he had heard on gray mornings when he was out on the rocky shore. It must have been Bronwyn MacKenzie 'singing away her sadness!' "I'll not tell; but I'd like to hear you play the harp some time, and your recorder."

"Maybe some day. But not now. It's also sort of a private time for me. I hope you understand."

"Yes, Bronwyn. I respect that." Then he gave her opportunity to be alone with her music. "This rain means I can't do the things I'd planned. So why don't you spend some time at home—perhaps with your harp—this morning. I'll 'mind the store!'"

She looked at him with a trace of tears in her eyes and said, "Max Ritter, you're too good to me! But I'll do as you say."

Max saw that she was about to weep as she left the take-away for her home. He took satisfaction from minding the store that morning, and on other mornings like it in the succeeding weeks.

A month flew by giving Max time enough to do most of the odd jobs around the Inn which had piled up since Duncan's illness. He continued to take his meals in the take-away. The day-to-day contact with Bronwyn consisted mostly of motel business matters.

Sundays, were their opportunities for more personal conversations. They customarily went to Riverton for morning worship. They usually continued on into Invercargill for the afternoon, and returned toward dusk.

One Sunday they visited the Southland Museum and Art Gallery in Queens Park. Max was especially taken with the Tuatara, one of the most ancient of living reptiles. They stood at the glass enclosure for the longest time trying to spot one. Finally they were rewarded with a glimpse of the wizened old creature peering at them. "It's as if it's looking at us from among the primeval rocks of a time before human history." Max said.

"I know! Wouldn't we like to know what he's thinking!"

Later that afternoon, they sat on a park bench without a lot to say, each in private reverie. Suddenly in the distance they heard the sound of a lone bag-piper. "Scotland the Brave," Bronwyn whispered.

Both were stirred by the distinctive combination of low droning sounds and the reedy melody in the higher range. Max happened to look at Bronwyn as they heard the piper. He discovered that she was weeping. She noticed his looking at her, and appeared embarrassed.

Max gently said, "Weep, my lass. Weeping tells God of your love . . ."

"For Duncan, and for my father—and for Grandfather. They are all on my heart when I hear the sound of the pipes! All three played them. But it is the piper at my Grandfather's graveside that always comes to mind. Grandfather was buried in the little cemetery outside Winton. I must have been about sixteen then. After the clergyman finished, we could hear in the distance a piper piping "Scotland the Brave. After that piece they lowered his casket into the open grave, while the piper played, 'Abide with Me.' Everyone wept. For we knew of Grandfather's military service in the Great War of 1914. He'd been in a Highland unit and had played the bag pipes for it. Since then, whenever I hear it I can't help but weep. I remember at the end of the service, the piper played 'God, Be with You 'till We Meet Again' as the workmen began shoveling dirt onto his casket in the grave."

In the silence that followed Max felt the edge of tears. He was thinking of Gwen and of his own failure to attend her burial. It wasn't like Max at all, but he found himself suggesting, "Let's sing away our sadness, Lass! Let's sing our sorrow to God!" With that he began to hum "God Be with You;" and then together they sang quietly as much of the hymn as they could remember.

After their singing they were quiet. Bronwyn, with her eyes still moist leaned over and kissed Max on the cheek and gave his hand a squeeze.

On another Sunday afternoon they attended a choral concert given by the Ionians, a Southland choir based in Winton. Again on that day Max could feel the emotion which music brought to Bronwyn. One of the numbers seemed especially to move her: "When you walk through a storm, keep your head up high." Music is her "Balm in Gilead", he thought.

On the first week-end in December their routine was radically changed when Bronwyn got a Saturday morning phone call during breakfast from one of the Riverton church elders: "Miss McKenzie, this is John Lindsay from the church Session.

"Ah, yes, Mr. Lindsay. What is it?"

"The substitute minister from Winton has fallen from his roof and broken his leg. We are in need of someone to lead our service tomorrow morning. Might you be able to help out with our service, Bronwyn?"

Quite flustered at such late notice, Bronwyn nevertheless agreed to take the service. But when she hung up the phone she did not see how she could come up with a suitable service. She told Max of the request and appealed to him: "I simply cannot prepare a service on such short notice. Do you think you could take the service? With your training and experience, I'm sure you could improvise."

This struck him numb. For a long moment he could not reply. Then he said: "What you're asking me is something I have dreaded since that last fateful Sunday in Tipton. I've been telling myself ever since that I simply can't—or won't lead anymore services . . . " He struggled to know how to go on.

She intervened, "Max, this could be a step in your healing."

"I'd have to admit that worshiping in your church has been a

healing balm for me. But to stand up there——and lead——and to
preach. I feel so unworthy now . . . "

"But the congregation is in need—worthy of the Word, Max.
Who is going to bring it to us this week? And it is the First Week
in Advent!"

Max said aloud, "Are you sending me, Lord? I'll try my
best . . . You'll have to pick up the pieces, Lord."

So it was that the Rev. Max Ritter returned to the pulpit for
this one Sunday. It turned out that Bronwyn provided him a great
depth of support, helping him ease back into the role which terrified him so after the cruelty of Tipton. That afternoon after worship Max was unusually quiet as they drove to Invercargill. Bronwyn
broke the silence, "Max, we truly had a good worship and preaching this morning! So many friends told me how much they felt
inspired by your message and your leading. I was proud!"

Max was touched by her words. "Thank you for that. Your
presence in the congregation is what carried me through! Again,
Bronwyn MacKenzie, you have been my healing balm!"

"You know it was God—not me."

"Yes, God; God through you; making me whole again!" Max
said, almost overcome with emotion. During their meal and walk
in the park Max felt closer to Bronwyn than ever before. He cautioned himself, reminding himself of Bronwyn's commitment to
Duncan.

That night Max was awakened by a rap on his door in the
early hours of Monday. He got up, put on his robe and found
Bronwyn also in her robe at his door with an urgent request.

"I've just gotten a call from the hospital in Dunedin. Duncan
has taken a serious turn for the worse. The nurse attending him
felt that I should know, and that if possible, I should come as soon
as I can."

"Why, yes, by all means, I think you should. Can I take over
here?"

"You could, but my problem is that I haven't driven that far at
night; and besides that, I really am feeling quite nervous about the

situation. Could you drive me there, Max? I feel that I can justifiably close the Inn for a few days."

"I can do that. You mean right away, don't you?"

"Yes, I know that is quite an imposition, but I really think I need to be there as soon as possible."

"Let's get ready and go. How much time do you need?" Max said taking charge of this emergency in Bronwyn's life.

"Thirty minutes should be enough."

"That would be a little after three. I'll be over."

"Oh, thanks, Max—so very much!"

At a quarter past three Max and Bronwyn pulled out of the Inn car-park; and they were on their way to Dunedin, a trip of almost two hundred and fifty kilometers. They remained mostly silent as each pondered the unknown soon to be faced.

It was nearly seven when they were driving through the outskirts of Dunedin. It was just beginning to become light. The sun was about to emerge in the north east over the Pacific.

Bronwyn directed Max to the hospital. When they arrived she said, "Max, I'll go right in and try to see Duncan. If it's too early I'll let the nurse know I'm here so that I'll get in as soon as I can. Why don't you find us a place to stay. Two rooms in a Bed and Breakfast would be good. That way you can have breakfast when you check in. I'll get a wee bite at the hospital."

"I'll do that. How shall I contact you?"

"Let's meet here in the main floor waiting room at three this afternoon. Then we can see what's next."

"I'll be back at three. I hope you find Duncan holding his own. It should do him good to have you there. So good bye for now."

"Bye, Max."

After Bronwyn left Max to see Duncan, Max found a service station to fill up on petrol and to ask about a B & B. He was directed to Magnolia House not far from the downtown area. He found this to be a very picturesque Victorian home which had been made into a bed and breakfast. He obtained two rooms and

was invited into the dining room for breakfast, which by this hour
he craved. After breakfast and a friendly chat with the proprietor
Max spent the rest of the time walking around down-town Dunedin

Later, when he met Bronwyn in the hospital waiting area at
three she said, "Take me somewhere away from here where we can
get something to eat. They found a small take-away nearby and
she unloaded her feelings: "He looks so bad, not at all himself.
They've got tubes in him every imaginable place. He's in intensive
care and hooked up to a heart monitor and to a respirator. He
recognized me, but couldn't talk. They let me in to see him for
only five minutes every half hour. No-one could tell me anything
for sure. I guess at this point they really don't know. I certainly
don't know how this is going to turn out. It's gotten me upset."

Max reached over and placed his hand upon hers and said,
"Sometimes reality is far worse than what we had imagined. I guess
this is one of those times. It's just good that you got here."

"Yes, it is, even though there's not much I can do."

"Just being there for him, where he can see you every so often—
that's surely going to help."

"I hope so. Did you find us a place?"

"Yes, I found a very nice B & B in an old Victorian house.
Called the Magnolia House."

"I think I'd like to go there and lie down for a little while.
After getting up so early this morning. I'll go back to the hospital
this evening for a while."

While Bronwyn slept Max arranged with Hugh Grayson, the
proprietor of Magnolia House for two evening meals. At half past
five Max gently knocked on Bronwyn's door to let her know that
they would eat at six. Soon afterward she joined him in the dining
room. "How are you doing now, Bronwyn?"

"A bit better, I'd say."

"I'm glad for that."

After eating together in the dining room of Magnolia House,
they returned to the hospital where Max waited in the waiting
room while Bronwyn visited Duncan. He had found a book on

New Zealand history at a book stall, this afforded him opportunity
to have a look at it.

For the next five days Bronwyn continued her routine of being
in the hospital as much as she could in order to see Duncan every
half hour or so. Meanwhile Max spent the time exploring Dunedin.
Saturday evening Duncan was moved out of intensive care and
into a regular ward. He was improving.

Sunday morning Bronwyn and Max attended worship at the
large First Presbyterian Church in the heart of the downtown.
Bronwyn was able to spend the entire afternoon with Duncan. By
evening she had much to share with Max, as they sat in the
Magnolia House lounge.

"He seems so different. This radical illness seems to have changed
his personality. He is so listless and morose. Much changed from
the way he was. He was previously quite bouncy."

"Perhaps only temporarily, don't you suppose. Could be the
medication. And of course anything that serious with the heart is
bound to make a difference in a person."

"He knew me, but you'd think we were strangers who had just
met."

"That must be hard on you."

"It is. His closest family member is his brother from Gore. He
has been asked to come tomorrow for a family conference with the
doctors. I guess that's when they will say what they can about the
future."

"Can you be at that conference, or are they strict about only
talking to family?"

"At first they said I could not attend. Then Duncan's nurse
intervened and explained how close I am. So they said I could
come, if the brother approved. He will, I'm sure."

"So, by this time tomorrow you should have some idea of what
is ahead!" Max said, more as a question than a statement of fact.

"I think so. But it makes me afraid to think about it."

Max surprised himself when he said, "Bron, would you want
me to pray with you?"

"Yes, I'd like that."

"Let's go out on the porch where we can be alone.

"Alright, let me get my jersey first.

They sat together in the dark of evening and Max, holding her hands prayed: "O God of mercy, be with your servant, Bronwyn, tomorrow. Give the doctors the best possible wisdom and understanding of Duncan's condition. And be with Duncan. Place your loving hand upon him, strengthen him, and above all make your abiding presence known to him in such a strong way that he feels fully supported and in your loving presence. And O God, whatever the outcome, I pray that you fill Bronwyn with your love and power, your comfort and your mercy. In the name of Jesus, the Good Shepherd, we pray. Amen."

After a long silence, Bronwyn looked into Max's eyes and said, "Thank you for that." With tears beginning to form in her eyes she said, "Now I can sleep. You have been my Balm in Gilead!" This had the effect of bringing a few tears to Max as well. With that they both arose and went to their separate rooms. There to be refreshed with sleep, to prepare for the revelations of the next day.

Bronwyn drove to the hospital alone to attend the conference with the doctors. By noon she was back at Magnolia House. She went to her room to spend some time on her own to think about what she had been told. Max had spent the morning in the local library. When he returned after lunch he noticed that the Subaru was back, but he decided not to bother Bronwyn, and to wait for her call. Sometime around the middle of the afternoon she phoned Max's room: "Max, this is Bronwyn. Might I pop in to tell you about the conference?"

"Sure, come right over."

When she arrived Max could see from the expression on her face that the news at the conference had not been good. "Sit down, and tell me about Duncan."

"What I was told is not at all encouraging; but I am going to have to face it."

"What were you told?"

"Physically Duncan is doing quite well. A fortnight or longer perhaps and he should be sufficiently healed and strengthened so that he can return home. But it seems that during his most critical time the blood flow to his brain was cut off briefly leaving him . . . ." she found it difficult to go on . . ."He'll be somewhat incapacitated mentally."

"That is very painful news. Do you know what sort of incapacity? Is it in any sense temporary?"

"I think it mainly has to do with his memory and his speech—like a stroke. We were told that a certain amount of this will be permanent, but therapy may be able to bring back some of his ability to speak; and certain of his lost memories may gradually return. At least at first he is going to need daily assistance; but in time he should be able to do some things for himself. As they said, physically he is going to be able to do whatever he did before. But mental tasks are going to be hard for him."

Max took her hand to offer his care and support. They both sat quietly for a few moments. She then, said, with an edge of anger in her voice, "In plain practical terms this means that Duncan can be a handyman, but not a minister. Those days are over for him, I am afraid. The neurosurgeon was quite blunt about that. He said, 'I should not expect that Mr. MacKenzie will ever be able to perform the basic functions of a minister again. His best hope lies in vocational rehabilitation, and counseling to obtain for him some other employment commensurate with his diminished capabilities.' When Duncan's brother heard this, he asked the doctor to put this in writing so that the church offices in Wellington and in Invercargill could be advised. When I heard it I felt as if a most awful black cloud had fallen upon Duncan and me." Bronwyn began to openly weep.

Max waited for a few minutes before asking further, "What are next steps? Do you know?"

Having regained her composure Browyn outlined what she knew: "In a few days he should be dismissed to a rest home here in Dunedin where he'll be given some therapy—speech and vocational.

After that he can come home where I will be the one to provide some daily assistance to him. But meanwhile . . . it may sound strange . . . but the psychotherapist on the team directed me not to have any contact with Duncan until he returns to his familiar surroundings . . . not even another visit, she said. Then, after he is home he's to have outpatient therapy at Kew Hospital in Invercargill as needed." Again with an edge of anger she concluded, "So that's it for me here in Dunedin. I'd better get back to the Inn, where I belong."

"I can sure sense how you must feel."

"And even worse, I don't have any idea what this means in terms of marriage and my future. In fact I'm terrified to think about it."

"You can't right now, Bronwyn. You've got to take only one little step at a time. Don't look ahead, if you can help it. And above all, don't make any far reaching decisions. Let's just get you back to Colac Bay now. We can leave right now; or wait for morning. I think morning would be better. Something to eat now and then try to get a good night's sleep. And I'll do the driving tomorrow. OK?"

"Yes." she said in meek compliance, glad to be told.

The next morning when they met for breakfast in the dining room of Magnolia House, Max saw a dramatic change in Bronwyn. She appeared rested and her countenance was surprisingly sunny. Both ate lustily the breakfast set before them, consisting of fried eggs and bacon with grilled tomato slices, toast, marmalade and fresh perked coffee—American style. While finishing a second cup of coffee Bronwyn said, "I tried not to look ahead, as you advised me; and after just a wee gaze at my questionable future I made a decision! I know, you told me not to do that either! But this is different."

"How so?"

"When I looked ahead all I could see was being tied down to a very steady routine of caring for the Inn and for Duncan as well. I could not see much in the way of a holiday in sight. So, I said to

myself—'Your holiday is right now! On your way home with Max
Ritter! Between here and Colac Bay you have no responsibilities.
Once you get there, you'll have duties enough! So—why not take
some time returning and enjoy yourself. It's your last chance!'—
And when I told myself that, I immediately felt better! I went to
bed and slept the whole night through! I got up, had a long shower,
and here I am ready to take you the long way home! What do you
think? Am I crazy?"

"No, you're not crazy. You make sense to me; and I'm willing
to play along. What do we do? Where do we go from here?"

"Here's my plan, Max. The Inn has been closed this long—
another three days won't hurt; so I'd like you to see some of the
tourist places on the South Island. I suggest we drive to Arrowtown
and Queenstown right now and on down to TeAnau where we
would stay two nights. That way, tomorrow we could drive up to
Milford Sound for the day. Then the third day we could get back
to Colac Bay easily. What do you think? When we get to the car
I'll show you on the map."

"You're the tour guide. I like the way it sounds. Let's check
out now and get rolling!"

They spent the next three days as Brownyn had suggested,
playing the tourist each mile of the way, stopping at scenic vistas,
hitting the gift shops and finding unique restaurants, taking pic-
tures, and yes, laughing and obviously enjoying themselves on
holiday. They found a quaint B.& B. in TeAnau, and booked two
rooms, causing the inn-keeper to wonder why two! For in every
other way they appeared to be newly-weds.

On Milford Sound they took the launch tour out to the Tasman
and "oohed and ahed" at the waterfalls along the way. They saw
the seals on the rocks as the boat glided by. Majestic Mitre Peak
looked down upon them through the mists benevolently as they
slipped by on their way out to sea and back again.

Finally on the third day at lunch in a little take-away in
Lumsden, knowing that it would only be a hour or two before the

reality of Colac Bay closed in upon them, they settled into a serious conversation.

Max opened with, "Bronwyn, we are almost home—or you are. I'm still half a world away from home, wherever that is for me now. It won't be long before Duncan is back and possibly able to do the handyman thing. I need to be out of the picture, I feel. And I need to face my real situation as you must face yours. And besides all that, my visa runs out soon after the new year."

"Oh, Max, I hear what you are saying. I know you are right, but that doesn't mean I have to like it!"

"No, I don't suppose either of us likes it, but that's the way it is, isn't it?"

"Yes, but not right now. There's still a fortnight—I think."

"A few more days to do a few more handyman jobs—right? Just teasing!"

" I'll try to find some complex jobs that will take you a long time! With Christmas holiday coming in a few days we shall be busy."

"How so?"

"Christmas school holiday is the time for lots of summer trips for families. Riverton Rocks is a popular place and we get our share at the Inn. In fact during the last few years we have been full because of one family group. They will be coming on 19 December, and will stay through New Years. It is a group of three families and the grandparents."

"They celebrate Christmas with you?" he asked incredulously, and he wanted also to know, "Where do they come from?"

"The older folks are from Gore, and the others are from Browns, Drummond and Otautau. Distant relatives of Duncan's. I give over the kitchen, dining room and lounge of the big house on the 24th and 25th for them to celebrate Christmas as a family."

"What do you do then?"

"Duncan and I often were at the Manse in Riverton for the day on Christmas. Christmas eve was mostly at church. This year— I just don't know."

"Whether Duncan will be back?"

"Yes, and if so, what will he be like?"

Not knowing what more he could say, Max was quiet. Then, "We better get started!" he said, getting up from the table and taking Bronwyn by the hand and leading her to the Subaru.

They returned to Colac Bay and to the work at hand. Max busied himself with routine maintenance chores while Bronwyn kept herself busy with the usual tasks. The days progressed rapidly. They took little time to talk of much besides the Inn matters.

The family group arrived as expected on the nineteenth, filling the Inn. It was made up of a mother and father and their two daughters and son, each with their spouses and children. The children were young school age, five of them, which provided a lively atmosphere. Their excitement increased as Christmas approached.

Christmas eve they all went in to Riverton to the annual family service including a traditional children's pageant—the kind with straw in a wooden box containing a doll, and children in bathrobes and towels for shepherds headdresses. Bronwyn went in for the service, leaving Max to watch over the Inn. He then went in to the late night service of Lessons and Carols.

When he returned after midnight he expected to find the Inn locked up and dark, but was surprised to see a light on in the takeaway. He found Bronwyn sitting at one of the tables weeping. He went up to her: "Bronwyn, what is the matter?"

"Oh, I guess I'm having an attack of loneliness. With the family over in the big house and you in town, there just wasn't anything to keep me from thinking about Christmas times in the past when my parents were alive and all of us were still at home. Now even Duncan is gone—perhaps forever, in a way."

There was nothing Max could say, he sensed. He sat down opposite her and took her hands in his, holding them as he allowed her to continue her quiet weeping.

"And, Oh Max, I know you are alone as well without Gwendoyln and away from home."

"Yes, but the closeness of new friends comforted me as I sat in worship tonight. The familiar words and carols seemed to bind me to my new family!"

"I am surely pleased that my church means that much to you.."

"Now, you had better get some sleep, Bron. It's almost one o'clock!"

"You are right. May I take my breakfast with you tomorrow morning, Max?"

"Certainly. I'd like that a lot."

When Max arrived at the take-away on Christmas morning, there was a small Christmas present at his place. He placed one at hers."Merry Christmas to you, Bronwyn MacKenzie!"

"And Merry Christmas to you, Max Ritter!"

After porridge and scones, and some good hot coffee they opened their gifts.

To Max Bronwyn had given a paua shell bolo tie from the Riverton Paua Factory. "Thank you, so much! I spotted these when we were at the factory store and thought I'd like one."

"I know. I noticed that. I had not even known what those were, but I guess you wear them in the US?"

"Yes, in the West, we do. Now open yours," he said grinning.

"What's the grin for?"

"You'll see"

When she opened the gift wrapping and found a jade necklace from the same place, she had to grin too. "It's lovely, Max. I suppose you saw me looking at this the other day?"

"Yes, I did!"

With that they both stood, and hugged in a manner most warm, but chaste, wishing each other: "Merry Christmas."

CHAPTER 11

The New Year came, and the Inn once again was occupied by a steady succession of one or two nighters seven days a week. The holidays kept Bronwyn and Max at the Inn on Sundays bringing to an end their Sunday afternoons together away from Colac Bay.

No further word had come from Dunedin until a few days after the first of the year when a nurse phoned Bronwyn to tell her that Duncan needed to remain in the rest home indefinitely. "Does that mean you don't expect him to be able to return?" Bronwyn asked.

"No, I think in another month or so, he will come out of this enough to return."

"What about visits?"

"The doctor still wants him to avoid any agitation, so he does not recommend visits at this time."

"I see," she replied sadly. "Thank you for ringing me. Please keep me informed as to Duncan's progress."

"Yes, Miss MacKenzie. I will do that." Days passed and the routine continued. There always seemed to be tasks for a handyman to do, and Bronwyn was kept busy with managing the Inn and also with her volunteer duties at church. To strangers who came to stay, Max and Bronwyn must have appeared to be an "old married couple" who were proprietors of the Inn. The bulk of their day-to-day contact had to do with matters regarding the Inn. Seldom did their conversations take a deeper, more personal turn. There wasn't time. Max felt that Bronwyn had become more reserved, and that she seemed often to avoid personal contact since their return from Dunedin.

Max knew from the calendar that his visa would soon run out, but he didn't want to think about that. But it was inevitable. What were those words from the hymn? "Time, like an ever rolling stream, bears all its son's away."

One evening soon after the first of the year, as the sun swung along its northern arc and sank lower into the western horizon, Max was sitting in his porch chair watching the glistening orange fringes on the steadily lapping waves. This time of the day immediately before dusk always saddened him. For this was the hour when folks returned home to be with each other for yet another evening. When husbands could anticipate the warmth and closeness of the night. Max recalled a poignant observation he'd heard once—that the best part was walking up stairs! He noticed the orange fading and the light lessening, when the door to the take-away opened and Bronwyn came out. She was wearing the full denim skirt and pink sweat shirt which she had worn the first time he saw her. Something inside him tripped as he looked at her coming toward him. There seemed to be such a gentle warmth in her expression, and yet there was that deep sadness in her eyes. She came over to his chair and sat on its arm and turned to Max as she spoke somewhat reluctantly: "Max, there was a phone call from Duncan's nurse. He's been told he can come home. And after a fortnight he can do some of his work again. 'Tis good news, isn't it?" she concluded without much enthusiasm.

"It is, Bron, it is." Max repeated her affirmation twice as if to try to convince himself of the truth of it. "Will you be going up to get him? Do you want me to drive you?"

"No, his brother from Gore has gone to Dunedin already. They should be here in a few days. Duncan will be home then."

Max then said what he had known for so long he'd need someday to say: "I'll need to find my way home as well, Bronwyn. The deadline for my return will soon be here anyway. January 18!"

Then Bronwyn said, "But, come now, let's have tea." Instead of leading him into the tiny-motel take-away, she led him to her own home and said, "Somehow, I felt we ought to have a proper tea tonight, so I set it up here in my dining room. Won't you join me for high tea, Max Ritter?" she said in mock formality.

"Why, yes, of course, Ms. MacKenzie, I will, indeed." And so the two dined together at the close of Max's odyessy on Colac Bay. The unspoken words in the silence of their unique union found expression finally when the meal was over and Max said,

"The time has come, dear Bronwyn, for me to return to Montana; and instead of putting it off as I have been for the past several weeks, I need to find a flight out of Invercargill as soon as possible, if I can get one."

"Yes, if you think you must, Max. But it will not be the same here after you've gone." she said softly.

"No, I guess not, with Duncan back home." He replied.

"No, that's not what I meant." Bronwyn countered. "With you gone, it won't be the same. You have been such a help around the Inn—and to me, Max" For a minute or two nothing more was said as they finished their meal.

"You can't know what my being here has done for me, Bron. That night when I first arrived, I was at the end of my rope. I needed far more than a room for the night. I didn't know it at the time, but I desperately needed someone to hold me back from the edge. In the awful lonely silence I needed to hear a voice, a reassuring voice, a human heart to connect to mine. Someone to tell me that there was still a place in life for me; a soft safety in which to bare my soul, a hand to pull me along. You have been all of that to me, and more. I can go back now knowing you are here and know that you will still be a part of my life . . . "

"Max," Bronwyn interrupted," I couldn't have been all that to you. I've just been living my life and taking care of things here as best as I can; and you entered my life in a very helpful way. But we have become good friends, haven't we?"

"Yes, very good friends, Bronwyn.

They remained for a while in silence, until it was time for Max to return to his room. Tomorrow he would find out how much longer they would have.

When he phoned the travel agent the next morning he half-way hoped she would find all the flights booked. But when she returned to the line after checking her computer she said, "As a matter of fact, Mr. Ritter, I have a seat out of Auckland available tomorrow afternoon at 3:24. I can get you on a flight to Auckland tomorrow morning at 9:05. Do you want me to book you on both of these?"

Max hesitated, knowing his need to confirm these arrangements, and yet reluctant to take the step. After a moment he said, "Yes, put me down for these. I have my return ticket to the US."

"That will be fine, Sir. I have you listed."

Max hung up and went to the Inn office to notify Bronwyn. "I have reservations."

"When?" Bronwyn asked.

"They are for tomorrow—9:05 out of Invercargill. I think there might be an early bus I can take into town."

"No, Max, I want to take you myself. I need to."

"You sure?"

"Yes.

The following morning Max was up early and ready to leave. He sat for one last time on the chair outside his room overlooking the bay. Bronwyn drove the car around to pick him up. He reluctantly loaded his suitcase into the boot and climbed in beside Bronwyn. "I guess this is it, Bron. It's good-bye to Colac Bay and its healing waters—my Gilead."

With a sadness in her eyes she replied, "Oh, Max, you'll return someday, won't you?"

"I'd like to, but I cannot even know what is ahead after my flight back to Montana." They drove away toward Invercargill.

Going east on the main street of Riverton they passed the church. Bronwyn said, "You'll be taking a parish again when you get home?"

"No I'm not ready for that. I really don't know if I'll ever be able to do that."

"Such a waste," she said."The Riverton folks really enjoyed having you conduct their service while you were here.

"I know, but that doesn't solve my problems with it." Wanting to change the subject he said, "Soon Duncan will be back. That should be good."

"I'm not sure. His condition makes him so different. Besides, I can't be sure his health will hold up. We almost lost him, and that could still happen, you know."

"Bron: with his restricted ability now, what will you do?"

"I can make it with just the Inn during the Summer months, but in winter its pretty slow. I'd have to get a job somewhere, I suppose."

"Where? Invercargill?"

"Maybe, but I have a cousin who works at the Paua shell factory in Riverton. Maybe I could get a winter job there. I'll manage."

As they drove toward the center of Invercargill they passed the Pizza Hut and gave each other a knowing look. "Seems like a very long time ago, doesn't it, Max?"

"So much has happened!"

They pulled into the air terminal car-park and went into the terminal where Max presented his ticket for Auckland. His scheduled flight would depart in about forty minutes. They went over to the food service area and had morning tea. There wasn't much left to say. They were quietly sharing the time; but their own thoughts were much to themselves. Soon the relative silence was broken by the sound of the 737 landing and taxiing toward the terminal. Over the loud speaker came the announcement which would bring an end of it.

"Flight 619 for Christchurch and Auckland is now boarding at gate 2. Have your tickets ready."

"Max, it's good-bye now isn't it?"

"Yes, Bron I guess it is." They walked toward the gate. Before he left the terminal to walk onto the tarmac Max and Bronwyn turned to each other in a moment of anguish. Then each encircled the other in their arms, They shared a poignant farewell kiss as they hugged. Neither wanted to let go, but it had to be. Both knew it; and as they separated each had tears to wipe away. Max waved as he began to mount the steps to the plane. Bronwyn returned the wave before turning to leave. Seeming to change her mind she walked to the window and took a seat facing the plane, watching the final boarding and pondering in deep reverie until both jet engines began to turn and the plane taxied out to the runway. Max was airborne—gone from Southland, and from her life. Her tears persisted as she walked out to her battered Subaru. She smiled as she remembered the strange way he had always pronounced Subaru. "That's the way I'll pronounce it now!" she thought as she drove away.

The plane circled over the sea and turned north while Max watched the green paddocks below him recede from view, scenes which had become so familiar to him. He purposely kept his mind from wandering or from jumping ahead into the unknown. Rather he held fast to the feeling and the image of their parting. As the plane emerged above the clouds into the sunlight Max let thoughts and memories wash over him until his reverie was interrupted:

"We have begun our descent into Christchurch. Please fasten your seat belts and remain seated until we reach the gate and the aircraft has come to a complete stop. We will be on the ground for thirty minutes. Those passengers continuing on to Auckland may deplane if they wish. Be sure to take your boarding pass with you."

Tomorrow Duncan will be home. She thought out loud as she drove west toward Colac Bay. What will that be like? How sick will he still be, I wonder. A gray wave of guilt swept over her as she thought about their reunion. I should feel utterly happy, but I don't. In fact I don't know what I feel. Really it is a sort of void, an empty feeling, almost a bit like being sick.

Her thoughts turned to Max. I feel as though I have lost something quite personal, an absolutely frustrating loss; for there's no way that we'll ever be together again. I have no way of contacting Max, for at this point he doesn't have a permanent address. He said as much.

As she slowed down and turned into the Inn she couldn't help but look longingly at the chair outside his room—now so empty and lifeless. But the bay is the same and the gulls were still diving this way and that. She entered the familiar kitchen in her house behind the Inn and said out loud, "Nothing has changed, really. My life is the same. This house, this town—everything is the same, except for Duncan. We will go ahead with our wedding plans. Oh, why can't I believe it?" She flung herself down in a chair by the table and began to weep uncontrollably. Fiona came out into the kitchen with her tail in the air uttered a plaintive "meow" and rubbed herself on Bronwyn's leg. Bronwyn absently reached down to give Fiona a half-hearted pet. The cat began to purr. Fiona got her wish. She was picked up and cuddled in Bronwyn's lap. But Fiona's feline bliss was soon interrupted when the telephone rang. Thinking it might be news of Duncan, "Hello, B. MacKenzie here."

"Bron, this is Max! I've got a few minutes on the ground here at Christchurch, and I wanted one last chance to talk to you." There was a silence and Max continued, "Are you there? Are you OK, Bron?"

"Oh yes, Max. I was just so taken aback—so overwhelmed that I needed to get my breath."

"Is it ok that I called? Can you talk?"

"Oh yes, Max. I'm thrilled that you called. I was feeling so sad that I'd probably never hear your voice again. And here you are!"

"Bron, I can't just never hear from you again. I simply must have a chance to keep in touch with you no matter what comes. I'll want to hear all about your wedding!"

"I feel that way too, but I don't know how we can?"

"As soon as I get half-way settled I'll send you and Duncan my address; with maybe something like a contribution to the parish which I can send to you with my return address. Do you think that would be ok?"

"I think that would be fine. I'm so glad that you thought of that. Then I could at least write you to let you know how things are here."

"Good. that's what I'll do. It may be a few weeks until I get things figured out, but I promise. I better go now; the plane is due to take off in a couple of minutes."

"Cheerio, Max, take care."

Max said "Good bye Bronwyn . . . I love you!" and immediately he hung up, without giving her a chance to respond.

Bronwyn slowly put the phone back on the hook in a daze, shocked, but somehow not surprised at what she had heard him say. Three words which would remain lodged in her consciousness in all her days to come. "I love you too, Max!" she said out loud. Fiona looked up and offered her opinion, "Meow." And then she assured herself that she still loved Duncan. But she had a deep foreboding that he had already been taken from her.

After hanging up Max had to run to get to the gate in time to board. He arrived in his seat just as the cabin door was being secured for departure. And only then did he have time to think of what he had said. He too was shocked at what he had impulsively said, but not sorry; for now he knew it was true. In that final moment after parting the old familiar refrains echoed in his mind and heart:

"God be with you 'til we meet again . . .

By his counsels guide, uphold you."

The aircraft reached its cruising altitude, speeding northward. Southland was now far behind. And now Max entered into a near impossible struggle within himself. A struggle against abject frustration, recognizing and admitting to himself his inner feelings, and yet knowing that he had no way of expressing those feelings in action; and furthermore he most likely never would see Bronwyn again. This struggle would permeate everything that Max would do in the coming days.

PART III

CHAPTER 12

A low hanging cloud had moved into the valley from the west, obscuring the mountains and making it necessary for Con Schneider to put the lights on in his office. He looked out his west window and could barely see the horse barns. A light snow had started, the first since November. It had been a brown Christmas, much to the disappointment of staff and guests alike. Now it looked as though January would bring winter. Con's disappointment, however, had had more to do with Lee's delay in coming out to Montana. As she had feared, her daughter needed her for a longer period of transition than Con had thought reasonable; but then what did he know of marriage and divorce? On the other hand it was right for Lee to spend Christmas in River Forest with both her children and their families. Her daughter, especially, would need this time at home. Con had celebrated Christmas on the 23rd with the annual staff party, which had come to be the high point of his season. However, this year the Christmas Eve service at Mill Creek had been very special for him.

Now the new year start-up business for Fairhavens occupied the director's attention. His accountant assured him that the year had ended in the black and that the new budget could be put in place. Among the items on the new budget was a handyman/driver position. It had been six weeks since Con Schneider had lost his driver-handyman. He had waited until the new year to pursue this need, wanting to find someone locally: but no one qualified had surfaced. His next hope had been Billings. Now, he'd have to wait a couple of days for some responses to the ad he had placed in the Billings Gazette:

WANTED Handyman/Van Driver. General maintenance
and repair.
Courtesy Van driving for a resort/dude ranch. Benefits.
Phone
Dr. Schneider, Director—406-333-9944
Fairhavens, Pray, Montana 59065

Just as he was thinking about the ad, the phone rang. His first
thought was that it would be an inquiry. "Hello, Dr. Schneider
speaking . . . Yes! Lee! Good to hear you!"

"Conrad, I've got reservations for Bozeman for this Thursday. I
hope that's ok?"

"Yes, that's great! I've been waiting."

"I know. So have I. But things just piled up." Lee said with a
note of apology in her voice.

"That's OK—especially now that you're coming! What time is
your flight arrival in Bozeman?"

"It's 1:15 PM on Northwest. I'm sorry this is such quick notice, but I couldn't get things arranged before this; and then when
I called I found an available seat on Thursday."

"No problem! I'll meet you at the terminal in Bozeman . . . I
know, but we haven't got a courtesy driver right now. In fact I've
just run an ad for one"

"Are you sure it will be OK?"

"I'm sure. There may even be others who need to be picked up
at that same time."

"OK, if you say so. I need to be running along now, but I'll see
you Thursday, Conrad."

"Right, I'll be there. Bye for now."

Whatever else Con had planned to do at the moment, seemed
to fade into unimportance. There was so much he wanted to show
her and to share with her about Fairhavens . . . and he wanted
time for them to become better acquainted personally as well.

Now he felt as if his life was on hold until Thursday. And
besides he had "itchy feet". Even though the day wasn't all that

great he got in his Ford Explorer to have a look around the Emigrant area. There had been some disturbing signs lately, and he wanted to keep up with what was happening.

From the Lodge he went up Emigrant gulch along which there were a number of private homes, most of them quite old. These folks were Fairhavens' closest neighbors. Most of them were re-tired. A few worked on ranches in the Emigrant area. As he rounded one of the sharp bends in the gravel road he discovered a large U-Haul truck backed into one of the yards. It was the home of Charles and Elizabeth Coats, retired, and long time residents. As he came closer he could see that the U-Haul was being loaded with all of their household furnishings and goods. It was obvious to Con that they were moving out. He had known nothing of this move and was quite taken aback by what he saw. Parking along the road he walked up to the house and there found Charles straining over some boxes he was moving out of the house to be loaded into the truck. "Charlie, what on earth is going on? If I didn't know better I'd say you were moving!"

Looking somewhat sheepish Charlie replied, "We are moving."

"You are! I had no idea. Where to? Into town, or where?"

"No, Beth and I are buying a place in Arizona, Green Valley; and we are moving there. Always wanted to go south, but never thought we could afford it. Now, we're selling this place and we're going for it!"

"You can't tell me you are getting enough for this place to move to Arizona!" Con wondered where enough funds were coming from for the Coats's.

"No, not just this place, but also that piece of pasture-land down next to you. You'd be surprised what we are getting for those fifteen acres."

By this time Con was quite suspicious and asked. "Who in the world is giving you a good price for your land?" The land had been suitable for running a few cows on it as Charles usually did, but so far as a marketable piece of property Con doubted it would go for much if any locals were to buy it. But . . . if an

outsider . . . Vermillian to be specific—that would be in a different ball park.

At this point Charles seemed even more embarrassed and hesitated before confessing, "Well, the truth of the matter is that this
Vermillian fellow came to see me a week ago, and I just couldn't
pass up such a good offer."

"I see. I guess he's got the bucks. Well anyway I'll miss you
and Elizabeth; and wish you the best."

"Thanks, Con. We'll drop you a line when we get there. Come
see us!"

The snow had let up and there were a few breaks in the clouds
through which the blue was trying to emerge. As Con Schneider
drove off he tried to remember how many separate holdings bordered the Fairhavens property. He could remember four in addition to the Coats property. But, surely there must be quite a few
more. With his suspicions aroused he determined to pay a visit to
the County Clerk and Recorder's office to get a line on who his
neighboring owners were. Before turning back he went up to the
end of the string of houses and discovered the small one on the
end to be vacated. He wasn't overly surprised, since this one had
been occupied by a ranch hand. It turned over frequently. but
yet—he wondered.

The next day Con found time to drive up to Livingston to
check the map at the county clerk and recorders office. He found
that eleven separate properties bordered the Fairhavens land. He
discovered that five of them were owned by the C bar V Land and
Cattle Company! He asked the clerk, "Can you tell me who this C
bar V is?"

"I don't know a lot about them, except that they have recently
been coming in with deeds to record after purchases they have just
made."

"Throughout the county or just in this area around Fairhavens?"

"Not all over. Mostly up Emigrant gulch as well as in your
region."

He looked at the properties in the gulch and found two owned by C Bar V. One was the Coats property; and the other was the rental he'd seen up beyond Coats!"

So C bar V Land & Cattle Co. is Vermillian! It figures. He examined the book more closely to check on the property which Fairhavens had customarily used to access forest land in the foothills to the east. He found that this piece, was still owned by the McMillan family , who now lived in Pasadena. Not C bar V—not yet! Before giving up the plat maps he took down the names of the remaining six neighbors.

As Con drove back he thought about the McMillan land and how important the use of their access road was. For this was the way guests could reach the wilderness areas, so important both for the therapy people and for the R. & R. guests. If Vermillian were to tie this up, it would add at least twenty miles to get to the National Forest. As he drove into Fairhavens he determined to contact MacMillans. In fact it might not be a bad idea to talk to all six neighbors.

The feeling of exhilaration Con always experienced when he returned to the Lodge was spoiled for him by a feeling of encroachment—forces unfriendly and menacing.

There were times when Conrad Schneider felt very much alone in his responsibilities for Fairhavens. He missed the collegiality he had enjoyed when he was on the staff at Deaconess in Billings, and earlier at Erie House. Now, his only peers where board members, and he saw them only at meetings of the board and once in a while in other connections. So far as the rest of the staff at Fairhavens, the therapists were all fairly young and seemed to stick close to their own association as mental health care professionals. The others were busy with their own tasks as resort hotel employees. As general manager of Fairhavens Con had always enjoyed a good and congenial relationship with his staff. Such positive work environment had been intentional, for Con believed that this would spill over into the mood and atmosphere which guests would experience. He'd been in restaurants and hotels where you could feel negative tension in the staff. It made those places less pleasant and inviting. He didn't want that at Fairhavens.

Nevertheless as project coordinator and long range planner Con remained pretty much alone and isolated. The original concept had been his and it remained his responsibility to implement. But he wished from time to time for someone with whom to discuss critical issues and future planning. The Vermillian intrusion presented him with one of those times when it would be good to have some colleagues, or family, with whom to mull over pressing concerns. He wondered if Lee would ever be someone close with whom he could share Fairhavens concerns—and personal matters as well!

CHAPTER 13

After landing in Auckland Max entered the terminal and retrieved his bags. He went to the Air New Zealand international counter to check in. He then dropped in to a restaurant in the terminal and took his final New Zealand meal. He made it a good one: lamb chops, swedes, mashed potatoes, cooked carrots, and, of course, tea. He finished with pav lova, that delightful dessert from down under—a meringue topped with exotic tropical fruit and whipped cream. After his feast he found a seat in the waiting area at his gate and tried to collect his thoughts—not easy! Images of Bronwyn intruded at every turn of his thinking. Anxiety over what he would do when he returned to the States; regrets about having left Montana without any negotiation with his Presbytery about his ministerial status; an aversion to going back to Tipton to get his personal belongings; wondering about what his obligation to Gwen's family might be. Almost hidden in the shadows was a still deeper struggle which was spiritual in essence. Where was God in all this? What might God lead him to do next with his life. These thoughts and still others pushed and shoved seeking to claim his attention. None of his thoughts were clear enough to provide any sort of resolution. And always in the background there was the gentle, warm and caring face of Bronwyn MacKenzie; and the touch of her hand upon his. And now the feeling of wrapping their arms around one another in that farewell hug.

He got up and went over to the News and Gift store. Browsing through it he came upon a rack of stationery and assorted office supplies. A letter-size notebook with a picture of a kiwi bird on it caught his eye. "Travel Notes" was embossed in silver on its dark blue cover. The sight of this notebook triggered his thinking.

One of his profs in Seminary had emphasized the idea of keeping a journal. Some of Max's classmates had picked up on the suggestion, and had begun to record their day to day thoughts. They had claimed great things for such a practice—sermon ideas, good for growing your own theology, therapeutic! Max had taken a dim view of this discipline while in seminary, but a time or two while at Tipton he had thought about it and wondered if such a practice might not be such a bad idea. Now, pondering his own mixed-up state of mind, journalling took on a new appeal. So he bought the kiwi travel notebook and returned to his seat in the waiting area. The long flight to the US would certainly give his journalling a start, he thought.

His Air New Zealand flight was finally called. Soon he found himself settling into an aisle seat in one of the center sections on the 747. Next to him was a family of three—parents with their daughter who appeared to be eight or nine. After the preliminary announcements and the video safety instructions were played, the huge aircraft rose from the tarmac and was airborne. Max took his kiwi journal and began to organize his thinking preparing for his initial entry.

Looking at the Kiwi bird on the cover made him think of the bird sanctuary in TeAnau into which Bronwyn had taken him. They had gone into an enclosed area which was kept completely dark. Standing before a glass wall they had waited for their eyes to adjust to the dark. Gradually the natural setting of shrubs and ground cover came into view, revealing finally a Kiwi bird pecking at the ground cover with its long beak. Such good memories! And then they had stopped at a little take-away for morning tea. Oh how he missed his "balm in Gilead"!

A gentle lurch of the aircraft brought Max back. He found himself trying to start his journal at a mid-point. Already some very significant events had occurred in his life since leaving America. He was conscious of some dramatic changes in his mood. His first thought was to go back and begin writing as if he were just leaving Tipton. But this struck him as unreal. He was now a different person. And so what he would write needed to be his thinking at this very moment. Closing his eyes and relaxing in his seat he began to sense a flow of thought emerging; in fact there raced into his mind thoughts and impressions which clamored to be cast in writing! He began:

I have been to the bottom of the world. I have gone as far away as I could travel. To get away! To get away from what? From Tipton and the mean spirit I felt there, meanness against Gwen and me there. From the struggle to minister in the name of Christ to a congregation set against me. I had thought God had called me to be their minister. It was a call I felt at the time. We were excited to take up the work there. The Monday morning after my installation stands out in my mind. The visiting clergy and elders had returned to their respective communities and the Tipton people were going about their work. I sat in my study and prayed for guidance as to what God would have me do next. I think I can honestly say that one way or another that prayer was fairly continuously in my mind and heart all during my time in Tipton. I thought I was trying to follow what I took to be God's directives. Then—almost as a negation of this—the people started opposing me and saying behind my back that I wasn't spiritual enough. But I didn't know that then. I learned it later. I wonder what they meant. And I wonder if perhaps they were right. I wonder if that really is the question—the challenge I have been running from. As it turned out they made their view-point stick by giving me the boot. And now I don't want to go back to Tipton—or to any other place as a minister. Does that mean they were right? Could that be? Has God disappeared from my life because I haven't been spiritual?

Max looked up and saw two of the flight attendants bringing the beverage cart up the aisle. Breaking his train of thought for the moment, he asked for ginger ale. Something in the appearance of the flight attendant who served him made him think of Bronwyn and her cheery disposition. Seemingly always cheerful despite the serious condition of her fiancé. She went about her tasks at church with a genuine joy, so unlike Gwen in that regard. Gwen! He felt impelled to write—

> *Gwen. You deserve a place in this journal of my deepest thoughts! I feel guilty that I haven't mourned your death. Maybe I was too hurt and resentful of your leaving me. But you were a part of me and you were killed. O God—forgive me. I don't deserve even to ask.*

Tears began to well up in Max's eyes. He closed them and in the darkness he prayed. Words at first; words fading into thoughts and memories; then momentary sleep. Some minor turbulence lit the seat belt signs and awakened Max. He returned to his journal.

> *This has been a time of severe loss for me. The loss of my ministry—not only at Tipton—but possibly a total loss of my calling. The other painful loss has been Gwen—first through separation, then through death. On the surface it appears that it was the life of a minister's wife in Tipton, Montana which Gwen rejected. But it was a rejection of me. That means that under the surface my love for her was not strong enough to overcome the obstacles she saw in her parish situation. I wasn't loving enough! Just as I wasn't spiritual enough. I'm not fit for another parish or for another relationship. And yet there is Bronwyn. Without knowing it she showed me that a loving relationship might be possible for me—someday. Might that be? I don't know. And when she commented upon my feelings about going back to the parish she had said, "Such a waste!" Those were affirming words for me, I have to admit. Will God ever call me again to ministry? I don't know. And now I have lost Bronwyn as well. I love you, Bron!*

Max closed his journal, put away his pen and waited for the evening meal to be served. What he had written had needed to be put down, before any other thoughts could emerge. In many ways the jottings in his journal represented a distillation of what had gone through Max's mind over and over again on most of the days he sat looking to the bottom of the world from Point of Rocks on Colac Bay. These were his expressions of grieving, grieving the death of his spiritual calling; the death of his most intimate relationship; almost his own death, in a way! Now they were written. In a strange way he felt relieved of their morbid curse! And so when the cabin was darkened, he slept, and slept soundly, but yet waking periodically through the night.

Sometime during the night he awakened to see on the big screen that the plane was crossing the international date line. When he observed this he thought about how he was being given a new day! At about the same time the plane crossed the equator and entered the northern hemisphere—his own, the hemisphere in which he had been born, and in which he would most likely live out his days. But a world away from Bronwyn.

Toward morning when he awakened to the new day, he saw on the graphic chart on the screen that the plane was inching its way toward the American continent. This day was a new date; and he was at a new location. Almost a sort of resurrection, he thought.

The hot towels were distributed, orange juice was served, and then a full breakfast. Passengers were raising their cabin shades one by one. The noise level in the cabin had increased. People were moving around. And the 747 inched closer and closer to LAX! The chart showed that an hour and forty-five minutes remained. Time enough to do some more writing.

Today I'll be home. Yet I am not sure where home will be. I know it won't be Tipton; but it will be Montana, at least at first. I don't know what I'll be doing. I'm not ready for parish ministry. I don't have any idea what my status with Presbytery is— if any. The way I ran, and disappeared, I'll have some explain-

ing to do, and I'm not sure I'm ready for that either. So for now,
I need to find something else. What?

I can't believe it, but I think I will be reduced to looking
through the help-wanted ads in the newspaper!

But, as I think about that, I feel some excitement. What
turns in the road am I being led to take. Led? Do I feel that
God is leading me? Perhaps so. Was it God who sent Bronwyn
to me? Was she some sort of angel? A messenger of God who came
to me when I needed someone to care for me; when what I most
sorely needed was God's grace? A little Christ, as Martin Luther
would say. A Christ with blue-gray eyes? Could be. I do know
that in some sense she gave me back my life. Am I being overly
dramatic? I don't know. I went down there totally alone. All I
wanted was to get away, as far away as possible. But because of
Bronwyn I was not alone. I was transformed from merely being
away to being involved in some meaningful work, and given
the opportunity to offer myself in a helpful way. And,——I felt
loved. Furthermore, I loved someone, authentically. And the
very fact that I am seeing this as a gift from God, a gift I did not
deserve, but one which lifted my life from the pits! Isn't that a
pretty good definition of grace? I think it is!

He heard the slowing down of the engines and felt the plane slope
to the right as the overhead speaker carried the long anticipated
message:

"We have begun our descent into Los Angeles. Our projected
arrival time at the gate is approximately twenty minutes. Please
remain in your seats with your seat belts securely fastened, with
your tray tables replaced, and your seats in the upright position."

Finally they were on the ground. The huge 747 came to a
stop. The cabin doors opened. Home at last! Coming out of the
customs hall he felt very much alone as he watched the joyful
reunions among his fellow passengers. Max took a terminal bus
from the international building and got off at Delta. There he
obtained a reservation and a ticket for Billings on a flight sched-

uled to leave in two hours. He chose Billings, because he was reluctant at this point to be seen so near to Tipton as Bozeman. As he walked to the departure gate he felt a strange solid sensation in his feet. "Terra Firma" he thought. This is real. No more running! It would be a hour and a half to Salt Lake City; thirty-five minutes between planes and the flight to Billings would be a little over an hour. That's all! Then life would begin again for Max Ritter.

CHAPTER 14

On Montana soil again! As soon as Max was in the terminal building at Logan International Airport in Billings he found a phone
and obtained a room in a favorite motel for the night. After retriev-
ing his bags, he took a cab to the Dude Rancher Lodge in downtown Billings. It was late afternoon when he checked in. After
taking his bags to the room he walked across the courtyard to the
café for an early supper. The Lodge and the café were built and
furnished in an old Spanish western motif with dark wood trim
and ceiling rafters. He sat at one of the small heavy wooden tables
next to a window looking out onto 29th St. A steady stream of cars
passed by heading away from the down town area. He surmised
that they were all going home for dinner. Max experienced a pang
of loneliness and felt the need for some familiar human contact.
For one fleeting moment he thought he was looking out upon Dee
Street in Invercargill. It seemed to him that until he exchanged a
few words with someone whom he knew he really wasn't home.
Back in his room he dialed a Tipton number.

"Hello, Kobers, Dale speaking."

"Dale, this is Max . . . right! . . . No, I'm in Billings . . . I've
been about as far away as you can get. I'll tell you about it some
day. Dale, please don't say a word to anyone about this call. Right
now I don't want to talk to anyone else. I just thought I'd hear
from you any news."

"Max, buddy, its good to hear you again. First off, I've got
your car in our garage; and your stuff from the manse is stored out
in the barn on our ranch. Some of the church board members were
all over me to get this stuff so that they could get the manse ready
for a new pastor . . . No, they still don't have anybody. The place

is still empty. But you can get whatever is yours whenever you want to. Somebody from Gwen's family came out and got her stuff. So the rest is yours."

"Thanks, Dale. I'm glad I don't have to hassle getting it from the manse. This way I can sneak over one of these days and get the car. The rest of it, I may have to store a while, until I figure out what I'm going to do."

"No hurry."

"Hey, Dale, you don't know how good it is to talk to you!"

"Yeah, it's good to hear your voice, buddy. Say, you got a minute? . . . Good. I've been trying to figure out what happened. How come they dumped you?"

"Dale, I don't really know. All I could get out of them was that they said I wasn't spiritual enough."

"That's a laugh. I know most of those guys. They hang around here all the time. 'spiritual enough!' It's them that ain't spiritual. I know 'em. You should hear them talk! Must be something else, Max. You didn't screw up; I know that!"

"Not, as far as I know, Dale. Would you keep your ear to the ground and try to find out for me?"

"Glad to. When you come over to get your car, let me know so that me and Maude can have you for a meal at the house. Maybe by then I'll have an idea of what really went on."

"Thanks, I'd like that. I'll let you know. But I need to go now."

"OK. See you!"

Max felt a little more at home; but he was still without a plan. Maybe tomorrow, he thought, I'll check out possibilities, if there are any.

The next morning after breakfast in the café Max bought a Billings Gazette and took it to the lounge in the Lodge. It was a warm comfortable room with a fire blazing in the fireplace. It had snowed overnight and through the window Max could see the cars making their way through the snow covered street. Everyone was going more slowly now than they had the day before. Reading the help-wanted ads he came across an ad which caught his eye:

WANTED Handyman/Van Driver. General maintenance
and repair.
Courtesy Van driving for a resort/dude ranch. Benefits.
Phone
Dr. Schneider, Director—406-333-9944
Fairhavens, Pray, Montana 59065

This could be it! He thought. Returning to his room, he
decided to phone immediately. "Hello, my name is Max Ritter.
May I speak to Dr. Schneider?"

"This is Dr. Schneider. How can I help you?"

"Yes, my name is Max Ritter. I am presently in Billings. I'm
calling in regard to your ad for a handy-man/courtesy driver. Is
that position still vacant? . . . Good! . . . Well, I'd like to
apply . . . Altogether I've had about nine years experience working
in the hotel business—various jobs . . . No, I don't have a car with
me here in Billings.

Conrad Schneider showed an interest in his caller and said,
"I'd like to have you come here for an interview." He then gave
Max directions for getting to Fairhavens: "If you could take the
Greyhound to Livingston, I would be glad to meet you and take
you up to Fairhavens. That way you could get a feel for the job.
Can you do that? . . . No obligation. If you like what you see and
I like what I see, we can sign you up to begin right away . . . There's
a bus, I think, around 10:15 out of Billings, which gets into
Livingston around one o'clock. Will that work for you?

Max felt a rising excitement and eagerly said, "Yes, where will
I meet you?"

Schneider replied, "After you arrive in Livinston walk three or
four blocks to the old NP depot where you'll find a restaurant. It's
called Martins."

"I'm familiar with it," Max offered.

"Good! Why don't you slip in there and get yourself a bite to eat.
I'll meet you there about 2:30. I have to pick up some lodge guests in
Bozeman around 1:15, and then I'll drive over to meet you."

Max replied: "I'll look forward to meeting you there this afternoon . . . Yes, Goodbye."

After hanging up the phone Max checked out of the Dude Rancher and walked the six or seven blocks to the bus terminal. His bus arrived as scheduled in Billings, and the ride to Livingston was uneventful, arriving there more or less on time.

In an earlier time, Livingston had been the Northern Pacific Railroad's gateway to Yellowstone National Park. Its' depot had been the major transfer point for tourists from throughout the country and the world on their way to Yellowstone. Martins, the depot cafe in the NP Depot in Livingston, has outlasted passenger service by decades. It retains the busy no-nonsense atmosphere of a railroad café of the 1930's with its high ceiling, white tile floor and a meat and potatoes menu. Max had been there before on some trips between Tipton and Billings. The depot itself was being transformed into a railroad historical museum.

Max finished his hot roast beef sandwich with mashed potatoes and remained at a table where he could watch the door as he nursed a third cup of coffee. He didn't have to wait long. Soon a man of medium height slightly balding entered the café. He wore a western cut suit with a bolo tie. It would be difficult to say who recognized the other first.

"Aren't you . . . ?" Max began.

"Yours was the table . . . ! Conrad added.

"Right! at the City Deli in the terminal at Salt Lake!"

"Well, small world, as they say. Anyway: Hello! I'm Conrad Schneider from Fairhavens; and you are Max Ritter? Am I right?"

"Yes, I'm Max Ritter, and I'm glad to meet you . . . again! . . . Dr. is it?"

"Yes, but my friends call me, Conrad. I have the van in the parking lot. Grab your luggage and we'll be on our way."

Max got up, paid his bill and followed Schneider to a Club Wagon with the Fairhavens name and logo on the door. He noticed that there were three other people in the van—a middle aged couple in one of the center seats, and a woman in her fifties in the front on the passenger side.

Conrad ushered Max into one of the seats toward the rear putting his bag in the back compartment. When they were seated and ready to go, Schneider offered some introductions: "This is Max Ritter from Billings," and pointing to the couple: "These folks are Bill and Ruth Jones from Spokane. And this is Leona Baxter from Illinois—the Chicago area."

Max greeted them as they offered a word of greeting to Max, while Conrad drove from the parking lot and entered Highway 89 to travel south out of Livingston to Fairhavens.

The only conversation in the van for most of the way was confined to the front seat between Dr. Schneider and Leona Baxter, and occasional remarks the Jones made to one another. Max remained silent lost in his own thoughts until they came to Emigrant where Schneider turned off the highway and drove eastward.

They, crossed the Yellowstone river and turned north following the river for a few miles to the gravel road leading toward the mountains. "That prominent mountain there in front of us is Emigrant Peak." Conrad said as he dodged chuck holes in the road. On either side of the van were dry grasslands. Soon they came to a ranch gate on the left. Hanging from the cross log at the top was a sign which read: A PLACE CALLED FAIRHAVENS. Once across the cattle guard the ranch road turned sharply to the right and brought them to the ranch buildings on the left and the main lodge ahead of them. They drove up to the side of the lodge and parked. Max noticed steam rising from a portion of the building beyond their parking place.

Like a tour guide Schneider told his passengers: "That is coming from the hot springs pool which is just inside that wooden enclosure," Conrad explained. "It is an outdoor plunge now. Fifteen years ago the roof burned and that left the pool out of doors year round. You should see it in the dead of winter! Snow falls to about a foot above the water and turns to a fine drizzle. People in the pool are quite warm, but when they get out they don't waste any time getting inside the changing house. You can see that later. Let's go into the Lodge."

He took the Jones's and Mrs. Baxter to the desk for them to register and he showed Max into his office saying:

"If you'll wait here briefly, I'll get these others settled and then we can talk."

In a few minutes time he returned and took his seat behind his desk and addressed Max: "Well, that was quite a while back when we met by chance in Salt Lake. I take it your trip worked out despite the delay?"

"It did, but in ways I had not dreamed of. I can get into that at another time."

"Yes. Tell me a bit about yourself, would you?"

Max really didn't know how much to tell, and so he just began in a relaxed manner: "Well, I've just returned from an extended visit in New Zealand where I spent a fair amount of time as a handy-man in a small inn on the southern shore of the South Island, a place called Colac Bay Inn. Before that I was in Tipton, Montana for five years. I grew up in Illinois where I graduated from college and from theological seminary. I am single again. My wife was killed this past year in an auto wreck."

"I'm sorry. Theological school? Does that mean you are a minister?"

"Is that a problem?"

"No, I don't believe so."

"Good," Max replied with some relief, "Yes I served the Presbyterian Church in Tipton as its pastor. But my work there ended; and I'm not sure I want to continue in the parish ministry. I really don't know what I want long term. That's why the job you advertised seemed to fit me at this point in my life."

"A couple of things come to mind as you talk, Max. One is a concern that you would be here for only a short term, before you decide what you want to do."

Max took this as a lead into his own thinking along this line. "Dr. Schneider, I honestly do not have any other plans. I am very open to the possibility of a more or less long term experience, if it works out."

"That's good enough for me," Conrad responded. "The other comment is a plus! Your training as a pastor would fit in with the rationale of Fairhavens. So, let me tell you something about this place before we go any further."

"I'd appreciate that."

"We use the term 'R & R' here to refer to resort and retreat— two levels of experience we offer here at Fairhavens: For many of our guests we offer recreation and fun—vacation, relaxation and all that. Others come here for retreat and a type of therapy. These most often are folks whose lives have been shipwrecked, which is where the name FAIRHAVENS comes from! I don't need to tell you, but just to remind you of the Apostle Paul's shipwreck on his way to Rome and his landing at Fair Havens where he wanted to spend the winter. It's in Acts 27. Let me quote the verses. They are well fixed in my memory:

"We sailed slowly for a number of days, and arrived with difficulty off Cnidus, and as the wind did not allow us to go on, we sailed under the lee of Crete off Salmone. Coasting along it with difficulty, we came to a place called Fair Havens, near which was the city of Lasea."

I'm not a student of the Bible, but the way I read this, it was either Fair Havens or shipwreck. And that's the way we see this experience for those who come for retreat and renewal. Come here to Fairhavens before you experience some form of shipwreck in your life!"

"I like that. You mentioned a 'type of therapy.' What does that mean?"

"In the first place a lot of what we do is group therapy. We have a team of psycho-therapists who do one-on-one counseling; but the group experience is the special type of therapy I referred to. It is a form of music therapy coupled with a therapeutic use of our isolated, natural setting. That is the element of retreat I mentioned."

Max was intrigued by what he heard, and thought that Fairhavens was the sort of experience he himself needed, from which he could benefit. But then he reminded himself that he was here for a job interview! "Can you tell me a bit about the job you have listed."

"It is a position with two job descriptions. The first is handyman. By that we mean general minor maintenance and repair about the lodge and other buildings. Nothing too complicated. We hire professionals for those kinds of jobs. And the other is driving the van, as I did today, taking guests back and forth from public transportation—mostly air travel in and out of Bozeman—or really Belgrade, where the airport is located. And then once in a while there are field trips in this region on which we take guests in the van, like to Yellowstone Park. Does that explain it enough?"

"Yes, I think so. What about my own living situation? On my own, or is this a room and board arrangement?"

"That could be either way. Some of our employees commute from Livingston or Gardiner, or from places they have found closer. Some room and board here. I think that's the way you would want to start out. Later you might find something else on your own." Conrad then went over the details of pay both with board and room and without. He concluded with, "Max, I'm satisfied with what I've heard from you. If you feel you want this position on the terms I've outlined, its yours!"

"I'm prepared to accept. In fact, I am really fascinated by the Fairhavens concept and I believe I could fit in."

"That's really what I hoped to hear; for in many ways I don't want this to be just a job, but a position in which you find you can make a meaningful contribution!" Conrad looked at Max Ritter to gauge his reaction and apparently was satisfied. "I've got a simple employment contract here for us both to sign, if you are ready."

After Max read it over, each signed. Dr. Schneider said: "Now, let me show you to your room."

Con took Max to the back of the lodge where they entered an adjoining building. "This is the Annex. There are some meeting rooms on the first floor and some employee rooms on the second. There is one of them ready for you. When they reached the room, Con unlocked it and gave Max the key saying, "Why don't you relax until dinner. There is a men's lavatory and shower room down the hall. Your next-door neighbor is Jackson Evans. He is our accountant and business manager. If he's in, I'll introduce you to him.

Fortunately Evans was in and introductions were made. "Jack, would you take Max down to dinner and show him the ropes?"

"Sure, be glad to," and turning to Max he smiled and offered, "Max, I'll come by for you around ten to six."

"Thank you. I'll be in my room ready for you."

Con concluded, "Max, I'll meet you after breakfast tomorrow and get you started. Meanwhile, have a look around and enjoy your evening."

Max opened his door to Jackson at ten to six and invited him in for a moment before the two went down to dinner. Jackson Evans was a man of medium height and build, in his late forties. His coal black hair was very carefully combed. It matched his dark penetrating eyes set behind horn rimmed glasses. His brown western cut dress pants were neatly pressed, as was his western shirt. There was something formal and precise about him, though not at all unfriendly. They exchanged initial information about each other as they walked to the dining room. When they entered through glass paned double doors into the dining room Max saw that about half of the tables for eight were filled, some with couples of various ages, others with single individuals, both women and men. At a few of the tables there were small children accompanied by their parents. The congenial sound of people visiting with each other echoing against the polished wood floor added to the pleasant atmosphere of the large old dining room. A low ceiling was held up by supporting posts about twenty feet apart. Above the dark brown wainscoting the wall paper seemed outdated. Along one wall eight tall windows looked out onto the grounds surrounding the lodge. For the evening meal white linen table cloths were used with complete place settings. Waitresses were serving tomato juice to those who had arrived,

Jackson led Max to the staff table near the kitchen entry, where he introduced him to staff members already at the table. A new era in Max Ritter's life had begun.

CHAPTER 15

In founding Fairhavens Conrad Schneider's first action had been to establish a board of directors. The first board action had been the selection of a site, which had been recommended by Schneider. Paradise Valley had always appealed to him. When he learned that the old Emigrant Inn had closed its doors, he discovered that the board could lease the Inn and its adjoining land. Emigrant Inn had been a dude ranch from the earliest settlement of the valley, but when Jake Cobb, its long time owner died the property was inherited by his grandchildren, who by that time lived in Oregon. They did not care to keep the business going, and so put it on the market for lease through a Livingston realtor. An agreement had been reached for an acceptable lease with the Fairhavens board.

The board renamed the inn, Fairhavens Lodge. It is located thirty miles north of the North Entrance to Yellowstone National Park. With Yellowstone it shares in some of the benefits of underground thermal activity. Hot springs wells supply a large outdoor swimming pool as well as hot tubs the year round. The lodge, built in about 1910, can house eighty guests and is equipped to provide full meal service in its turn-of-the-century dining room. In addition to the lodge, the Fairhavens Board took over the pool facilities and horse barns left from the original dude ranch. Since its founding the Board has built five individual family log cabins, and the Annex with conference center facilities and the employee dormitory on its second floor.

Paradise Valley is a broad grassy valley along the Yellowstone River which flows north from Yellowstone Park to Livingston where the river bends eastward toward Billings, and from there north-east into eastern Montana. After flowing through much of eastern Montana the Yellowstone converges with the Missouri just across the North Dakota state line approximately seventy miles south of the Canadian border. From there the waters of Missouri flow southeast into the Mississippi, and thence to the gulf of Mexico in the Atlantic ocean.

Paradise Valley is bordered on the east by the Absoroka Range and on the west by the foothills of the Gallatin Range. Significant forestation is to be found only in the higher elevations of the Absoroka. The valley itself is covered mostly with grasslands spreading over gently rolling hills on either side of the Yellowstone. The river is broad and placid, unlike the Gallatin to the West, which is a more typically turbulent mountain stream. The Yellowstone carries the waters from melting snow from the mountains as well as run off from thermal activity of the high country in the national park.

Paradise Valley had not been heavily populated, containing only far-flung ranches, until recently, when more and more recreation homes began to spring up along the river. Emigrant Inn had been built at the mouth of Emigrant gulch, the site of some very active gold prospecting and mining in the 1860's. These mining activities flourished until the price of gold plummeted in the 1930's. Some of the remains of that boom and bust period are still to be found along the gulch up the mountain valley from Fairhavens. After the miners moved on, the cattle ranchers brought in their herds to feed on the lush native grass. Next the homesteaders found their way into the valley. Following the farmers, have come those who are looking for recreational pleasures in the valley of Paradise. With the coming of Fairhavens still others have come to the Valley for short term experience. In addition to those coming to Fairhavens for recreation are the broken ones seeking retreat, renewal and the re-building of their lives.

Towering above Fairhavens and its seekers of recreation and renewal is Emigrant Peak reaching into the sky almost eleven thousand feet. It is one of the crowns of the Gallatin National Forest with its east face within the Absaroka Beartooth Wilderness. This region bordering Yellowstone Park is a Mecca for back-packers.

The capacity of the Lodge dining room is a little over one hundred. The average number of lodge guests at any one time runs between sixty and eighty. Professional staff generally eat in the dining room with guests, while the support staff take their meals in a small dining room on the first floor of the Annex. Because guests are welcome to sit wherever they please in the dining room, there is a fair amount of mixing of family groups and individuals. No distinction is made between those registered for renewal experiences and those coming for vacation activities. Dr. Schneider and some of the professional staff often eat with guests, circulating among the tables from meal to meal.

Thus, on the evening of their arrival, Leona Baxter and the Jones couple found a table together. Dr. Schneider joined them. This gave Conrad opportunity to offer information and lore about Fairhavens which he liked to share with each new person as they joined the Fairhavens "family."

Jackson Evans, considered professional staff, had been asked by Conrad to include Max Ritter among professional staff when he brought Max down for his first meal at Fairhavens. Evans thought this a bit unusual since the former handy-man-courtesy driver had been considered support staff, taking his meals in the Annex. But, then Schneider was the boss and he had an uncanny way of making wise decisions. When Jack guided Max to the staff table where four of the therapists were already seated, he chose not to say very much about Max's position. Rather he steered the discussion at the table to the young therapists and their background and interests, something they seldom tired of expounding!

At a nearby table Con Schneider was giving some of the local history to the new arrivals. "As far as I can ascertain Emigrant Peak got its name from wagon trains of emigrants who passed this way in the mid-eighteen hundreds. I do know that in 1862 a Thomas Curry discovered gold in this gulch leading down from the peak, which was then named Emigrant Gulch. This was in the same year that the first big gold strike in Montana Territory was made on Grasshopper Creek, where the town of Bannock was started. Thus, Bannock became the first Montana territorial capital. It is significant, I think, to note that Emigrant gulch was developing as early as Bannock. And if you go up the gulch any distance you'll find some of the rotting wood from the early gold mining activity. When you go up there you really feel you are in a ghost town. In those days there was another attraction here at the mouth of the gulch—crude vats had been constructed to hold the waters from hot springs, which the trappers and prospectors used for bathing."

Lee Baxter broke in, "Would you say that those were the original version of the hot springs pools which Fairhavens now has?"

"That's exactly right!" That water has been running for centuries and it's been used for well over a hundred years! Really, much longer. Legend has it that native Americans had used the pools for centuries."

When the main course was served, the conversation turned to informal talk during dinner. As they were finishing dessert, Bill Jones asked, "Besides the pool, how do your guests spend their time here?"

"Some like to ride. You can check out the horse barns in the morning. Do you like to ride?"

"I don't know, but I'd like to try that."

"We have a wrangler who takes groups out on the trail each morning. There are quite a number of horse trails leading out from our property. They cross other deeded lands before extending up into the forests up the side of the mountains to the east. Some trails go west, crossing the road and then leading up into the Gallatin foothills. There are also hiking trails in almost all directions. Oftentimes guest have enjoyed painting or photography. And, of course, with Yellowstone so close, only thirty miles to the entrance, many spend time in the Park."

"Even in winter?" Leona Baxter asked.

"Yes. Mammoth Hot Springs is open all year, and you can

drive to Tower Junction and out the North-East Entrance to Silver Gate and Cooke City year round.

Ruth Jones asked, "How do those of us who flew in manage a tour of Yellowstone?"

Our courtesy van will take you and pick you up whenever you want to go. In the summer Park buses can be gotten at the Mammoth Hotel at the north entrance of Yellowstone. That way one can get around the entire park. We have specific information in the office if you are interested."

Lee Baxter wanted to know what sorts of activities are available at Fairhavens itself.

"Three evenings a week we have a campfire program, this time of the year around the fireplace in the lounge which you walked through to come in here. We follow the Park Service model and have people give illustrated talks on various wild life and nature subjects, sometimes history; and these evening programs include music, both singing and instrumental. Since we are family oriented there are various recreational activities during the days like volley ball, soft ball, and badminton in the summer; sledding and cross country skiing in the winter. For the younger children there are games. One of our staff is ready to help with this when there are kids wanting such things. And I guess we also need to say that we promote relaxed, sitting around, reading, meditating or conversation. That's the retreat part. RECREATION, RETREAT, RENEWAL—these are the three R's of Fairhavens! Renewal is quite a bit more programmed, with specific group and individual sessions for the folks who have come here for that purpose."

"That raises a question I've had." Leona interjected. "Don't you tend to have a sort of two tiered group here? You know—the vacationers, and the people registered for therapeutic reasons. How do they regard each other?"

"You've pointed to an area we intentionally work at. We try very hard not to make distinction between the two kinds of guests. We all eat at the same times and sit with whomever we want to. Each family or individual goes about their own daily activities;

and no attempt is made to draw any lines, so to speak. The therapists are called program staff and some of them provide leadership
for vacationer activities as well as for renewal folks, like the therapist who also leads children's recreation and sports. The one thing
I haven't said much about is the music therapy component. A fair
amount of this is just a part of the public atmosphere of the place.
You can hear some of it now over the sound system. In addition to
the campfire programs we sponsor musical events every so often
which are here for guests of both types."

Lee seemed satisfied with Con's answer.

"Well, that's enough lecturing from me for tonight. You probably are ready to relax for the evening. Breakfast is at 8."

Mr. & Mrs. Jones rose and walked out into the lounge to have
a look around. Con asked Lee, "Would you care to have a bit of a
walk around the grounds? It looks like a pleasant evening!"

"I'd like that."

They put on their winter coats and took the path behind the
horse barns which leads up the hill in back of the lodge. When
they reached a point overlooking the lodge and the entire cluster
of Fairhavens buildings Con stopped to point out various of the
buildings. When the two resumed their walk he said, "It is so very
good to have you here at last, Lee."

"I know. I feel that way too."

"What do you think of it so far"

"I'm impressed. I so much want to know more about it—
especially the retreat and renewal part."

"Feel free to visit with people as you meet them around the
place or at meal times. You might be able to guess which ones are
here for therapy. Some of them will be quick to share with you
something of their journey."

Con was eager to tell Lee about Max Ritter. "I've just hired a
handy-man/van driver. You met him in the van when you arrived."

"Yes, I remember; but he didn't strike me as the handy-man
type."

Con laughed, "You mean there's a handy-man type?"

"Oh quit it! You know what I mean."

"Yes, I do; and you're right. I see Max as having the potential for a position of greater responsibility. Maybe my assistant! Which at this point I don't have—and need!"

"I should think you would need help like that."

"I do—but enough of business for now. Lee, I have to say that I have missed you, and you're coming here means so much to me personally."

"Oh, Con, since your Chicago trip and our meeting, my life seems different; and you have been on my mind constantly. For the first time since my husband died I can honestly say that I am happy. Your coming to me that day in River Forest was a gift!"

Con took her hand in his and said, "I can hardly believe what you have just said, Lee! Talk about a gift! You are a gift from God to me. I don't want to sound foolish, but it is like there is something big and real—palpable—that is hovering over us and between us and uniting us," Con said in a hushed voice, almost in a whisper lest his boldness offend her.

"You're not foolish, Con. I know what you refer to. But to me it is more like an invisible band which encircles us and seems to pull us together."

"Yes—," Con said wistfully.

"And the cord is fragile—made of glass—we have to let it pull with its own strength—at its own pace!" Lee cautioned.

"On a very practical level, I guess that translates to 'cool it! Especially, when we are among any of the Fairhavens folk!" Con offered.

Next morning after breakfast Con invited Max into his office to give him a briefing on what would be expected of him: "Bring your coffee into my office and we'll talk about your job, Max."

When Max was seated Con began: "The last person who worked here as a handy-man did good work, but he wasn't a self-starter. He needed someone else to discover the problems, and then he would follow orders and take care of whatever maintenance and repair jobs he was given. Since meeting you yesterday, I've made a decision which I hope isn't going too far out on a limb! And I hope it's not more than you've bargained for."

"What is that?"

"I'd like give you the title of 'Superintendent of Buildings and Grounds.' And by that I don't mean just a change of title. What I mean by that is, that your job would be to keep tabs on the physical condition of the place and take care of repairs and maintenance issues as they arise. Many of these, I assume you can do yourself. But there will be things that require professionals like plumbers or electricians. When that kind of help is needed, it would be up to you to determine; and then to line up the right repair person for the job."

Max looked a little startled at this job description.

"Well, what do you think?"

"You take me by surprise, but I guess, when you come down to it, if I can fix a thing, I ought also to be able to discover what is needed!"

"That's it exactly."

"But, I'll need some time to become well acquainted with the buildings and grounds, and to get to know what sort of professional repair people are in the area."

"Of course; and I'll do all I can to help get you oriented."

"OK, why don't you give me three months, and then let's evaluate whether this is working out."

"Fair enough! By the way you may have wondered about Jackson bringing you to a staff table in the main dining room last night and this morning instead of sending you out to the Annex. My reasoning was that if you were to be named Superintendent of Buildings and Grounds, that really is a professional staff position and you might just as well begin on that level."

Con began to shift in his chair and absent-mindedly to sort through some papers on his desk, a clear indication to Max that it was time to get started.

Con dialed the phone, "Jackson, can you take time this morning to show Max Ritter around the buildings? . . . Good, I'll send him up to your office."

"Jackson will show you around. His office is up the stairs and to the right. And I'll get Everette Engstrom, our wrangler to tour the grounds with you this afternoon. You can get together with him at lunch. Now, Max, I think this is going to be good. I hope you have a good look-see today!"

The rest of Max's day went as planned, and by evening he had a pretty good handle on the place and his responsibility as superintendent. After dinner he retired to his room, kicked off his shoes and lay down on his bed to review his first day at work. A good one, he thought. A fairly clear picture of what's ahead. Nice people to work for and to associate with. He anticipated getting started the next day on arranging for himself a combination office and shop. Two or three locations had seemed to be possibilities along this line; tomorrow he would decide. Fun! He thought. With that he put Fairhavens out of mind, closed his eyes and thought . . . of what had transpired in his life over the past few days . . . of what might lie ahead . . . and of his journal. He found it in his suitcase and began to write:

> *Wow! Here I am in a little 14'X14' cubicle at Fairhavens, a resort in Montana, with a job here—Superintendent of Buildings and Grounds! How's that for a development from Handyman at Colac Bay Inn—Southland, New Zealand! Colac Bay—I'd rather be there . . . (with you) . . .*

At this point he stopped, read what he had written and realized that he had not written this to himself in the manner of a journal, but he had written this to Bronwyn MacKenzie in the manner of a letter! He continued:

> *But, I can't. Nor can I write a letter either. So these journal entries will be for you, Bronwyn, as well as for me! Though I doubt you'll ever read them—sad to say.*

He closed his journal, put it back in his suitcase, and went to bed. At the close of Day 1 at a place called Fairhavens.

His nightly journal entries would provide him a record of his first days in his new life, and these would be moments with Bronwyn as well. Time in his new setting passed quickly for Max. Soon it was Day 7!

Most of the guests had come down to breakfast and were seated throughout the dining room when Con broke away from some early office work to take some breakfast. Max was at a table with Jackson Evans and Everette Engstrom. Max was discovering in these two men the opening up of friendship. Close friendship had until this time been rare in his life. The three took most of their meals together.

Sometimes Con joined them, but on this morning he chose to take an empty seat at one of the guest tables. The Jones's and Lee Baxter had selected a table together as they had done often during their stay. Con came up to their table, "May I join you?"

"Certainly. We'd like that." replied Mrs. Jones.

Lee chimed in, "Honored!"

"Well, what's on your agendas for today?" Con asked.

Ruth Jones said she and Bill planned to take a winter hike during the morning and spend the afternoon at the pool. "We have only three more days. This has been one of our most relaxing vacations ever. We hate to leave,. but we'll be going back to work in far better shape than when we took off a week ago!"

"Great! That, of course, makes us happy here at Fairhavens. I hope you'll come back another time!"

"Oh, we plan to."

"And, Lee, what about you?"

"I have to return to Chicago. I have reservations for the day after tomorrow. But this has been such a good experience. I really feel that I've gotten to know Fairhavens."

Con explained to Ruth and Bill Jones, "Mrs. Baxter had heard of Fairhavens through some of her volunteer associations in the

Chicago area, and when she contacted us, we assured her that an on-site visit would really show her what we are about."

"Yes," she said, "I have been here as a dude, but my interest has been in the therapeutic track which Fairhavens provides, and I've had opportunity to get to know something of the renewal emphasis this week as well as to give myself some relaxation. And I can say truthfully, that I am impressed."

"I'm glad to hear you say that. If you have any further questions, be sure and ask me, before you get away."

At this point the Mr. & Mrs. Jones took their leave so that they could dress for their hike.

Con then suggested to Lee, "Since you have only a day remaining, I'd like to take you on up to Yellowstone before you leave this area. How about it?"

"That would be fun, but are you sure you can take the time?"

"I'll make time. Not only for you to see a little of Yellowstone, but for us to spend a bit of time together away from the curious!"

"OK, I'm game! When do you want me ready?"

"If we leave here after lunch we can get to the North East Entrance by dinner time. I have a friend who runs a motel in Cooke City and I'll get a couple of rooms there for tonight; and then tomorrow we can return to the Mammoth area, and maybe do some skiing."

"Whatever you say!"

"Lee, have you ever cross country skied? Would you like to?"

"I'd like that, I think. Some years back I tried it briefly."

"I'll take a couple pair along and we can do that in the Park tomorrow."

Soon they were on their way up the valley to Gardiner at the North Entrance, and five miles further into the Park to Mammoth where they stopped for a coffee break, before driving over to the North East Entrance.

That evening after dinner in Cooke City they checked into Soda Butte Lodge. They spent a leisurely morning with breakfast in Cooke City and a drive back to Silver Gate. The sun was out brilliantly with the temperature in the teens and no wind. They stopped a few times between Cooke and Silver Gate to get out and feel the freshness of the mountain air and to poke around a bit in the woods near the road. They found a place open in Silver Gate for a light lunch.

Driving through the Lamar Valley toward Tower Junction they stopped to watch a herd of bison pawing through the snow getting the grass underneath. After turning west on the road to Mammoth they found a good place to stop for some cross country. After a couple of hours of cross country skiing on fresh white snow under a gorgeous bright blue sky they returned to the car ready for the thermos of coffee they had filled in Silver Gate.

The sun was beginning to sink in the west creating a vivid array of oranges and pinks turning to purples as they drove westward. They arrived in Mammoth in time for a gourmet dinner in the Mammoth Inn Dining Room. A sprinkling of winter guests were seated at tables throughout the large room. Western Prime Rib for Con. Mediterranean Chicken for Lee. And all the trimmings and special touches, which always make dining in Yellowstone Park hotels so special. After a dessert of raspberry torte and gourmet coffee, the two from Fairhavens lingered for a few minutes in the dining room before continuing their homeward drive down the Yellowstone.

Lee took his hand in hers. She said, "Oh, Con, these days have been the best I've had since . . ." becoming emotional she couldn't quite finish.

"That's all right, Lee. I think I can sense something of you're feeling."

They were silent for a while. They could hear the classical music coming over the sound system, as well as the muffled sound of the other guests in the dining room, as they sat quietly.

Lee continued: "These have been very lonely years for me. Oh, I've kept busy with volunteer work at church, at the Evanston home and some community things, but on a deeper level I have felt the loss of personal relationship. I don't want to embarrass you, Con, or to be too forward, but from our first contact, I've felt in your presence the restoration of a warm personal connection—missing in my life since Hunt died."

This took Con by surprise; and when he looked into her eyes he could see faint traces of tears. "I don't know what to say. To say 'me too' would sound dumb, although true. I have felt that too, Lee, but hadn't been able to put it in words, as you did. Personal connection! That has to be two ways. And I'm feeling such a connection with you." They were silent again. He could feel her hand tighten on his. He responded in the same way.

The lights from the chandeliers glistened against the windows now reflecting the shiny black of the winter night.

"We have about an hour's drive, Lee, so I'm afraid we are going to have to leave this place."

Alone together as they walked out to the car in the darkness. When they reached the car Con took Lee in his arms and the two gave each other a very warm embrace before getting in for the drive home. Their embrace was accompanied by what would be their only chance to kiss good bye.

The drive back to Fairhavens in the dark was a quiet one. Each pondering deep and personal thoughts. As Con turned off the highway to head on up to Fairhavens he said, "Tomorrow you'll be leaving and who knows when we'll see each other again. But, believe me, I want to see you again, Lee."

"I want you to come to Chicago, Con, whenever you can. We need some good times together!"

"Yes, we do."

"Are you on E-mail?"

"No" Con replied, "Are you?"

"Yes, I am, and if you could get on, then we could 'talk' on a regular basis."

"I've thought of it, and now you give me the added incentive. Give me a chance to work that out. Meanwhile can we write?"

"Let's do, but I'm not so great a letter writer. But I think I could do better on E-mail. There is something about E-mail that makes it easier," Lee observed.

It was quite late when they got back to the Lodge. A couple of guests were still up in the lounge reading, but the rest of the place was asleep. Lee went up to her room and Con stopped by his office to check messages before retiring to his room. He was glad that there were no messages. He didn't want the spell to be broken.

CHAPTER 16

In his first weeks at Fairhavens Max threw himself into his work with unremitting zeal. He carefully examined each of the structures and noted repairs needed. He was getting a feel for the sort of maintenance program he wanted to work out. A ramshackle toolshed behind the lodge would eventually serve as his base of operations He would need to provide for some heat in this building for winter use. This he arranged with a Livingston electrical contractor to be put in as soon as possible. He felt an immediate need for a telephone, so that he could easily make his contacts with professional repair people when they were needed. Con Schneider very happily authorized this and Con had U.S. West out from Livingston to put a line into the shed.

He found himself putting in eleven and twelve hour days, which left him little energy or time to think about much else; but, that suited him, at least at first.

One evening at dinner when Con was at the staff table he said to Max, "A couple things, Max: You're working longer hours than you're expected to. You ought to have some time to yourself; at least your evenings. And give yourself a day off besides Sunday each week. Fit that in to your schedule—just let me know when. Everette can serve as a back-up for any emergencies when you're gone, Max. The other thing is that there are two small cabins up above which are unused. If you want to take one over for yourself, that would be fine with me. They both may need some fixing!"

"Thanks, Con, for both ideas. I think I've got things in hand and I can let down a bit like you say. I know the cabins you're talking about; I'll take a look tomorrow."

The cabin he chose needed a week of evenings to get it in

shape, but it promised to be a very private spot for Max, nestled in a grove of aspens, high enough up the hill behind the lodge to give him a view of the Gallatin foot hills across the valley. Everette helped him with some of the fix-up. While working together, Everette identified a mountain peak visible from the cabin as Hyalite Peak, just about on a direct line west from Fairhavens. "Sometime when you get a chance you ought to drive over to Bozeman, and just south of town you can get into the National Forest by driving up Hyalite canyon. There's a dam a ways up with a reservoir. People camp up there and fish. Further up there's a natural lake, Hyalite Lake. Anyhow all that's just over the hill below the peak you see from here.

Max remembered some of the folks from Tipton talking about the Hyalite area, but he chose not to reveal his Tipton past. "I'll have to do that on some day off."

The following week Max took Thursday off, returning to his cabin after breakfast. He'd found a discarded writing table which he had repaired and placed in his cabin under his west window with a view of the Gallatin range. The hill dropped off immediately in front of the cabin; and from its edge he could see the roof of the lodge and the pool. To the north he could see the horse barns and the corral. From inside the cabin no other buildings were visible, except the other small cabin ten or so yards to the south.

It was a quiet morning with only the twittering of some finches in the aspens. The sun illuminated the hills to the west under a bright blue cloudless sky. What could be better, he thought. Taking his journal out of the drawer in the writing desk he began:

> *As I look out of my window I see nothing but the natural surroundings, a scene most beautiful to me. My former life far beyond those hills is unseen, and unremembered—almost. I don't even see much of my present life from here! The Lodge and all its repair needs are almost out of sight! Here I am with only my thoughts. Nine o'clock in the morning, March 4th—Park*

County, Montana—Paradise Valley. Let's see—in my other para-
dise—Southland, New Zealand—it's tomorrow morning—4
AM—in the middle of the night. You are asleep? But where?
Dunedin? Colac Bay? Or where? I wish I was there. I wish you
were here!

This sudden thought of Bronwyn derailed Max's journalling as he
thought about his promise to send his address through the church
at Riverton. He really didn't want to use the Fairhavens address.
What he needed was a post office box of his own. He thought
reluctantly, I hate to think of being anywhere near Tipton, but the
time has come, I guess, to check out my stuff and pick up the car.
Max made up his mind to phone Dale to make arrangements to
slip over on his next day off.

The following week Max was quite touched by the way in which
Maude Kober had gone all out to provide a festive sort of dinner for
him when he arrived to pick up his Subaru. They were plain people;
but using her heirloom china and silverware, Maude served a delicious roast beef dinner with mashed potatoes, string beans and cot-
tage cheese salad. She made a good cup of coffee and the berry pie
afterward could not have been better. Their sixth grade daughter helped
her mother to serve, and their teen-age son, whom Max knew from
the church youth group, sat at the table, a miniature replica of his
dad, both of them sat at table like "lords of the manor!" The kids left
to take up other more exciting activities after dessert and Maude and
Dale remained with Max at the table over another cup of coffee.

Dale opened up the subject, "Like I said I'd do, I nosed around
and I think I've come up with the stuff that turned things sour for
you, Max."

Max was eager, and yet reluctant to hear Dale's revelations.
"Tell me, Dale. What did you find out?"

"Well, do you remember the Junior High teacher . . . Pearle, I
think was his name, Aaron Pearle?" Dale began.

"Sure I do."

"It seems that some of the parents of kids in his class got upset with that world religions unit he taught and they tried to get the school board to get him to drop the unit. And you publicly defended his right to teach world religions. Not only that, but you had befriended him; and they couldn't stomach that! You know why?"

Max gave a flicker of realization.

"You guessed it! Because he was Jewish!"

"Max's anger was re-kindled just hearing of this again. "That's right and I'd do the same thing again!"

"Good for you!" Dale applauded, "They've never forgiven you for that, Max; and then there was the time when the new high school principal canceled plans for a baccalaureate service; because it was against church and state separation, I think he said. This got everybody mad; and then when you said something in church about agreeing that the school had a right not to have a baccalaureate service. That did it for you. That signed your walking papers."

"That's another one I'd do again, Dale. What I did do then was to hold a baccalaureate service in church the Sunday evening before graduation for our own high school seniors, and it was, of course, open to any others."

"They never even mentioned that."

"That's because hardly any of them came! . . . So that's what not being spiritual enough really means! Is that your thought too, Dale?"

"Right! They were too 'chicken'" to bring up the real reasons especially the Jewish business. So they pinned 'not spiritual' on you!"

Maude added, "Max, if it makes you feel any better, you can be certain that we think you were right both times. We're just sorry we didn't know what was going on. Or we would have put in a good word for you then."

"Thanks for that, Maude; and for your sleuthing. It makes me angry, but I feel better knowing what it was."

"We're glad it helps," Maude affirmed.

Dale had an additional thought, "And you know, there is something else. We know, because we came from somewhere else too.

"What's that?" Both Max and Maude said, somewhat surprised.

"Well, you know what I really think? I think it was because you and your wife were outsiders. And these folks have a hard time trusting outsiders."

Maude added, "I think you're right, Dale. That's one reason why preachers don't seem to stay long in towns like this. With us it was some different. We had the kind of work which fit into their daily farm and ranch activities, and they came to accept us not too long after we moved here."

Max thought about this for a while, and seemed to be thinking out loud as he added, "That explains some feelings I used to pick up now and then . . . and even more so I imagine that Gwen must have felt that pretty strongly . . . it must have been one of the reasons she never seemed to be happy here," and then as if to himself, "In a way that's part of what I did to her by bringing her here."

Neither Dale nor Maude knew what to say.

Before tears began to form Max changed the subject, "Now, I better head back to the Paradise Valley. I've got a job there, by the way. You two will never know how much both this banquet and this talk mean to me!

"Oh we love having you," Maude replied.

"That's right, buddy! Any time!" Dale chimed in.

"Thanks so much! I know I'll be back."

On his way back he thought a lot about what he'd heard. I need to do some journalling on this issue, he thought, just to help me get it out of my system. When he got near Fairhavens he stopped in at the local post office, rented a box, put his return address on an envelope and put a check inside to the Riverton Church, and sent it.

"Somehow, someday, maybe I'll hear. No matter what, it won't be at least for three weeks considering mail time." he thought as he drove the few miles along the East River Road to Fairhavens.

The topic of alarmed conversation around the staff table that evening was the Cody Vermillian development. Everette had reported, "When we got to the property line on our way up the hill to the east we found the south gate closed, locked and posted, 'Private Property. No Trespassing.'"

Jack Evans said, "That's illegal! Charlie Coats owns that and we have written permission from him to use his property for our horse trails!"

"Illegal while it belonged to Coats'" Con corrected, " but he told me that he had sold his fifteen acres along with his house on Emigrant Creek to Vermillian! Did you try the north gate?"

"Yeah, we went over there and it was also posted; but the gate was open, so we went on up as usual, since Sorensons have always allowed us through."

Con continued his questioning: "Did you get near the Sorenson's house on the trail?"

"We did, but the funny thing was, it looked deserted." Everette replied.

"Another sale, I'm guessing. We are going to be hemmed in by the Vermillian outfit," Con said with obvious distress. "Have you been up on the Mill Creek trail lately?"

"No, but I can try that tomorrow. If that's closed then we know we're blocked."

"That's Nelson land." Jack interjected. "Or it was!"

"Jack—is tomorrow your banking day in town?" Con asked.

"Yes, in the afternoon."

"While you're in, why don't you check at the court house and see who's listed as owning both the Sorenson and Nelson pieces."

The next evening Everette gave an account of his attempt to ride up to Mill Creek. "That area isn't fenced, so the trail has always gone from our property out into Nelsons' without any obvious change—until today, that is. As soon as you get off of our land the trail is blocked with a bunch of downed timber and rocks. More than you could put there by hand. You could see bull dozer tread marks."

"Looks like more Vermillian!" Con concluded. Turning to Evans Con asked, " What did you find out, Jack?"

"Vermillian's group has both places!"

"So . . . Do we have any legal recourse, do you suppose?"

"Not unless there's a deed restriction—a covenant that provides access." Jackson offered. "I could have Mark Eagle check that out for us in the morning."

"Do that!" Con agreed.

Late the next afternoon Jack Evans came to Con's office. "It turns out that the deed restrictions were written poorly. Rendering the deeds subject to interpretation."

"What does that mean for us? Con asked.

"Mark said that the only way to obtain access from the new owners would be to sue, and let a judge decide."

When Con was told this by Jackson Evans he said, "And that we don't want to do—not at this point. Let's lay low and bide our time first."

After Jackson left the office Conrad went down to the horse barns to see Everette. "Ev, we're not going to be able to use any of your three trails—at least for now. What else can you do?"

Everette thought for a moment and said, "It's a lot longer, but I can get into the forest on Sixmile creek. Possibly the Bridger Hollow road. I could give that a try."

"Good. We don't want to be licked by the Cody group! . . . yet . . ."

At dinner that evening, when the subject of access came up, Max asked, "What's up there, that you will lose if this closure sticks?"

Everette said, "Mainly, its our way of getting into National Forest lands. But, there's some interesting stuff on the private property involved. Some ghost town ruins, if you like that sort of thing."

"Is that a loss?

"Dudes love it, and it would be a shame if they could not get in to see it."

Con remarked, "There's the irony. Our dudes don't get to

poke around some authentic mining era remains, because Cody Vermillian is putting up his fake ghost mining town theme park!"

"These Californians!"

"Wait a minute, Jack!" Con cautioned, "Cody's from Nevada."

"Las Vegas! That's more California than Nevada," Jackson countered."

Con went on, "Some of my best friends are Californians! And better yet, some of our best customers are Californians!"

"Especially on the therapy side." Ev chimed in.

"Max, careful what you believe from these guys! The truth of the matter is that many of the first people in this Emigrant area were miners coming here from the California gold fields—'49ers looking for the perfect bonanza strike. So, you might say, without the Californians we might not be here!"

"Ok . . . Ok, let's turn to North Dakota jokes instead." Everette suggested.

"Careful! That's Evan's birth-place!" Con warned, as Jackson feigned deep hurt.

Con had the last word. "Let's be fair. Cody is really Nevada's gift to Paradise Valley, not California's!"

"Same thing!" Everette quipped.

The conversation turned to small talk, while each man held the Vermillian matter for later pondering.

Max continued his work of refurbishing the lodge and other buildings on the grounds. More than once Con Schneider expressed his appreciation to him for the work he was doing. Max found himself increasingly contented with his new life at Fairhavens. There were some loose ends which he kept putting off, like his dangling relationship to his Presbytery, and his personal items and house-hold things still stored at Kobers in Tipton. But the less he thought about these left-overs from his former life, the more he felt re-newed in his new associations at Fairhavens. Even New Zealand and Bronwyn had begun to fade into a sort of lifeless, sterile memory, like an old Valentine stuck in a drawer. Now, he seldom removed his New Zealand thoughts from the pockets of his mind.

Meanwhile Conrad Schneider was entering a new phase in his
life—cyberspace! After Lee Baxter's challenge to him to get on
Internet, he had gotten a TV and Radio appliance friend in
Livingston to get him a modem and connected with the internet.
His computer mentor had suggested that Fairhavens would qualify
for a church-related carrier call CONVENE. His first note was, of
course, to Lee Baxter:

> LEE!
> DO YOU READ ME? I'VE JUST GOTTEN HOOKED
> UP FOR E-MAIL AND YOU'RE THE FIRST TO GET
> A NOTE. THAT IS, IF I'M DCING THIS RIGHT. LET
> ME KNOW IKF THIS IS WORKING?
> Con [cschneider.parti@ecunet.org]

The very next day after Con went online he received his first note
from Lee Baxter:

> CON!
> YOU'RE ON. NOW WE CAN "TALK" IF YOU GET THIS!
> LEE [LEONAB@AOL.COM]

On his third day in cyberspace Con Schneider entered a modern era
of communication with Lee Baxter when he received her note! A
schoolboy's delight swept over him as he realized how easy it was
going to be to "sneak" messages daily—back and forth with this new
and delightful friend! Something more than friend, he thought.

Conrad Schneider had grown up in a time when the Puritan Work
ethic pervaded everyone's conscience! This prompted him to write
his notes to Lee after hours, because this would be pure pleasure,
not work! Even though at first much of their conversation centered
around Fairhavens.

      So it was that just about every evening after dinner he returned
to his office and "talked" to Leona Baxter. And, he was pleased to

realize, she sent notes just as frequently! One of their earliest exchanges had to do with the music therapy emphasis at Fairhavens:

> DEAR CON—
> ONE OF THE THINGS WHICH I REALLY DIDN'T HEAR ENOUGH ABOUT WAS YOUR MUSIC THERAPY PROGRAM. TELL ME MORE ABOUT THAT. I FIND THE IDEA INTRIGUING. AND UNIQUE, I MIGHT ADD.
> LEE

> DEAR LEE—
> AS A MATTER OF FACT IT IS UNIQUE. THERE IS A NEWLY DEVELOP-ING FIELD OF MUSIC THERAPY, BUT THIS IS DIFFERENT. IT DOES NOT HAVE SO MUCH TO DO WITH THE PLAYING OF MUSIC BY PATIENTS AS IT DOES LISTENING TO MUSIC. AND THAT INCLUDES A SUBLIMINAL LISTENING AS WELL. BY DEFINITION THE FOLKS WHO COME HERE ON THE THERAPY TRACK ARE TROUBLED TO VARYING DEGREES. THE IDEA OF FAIRHAVENS AS A SAFE HARBOR PROTECTED FROM THE STORM MEANS THAT WE TRY TO PROVIDE A CALMING ATMOSPHERE. NO MATTER HOW STORMY THEIR LIVES HAVE BECOME, WE TRY TO BRING THEM INTO A SAFE HARBOR. IN ADDITION TO THE MOUNTAIN RETREAT SETTING, SAFE HARBOR IS CREATED BY THE MUSIC WHICH IS HEARD. MUCH OF THAT MUSIC IS BACKGROUND SOUND DURING OTHER ACTIVITIES LIKE MEALS, FOR EXAMPLE. SOME OF IT IS VERY INTENTIONAL, TAKING THE FORM OF VERY INTENTIONAL TIMES LIKE RECITALS AND CON-CERTS TO WHICH THE PEOPLE IN THE THERAPY TRACK ARE EN-COURAGED TO ATTEND. THESE MUSICAL EVENTS ARE OPEN TO THE VACATIONERS AS WELL. IT IS OUR HOPE THAT BOTH THE FORMAL AND INFORMAL EXPOSURE TO MUSIC WILL HAVE A CALM-ING EFFECT AND PROVIDE A THERAPEUTIC ENVIRONMENT. WHILE YOU WERE HERE YOU HEARD SOME OF THE BACKGROUND MUSIC, BUT THERE WEREN'T ANY CONCERTS DURING THAT TIME. HOPE-FULLY NEXT TIME!
> CON

DEAR CON—

AND I HOPE THERE'LL BE A NEXT TIME!

WOULD YOU SAY THAT THE HELPFUL ASPECT OF MUSIC IN YOUR MUSIC THERAPY PROGRAM IS TO SOOTHE? WHAT KIND OF MUSIC DO YOU USE FOR THIS? OR IS ANY KIND OK? I HOPE I'M NOT ASKING TOO MANY QUESTIONS! BUT, ONE REASON I'M INTERESTED IS THAT I WONDER IF THERE MIGHT BE A USE FOR THIS APPROACH UP AT THE EVANSTON HOME WHERE I DO A LOT OF VOLUNTEER WORK.

LEE

DEAR LEE—

I'M NOT SURE HOW THIS MUSIC THERAPY FITS INTO YOUR INVOLVEMENT WITH THE EVANSTON HOME. BECAUSE THAT WOULD DEPEND UPON WHAT YOU ARE TRYING TO DO—JUST GIVE AN ENTERTAINING SOUND, OR TRYING TO AFFECT CHANGE IN THE LIVES OF PEOPLE.

WE USE ALMOST EXCLUSIVELY MUSIC FROM THE BAROQUE PERIOD. IT'S A LONG AND COMPLICATED RATIONALE—MORE THAN YOU WANT TO KNOW I"M SURE.

WE ARE NOT JUST TRYING TO SOOTHE. RATHER WE USE MUSIC TO HELP BRING ABOUT RESOLUTION TO PEOPLE'S UPSETTING SITUATIONS AND CONDITIONS. THAT'S WHY BAROQUE IS USED. EACH PIECE OR MOVEMENT ALWAYS VERY EMPHATICALLY RESOLVES! BUT, I THINK THAT WITHIN EACH PIECE THERE IS SOMETHING UPLIFTING. IN FACT THE IDEA FOR THIS KIND OF MUSIC THERAPY CAME TO ME DURING ONE OF MY FIRST WEEKS HERE BEFORE WE REALLY HAD A PROGRAM IN PLACE. I HAD TUNED IN TO NATIONAL PUBLIC RADIO DURING THE PLAYING OF BACH'S BRANDENBURG CONCERTO NO. 4. AFTER THAT DRAMATIC RESOLVING CHORD AT THE END, THE ANNOUNCER COMMENTED: "MUSIC THAT HAS THE POWER TO LIFT A HEAVY HEART." THIS WAS THE SEED PLANTED IN MY MIND THAT DAY WHICH HAS GROWN INTO THE PRESENT APPROACH TO HELPING PEOPLE WITH "HEAVY HEARTS" SO TO SPEAK.

NOW I'VE TOLD YOU MORE THAN YOU EVER WANTED TO
KNOW! ENOUGH FOR NOW!
CON

DEAR CON—
THANKS—I THINK I GET THE PICTURE. YOU HAVEN'T BORED ME
AT ALL. OUR EVANSTON PEOPLE HAVE THE WEEKLY RE-RUNS OF
THE OLD LAWRENCE WELK SHOWS FOR SOOTHING ENTERTAIN-
MENT. SOME FOLKS NEED SOME RESOLUTION AND YOUR IDEA
MIGHT HAVE MERIT. I MIGHT TALK TO THE DIRECTOR ABOUT
THIS.
    TELL ME HOW THINGS ARE GOING FOR YOU, CON!
LEE

Con shut off the computer. He thought about the conversation
he'd been having over the past week. All about Fairhavens; but so
many of their other exchanges lately had been on a more personal
level. She had shared with him her concern for her daughter after
her recent divorce. Having no children of his own, he was eager to
get to know about Lee's family. Now he pondered the change which
was taking place in his life. He no longer felt quite so alone. His
relationship to Lee Baxter was growing in a way which was very
new in his experience. He felt a nameless anticipation of good
things ahead.

CHAPTER 17

Fairhavens occasionally accommodated conferences for groups of educators or religious leaders. Most years the week after Easter was reserved by clergy groups for retreats. Often the Lutheran pastors in the state scheduled such a conference. With less frequency the Presbyterian pastors of Montana came to Fairhavens. However, a Yellowstone Presbytery group came in during Max's first year on the grounds. He'd seen the entry on the master calendar: "Yellowstone Clergy-Spouse Retreat." It had not occurred to him that this might include some people he had known while at Tipton. So it came as a surprise to him when he recognized some of the ministers, on the first Monday in April as clergy began arriving. He did not make any contact with these folks at this point in his new life. Since Max did not have direct involvement with guests it was possible for him to avoid any contact with the ministers who had come for the retreat.

However, during one afternoon during the clergy-spouse retreat Max ran into a man he had known slightly in Yellowstone Presbytery. He was the minister from Terry who was taking a walk above the horse barns during his free time. Max couldn't avoid recognition and so he openly greeted him, "Hello, Art!" When he saw that the man was bewildered, Max went on. "You probably don't remember, but I used to be at Tipton."

"Oh, now I remember. You are Max Ritter!" He noted with obvious surprise. "We lost track of you. Nobody knows anything of your whereabouts. So this is quite a surprise."

"I'm sure it must be. I owe you an explanation, I suppose. And maybe you can fill me in on what's going on. Can you come to my cabin. I'll fix us a pot of tea?"

"Why, yes, I suppose I could. I don't have anything until the supper hour? Are you staying here—for the conference?"

"No I'm on the Fairhavens staff."

The two men retired to Max's cabin and Max shared some of his story with Art Simpson. And then he asked Art, "What can you tell me about my status with the Presbytery. I wouldn't be surprised if they've kicked me out, except that I guess they can't do that until they find me!"

"So far as I know," Art told Max, "we dissolved your pastoral relationship with Tipton and put you on the list of ministers without calls."

"That's tame enough, I guess. What, if anything, was said about the Tipton situation?" Max asked with a eager urgency in his voice.

"Not much, really, just that the leaders of the congregation said you weren't spiritual enough. But, Max, people are always saying that about us."

"That may be, but you're still at Terry! No, in my case I guess they thought they had a valid reason. But it beats me to figure what I should have done differently. The stands I took, I'd take again."

"Far be it from me to answer that. 'There but for the grace of God go I!'" Art offered, both as a self-induced warning and a way of trying to lessen the pain he saw in Max's face.

"Well, anyway I didn't fall too far out of the good graces of Presbytery then?"

"No, really not. You know, you are on the list of people the Committee on Ministry writes to once a year to find out what, if any, volunteer involvement you have in a congregation—that is, if they have an address!"

"I'm on the list, but no one knows my address. I suppose I ought to let them know. Here, why don't you take my address and give it to the Stated Clerk for me?"

Max wrote on a paper napkin and gave is to Art: Max Ritter, P. O. Drawer Z, Pray, Montana 59065. "Quite an address, isn't it *Pray*! I guess after being told I'm not spiritual enough, I've found the right place for a remedy!" Max said with a grim sort of smile, which Art did not know how to interpret.

"Maybe so. You said it. I didn't," Art said, "Anyhow, I'll be glad to give this to our clerk. Now I need to get back to my room before dinner. It's been good to see you again, Max. Be glad to see you at Presbytery meetings—how about it?"

"I don't know . . . thanks, though."

After Art left Max remained in his cabin for a while thinking over the conversation, mostly about his old nemesis—"not spiritual enough!" That phrase still haunted him. Pray, Montana—hah! Why don't you pray, Max! That might be more to the point. He thought also about Art's reference to the annual reports ministers without calls are required to make to Presbytery. What will he report? That he's a handyman? At least it's at a place that helps people; but that won't fly. He found himself "journalling" in his mind, as he went back to his afternoon work.

When he returned to his cabin after dinner that evening he got out his journal to work out his "presbytery problem."

> *I've set the wheels in motion so that soon I'll be getting a letter from the Stated Clerk of Presbytery asking me about my church involvement. Either I say "zero" or I get involved. That would be fake; but I really ought to attend somewhere. At the moment I'm not spiritual at all, let alone enough.*

The following week-end Max made the decision to find a church to attend. He'd seen the Mill Creek Community Church as he had driven the East River road. He found the worship time listed in Saturday's Livingston paper; and the next day made it to Mill Creek in time for the morning worship. The service was not at all what he had been accustomed to. The music was made up mostly of old time revival choruses, sung by a small choir and a congregation of about thirty. The atmosphere was emotionally charged as the singing was done with zestful energy. But, he had to admit to himself that there was something catching about the

service. By the last hymn Max was singing with as much enthusiasm as he had ever sung hymns. The sermon, he thought, was
surprisingly helpful. It wasn't the old familiar and worn out revival
message, but one which had more to do with facing contemporary
problems. The minister was a man in his sixties who possessed a
gentle manner. Max found him easy to listen to.

After the service it was obvious that most everyone knew each
other quite well. They seemed to be an assortment of local ranch
families and a few regular vacationers. A good mix of ages, too. On
the whole they were friendly and welcoming to Max, but it wasn't
overdone. He felt comfortable with the experience. When he was
greeted by the pastor Max felt a very real warmth in the way the
minister spoke to him. He asked Max if he lived in the Valley and
Max told him that he lived and worked at Fairhavens. This seemed
to interest the pastor who said that occasionally he had attended
some clergy conferences there and had always enjoyed the place.

On the way home Max had mixed feelings about his morning.
While the service had provided him with a good feeling, it also left
him wondering why he had never felt as enthused as the people in
this congregation certainly seemed to feel. He had to admit to himself
that the enthusiasm seemed authentic—not contrived, as he would
have pre-judged. Their honesty and good feeling showed itself not
only in the singing but in the way people were engaged with each
other in the fellowship following the service. It was obvious that the
members of this congregation enjoyed their worship and felt a genuine warmth for each other. As Max thought about this there popped
into his mind the two Great Commandments as Jesus had identified
them! Love God with all you are and love one another! That seemed
to sum up what he saw in the worship and fellowship of the morning!

In the week following, the emotional high left him, while there
remained his self-doubt in its place. This was the sort of service of
which he had always been critical. Too much emotion, he had
always felt. And yet that seemed to be the very thing he had to
admit he envied in these people. Is this the sort of spirituality the
Tipton folk had accused him of lacking? Maybe so; but if that was

so, he probably never should have gone to Tipton in the first place. But yet, if the Tipton people had been more like these Mill Creek folk, it would be hard to imagine them being so critical of him. His own self-doubt seemed to be balanced by some insights he was drawing from the morning's experience. And then there were the issues Dale Kober had said bothered the Tipton folk. However, Max was unwilling to let the "spirituality thing" drop.

After dinner Max retired to his cabin to spend the rest of his day off alone with his thoughts. He took out his journal:

> *After my experience at Mill Creek, I am struck by the comparison, or contrast, between the congregations at Mill Creek and Tipton. Somehow, even though Mill Creel wasn't my style, I felt that it was right and real for them. It appeared to me to be an authentic spiritual expression—not phoney. They accepted me in a way Tipton never did. What's the difference in this? I wonder. Could it be that the fact that Mill Creek was real, they were not threatened by someone like myself, who was not quite like them? And on the other hand Tipton was threatened by my difference, because their spirituality was not as real as they had liked to believe? Until they could force me to be like them, they would be uncomfortable. Do I think this? Or is this just my way of rationalizing? I get the feeling that I would be "spiritual enough" for the Mill Creek people, but not for Tipton? The important question is what should I be for ME? How can I be authentic? Am I? I was authentic with Aaron Pearle and all that school business, wasn't I? The more I think about Mill Creek, the more like Bronwyn's congregation in Riverton it seemed to be! As I reflect on Riverton I think I felt authenticity in those folk. Certainly that was one of the most appealing things about Bronwyn. There was nothing artificial about her; and yet she was spiritual in her own special way. I guess I'm learning that true spirituality must be authentic—real, or it's so much warm air! Just as God is REAL so my relationship to God must be real. It can't be fake. That would be a contradic-*

tion in terms. How can I be spiritual in my own way—a way
that is real?

Max closed his journal wondering why things always ended in a question!

Overall the experience at Mill Creek Church had been positive, so much so that he began attending Sunday worship fairly regularly.

Not much that staff members did escaped the notice of others on staff. One Monday morning at breakfast, Everette asked Max, "I see you are going down to Mill Creek on Sundays. How do you like it there?"

"I'm getting to like it quite well. At first it was different from what I was used to. But now its good. The people are really friendly."

"That's good. I attended there for a while, but lately I've been involved in what you might call a "house church." It's a group of about nine people who meet up at the Hostetter ranch. There was nothing wrong with Mill Creek, but I got invited up to Hostetters one week and I liked the feel of it. So I've kept going."

"That's interesting. What kind of group is it? Are they hooked up with some denomination?

"I didn't think so at first, but I discovered after a few times that most of the people attending are Mennonite in background. But that really doesn't enter into it."

"Do they have a minister?"

"No, but there's a university professor who comes over from Bozeman who leads it. A man by the name of Yoder. He teaches in range management. He's really good. Knows his Bible."

"Is there anything special about it that is Mennonite, do you think?"

"Well, I gather that it is the peace emphasis and the simple life style. No big thing about worldly goods, and fancy clothes—that sort of thing."

"Is that what attracts you to the group?"

"No, not especially. I think its that the people seem so down-to-earth. Not sophisticated. And not super religious either. And yet there is a genuine enthusiasm about the group and their Christianity," and then Everette added an observation which hit Max, "The people all seem so real!"

"Strange that you should put it that way, because that's the way Mill Creek strikes me." Max declared.

"Yeah, I suppose there is a similarity, now that you mention it," And seeming to want to change the subject Everette continued, "By the way there are some problems at the horse barns I'd like you to see, Max. Can you drop around this morning?"

"Sure, Ill be down in a little bit.

"I'll be there. In fact I've got to get down right away." Everette said as he got up to leave the table.

During this conversation Jackson Evans and Con Schneider, also at the table, had been discussing some business questions. When Everette left, Con went over to one of the guest tables to visit for a few minutes. Jack turned to Max and said, "I used to go to the Mill Creek Church but haven't been for a long time. Don't go anywhere now."

Max dared to ask, "What happened? Did you have a falling out with the church?" As soon as he asked it he wished he hadn't. It wasn't his business. It must have been the minister in me, he thought, that prompted the question.

However, the question didn't seem to phase Jack. He answered quite frankly, "I just wasn't getting enough out of the services. I had grown up in a big city and this outfit at Mill Creek was just too rural, I guess."

"What do mean—rural?" Max asked even though he more or less knew what Jack meant. His answer was surprising. "I just didn't feel at ease with the people. They wanted to be too friendly. I was used to sticking pretty much to myself. They were always wanting me to come to pot-lucks and that sort of thing. I know it's a flimsy excuse!"

"No, no! I didn't want to make you feel guilty. Just interested, because I was sort of taken with the church there."

"I guess I'm feeling guilty because, I haven't been going anywhere else. Easy to get out of the habit."

"You're right. I hadn't been going to church for quite a while until I went to Mill Creek a few weeks ago."

Con returned to the table and picked up on the drift of conversation. Con knew of Max's ministerial experience, but had pledged not to share that with anyone. Max had indicated that he wanted to keep that fact from affecting his relationships. Now, Con was surprised at the subject being discussed and said, "First time I've heard this much talk of church in ages!"

Max, somewhat defensively, said, "Blame it on Everette! He mentioned to me about my going down to Mill Creek for church."

"I see, but it seems to have hit a nerve."

Jackson replied to that challenge saying, "Well, it did—my guilty conscience!"

"I've long since quit feeling guilty about that." Con said. The other two made no comment. And so that ended the conversation. Con then said, "Well, I've got some office work to do."

And of course, so did Jack. And Max needed to get down to the horse barns to see what Everette had in mind.

Back in his office Con thought about Lee. He wondered what she would have added to the conversation. What would it be like, he thought, if Lee were here with me all the time—married! And visiting with the staff at meal times. How would my life be different? These thoughts both scared him and enticed him. As the days progressed he found the idea growing on him.

CHAPTER 18

One drizzly snow-flecked morning in late April Max was up on the northern boundary of Fairhavens property fixing fence. He had not previously been in this area. The fence line ran along the crest of a knoll, so that to reach the fence he had to climb a steep embankment. Once up to the fence he found that he was on a relatively flat expanse of grass land which stretched beyond the fence and extended far off in the distance. On this level the drizzle had turned to a light snow-fall. The swirling snow-laden wind caused the dry, almost white, autumn grass to wave like white caps on the ocean. Max had never seen anything quite like it,

Perhaps it was because he was literally miles from anyone; or it could have been that along with the light swirling snow the heavily moisture laden clouds were unusually close to the ground. But whatever it was, he found himself overcome with an eerie feeling, a vague impression of not being alone even though he knew he was very much alone. He had the feeling of having been transported into another world—possibly a different time as well. The rain turning to snow made seeing beyond the fence he was fixing diffi-cult. At the very least he seemed to have come into a an unknown place—of mystery—on this particular morning.

As he worked his way along the barbed wire fence he came to an old gate which apparently had not been used for years. Formerly it had provided access for a narrow ranch road now overgrown with tall grasses and weeds. However he could still read the prohibition on the rusty sign: "NO TRESPASSING—KEEP OUT." Treating the message a good bit like the proverbial Wet Paint sign, he succumbed to the temptation to "touch." He slipped through the sagging fence next to the gate and entered upon land belonging to someone else. At this particular point the ground rose before him as he climbed to a higher crest of a foot hill, not really recognizing the crest until he reached its ridge. Low clouds draped over the far side of the hill like a shroud. Once atop the crest he tried to look down the other side, but he could not see much beyond ten feet ahead of him, so thick were the clouds and so dense the swirling snow. Soon he began to make out the dim outline of a building ahead of him. There was something oddly familiar about what he saw in the mist before him. It was a low building with its broadside facing him. There appeared to be two front doors facing him, each flanked by windows. The roof was covered with cedar shakes and the overhang formed a canopy over a ground level porch in front of the doors. It looked like an old motel. He thought that it might have been a bunk house or some miner's cabins. He couldn't determine why it seemed so familiar. Certainly he had never been here before. Nor did it appear that anyone else had been near the deserted site for a very long time.

As he came closer to the ghost-like structure he saw an ancient wooden chair on the porch next to one of the doors. Then it clicked! His room at Colac Bay! He stood transfixed. His mind must be playing tricks on him, he thought. "Next thing—I'll see Bronwyn." he said out loud. At that point a slight wind came up and blew one of the doors in about a foot. It was the door next to the one with the chair. As he saw this he was reminded of the small take-away where Bronwyn had fixed light lunches. A chill went down his spine when he saw a movement through the open door, a move-ment which he could swear was Bronwyn. He stood quietly—very still. He didn't want to do anything to disturb this moment of apparition. Only the sound of wind. The building was still shrouded in the snowy mist.

Finally Max crept up to the door and slipped inside. In the center of the small room he saw a table covered with dirt and dust. He lifted his eyes to the wall beyond the table where he saw hang-ing an old and tattered denim jacket. Apparently, it was this which the wind had rustled. Bronwyn's denim skirt, he thought.

The mystery of the place and the slight tinge of fright which
accompanied it began to melt away into a soft nostalgia. Max stepped
up to the porch and sat down on the chair outside "his room" as he
had done so often before. A half a world away. As he looked out away
from the building the angle of the terrain was such that he looked
over the grassy waves and into the horizon—almost as if he were
looking toward the sea! In his reverie he was at the Inn on Colac Bay.

How he longed for Bronwyn. It made him realize that his life
had been shear frustration and heartache; but he had been unwilling to admit it. There had been no word from Bronwyn since his
arrival at Fairhavens, even though he had sent his address to the
parish treasurer in Riverton. That was literally months ago. Taking
her place in Max's life was his work. It had become his major commitment as he lived from week to week. He had no desire to culti-
vate friendships other than the normal amount of friendly rela-
tions with others on the staff. His remedy for the loneliness of his
evenings in his cabin was to purchase and install a fairly sophisticated stero system in his cabin and to begin building a library of
classical CD's. Whenever he had reason to be in Livingston he
dropped in to the public library. Thus, he always had a variety of
books on hand to read. His favorite reading for escape consisted of
English murder mysteries. In addition, Sunday worship at Mill
Creek had become an important part of each week. Occasionally
he had taken in programs or fellowship events at the church on
week-day evenings. His journalling not only filled up some time,
but it afforded opportunity to express himself. Not that anyone
would ever read it! But it kept him thinking straight. Certainly
this mysterious discovery of this deserted building—a Colac Bay
Inn look-alike, would be grist for his journalling mill!

His reverie was cut off by another gust of wind which squeaked
the door shut against its ancient jam, sending a shiver down Max's
spine. Reluctantly, Max got up and trudged down the hill through
the snowy mist to resume his fencing chores. But there remained in
his consciousness a strong sensation of having been with Bronwyn in
the familiar surroundings of her take-away at Colac Bay.

As weeks blended into months and Max became more and more an integral part of the Fairhavens operation. He did not soon return to the deserted building on the other side of the hill. He found himself thinking of Bronwyn less and less. In a somewhat cynical frame of mind he misused a scriptural verse to apply to his frustration with Bronwyn. "Let the dead bury the dead."

But then there were times when he had what he called "memory flare-ups." Often when he smelled the smoke from a fireplace or wood stove, he immediately was transported to Southland where so much of the home heating was done by wood stoves. He came to enjoy these serendipitous cameo memories.

Every few days when he was out on the East River Road for other reasons, he took the opportunity to stop by the post office in Pray to see if any mail had arrived for him. At first he quite anxiously anticipated what he would find, always hoping for a letter from Bronwyn; but after weeks of frustrating disappointment he had more or less given up. His mailbox was usually devoid of personal mail, only ads. He marveled at how quickly his address had gotten onto junk mail lists.

One afternoon after picking up supplies in Livingston he stopped by to check his box. This time he pulled out a light blue overseas air mail folder with red printing on it, and in black ink:"B. MacKenzie, 19 St. Andrew Street, Dunedin, NZ!" He quickly stuck it in his shirt pocket, got in the pick-up continuing south to Emigrant where he drove across the river. Instead of heading north on the East River Road, he turned south until he reached a good place to stop. He pulled out the letter. His hands were shaking, as he read Bronwyn's reply.

M. Ritter
P.O. Drawer Z
Pray, Montana 59065
U.S.A.
Dear Max,

I am so very sorry that I have not written you sooner than this. It was only this morning that I found the record of your parish donation, which showed me your address. O Max, please forgive me! It was so long ago that you wrote the parish. By this time, I am afraid you must have given me up. But then, you might just as well. For my life has taken a very sharp turn. In many ways I think I must seem to be a different person.

Let me explain. The day after you left, Duncan was brought home; but he did not seem at all well to me. In the days following he tried to do a bit of work for the parish, but tired so quickly that I could see that he was of little use to the parish. He felt guilty about this, and asked me to call a special meeting of the Session a fortnight hence. It was to be held in the Session Clerk's house in Riverton; but it was canceled because within that fortnight Duncan was back in the hospital in Dunedin suffering from a massive stroke! He could not speak. He could not walk or even stand. And so, he was totally bedridden. The doctor said that there was little chance of any substantial recovery for him and that I would have to find a nursing home for him as soon as possible. I found one near downtown Dunedin, which fortunately had a bed available. So he was moved to The Isabel Austin Rest Home. Well, the Session members then met and did what they had to do, and that is to retire Duncan to the care of Southland Presbytery. Those people were very good to him and to me, but of course the basic situation remains dismally the same.

I returned to Colac Bay and tried to keep the Inn going, but business was really down; and without any help, like the fine handyman you were, I decided to close it for a while. I felt the need to be closer to Duncan and so I thought I'd temporarily move up to Duneden and find work there, so that I could be near him; though I really don't know what good it does. When I visit, there is no communication. I just sit there, and he just lies there staring at the ceiling. They take good care of him—for what good reason I don't know. I am ashamed to say what I wish, but maybe you can guess. No such chance. They say he has a strong heart. I found a job at a new small hotel near "The Olveston" called, "The Olveston Arms." I have been made housekeeping manager and I have three chamber maids under my supervision. Not a bad job but there is very little time off, about six days a month as it works out. I'm on my first double day off today, but need to be back by tomorrow morning. I work from seven to six. I have found a tiny apartment within walking distance. After tea, I take the bus out to the hospital every evening, and come back to the apartment by half past nine. When I am fortunate enough to have a Sunday off, I can attend services at the big church downtown, which I enjoy.

So, that's my life as it stands now, and as I think it will be for the foreseeable future. How about yours? Write me once in a while if you feel like it. I hope you are well. I'm sorry.

As ever,

Bronwyn

P.S. Here is my address: Bronwyn MacKenzie, 19 St. Andrew Street, Dunedin, New Zealand.

After he read it, he slowly folded it and put it back in his pocket and sat looking out the windshield at the river in the foreground with the mountains as a backdrop in the distance. He had a dazed sick feeling as he pondered the news which had come to him. All his former feelings for her rushed back. In his mind he was in New Zealand again looking out upon the sea as it stretched endlessly toward Antarctica. Bronwyn was there with him in her full denim skirt and pink top, her loosely falling hair swirling in the breeze. The silence was gently broken with "Max Ritter, won't you come in for tea?"

"Is it that time already?"

"Oh yes! Half past six it is, Max. Are you not a bit hungry, now?"

Just then a pick-up rushed past and Max was shaken loose from his dream state. He looked at his watch. 6:30! Time for dinner. He started the engine, turned around and headed toward Fairhavens.

Deep in thought Max ate his dinner as rapidly as he could without causing undue notice. As soon as he could, he returned to his cabin, put on a tape of New Zealand's Maori music he had brought back with him, and sat down to reply to Bronwyn MacKenzie.

Bronwyn MacKenzie
19 St. Andrew Street
Dunedin,
New Zealand
Dear Bronwyn,

Your letter arrived in my post office box today. I am relieved to hear from you, to say the least! The long silence is now quite understandable to me and you need not give it another thought. In the first place you don't owe me a letter I have no right to expect that. But to get your letter is "icing on the cake" as we say here. Better yet: sheer joy!

I am deeply concerned for you and Duncan. Yours must be a very difficult watch to keep, as he is so separated from you in his physical state. How do you keep going? It sounds as if you like the work you have at the hotel. Maybe it's better that you don't have a lot of time off. At least that's the way it is for me here. I am fully occupied with my work six days a week. During most weeks Sunday is the only day I take off, although my boss wants me to take an additional day. I'm the handyman (they call me Supervisor of Buildings and Grounds! But handyman covers it!) for a resort and retreat house located in a broad river valley thirty miles from Yellowstone National Park. It's about eighty miles from the church I had served as pastor.

The buildings and grounds include an old lodge, a swimming pool and bath house, horse barns, an assortment of utility sheds and eight cabins. We have quite a number of acres of fenced in pasture land in addition to the grounds surrounding the buildings. So, it is plenty to keep me more than busy!

I'm glad you get to enjoy a good church service at least occasionally. I also have been attending church. In my case I've found a small country church. The building reminds me of the little parish church in Waimatuku. Do you remember it? No one here, except the general manager, knows that I am an ordained minister. I like it that way, as you can guess! I still don't feel too good about that whole part of my life. Though I'm making some progress.

I wish there were some way that I could make things better for you. But, of course, there isn't. Meanwhile, it would be my understanding that Duncan would have some awareness of your presence, even though he can't acknowledge it. That means to me, that you have the capacity to make him happier even in the midst of his condition! In that respect Duncan is fortunate.

You certainly made my life happier while I was in New Zealand! And hearing from you now has given me a boost!

I'll run down to Pray tomorrow and mail this. Isn't that a name for our little community! In Paradise Valley! Write me if you feel like it.

All for now—

Max

The next day Max mailed his letter to New Zealand. He calculated that it would be ten days or so before it reached Bronwyn. That is what hers had taken. And if she would be willing to write back, it would be at least another ten days. The best he could hope for was a three week interval, and in reality it probably would be more like a month.

Bronwyn replied as soon as she heard from Max, much to his delight. Thus a correspondence began between the two, in which Bronwyn asked a good bit about Fairhavens: what sort of activities and program it sponsored, what the staff folks were like; and something about the guests. Max was kept apprized of Duncan's condition and of Bronwyn's mood during her long ordeal.

Then one day there came this letter to Max from Bronwyn:

> Dear Max,
>
> Last evening Duncan passed away in his sleep. I was not there with him. Since I have no telephone, the nursing home could not inform me until this morning when I went to visit on my way to work. I have mixed feelings. Sorrow (because I'm supposed to feel that), relief, and guilt that I feel relieved! Perhaps if I had been with him at the last I wouldn't feel quite so guilty.
>
> His brother has come from Gore and is making all the arrangements to have him taken to Gore for the funeral and burial on Monday next. He is a "take over" type person and I have not had much say in all this, which is suitable to me—I guess. Once the funeral is over I doubt if I'll have much to do with Duncan's family. They really never accepted me.
>
> At this point I do not know what is next for me. I need to sort it out. I'll keep you posted. Pray for me.
> With my love to you, Max,
> Bronwyn

Max knew he needed to get in touch with Bronwyn. A letter would simply take too long. But how to reach her by phone was a question. He knew the Colac Bay Inn number, if by chance she should have returned. He checked his watch and calculated that it would be around noon in New Zealand. There was a public phone in the

Lodge lounge. He would use that with his phone credit card. Fortunately there were very few people in the lounge, to wonder what
he was doing. He dialed the international operator and gave the
Colac Bay number. After a series of electronic signals tracking the
call on its way southward he heard the familiar double ring. He
waited through five of these and hung up, concluding that she
had not gone back to the Inn. Her job in Dunedin probably would
keep her there for the time being. But she had no phone in her
room. However, she might be reached at work. He got the operator again and asked how to find the number for the Olveston Arms
in Dunedin, New Zealand. He was given the number surprisingly
soon. He decided not to phone until after two in the afternoon her
time, to make sure that she would be back to work. He would try
again after dinner, around seven that evening. He could think of
nothing else, but Bronwyn's pain. He wanted so much to share in
some of it for her.

After his evening meal, as he went back to his cabin he kept
thinking of Bronwyn alone during this time of grief and sorrow. If
only he could go to her. But a trip to New Zealand at this time
would be out of the question. His work—the expense—? Or would
it? He had things at Fairhavens pretty well under control. If the
right person could be found to step in for a couple weeks, it might
be possible for him to be away from work for a few weeks. The
money? A little savings left plus a two thousand or so personal
loan. He wondered if that could be arranged. He still had the
savings account with the bank back home. He could talk to his
banker friend. First the phone contact to talk to Bronwyn and see
how she is managing.

By 6:45 Max was leaving his cabin to go down to phone when
Everette drove up hurriedly, jumped out of his pick-up and shouted,
Demmings' house is on fire! We need all the hands we can find.
Can you come with me Max? Max could not refuse. He quickly
got into Everette's pick-up.

Demmings rented one of the houses on the gulch from its
absentee owner who lived in the Twin Cities. Demmings were new

to the area, having moved in from somewhere in Wyoming. Bob Demming worked for one of the ranches in the valley. Sue and their three children 7, 4, and 1 were at home most of the time. She helped out in housekeeping at the Lodge when they were short-handed. They were barely making it, and so a fire would wipe them out, and could force them to move away, Max thought. When Everette drove a half mile up the gulch they could see the smoke and the leaping flames against the night sky. The local volunteer fire truck was there, but the volunteers could do very little, except to keep the fire from spreading to other houses in the gulch. Help was needed to bring water up from the creek. Everette and Max joined Bob Demming in a water brigade.

Sue Demmings and her kids were huddled under a blanket on the grass far enough from the house to be safe. The two younger children were crying. Their two dogs were barking continually at the commotion. Three of the neighbor women were comforting the bereft family. Fires always seem to bring out more people than one thought lived in the area. A crowd had gathered, some hoping to help, others simply curious. It would be some time before it would be safe to enter the charred remains of the house to rescue anything of value which might be left.

While Max and Everette were helping on the bucket brigade, Con Schneider hurriedly arrived at the scene. He immediately went up to Sue and offered a room in the Lodge for them until something more permanent could be worked out. When the fire was under control and no more water was required from the creek Max and Everette helped Con gather up the Demming family. Con took them back in the Lodge van. Everette and Max waited until Bob Deming felt he could leave to join his family back at Fairhavens. As the three men returned to Fairhavens Everette asked Bob, "I know it's too soon to know, but what will you do?"

"I don't know. We have no one around to bunk with. It's great to be offered a room in the Lodge, but we can't stay there for very long."

Everette offered, "Bob, let me talk to some friends and see

what we might be able to do. I might have an idea by tomorrow afternoon."

"You don't owe us a thing, but whatever you come up with might help." Bob said despondently.

By the time Everette dropped Max back at Fairhavens it was too late to phone Bronwyn. She wouldn't likely be at work this late. So as soon as he could the next day he would phone Bronwyn—sometime during her work day.

That night, lying in bed, Max found it difficult to settle his mind for sleep. He prayed. A first for him in a long time! He prayed for Bronwyn. He prayed for the Demmings. His thoughts were muddled. He saw flames and smelled smoke—Bronwyn—the Demmings children crying—Sue huddled—flames—smoke—Duncan in bed unable to talk, now no longer alive—Bronwyn alone—Bob Demming distraught—and then finally sleep, though disturbed.

Max would be unable to reach Bronwyn at the Olveston Arms until afternoon. After spending his morning at work, he joined Everette and Con at the staff table for lunch. Max had had a crazy morning with plumbing problems in the Lodge and an electrical problem at the pool. Everette was saying as Max sat down, "I've got a group of men who want to come in as soon as it is safe to rebuild Demmings' house. And there is a family south of here who have room and want them to come and live with them as long as it takes. Plus—we have located enough basic furniture and clothing to get them set up again."

"Amazing! How did you get all that so quickly?" Con asked.

"I'm going to this house-church on Sundays and they are great for this sort of thing. All I had to do was phone one of the members and when I phoned back just now I got word of the help they have ready! In fact, we plan to move them after work today."

Max asked, "Do these people know the Demmings? Are Demmings by any chance involved in their church?"

"No to both questions, Max."

Max was noticeably moved by this massive expression of help. "The Mennonites?"

"That's right. You can always count on them in times of disaster."

Con asked with a streak of disbelief in his voice, "So the church people want the Demmings to start coming to their church?"

"Oh no. That doesn't even cross their mind, I don't think." Everette declared. "They're welcome. Everybody is. But no way is that expected of them. Their helpfulness is with no strings attached."

More to think about for Max. He ate as quickly as he could so that he could get his work out of the way by three, when he would take a break and try to phone Bronwyn. It was closer to four by the time he was free. The call went through: "Good morning, Olveston Arms, here. May I help you"

"Yes, I'm calling from the U.S. Is it possible to speak with Bronwyn MacKenzie in housekeeping?"

"I'll connect you, Sir. I'm not sure she is here today."

Max waited, hoping to hear a familiar voice. He could hear the extension phone ringing; but there was no answer. The hotel operator returned after a few rings and said, "Let me ring the staff dining room. She may be there."

Max heard the extension phone in the dinning room, and waited until: "Yes, this is the staff room. Whom do you wish?" The voice was not familiar.

"Could you tell me if Bronwyn MacKenzie is there?" he asked tentatively.

"This is Bronwyn . . . Max! Is that you?"

"Bronwyn! It didn't sound like you!" he said excitedly.

"I can't get over that it's you, Max. Where are you?"

"In Montana. But I just got your letter telling about Duncan, and I simply had to talk to you directly. A letter would take too long. I am so sorry. How are you doing? Tell me, Bron."

"I'm managing pretty well." She lowered her voice and said, "I have decided to stay on here for the immediate future. I need the income. But I really would like to go back to the Bay—at least by the next Summer season."

"But, do you have anyone there in Dunedin—to keep you from being entirely alone?"

"Not really, Max. I have made a few acquaintances, but these are casual. They all have their own lives, and I don't want to add my troubles to theirs."

"Troubles, tell me, Bron!"

"Not troubles exactly, but I do get depressed and lonely, mostly in the evenings after work. A city like this doesn't do much for me. I'd be better off in Riverton, or even Invercargill, don't you think?"

"Yes, I wish you were back in Southland! I'm so sorry! I just wish I could be there with you."

"I do too, Max. That would be so good." she said with a slight trip in her voice."But I know you can't."

"I'm just now getting my work in hand and to be away for any length of time would pose a problem for Fairhavens . . . I think."

"I'm sure you are right. But we can write, can't we?" Bronwyn pleaded.

"Of course. And perhaps a phone call like this once in a while. Would you like that?"

"I certainly would, but it is so expensive."

"Let me do the phoning. But I need to know where and when the best times for that are for you. I know it must be awkward talking from where you are right now."

"It is, but it's the only phone where I can be reached. Five PM my time would be a good time, though. I am so very glad you called."

"That would be ok—mid-night here; I can do that gladly, Bron." he said. "But I guess now I better let you go. I'll phone in a few days."

"Thank you so much for the call, Max. This has been so very good! I'll look forward to the next time. Goodbye."

"Goodbye, Bronwyn. I'll phone again soon."

A phone call can't go on forever, especially overseas, he thought as he went back to his work. There was so much more he should have said. But he assured himself that she had been more than glad to have his call. He thought of her spending lonely evenings and nights in a tiny apartment in a strange city. He wondered who the new acquaintances might be, and whether these would develop for her. When should he phone again? How often? Now, he needed to write her at length. How he wished he could go to New Zealand. But with her in Dunedin, wouldn't he be in the way; and she would be working all the time. But if she were to return to Colac Bay, then a prolonged visit would work—if he could manage—time and expense. But when did she say she would be returning? She didn't. No, she said she would like to be there in the summer. That would be in seven or eight months.

The idea of going to New Zealand at the time of Bonwyn's move back to Colac Bay began to take shape in Max's mind. That way he could help her re-open the Inn. Something he might mention after he was sure enough that he could do it. Meanwhile there was his own work to do.

CHAPTER 19

Work for Max settled into a predictable routine as he took responsibility for the physical needs of Fairhavens. This routine was broken up only by his van runs into Livingston, or to Bozeman to pick up and discharge guests. These runs were more frequent during the summer months. Sundays he regularly worshiped at Mill Creek church. From time to time his inner doubts about spirituality surfaced. These were often the occasion for journal entries. Bronwyn was a constant presence in the back of his mind, in many ways keeping him from being entirely alone. The correspondence between them kept each of them well aware of each other's activities and moods. Max had become at ease with his life and was reasonably happy. Ready for another advance in his journey toward self-understanding and perhaps even toward his return to ministry.

As a result of his chance meeting with Art Simpson he received an announcement of a presbytery meeting with its accompanying packet of reports from the Stated Clerk of Yellowstone Presbytery. When he picked this up from his postal box, his first reaction was to throw it away, but on second thought curiosity led him to open it and to have a look at what was happening in presbytery. The regular meeting of Presbytery was to be held at the church in Jordan, Montana in two weeks. Aside from the usual business, the theme of the meeting was to be "spirituality." A panel of clergy and elders were to lead in this discussion. Each congregation was to share its experience and program in the area of spirituality. It was to be a two day meeting over a Friday night. Max would be able to take that time off.

He decided to attend, and sent in his registration. This could amount to another step on this pathway to recovery, he thought. What would come of it he could not tell; but he resolved to go with an open mind. A resolve, which would be difficult to honor and one not every member would make, he was to discover.

In Montana, especially eastern Montana, there is typically only one route to take to a particular destination, and places to stop for coffee are miles apart. This means that when one stops for coffee one is apt to meet acquaintances, or people who are going to the same meeting. This was the case when Max pulled into the roadside cafe on the east edge of Harlowton on his way to Jordan. While having coffee at the counter the man next to him struck up a conversation. In his early forties and wearing clean levis and a colorful western shirt, he was a friendly sort. He asked Max, "Where you headed?"

"Jordan."

"So am I!" the man replied.

Jordan isn't big enough for more than one reason to go there. As it turned out the one reason was presbytery.

"So, what's in Jordan? Wouldn't be a presbytery meeting would it?" Max guessed.

"That's it. You too? My name's Jerry Krone."

"Yes. I'm Max Ritter. Where you from?"

"I'm from over to Tipton. Know where that is? How about you?"

"I know Tipton! I'm from south of Livingston. Have you lived in Tipton long?" Max asked, because he did not recognize the man as anyone he had previously known.

"Not too long. We moved up from Ennis a few years back. I'm a new member of the church. They just made me an elder, and sent me off to presbytery."

When Max discovered that Jerry Krone was a new member and elder from the Tipton church he told him, "I used to be a pastor there, but I guess that was before your time."

The two fell into an animated conversation about Tipton and the church. Since his new acquaintance had only recently moved to Tipton, Max felt he could skip telling any of the details of his own experience there. When Max learned that Jerry had just taken a job as a mechanic for Dale Kober at the Conoco he was glad to let him know that Dale was a friend of his. When the conversation turned to the church Max gained some significant insights into the current church situation.

"Even though I had just joined they put me on the Session. I'd been an elder in Ennis where I came from. Then I was elected to the Pastor Nominating Committee. They had been told the committee needed to represent everybody; so I was the new kid! Quite an experience."

"How so?" Max asked, wanting to hear as much as he could.

"Well, to begin with the committee had its mind set. They wanted somebody spiritual. I thought any minister would be spiritual. But, 'No' they said. 'A lot of them nowadays aren't,' but I'm not so sure about that. Anyway, that's what led them to choose our new minister."

"Tell me about him."

"His name is Stephen Cochrane—about 45 years old—comes from Tulsa, Oklahoma where he went to school. He preaches good sermons, but the church services aren't what I was used to—sort of informal. Almost holy-roller type."

"I see. Did he come from a pastorate in Tulsa?"

"Yes, part time for a small congregation. In addition, was some sort of coordinator for a Christian organization of some kind. Did a lot of traveling to conferences. In fact he's been asked to speak tomorrow morning at the Presbytery meeting."

"Do the Tipton folk like him?"

"They seem to. Lots of new faces coming to church—young couples. He's gotten some of them on the Session. They are his pet cheering section. Between you and me, I think some of the old timers aren't too impressed."

"You seem to be taking a 'wait and see' attitude. Am I right?"

"Yeah, you could say that. We'll see."

Max concluded the conversation with, "We'd better get with

it. I figure Jordan is a little over 180 miles yet to go. The meeting
starts at 1:30. See you at the meeting."

"Right!" At that they got up paid their bills and each hit the
road again for Jordan.

The afternoon session was spent on presbytery business items.
The evening was a worship service with communion. Fortunately
Max was made to feel quite welcome and at ease. He renewed
acquaintances with some of the pastors and elders with whom he'd
been friends previously. He had the feeling that the subject of
Tipton was being carefully avoided by his friends. The new people
assumed him to be a regular attender.

At the afternoon coffee break Max introduced himself to the
moderator of the Committee on Ministry. Later during his report
the moderator of the committee introduced Max and invited him
to say a few words about Fairhavens. Max sensed considerable interest in the Fairhavens mission. During the supper served in the
church basement Max sat with Jerry Krone and asked him if the
Tipton minister was at the meeting.

"No, he's not here today. He said that he couldn't get away,
but would come for part of tomorrow's meeting."

After a supper of roast beef, mashed potatoes, and green beans,
topped off with lemon pie—a menu rural churches seem always to
serve—the presbytery moderator announced: "Tomorrow morning
we convene at 8:30 for the spirituality workshop. We were to have
a panel of ministers and elders lead us, but when we were told of
Dr. Stephen Cochrane's experience in the field of spirituality the
Council decided to give the morning over to him. This evening's
service begins at 7:30 upstairs." The Jordan pastor then announced:
"After the service all of you are invited to the manse across the
street for refreshments and conversation. A continental breakfast
will be served here in this room tomorrow morning beginning at
7:30"

During breakfast in the church basement the next morning
the sound of a small plane could be heard flying low over Jordan.
It seemed to come and go. One of the Jordan men sitting near

Max and Jerry said. "I've got to get out to the air field. That's someone circling the town signaling for a ride into town." After he left the table, Jerry Krone said, "I imagine that's Dr. Cochrane flying in for his presentation!"

"Oh?" remarked Max.

"He flies his own Cessna, and told me Sunday that he'd only be able to be here for his presentation; and then he would have to fly back."

"What's his hurry?"

"He's got one of his training sessions starting tomorrow in Portland."

After morning prayers, Max took a seat in the back of the sanctuary and thought to himself, "Well, now I'll see for myself what the good doctor is like!" The sanctuary door behind him opened and two men entered and took a back seat across the aisle from Max. It was the man who had left to pick up Cochrane, and apparently it was Stephen Cochrane next to him.

The moderator of the Congregational Ministries Unit rose to begin the workshop on spirituality: "I'm very happy to introduce to you Dr. Stephen Cochrane, the new pastor at Tipton, who will lead us this morning in 'Achieving a Higher Level of Christian Life." He comes to us from Tulsa where he has been assoicated with *REALM of the King Ministries.* A native of Oklahoma, Dr. Cochrane received his degrees from Oklahoma schools. But since that time he has traveled the world leading training conferences sponsored by the R O K MINISTRIES. We are very fortunate to have him here, considering his busy schedule. Dr. Steve! Welcome!"

Hesitating a few moments as if to wait for applause, which didn't happen, Cochrane then hurried down the aisle with his rich looking leather attache case at his side. He mounted the pulpit and acknowledged the "warm introduction." He was wearing a blue blazer with light beige slacks. His button-down powder blue oxford cloth shirt was open at the collar without a tie. When he gestured a yellow monogram could be seen on his shirt pocket. He was a man of 45 or so with styled brown hair slightly streaked

with gray. Surprisingly he spoke without a drawl. Rather with the
soothing tones of a television anchor. He began with this stunning
invitation:

"I am here to give you the opportunity to join the greatest
renewal movement to appear in our time. The Spirit is at work all
over the world bringing a new and amazing spiritual dimension to
the lives of thousands of God's children. And He is here in this
room ready to renew your spiritual lives! Yes—right here in this
place . . . NOW! I know you are asking—right at this moment—
HOW, Dr. Steve? That's exactly what we are going to answer today.
I'm going to teach you the five golden Bible steps that will bring
you into the spirit realm. And when you are in the REALM you
will say as hundreds are saying today: 'How could I ever have
thought that the church life I had before was *of God* and Bible-
based? Because now I really feel the Spirit!"

A warning bell sounded in Max's mental ear when he heard
this last claim. At first he had felt a pull as Cochrane spoke, strangely
drawing him; but that mysterious magnetic force was broken for
Max when Cochrane cast his negative judgement upon the traditional church. He noticed the rapt attention in the group as
Cochrane continued to "teach" the "five golden Bible steps." Max
took verbatim notes during this lecture. That evening in his motel
Max put Cochrane's outline in his journal:

FIVE STEPS INTO THE REALM

1. R—real prayer—"not those prayers preachers get out of a book.
   Remember! REALM begins with R E A L !"
2. E—effective sacrifice—"don't hide behind the 'time and tal-
   ents' cop-out. Sacrifice your financial resources, your MONEY!
   And don't just give your money to any good cause or church;
   The most effective gift you will ever make is to the REALM!—
   R O K MINISTRIES!'
3. A—attitude adjustment—"make your attitude show that you
   are in the REALM. Think positive—show joy—share the
   REALM!"
4. L—lively worship—"not the stuffy dead worship of some church

tradition or other—worship is lively—power-filled—when you
are in the REALM!"
5. M—meditation—"without ceasing, Paul said, meditate on the
REALM of the King!"
Remember REALM

At the end of the lecture there was applause while Dr. Cochrane
walked down the aisle to his seat at the rear. The Moderator of
Presbytery rose to thank him. She announced, "Dr. Cochrane has
been kind enough to bring along copies of his latest book, *There's
Power in the REALM* which you can purchase at a special book
table downstairs." And then she announced," There will be a 30
minute break with refreshments in the basement." She added, "We
have the conclusion of our business to care for after the break and
we should be finished by 1 o'clock. Please, everyone remain for
this final session!"

When Max stood up and turned toward the rear door to go
downstairs he noticed that Cochrane had already left the room,
probably downstairs he thought. But he did not find him among
the people in the fellowship hall below during the break. As Max
mingled with the group during the break he found a number of
the younger ministers enthusiastically talking about the lecture,
as they gravitated to the book table. However others seemed to
have left the subject behind and were discussing other matters.
Max took a seat at a table where three ministers were discussing
Cochrane. One said, "I found him kind of scary!"

A second added, "I felt manipulated, and that always gives me
a fearful feeling."

The third, a counselor in a Pastoral Counseling Center in Billings remarked: "I know what you mean. In fact I had a very uneasy
feeling, which led me to remember something Scott Peck wrote
about some people with whom he has counseled over the years,
how their early unresolved issues resulted in some very troubling
personality configurations.

Max added, "I was disappointed that we didn't hear an assortment of people on the subject. I have been thinking lately about

the way spirituality has to be varied to fit persons of differing na-
tures. And this man gave a 'this is the only way to go' approach!"
All three agreed with Max on that.

When the meeting resumed upstairs the sound of a light plane
could be heard passing over town. Max thought, "There goes one
member of Presbytery who won't be here for the business of
Presbytery. His own business is obviously too pressing—and
important—more spiritual!"

The meeting of presbytery adjourned at 12:20. Most of the
commissioners stayed for a light lunch in the basement before
starting out for home. For some who lived in the west end of
Presbytery the trip home would entail eight to ten hours. Those
closer would spend anywhere from two to six hours travel time.
Most of the ministers would need to be in their pulpits the next
morning. Needless to say it was a quick lunch followed by hasty
"good-byes." Max figured six hours to Fairhavens. And he estimated also that Dr. Stephen Cochrane would be at home in Tipton
within the hour.

Max walked out of the Jordan church building and got in his
Subaru for his long drive home. Reflecting on the two day meeting, Max realized how much he had enjoyed conversations with
other ministers and with the elder commissioners as well. Some he
had known before, while others were new to him. The coffee breaks
and meal times had not been nearly long enough! He had dreaded
returning to this group of peers; but was only too happy to find
them entirely congenial to him, despite the circumstances of his
leaving Tipton.

When he got to Livingston around 6 o'clock he treated himself
to a gourmet dinner at the Winchester Cafe in the Murray Hotel.
The waiter showed him to a table for two. After ordering he sat
back to enjoy the ambiance of the Winchester's authentic 1910
decor. He looked across his candle-lit table covered with an elegant
linen cloth. A turn-of-the-century polished wooden chair opposite
him was empty. He envisioned Bronwyn seated there. He felt very

much alone. Later when he would return in the darkness to his cabin at Fairhavens he would be alone there as well.

Autumn had always seemed to be a time of solitude for Max. As the aspens which surrounded his cabin began to turn golden yellow Max felt the need to draw apart from his associates, to spend some time alone with his journal. As he had enjoyed his solitude at Point Of Rocks on Colac Bay at another time, he now felt drawn to the deserted building on the north boundary, which had reminded him of his favorite bay at the bottom of the world.

On a day off in late October Max went to his office and picked up a wooden sign he had made. He then packed a lunch, stuck in some books he'd been reading and his journal, and drove up to the fence beyond which he walked to the deserted building to spend an entire day alone with his thoughts. The first thing he did when he arrived at the deserted building was to nail up on the front of the old building the sign he'd brought with him. It read: COLAC BAY INN.

The leaves of the aged cottonwoods behind the building had turned to yellow. By this time of the month many had already fallen, exposing the intricate lattice of branches against the blue-gray sky of autumn. In the distance beyond the row of cotton-woods the heavy green band of the pine forest on the side of the mountains rose to timberline above which the rocky peaks were already dusted with snow. Autumn with an early touch of winter was in the air. A time to reduce life's pace. A time for introspection, it seemed to Max as he settled into his chair on the porch of "his inn."

It was during this day at his own "Colac Bay" that Max decided definitely to return to New Zealand. He strongly felt the need to go to Bronwyn and to help her in whatever way he could. He guessed that she would soon be moving back to Colac Bay and that her re-entry into her former haunts could very well be a time of poignant sadness for her; and a period of inner turmoil as she adjusted to her new life at the Inn. Besides the personal trauma there would be a daunting amount of work to restore the inn to her accustomed standards. If not on the personal level, certainly in connection with the inn refurbishing, he knew he could be of substantial help. Furthermore, he realized that both he and Bronwyn were so entirely alone in the world, more so now than when he had first arrived at the bay looking for a room. As he thought of those months, it came to him so strongly that they had each had serious emotional needs at that time; and to a large extent they had supported each other in those needs. Perhaps that is why, he realized, the bond between them which had developed mysteriously in a relatively short span of time, a bond so strong which the separation of a half a world had not weakened. His phone calls and their correspondence since Duncan's death had confirmed this. Judging from her responses to his calls and letters, as well as his own feeling, he concluded that they simply must be together again. Most likely, it would be around Christmas that she would move back to Colac Bay.

CHAPTER 20

As the Christmas season approached Max knew that for Bronwyn this was the coming of summer when she had wanted to move back to Colac Bay to open the Inn before Christmas. However in a letter in November she had written to say that she needed to remain working in Dunedin through Christmas before returning to Southland. Before making any promises to himself or to Bronwyn, Max needed to discuss with Con the possibility of his taking some time off around Christmas. When Con considered Max's request, he asked him to wait until after Christmas; for the holiday season was a time of increased bookings.

After his conference with Con Max telephoned New Zealand in the evening:

"Bronwyn!" he said after she answered, "I want to come to New Zealand to help you move back to the Inn, and to help you get it ready for opening! Will you have me?"

"Have you!" she said in surprise."You know you are always welcome, and besides that, I really am keen to see you, Max. It has been so lonely here. But are you sure you can come?"

"All I need to know is when you plan to return home."

"My latest thoughts have been to shift in early January. The one part of my Dunedin experience which I have enjoyed is First Church here; and I really want to be here for the Christmas services," she said somewhat apologetically. "Can you understand my feeling that way?"

"Yes, I certainly can. But I'm afraid I don't have such an anticipation. This little Mill Creek church I'm attending won't have that much going on for Christmas. I wish I could join you in Dunedin for Christmas!"

"Oh, could you, Max? That would be so good."

"I can't, Bron. This place is busy during the holiday season. Con doesn't want me to leave until after Christmas. But in January I can come down."

"I'm sorry about Christmas, but what date can you come?"

"I could try for January 5th. That means I could be in Dunedin on the 7th."

"Please come, Max! I'll plan on the 7th, if you say so."

"As soon as I have reservations, I'll let you know."

And so it was! Early in the morning on January 5th Max boarded the Delta flight at Bozeman for Salt Lake City, the first leg of his return to Colac Bay.

Twenty-four hours later he awoke to a new day in more ways than one. While he had slept the huge 747 had carried him thousands of miles southward into the Southern Hemisphere toward the islands of his dreams. The numbers on the big screen showed forty-five minutes flying time remaining to Christchurch. Soon he was looking down upon the world below where he could see the grey-green paddocks, and fields of grain laid out almost like a giant checkerboard. The Canterbury Plain, he remembered.

Just then the flight attendant announced: "Please make certain your seat belts are securely fastened and your tray tables are securely folded away. We are beginning our descent into Christchurch!"

His original plan had been to take a connecting flight to Dunedin: but when Bronwyn had heard of his plans she immediately wrote to say that she would come to Christchurch and meet him when he first set foot in New Zealand again! At first he had protested, but then he'd agreed. Now, after seventeen hours in the air from LosAngeles, he was more than glad for her suggestion. In less than an hour he would be seeing Bronwyn MacKenzie after so many months. The entire span of the globe had kept them apart physically; and now that great distance had melted away!

The flight from continent to continent, from north to south, from winter to summer through the night seemed to produce a metamorphosis in Max. In many ways he recognized himself as having become a different person since leaving these shores, he thought; and Bronwyn herself had gone through heart-wrenching changes. But yet, now as once again he felt the 747 steadily descending to the South Island of New Zealand, some of his former feelings were returning to consciousness. Feelings he had experienced when he first had stepped onto this beautiful and captivating island down under. Still other feelings were kindled by his memory of the warmth and openness of this wondrous person with her compassionate gray-blue eyes who had been his rescuing angel, this one who had been his "Balm in Gilead." Bronwyn, dear Bronwyn! Would she look the same? Hardly, she had been through so much personal pain and anguish. Hopefully, much would be as he remembered it. Colac Bay and its view of the endless stretch of the South Pacific to the Antarctic. The calm serenity of this southernmost shore which had so soothed him—that would be the same, but no longer the fringe of the world, Colac Bay had become the center of his world of dreams. How often he had imagined himself out on the Point of Rocks, on the porch of the Inn, with Bronwyn in the take-away sharing a simple meal. At worship in Riverton with her beside him. Now, in a moment he would step into that other world he'd dreamed of so fervently!

As the ground rose, he saw the runway on which the plane would soon touch down. The terminal building swung into view. Activity on the ground was coming into focus. The sound of the landing gear deploying. The ground was almost under him. Soon the double thud of the landing gears touching down, the rush of the jet engines reversing, the aircraft slowing down on the tarmac and swinging toward the jet-way, and then the slow and gradual coming toward a stop.

Background music began to be heard over the sound system. Max identified it as a Maori singing group. Then the music was interrupted, "Kia Ora!—Welcome to New Zealand. Please keep your seat belts fastened until the aircraft has come to a complete stop and the seat belt signs have been turned off. On behalf of your entire Air New Zealand crew, we wish you every pleasure during your time here in New Zealand." The choral music of the Maori resumed.

Soon the general exit began. He was making his way through the aisle, and stepping out of the cabin and into the jet-way. Sea legs for a few steps to the terminal and into the Hall of Customs, so strangely quiet as he waited in a queue to be processed. He presented his passport at the customs window, after his luggage had been unloaded onto the carousel and returned to him. "Good morning, sir. May I see your return flight ticket?" He showed his ticket with reservations for three weeks hence. "Thank you sir, enjoy your stay in New Zealand." Max then picked up his luggage and walked out of the Customs Hall into the waiting crowd.

It was an instant of glorious recognition!

"Max Ritter!"

"Bronwyn MacKenzie!" Without any forethought, they joined in a warm and extended embrace. Joy from deep within two lonely people welled up in wordless expression! Each shed tears of joy.

"Oh, Max, I've thought about this for so long! And now you are here!"

"Bron, it is the same with me. How could anything be better?"

The flash of excitement from anticipation fulfilled turned to embarrassed silence as they hurried through the terminal and into the bright sunlight of a summer afternoon in Christchurch.

They crossed the circular drive and entered the car park

"This way to my wee car." Bronwyn directed.

"You mean you have a different car?"

"Oh yes! I traded for a wee Toyota in Dunedin. It's the red one over there."

"I like it! My old Subaru would look pretty shabby next to yours!"

"I bought it second hand, but it runs!" she announced.

They loaded Max's luggage into the boot, left the airport area and Max was once again traveling the roadways of New Zealand. Bronwyn headed south-west on Highway No. 1 out of the city. "I know you must be tired from your long flight, so I thought we might stop for the night at Timaru. Then we can get into Dunedin early tomorrow. That will give me time to pack my things before we make the trip home!"

"Sounds good to me. I'm here to be your handyman; so you give the orders!"

"Max! You are far more than that. I don't want this to be all work for you. We must have some fun while you are here!"

The next two and a half hours were filled with eager conversation as they shared the latest in their lives. The only thing that brought their talk to an end was Timaru and the Cedar Motor Lodge on King Street. After checking in to their two units and each receiving the customary bottle of milk, they bought some meat pies at a nearby take-away and served themselves tea in Bronwyn's room. "Bronwyn, it's like the old days in your take-away at Colac Bay!"

"I know! It is, isn't it?"

The next morning, Max joined Bronwyn again for breakfast which she had ordered to be brought in from the motel office. As the tray was put before Max he exclaimed: "I knew it! Porridge!"

"Yes, and guava juice." Bronwyn added.

"Familiar tasting New Zealand coffee too—freeze-dried!"

By nine they were on the road to Dunedin. Bronwyn explained what would be involved in moving out of her apartment. After listing for Max the items to be moved he said: "It will never fit into your wee car!"

"I've been fearful of that."

"I'll be glad to hire a car to carry the rest of your things. We can both drive. I'm sure one of the major companies like Budget will rent on a one way basis, and I can drop it off at Invercargill after we've unloaded."

"A good idea; but I'll miss having you here next to me, Max."

"Can't be helped. But we'll make up for it."

Stopping for a noon lunch at Moeraki Point they spent some time walking among the famed Moeraki boulders. They read the descriptive signs and learned that these near-perfect spheres strewn across Hampden Beach were the product of the gradual concretion of lime salts around lime crystal cores around 60 million years in age. After a short walk to the ocean shore they returned to the visitor center and sat down to fish and chips in the small restaraunt overlooking the sea.

As they finished a pot of tea and some sweets, Max said, "You are looking more relaxed than when I first saw you yesterday.!"

"I feel more relaxed. It is good to think of returning to Colac Bay. It has been months. There just is something very special about home, isn't there?"

"I sense how much that means to you. But, I simply don't have that kind of place which has remained home for me," he confessed. "But, on the other hand, I'm eager to return to Colac Bay. In many ways it was a place of new life for me. In that sense— I'm returning to my birthplace!"

"It makes me happy to hear you say that!"

"So, let us be on our way to Dunedin, Bron."

By early afternoon both vehicles were loaded, Bronwyn had settled up with her landlord and they were back on Highway 1. They stopped for tea in Invercargill. Their anticipation was at a high pitch as they left Southland's big city for Colac Bay. Arriving well before dark, they were able to unload into the house. Bronwyn opened up Max's cabin. A rush of nostalgia filled him as we walked onto the porch and into "his" New Zealand home again.

The next couple of weeks were spent in getting the Inn back in condition for summer guests. There were a number of fix-up and repair needs to occupy Max's time, while Bronwyn cleaned, polished and painted to make attractive once again this resort by the southern sea.

On Sundays they resumed their former routine of worship in Riverton. Max was especially touched by the warm and caring way with which seemingly everyone in the congregation gathered around Bronwyn before and after worship. He also felt their genuine welcome as they greeted him, and inquired about his life since his last visit. They took their noon meals in Invercargill and spent relaxing Sunday afternoons somewhere in the area.

On one particular Sunday, what really struck Max and moved him to a new depth of self-understanding was a quote from Augustine, which the minister printed in the bulletin to go along with his sermon. Max read and re-read these words, words which he concluded had been sent to him by God Himself: "True, whole prayer is nothing but love."—St. Augustine

The sermon had been on the two great commandments: To love God with all that you are; and to love your neighbor as yourself. Praying for God's grace to follow these two commandments, the minister had proclaimed, "is the very essence of spirituality!"

These words together with Augustine's statement penetrated Max's consciousness like an arrow into the heart. After worship and through dinner he could hardly think of anything else. Until Bronwyn asked him as they lingered over coffee in the restaurant: "You seem so pensive. Have I done something to disturb you?"

"Oh, no! I am sorry you even questioned that. No, I believe that in the service this morning one of my most haunting self-doubts was addressed—and to some extent resolved!"

"Tell me more."

"You know how I have wrestled with the charge made by the Tipton people that I wasn't spiritual enough?"

"Yes, I know. Has that continued to bother you?"

"It has, on and off; and now this morning the idea that spirituality is really praying for God's grace to help you love God and your neighbor hit me solid between the eyes. It's not some big show of piety; its loving! How simple can it get?" Max declared. Then he reached in his pocket for the church bulletin and showed Bronwyn the quote: "Did you read this, Bron?"

"Actually I didn't," she confessed; and then she read aloud, "True, whole prayer is nothing but love."

As she pondered those words Max paraphrased them: "Spirituality is nothing but love." he intoned. "If this is so, then my problem with not being spiritual enough is resolved. Do you think I'm on track; or am I trying to convince myself?"

Bronwyn took a while to reply. It was apparent to Max that

she was taking his question very seriously. After a few moments she began: "Did you ever study logic? . . . Good, then you may remember the syllogism: A=B, B=C, therefore A=C . . . I can see I'm getting you confused. So, substitute for the letters these words: Spirituality is prayer, prayer is love, therefore spirituality is love! In other words, I think you are right when you say 'spirituality is loving.'" she assured him."

Max looked into Bronwyn's eyes and saw reflected his own sense of relief over a restoration of self-worth. "Thank you. Once again you have rescued me. Now let's go find the ocean. I want to walk the rocks."

They spent the rest of the afternoon at Bluff looking out over the sea, before returning to Colac Bay for another week of work.

Ironically the first to register as guests were Americans from Wyoming. Max enjoyed meeting them and trading stories of the Rocky Mountain region. A retired couple from Jackson Hole, they were on their first visit to New Zealand after their daughter, a University of Wyoming student, had spent her junior year at Otago University. Elmer and Ruby Johnson stayed a week, taking in the beauty of this isolated coastland. "We like to get away from the beaten tourist paths." they had said.

The day before the couple departed, Bronwyn prepared a picnic lunch for them. They invited Bronwyn and Max to join them for a mid-day meal on the rocks looking out over the Pacific. After their meal they rested back on the rocks and shared impressions of New Zealand and of the American west. It was Elmer who commented: "You know, there are some remarkable similarities. The area up around Alexandra reminded us of Laramie, Wyoming!"

"And this coastal shore line," Ruby added, "makes me think of parts of Monterey Bay in California.'

"You're right—Pacific Grove!" Elmer concluded.

"And when you get to Queenstown, you are going to think you are back home in Jackson!" Max said, guessing out loud.

"Queenstown! That's where we are going tomorrow, isn't it Rub?"

"Yes—we have reservations at the Earnslaw Lodge in Queenstown."

"How far is that from here," Elmer wondered.

"Oh, about three hours, 150 kilometers, wouldn't it be?" Bronwyn estimated.

Then Bronwyn complained, "You three are leaving me out! But you are giving me a more and more desire to see the U.S."

"Well now," Elmer offered, "Ruby and I would just love it if you two would visit us in Jackson Hole! How about it?"

"I just may do that," Max admitted, "since I live about as far from Jackson as Queenstown is from here. How about it, Bronwyn? Put America in your future!"

Bronwyn smiled sadly, "I wish I could."

"Well, you both know you are welcome." Ruby said, sounding a bit confused.

On the evening after Elmer and Ruby Johnson left, Bronwyn joined Max on his porch for his nightly meditative view of the ocean. "The Johnsons were very nice people, weren't they?" She said as she drew up a chair next to his.

"Yes, they were. And are you going to accept their invitation to visit?"

"I don't see how I can, and besides . . ."

"I know, I have been remiss by not having invited you first; but I have been so aware of how difficult such a trip would be for you, that I didn't want to bring it up. But now that the subject has come up, what do you think, Bron? Nothing in this world could make me happier than to have you come to Montana—for a visit—or permanently!" Max added, surprising himself as well as Bronwyn.

"Max, there's no money for that. What would air travel cost?"

"About $1,700 NZ—one way."

"It would be a very long time before I had that much in the bank to spend on myself. It would take at least $4,000 for the trip including everything, wouldn't it?" She added, "And besides, I'd not be able to stay very long, now that I have the Inn to keep."

"I know it is more or less impossible—at least at this point.
but lets just talk about it. Talk is cheap. If you didn't have the Inn,
what else would hold you to New Zealand. Besides that it is home,
I mean?"

"If you mean, family: no, there is no one close enough to keep
me here. Other commitments like church: these were all given up
at least temporarily since moving to Dunedin. Friends? None that
I would miss particularly. Just talking about it this way,
Max . . . makes me realize . . . that you have become family and
friend for me!" she said somewhat hesitantly.

"Bron—I could say the same thing!"

"This is still my home; but without the Inn and with enough
money I would surely like to visit the US. And Montana—to see
you, Max. Perhaps even for an extended time!" she said wistfully
looking out over the sea. She went on, "But I'm dreaming. I need
the Inn to keep bread on my table; and there's no way I'll ever
have any extra funds. I am afraid Montana will always be somewhere far away—only in my imagination."

Max hesitated . . . and then went on to say: "There was
something else about our picnic on the rocks with Elmer and
Ruby—-"

"What was that?"

"The way they treated us—you might say their assumptions—
made me feel like you and I were a long-time married couple!"

"I know——when they invited us to Wyoming, it took them
by surprise to hear each of us answer in a different way . . . Was
their assumption a new idea to you, Max?"

"Not exactly. The thought had crossed my mind, but like so
much of my life I am so tentative. The ministry: I still don't think
I could ever be in a parish again. A permanent relationship: I think
of my failure to make it work the first time, and I wouldn't want to
foist myself on someone else—especially you."

"Max! It wouldn't be foisting."

"Sometimes I think it would be much worse. When I think of
Gwen's death, I keep thinking that if we'd never married, she'd be

alive today. Or, worse yet, if I'd been a better husband, she wouldn't have gone back home . . . and been killed."

"You can't think that way. It's not fair to yourself."

"But I do, and it makes me feel that I must never put anyone else in the same position," Max said in despair, and added in a partial whisper as if to himself: "I'm not fit for marriage."

"You are much too hard on yourself," Bronwyn assured him. And yet she added, "But I know what you mean by being tentative. I'm not over Duncan yet. Granted, I had a lot of warning, and for a long time he was really gone—but still when he died I felt grief, as I did when my parents died. In this condition I'd be no prize." They were both silent for a while as they listened to the steady lapping of the water as wave after wave came in. The waning light of dusk was almost at an end. One by one stars began to appear in the darkening sky. Max looked up wistfully until he spotted the Southern Cross, under which Bronwyn had been born and under whose beneficence she would likely live out her days, he thought.

"Only two more days, and then I leave."

"From Christchurch, is it?"

"No, Invercargill."

"That's better. I can see you off."

"Good," Max replied. Then he shared something deeper. "Bronwyn, our talk tonight gives me a feeling down deep, which is so good. Just to realize that we both would consider being together if the obstacles within each of us were not there—that warms my heart."

"I know what you mean. Strangely, it makes your leaving a little easier, Max."

"Yes—maybe so, All the same, I hate to leave you again."

She looked startled and said, "Max, we should be going back to the Inn, before I cry!"

At that they both rose and facing each other briefly, they involuntarily reached out to hug. And they kissed. Not just a good night kiss but one which amounted to a pledge.

Max sat on his porch under the dark sky for a long time that night—two days before leaving Bronwyn. Forever? he wondered. Perhaps so. At least he would have to assume such, unless circumstances changed. But, he told himself, there's no chance of such a change.

For the second time in their lives Browyn MacKenzie and Max Ritter stood before the plate glass window in the air terminal in Invercargill. For the second time they waited for the Air New Zealand flight which would separate them by half a world.

It was one of those awkward times when there was so much each wanted to say; but neither could think of anything much to say. Each not wanting the jet to land, and yet impatient for the plane to arrive, and for it to depart again.

Eventually they heard the slowing-down sound of the engines in the sky above the tarmac a moment before the loud-speaker crackled on: "Your attention please, Air New Zealand flight No. 37 from Christchurch is due to land momentarily and will be deplaning at Gate No. 2. Just then the 737 rolled into view and slowly came to a stop in front of the terminal gate. Soon a trickle of passengers were walking across the tarmac making their way to the terminal. In about ten minutes time the speaker came on again: "Flight No. 38 for Auckland is ready for general boarding at this time."

Bronwyn and Max stood up and embraced each other and they kissed their good byes to each other with tears in their eyes.

"Good bye, Bron . . ."

"Cheerio, Max . . ." her voice cracking.

"Write me!"

"I will," she said, "and you be sure to write."

"You can count on it!"

Reluctantly they let go of each other and Max walked out to the waiting aircraft.

Bronwyn, holding back her tears, watched in silence.

"Flight No. 38 is in its final boarding process. All Passengers need to be on board immediately."

The engines began to rev up; and the 737 began to move, swinging out toward the taxi lane. As Bronwyn stood at the terminal window waving,. Flight No. 38 was on its way. Max looked out the cabin window and waved without seeing Bronwyn again as the plane rolled away from the terminal, lifted off, and veered northward, disappearing into the clouds.

Northward, soon above the clouds and into the sun he flew. He would be airborne until the sun would be in the south again and he and his angel of healing would be half a world apart from each other. Possibly forever.

The terminal was almost empty when Bronwyn turned from the window through which she had been looking out onto the tarmac. She walked to the door and to her car. As she drove along Dee street, everything seemed gray and devoid of life. At Gala Street, on impulse she turned in order to drive through Queens park. She remembered the Sunday afternoons they had spent together here. Once again on Dee she turned in at the Pizza Hut. And for an hour or so she "nursed" a small pizza and coke, remembering that first Sunday and Max's delighted surprise when she had taken him there. She returned to Colac Bay, went to her bookshelf and took down *Jane Eyre.* a favorite, and sat on Max's chair thinking, remembering, and finally reading; but she was not able to look ahead. That would have to come later.

PART IV

CHAPTER 21

The morning after Max's return to Fairhavens Con asked him to come to his office. After closing the door behind Max and having him sit down, Con said: "There are two developments which I want to share with you before you pick up any stray gossip. The first has to do with me personally. The second concerns Fairhavens. Let me start with the second. As you know the Vermillian group has been trying to buy up as much property in this vicinity as they can. Their buying activity has been on the increase; so much so that there is only one parcel bordering our boundary which is not owned by them. With the exception of one hundred yards of property line, we are surrounded. That puts our access to public lands in jeopardy."

"You mean they are keeping our people out?" asked Max, taken aback.

"That's right. The fence lines are posted—NO TRESPASSING all over the place. And they are trying to buy the last piece."

"How much chance of that is there?"

"As of the moment, the ball is in our court. The owners have given us first option to purchase. They know how we need this parcel for access. It stretches from our property line all the way to the National Forest. But we must come up with the purchase price—now!"

"How much are you talking about?"

"Only eighty thousand, and I pretty well have that in hand. It means a trip to Chicago—again. You weren't here then but we were up against a similar ultimatum on the Fairhavens property itself. A donor was found in the Chicago area."

"Yes, Jackson told me something of that story."

"And now this brings up the other matter I wanted to share with you."

"What is that?" asked Max, curious to know what more could be in the air.

"I am planning to be married! And I'd like you to perform our ceremony."

"Where?" asked Max, buying himself some time before facing this awkward request.

"Either here at Fairhavens, or possibly at Mill Creek Community Church."

"The other more important question, Con, is "who!"?

"She has visited here once, and I think you met her then. It is Leona Baxter from Chicago—or River Forest, really."

"I vaguely remember her. So, you'll be seeing her on your up-coming business trip?

"Right! I leave tomorrow, and that's why I'd like to have this settled before I see her. What do you say? Is your standing such that you can still marry people?"

"That's no problem. In fact under Montana law you can even make your vows to each other without someone to officiate!"

"Is that a fact?" Con responded in amazement.

"Yes, I checked it with the court house in Billings one time when an acquaintance told me he had married on the rims over-looking the city—just he and his wife-to-be, and two witnesses. So long as the license was legally signed and witnessed, they told me! I couldn't believe it."

"But in our case we want you, Max!"

"Don't get me wrong, I'm not suggesting a do-it-yourself wed-ding! However, you confront me with a tough decision. Up until now I haven't let anyone know that I am clergy—only you know that. Because my leaving Tipton was so painful—and still is—I have more or less rejected that part of my life; and I am really reluctant to take it up again. But for you, I'd like to. Let me think this through this afternoon. I'll get back to you tonight before you take off for Chicago—would you give me that bit of time?"

"I don't want to push you into a spot you don't want to be in—but on the other hand, I really hope you'll agree, Max. Let's hear from you after supper."

This request struck at the root of Max's internal struggle over the ministry in which he felt he'd failed dismally. Almost the last thing he'd done in Tipton was a wedding. It was during that wedding that Gwen had left.

Thinking about doing a wedding brought back his feelings of failure and inadequacy both as a minister and as a husband. This was the inner struggle which had sent him south to the end of the earth—and to Bronwyn!

As Max went about his work he mulled over Con's request. He found himself wishing so much to be with Bronwyn—to ask her help. She would want him to take the wedding, but she would not violate his feelings. She had said more than once that "it is such a waste" referring to his unwillingness to go back to ministry.

His afternoon task was to check fence. He chose the most isolated portion of the Fairhavens property in the north east, where he had discovered the deserted building. The mysterious place where he had been transported in his imagination to Colac Bay. As he followed the fence line there, and came to the overgrown path to deserted buildings. On his return to this wilderness perhaps he would feel himself looking out to sea again, and could it be that he could "talk to Bronwyn?"

He saw the sign he had put up—COLAC BAY INN—and found the ancient chair on the deserted porch on the north side of the decaying cabin, the chair in which he had previously felt mystically transported to New Zealand. A breeze stirring the trees was the only sound. As he sat entranced, the gentle sound of the wind in the trees seemed to increase in intensity until in his mind he began to hear the waves as they surged upward onto the flat moist sand of Colac Bay. Facing the mid-day sun he felt the brief chilling effect of a cloud which passed over, momentarily obscuring Max's sense of direction. When the sun broke forth from behind the cloud he felt a changed sense of direction—this time the sun appeared to be arching across the northern sky over the sea. And mysteriously almost as it had been when he was at Colac Bay, he felt Bronwyn's presence as she came up and stood near his chair on his cabin porch!

"Max Ritter! I think that you look troubled. Might there be some way I could help you?

"Bron—what shall I do

"What do you **wish** you would do?—not **want**, but **WISH**?

"Aren't they the same?"

"Not exactly, Max! I think 'want' is what you want now. That's not to have to do the wedding, isn't it? But what you wish is to have things resolved, and for you to have an easy time of it after your struggle is over, isn't it!"

"Yes—an easy time of it! If my struggle were over I'd perform Con's marriage."

"And . . . ?" she seemed to probe more deeply. "What else would that mean for you, Max? . . . if your self-doubts were satisfied?"

"I guess, what you are telling me is that I'd be ready to take up the ministry again. Is that it?" he asked cautiously.

"Is it?" Is that what you **WISH**?" At that point the sound of her voice began trailing off.

Max was quiet a long time. He could almost hear the waves and see the gray sky stretching southward forever. Over the sound of the waves he began to hear music faintly, an alto voice singing . . . Bronwyn singing:

> Don't ever feel discouraged,
> For Jesus is your friend,
> And if you lack the knowledge
> He'll not refuse to lend.
> There is a balm in Gilead to make the wounded whole,
> There is a balm in Gilead to heal the sinsick soul.
> If you cannot preach like Peter,
> If you cannot pray like Paul,

You can tell the love of Jesus
And say, "He died for all".

The breeze intensified, making the quaking aspen sound even more like the waves of the sea! The music was Max's own, as he sang to himself:

There is a balm in Gilead to make the wounded whole,
There is a balm in Gilead to heal the sin sick soul.

"Thank you dear Bronwyn, Bronwyn, my angel," he whispered in the deserted silence of the place." He rose to return to Fairhavens to tell Conrad of his decision.

Recommitting himself to the ministry would not be without complication. He did not want to leave Fairhavens; he would need to make himself available for supply preaching and other tasks the Presbytery might find for him to do.

To the surprise of everyone Conrad Schneider returned to the Paradise Valley after his Chicago trip accompanied by Leona Baxter, whom he introduced as his bride-to-be!

The surprise was further compounded on the wedding day when the Fairhavens staff and many neighbors from the valley arrived at the Mill Creek Community Church to discover that the officiating clergy person emerging from the side room in a clerical alb and white stole was Max Ritter—handyman, courtesy van driver and supervisor of building and grounds at Fairhavens! Strangely transformed, Max assumed a holy authority over the two standing before him that day as he conducted the traditional service of marriage, and in the end pronounced:

"By the authority committed unto me as a Minister of the
Church of Christ, I declare that Conrad and Leona are now
Husband and Wife, according to the ordinance of God,
and the law of the State: in the name of the Father, and of
the Son, and of the Holy Spirit. Amen"

Afterwards as Max retired to the tiny ante-room to take off his ministerial gown, he felt a sense of exhilaration. He wanted to share his feeling of victory with the one who had brought him to this point!

It was to Max's relief that he found most of his friends having a very favorable response to the unveiling of his identity as a minister. Everette said, "I sort of wondered. The way you talked about things sometimes when we got in deep discussions."

Jackson Evans suddenly began to put Max on a clergy pedestal, until Max spoiled his efforts by saying to him, "Jackson, I'm no priest, just the same old guy I've always been. It's just that I trained for a different job than the one I've got!" Afterwards, Max had some misgivings about what he'd said to Jackson. He thought to himself, "If the thing is no big deal as I implied, then why did I have such a struggle reclaiming my ordination?"

The therapists were less than impressed. Max guessed that his perceived change in status tended to encroach on their professional monopoly.

For Max himself there came a new sense of freedom, freedom to be who he really was. This new authenticity helped him to take up occasional ministerial duties as these presented themselves to him. Duties such as supply preaching for congregations in the area on Sundays when their ministers were away. The Mill Creek minister called upon him occasionally for funerals and weddings. Once in a while someone working at Fairhavens sought his counsel.

In time Max felt as if he had emerged from a dark tunnel, which was now far behind him as his sense of vocational confidence began to increase. This did not include any thought of returning to a parish ministry, however. That and the thought of his own marriage remained enemy territory in his mind.

It was good to be back at work at Fairhavens. Max enjoyed his responsibility for buildings and grounds; and the courtesy van gave him contact with the guests.

On the Tuesday after Con and Lee were married and while they were gone on a short honeymoon Max had a pick-up at Gallatin

Field in Bozeman. Only one person was arriving and he met her in the baggage claim area after the mid-day Delta flight had arrived. His Fairhavens wind-breaker helped arriving guests to identify him. A smartly dressed woman in her early thirties came up to him and introduced herself:

"I'm Anna Vermillian. I am to go to Fairhavens. You're my driver?"

Max bristled at the condescending way she addressed him, but regained his composure and replied: "Yes, Ms. Vermillian. We have been expecting you, and I shall be happy to get you to Fairhavens." He continued, wanting to set the record straight: "I am Max Ritter. I'm superintendent of buildings and grounds. And when feasible, I like to meet guests on their way up to Fairhavens. If you'll point out your baggage I'll carry it for you."

They waited in silence at the carousel until she spotted her two matching pieces of leather-bound luggage.

"Is this your first time at Fairhavens?" Max asked as they drove eastward on the frontage road before entering the Interstate at West 19th.

"Yes it is. In fact this is my first trip into Montana. I've flown over it many times, I'm sure."

"Lots of people do. Where is home for you, Ms Vermillian?

"Clovis, just outside of Fresno."

"I see. That's in the productive Central valley, isn't it?

"San Joachin." She added.

There was something about his passenger which made conversation somewhat strained. Max sensed a reserve in Anna Vermillian, a reserve which somehow challenged him. "It always is interesting to discover how our guests hear of Fairhavens. We don't do a lot of advertising. We find we don't have to." He paused to give her a chance to volunteer information, but she remained silent. "Did you hear of us through a travel agent?"

"No, I didn't. I usually make my own plans and deal directly with Delta."

Not to be put off Max returned to his quest and said, "Of

course word of mouth is the best advertising, and there are a number of new guests each year who come on the recommendation of someone they know. How about you?"

"Yes . . . I have a relative who knew about Fairhavens," she said reluctantly.

"Oh, so was he a guest at one time?"

"No, I don't believe so.

Max decided that he had beaten the subject to death and that he'd wait for her to say more. But she did not.

As they pulled up to the Lodge, Max told her that he would wait until she had checked in before taking her luggage to her room. He customarily said this to new guests when he did not know whether they were coming for vacation or for therapy. Most of the guests coming for therapy were housed in the A-Frames on the crest of the hill east of the Lodge, while the Lodge was usually the place for the resort folks. When she came back out to the van she told him that her room would be No. 24 in the Lodge. He carried her bags up to the room and concluded his responsibilities saying:

"Dinner is in the Dining room at six o'clock. If you need anything phone the desk and I'm sure it will be taken care of. I hope you have a really enjoyable stay, Ms Vermillian."

"Thank you, Mr. Ritter."

As Max returned to the lounge on the first floor he wondered if she could possibly be related to Cody Vermillian. He didn't think Cody would be her brother, since she was staying at Fairhavens instead of with Cody. Yet, she had the same name. Something didn't add up. When Con returns, I'll have to talk about this with him. Meanwhile Max would keep a curious eye on Anna Vermillian.

Not much had been heard of about Cody Vermillian lately, except for indications of his purchase of one piece of property after another. And some increased activity along the Emigrant Gulch road had been observed. Someone had erected a temporary wire fence with a yellow caution tape along the road in front of those houses,

which had recently been vacated. A county road grader had been
up and down the road a number of times lately, which was unusual. Generally when the road had gotten washboardy, Max had
had to call the county road office to get the grader to come out.

Coincidently, a few days after checking Ms Vermillian in, Max
was awakened at 6 AM by the distant noise of heavy earth moving
equipment: the intermittent roar and idling sound as well as the
warning beeping when backing. He looked out his window and in
the direction of the gulch he could see puffs of dust in the air,
coming as he later discovered from heavy earth moving tractors.
More to tell Con, he thought. He decided that after breakfast he'd
drive up that way and have a look.

By the time Con and Lee returned from their honeymoon
Max had determined to a fair extent what was going on. He gave
an account to Con: "It looks like Cody has begun work on his
resort hotel up the Gulch. He's leveled the land, tearing up the
sod and natural ground cover—really making a mess of things.
Yesterday cement trucks, one after another were going up the road
to pour the basement foundation. This morning two construction
shacks were hauled by."

"Who's the contractor? Could you tell?" Con asked.

"No, it was funny. There wasn't any name on the trailers; but
they had county "3" licenses."

"I figured he'd get his work done out of Billings. The Livingston
Chamber is all for the development; and then he goes to Billings
to buy his help! Just to keep track of him, I think we ought to
watch to see where his carpenters come from," Con advised, "I
doubt if there'll be a "49" license in the bunch."

Max agreed, "You may be right."

The next day the dust on the road up the gulch wouldn't quit
in the early morning while one pick-up after another sped past the
Lodge. You could tell they were carpenters. Each truck had a gun
rack in the rear window. Many with rifles; all with long carpenter
levels. Max took it upon himself to watch who went by. None of
the pick-ups had any construction names. The assortment of plates

was outstanding. Three Wyoming counties, a couple of Idaho plates, a number of eastern Montana counties, mostly from rural areas like "45"—Terry and "50"—Jordan. Max wondered what accounted for such a variety. It wasn't many days before it became evident.

After the builders' pick-ups reached the work site above Fairhavens another group of vehicles began to appear on the lane into Fairhavens. Max recognized them as cars driven by Board members. These came as a surprise to Max. This wasn't the time for the regular board meeting. While the members were gathering in the conference room behind the lodge an unfamiliar car drove up. It was a Gallatin County car with a Prudential Realty logo on the door panel. The driver asked Max to direct him to the Board room.

"Thanks," she called to Max as she grabbed her brief case and hurried down the sidewalk to the conference room.

Max didn't think much about this at the time.

A few days later around noon he saw the Prudential Realty car parked outside the lodge. Later in the Dining room he noted that the woman from Prudential was having lunch with Con.

Con was not normally a secretive sort of person, Max thought but in connection with his association with the Prudential woman, there was something furtive in his demeanor. Max did not know what to make of this. There was something ominous in the air, he felt.

CHAPTER 22

"There's trouble at the Vermillian job site. Bad trouble, I'd say!" Everette warned as he took his seat at the staff table. Max and Jackson Evans had joined Con and Lee for lunch a few minutes earlier.

The Schneiders had settled into a routine of taking their noon meal with others on the staff. They very much wanted to develop good relationships between staff people and Leona. It was not Con's nature to "pull rank," and with that Lee was in full agreement. They hoped for a collegial relationship.

"What kind of trouble? What do you mean—bad trouble?" Con asked.

"It seems that there is a bunch of union members setting up picket lines."

"Where are they from?" Jackson asked.

"As near as I could tell they are from Butte, Anaconda and Great Falls. From what I could tell when I saw three extended cab pick-ups registered in those three counties."

"There's our answer!" Con said, directing his remark to Max.

"Vermillian has hired non-union. That's why he's got them from all over."

Everette re-joined the discussion: "I was up the gulch with a string of dudes on horseback. That's a favorite ride. But just going by up there puts a damper on the feel of it. Here we are trying to provide people with a relaxed western back-to-nature experience; and what happens? We ride right into a labor union picket line, scabs, and all."

"That's bad enough now. But what if it really turns messy?" Jackson commented.

"I know," Everette continued, "That's what I mean by bad trouble. Remember that non-union house construction in Laurel back some years ago?"

"I remember," Con said. " I was working at Deaconess in Billings that night. Six men were brought into Emergency!"

"That one got nasty," Everette agreed. "And the union people were from out of town that time too!"

A siren was heard in the distance. It was getting louder and louder. Jackson ran out to the lounge to see if he could spot it. The siren peaked as it went by, and receded as it sped further up the gulch creating a cloud of dust. Jackson came back to say, "That was a sheriff's car!"

Before lunch was ended two more sirens amidst swirling clouds of dust streaked by. Two more cars from the Sheriff's department.

"Not your quiet 'get-away-from-it-all' retreat house Is it?" Lee said to no one in particular as she and Con rose to leave the dining room.

As Max was leaving the dining room he met Anna Vermillian coming down the stairs from her room. She looked troubled as she asked, "What were the sirens for?"

"They were sheriff's cars going up the gulch." Max replied, not really wanting to say much about it. But he knew she'd want to know more.

"How often does that happen?"

"Very rare."

"Do you know what the problem is?" She persisted.

"Well, not exactly; but I do know that there seems to be a bit of union trouble at the job site up the gulch. Picket line, I understand."

And then under her breath Anna muttered something Max could barely understand. It sounded like: "——come to this."

Max hadn't seen much of Anna Vermillian since she had arrived. She had been keeping to herself. A day or two after she had come to Fairhavens she had asked Max for a ride into town so that she could pick up a rental car. During the forty-five minutes it took to drive to Livingston Max tried to open conversation; but her reticence and evasive answers left the two in silence for most of the way in to town.

She had returned with a dark green Ford Escort at her disposal. On most days she would take off after breakfast and again after lunch. She had become an enigma to Max. She did not fit the customary patterns which he had come to associate with Fairhavens guests, either of the recreation or renewal varieties. Often when she drove off, he would try to catch sight of her direction. He could determine no consistency. Sometimes she headed up the gulch; but just as often she drove down toward the highway. whether to Livingston or south to Yellowstone he had no way of knowing.

Now when she heard about the union trouble she hurried out of the lounge and got into her rental car. Max was curious after hearing the remark she had mumbled. He positioned himself at a lounge window to see which direction she went. She drove up the gulch toward the construction site traveling faster than her usual speed. As Max turned from the window Con approached him: "Max, I'm concerned about Everette's information. This could be the beginning of something we don't need!"

"You could be right. But there's nothing we can do, is there?

Con thought a moment and replied, "No, but it occurs to me that we need to keep on top of this. Do you have time this afternoon to take a drive up there and find out what you can?"

"I could do that." Max was glad for the opportunity to see first hand and to check out where Anna Vermillian might have gone.

Within minutes Max was in one of the Fairhavens S-10 Chevy pick-ups on his way to the Vermillian development up Emigrant gulch. Not far beyond Fairhavens he passed by the houses along the road which former residents of the gulch had sold off to the Vermillian outfit. These had been cordoned off, waiting to be renovated and incorporated into the "old town" part of the project. Above them the valley opened out into a relatively flat plain. It was here that the resort hotel was being built. The work in progress was blocked by picket lines. Max was stopped on the road near the construction site by the three Park County sheriff's cars. Seven or eight sheriff's deputies were out of their cars and standing in the road. Max saw that they were confronting a crowd gathered around a pick-up which had been overturned. Max eased his pick-up into a relatively shallow stretch of the barrow pit and got out. He asked the first bystander what had happened.

"I'm not quite sure, but I'm guessing that those picketers overturned that truck when the driver tried to break through the line to go to work."

"Who's the driver?"

"I can't tell; but it's a local vehicle."

Max hurried on up the gulch on foot getting as close to the accident scene as he could. No one seemed to be hurt. The sheriff's deputies were talking to the union men near their police cars. A group of workers had gathered near the overturned pick-up, at a safe distance from the union crowd. In the middle of that group was a young carpenter on the ground holding an injured arm as if in a sling. He apparently had been the driver of the overturned truck.

As Max watched he saw Anna Vermillian come up to the group of workers. She singled out the injured man and was talking to him. One of the sheriff's men broke away from the union picketers and came over to talk to the injured man. Max was surprised to see that Anna and the sheriff's deputy appeared to fall into serious conversation. They moved over to his nearby patrol car. Max stepped a bit closer so that he could observe what was going on. The officer was filling out a report form on a clip-board, asking Anna questions as he filled in the form. By this time Everette had joined Max and asked, "What have you found out?"

Max told Everette as much as he could gather as an outside observer on the fringe of this incident. And then he said, "The thing that has me wondering is what Anna Vermillian's involvement in all this is. She's been in the cop car while the sheriff's deputy seems to be interrogating her."

"Who is she?" Ev asked.

"So far as I know she is just a recreation guest at Fairhavens. I brought her down from Livingston just the other day."

"But, with a name like Vermillian, she must be tied in with Cody, don't you think," Everette commented.

"That's what I have been thinking. But the fact that she never said as much, has kept me from thinking so, until now." Max admitted.

"The fact that they are taking her information down, clinches it for me." Everette declared. "And not a sign of Cody. That's strange. So they've got her in the car instead!"

"You're probably right. We'll hear one of these days. But I think this is about all we are going to find out. I'm going back," Max said as he started walking back to his vehicle.

"Who's it that's injured?" Everette wanted to know before Max left.

"I don't know who, but one of the carpenters, I think. He'd been the driver of the overturned pick-up."

"Hope not too serious!" Everette concluded as Max turned to walk back to the Blazer. On his return down the gulch to Fairhavens Max met an ambulance coming up, probably to carry out the injured carpenter.

Conrad's reaction to all this, when Max told him, was to call Cody Vermillian. A sophisticated feminine voice answered, "Good afternoon, Vermillian Park County Enterprises!"

"Yes, may I speak with Cody Vermillian?"

"I'm sorry sir, Mr. Vermillian isn't taking any calls just now. You may leave a message, and he'll get back to you as soon as he can."

"This is urgent and I believe it is in his best interest to hear what I have to report."

"I'll try to ring him."

After an all too brief a moment she continued: "He must have stepped out." Then she added as if by rote. "If you will leave your name and number I'll have him call you."

"This afternoon?" Con pushed.

"I can't promise. He has a busy schedule."

"Do you have his home phone number?"

"I can't give that out, sir."

"I'll call again," Con replied as he hung up.

The next morning before going in to breakfast Max stationed himself at the end of the lodge porch so that he could count the incoming vehicles. He counted seven "foreign" pick-ups—that's what locals call vehicles from other counties. Almost all of them had at least one passenger besides the driver. Again these were either from counties "1", "30", or '2"—Butte, Anaconda, Great Falls. Jackson had remarked that there were more union members in those three towns than in all the rest of the Montana counties combined. As Max watched, two sheriff's department Ford Broncos went by. "Another day of mounting tension," he thought. Just so we don't see any violence."

But that hope was shattered by mid-morning when the noise of a rotor blade was heard overhead, as the "H E L P" helicopter from Billings chopped its way up the gulch. Max rushed out to the Blazer. Reaching the job-site as soon as he could he found the EMT's loading an injured person onto a stretcher and into the helicopter. Soon the rotor blades began to move and the unwieldy craft rose and twisted its way northward most likely to one of the hospitals in Billings. Max joined the hushed crowd. The sheriff's deputies were hand-cuffing three of the union picketers and putting them into one of the patrol broncos. Finding a familiar face Max asked, "What has happened?"

"Al Dexter was shot as he crossed the line!"

"Hurt seriously?"

"Lost a lot of blood—unconscious—He's on his way to Emergency at Billings Deaconess!"

Another bystander added, "Tragic, senseless violence. It's not the unions I blame. It's this whole lousy development. Look what's happening to our quiet valley!"

Returning quickly to Fairhavens, Max turned over in his mind the name, "Al Dexter," thinking that it sounded familiar. When he went in to Conrad's office to report what he had heard, Con was much alarmed: "That's Connie Dexter's husband! She's one of our cooks. I doubt that she's heard!"

Max hesitated and then offered: "Do you want me to give Connie this information?"

"Would you?"

Max entered the kitchen and found Connie working on the noon meal. "Connie," he said, "I need to talk to you. Can you stop what you're doing for a minute?"

"Yes, what is it?"

"I've just been up to the job-site and discovered that Al has been hurt and they've taken him to Billing Deaconess in the helicopter."

"Oh Lord! How bad is he? What happened? Did he fall?" she asked fearfully.

"No it wasn't a fall. It was some of that union trouble. Apparently they shot at him as he crossed the line."

Dazed by this news Connie pulled out a chair and slumped into it as she was consumed with weeping. Between sobs she said, "I've got to go to him!"

Max quietly stood next to her, put his hand on her shoulder and said, "I'm so sorry! I'm sure we can get you to Billings just as soon as you can leave."

"Oh, please—yes! I want to go right away."

"Connie, you are going to need to be prepared to stay. So do you need to get some things at home?" Max suggested.

"No, if you can get me there, I'll manage with what I have with me. But I'll have to make a phone call to get my neighbor to baby-sit for me while I'm in Billings."

"OK. Make your call and then meet me out in front of the Lodge. Fifteen minutes enough time?"

"I think so."

"I'll meet you as soon as you can make it. And we'll leave."

In his office Conrad reached for the phone determined to bring Cody Vermillian face to face with what was going on up at his project.

"I'm sorry, sir, Mr. Vermillian is not in the office today."

"Can you reach him? It is urgent. There has been a serious injury on the job-site of your project at Emigrant. A criminal investigation is pending. Your company could very well be liable." Conrad replied in an angry rapid-fire voice.

"I will leave him a message." she replied curtly.

"That is hardly adequate. Have him go directly to the job-site." With that Conrad Schneider banged the phone down. He concluded that he had done all he could. The rest would be up to the Vermillian outfit.

When Max and Mrs. Dexter arrived at Deaconess in Billings, he took her into Emergency. They found that Al had been admitted to the hospital and was in I.C.U. Connie was permitted a brief visit, while Max waited in the I.C.U. waiting room. When she came out she was obviously distraught. Max ushered her into a small private room where she told him:

"He's unconscious. They have him on a heart monitor and all kinds of tubes and wires. The nurse told me that they are taking him into surgery in a few minutes. I guess to remove the bullet."

Max tried to reassure her: "I should think that once they get the bullet out and have a chance to take care of the area that's been hurt, he should be in a better condition and ready to improve."

"Oh, I hope so!"

"Did they tell you where he was hit?"

"No, they wouldn't say."

Did they tell you how long he'd be in surgery?"

"No. They told me to stay here, and they would come out and talk to me after he's in recovery." She seemed resigned to a long wait.

Max found a place in the waiting room and got a couple of coffees from a little courtesy alcove in the room. When he returned to Connie he sensed that she would just as soon talk about something else. He asked, "Connie, I really don't know you very well. How long have you been at Fairhavens?"

"Just two years. Al and I moved out here from Missouri. He'd run out of jobs there and heard of work out in Montana. He found a job in Livingston and then I got a cooking job at Fairhavens. I'd cooked in a hotel back in Missouri."

"Do you like it here?"

"Yes—we did until this union trouble came. Al really had a struggle with himself about going to work during the picketing. It wasn't that he was afraid. He's sympathetic to the union, but he simply had to work. We need the money bad—especially since the baby came," she said, almost in tears.

"You're first? How old?"

"Eighteen months. Baby boy—Christopher. Our first." Just mentioning the baby seemed to bring a bit of joy to Connie. Then she asked Max, "How long have you been at Fairhavens?"

Max gave an abbreviated account of his Fairhavens experience: "A shorter time than you. I came back from an extended stay in New Zealand and needed work while I decided what I—"

"CPR TEAM TO ICU!"—he was interrupted by an urgent call over the loudspeakers in the ceiling. "

—while I decided what to do next. I saw an ad in the Billings Gazette and took—"

"CPR TEAM TO ICU" Max was aware of the meaning of the call coming over the sound system; but without knowing for whom the team was sought he could only wonder if possibly it was for Al.

He continued his story: "I took the job they offered and I'm still here. I guess this is what I'm doing next!" Max concluded, sensing that Connie by this time needed some quiet time alone. "Now, I'm going to go downstairs to make some phone calls, but I'll be back up in a little bit."

After phoning Con to give an up-date on Al Dexter, Max went into the cafeteria for a cup of coffee. As he sat musing over the situation, he spotted a familiar face across the dining area . It was Anna Vermillian. She was at a table with two men. One he later was to discover was her brother, a banker from Fresno. The other he recognized as Cody Vermillian's lawyer. Curious, he thought. Was this coincidental—or what was her reason for being here? He considered going over and identifying himself, but before he could do that she and her companions had risen. The two men started for the door, while Anna dropped around Max's table and greeted him and immediately asked, "Tell me how Mr. Dexter is doing."

"At this stage we don't know. He is in Intensive Care. Frankly, it could go either way!"

Aghast at what she was hearing she double checked, "You mean he could die?"

"Yes, I think that's a possibility."

"Oh my, I had no idea." She was obviously devastated by this news. Max wondered why this touched her so deeply, as she dismissed herself from his presence and walked rapidly to catch up with her companions. A grave look came over the lawyer's face as he apparently was given a report of Dexter's condition.

Why is all this so important to these people? he pondered as he remained seated, finishing his coffee before rejoining Connie Dexter.

"I can't believe it! It's Maxwell Ritter!" A tall man with graying hair and a full beard stood at Max's table.

Max immediately recognized Calvin Munson, and stood up to greet him, "Cal! I haven't seen you in years—since seminary. I didn't know you were in Montana. What are you doing? Sit down if you have time."

Cal Munson, dressed in cowboy boots, Levis, and a tweed jacket over a maroon turtle neck, pulled out a chair: "I'm a pastoral counselor in private practice; but I do some work here for the Pastoral Care Department."

"You didn't go into the parish ministry?" Max asked.

"No, I just couldn't stomach the narrow, naive conservatism. In fact I sort of lost my faith by the time I graduated. It seemed to me that religion, church, prayer, spirituality and all that were really tools we use to maintain a healthy, balanced life. So I decided psychotherapy would be a more effective way to do that; and then I joined a Unitarian fellowship, and that's just right for me."

"I can go along with your feelings about conservatism, but I couldn't go as far to the left as you. To me that's throwing the baby out with the bath."

"To use your analogy, the baby was already gone—for me!"

"So, do you have someone here in the hospital?

"No, I'm here to meet a client and some of her family. We are preparing for an intervention over in the psych unit this afternoon."

"Chemical abuse counseling a specialty, then?" Max asked.

"Yes, I seem to get into that quite a bit. No let-up in that market!" and then, typical for his profession, he switched the conversation to the other person, "Tell me about yourself."

"Well, after seminary I pastored a congregation not too far from here for a while. Then I spent some time in New Zealand—"

"New Zealand! I've always wanted to go there. So finally next year! I've got a trip in the planning stages. I'd like to talk to you about that sometime."

"I'd be glad to. Anyway after New Zealand I came back here and took a job in the Paradise Valley at Fairhavens."

"That's interesting. I've referred some clients to Fairhavens. I have gotten a good impression of what goes on there."

"Great! You'll have to come over and see us."

"What do you do there? Counsel?" Cal asked.

"No. Handyman and van driver, if you can imagine."

"Yeah, I can imagine. Some days, I wish I had a job like that! What brings you here to the 'Deac'?"

"The husband of one of our cooks was seriously injured. I brought her down this morning, and—"

"Oh, I see my client looking for me, I'd better go. Let's keep in touch. Here's my card. See ya."

Calvin Munson, counselor, very quickly left Max and walked across the dining area and to the three people who were obviously waiting for him. It was with a knowing sort of recognition that Max saw that the client Cal was meeting was Anna Vermillian! A chemical abuse intervention, he pondered, Who else but Cody! Alcohol?

When Max returned to Connie Dexter. She reported that the

surgeon had told her that Al was in the Recovery Room and would soon be returned to Intensive Care; and that she should make arrangements to stay near the hospital for a the next few days.

She appealed, "Max, I don't know anything about Billings. How do I find a room?"

Max assured her: "Are you ready to find a room now?"

"Yes, there's nothing I can do right now. If I can get a room and then come back . . ."

"Let's go across the street. I'll help you get a room at the Cherry Tree Inn. From there you can walk back and forth to the hospital and get your meals in the hospital cafeteria."

"I don't have that kind of money."

"Don't worry. Between Fairhavens and Workman's Comp, you'll come out ok. For now let me advance you this from Fairhavens," Max said as he handed her six twenty dollar bills.

Max checked Connie in and paid for her room on a Fairhavens credit card. Then asked her, "Will you be ok now, if I go back?"

"Yes, Max. Thank you so much for your help."

Conrad Schneider met Max as he got out of the Blazer and began walking into the Lodge: "What is the news from the hospital, Max?"

"Al was put into intensive care. I got Connie into the Cherry Tree. She'll be ok for a couple of days until Al is in a regular room—that is if he makes it."

"He's in that serious a shape?

"I have a feeling he might be." Then he added, "In a few days I think we can see how to help her further."

"Thanks for going over to Billings for us, Max. I guess we'll just have to wait and see."

"That's right."

As Max got up to leave, Con said to him, "Lee and I would like to invite you to our home for dinner this evening. Could you come over?"

"Why—yes, I suppose so, if you're sure . . ."

"We're sure! 6:30."

"I'd like that. I'll be there."

During dinner Leona pressed Max about Bronwyn. "What do you hear from Bronwyn? Con has told me about her."

Con added, "I don't think you have mentioned her since your return from New Zealand."

From anyone else this might have sounded pushy, but he knew Con to have a genuine interest in his relationship with Bronwyn. "I haven't heard much, Lee. In fact we just haven't been writing since I returned. And I don't know why.'

"That's too bad."

"I guess when we parted we both knew that if we were honest we realized we probably wouldn't see each other again. Neither of us has the means, and Bronwyn is tied down to the Inn. I haven't wanted her to put herself on a shelf because of waiting for me, and so I haven't written."

"You mean that it's only a matter of money!" Lee declared: "Come on Max! Where there's a will there's a way."

"Well, to use that slogan in another way: 'Where there isn't a way there isn't a will.'"

"That's not in my book of slogans, Max! *When* you write and she writes, let me know how she is!"

When dinner was over Max could sense that there was something more to this occasion than a social time around the table. The three took their coffee into the living room and Con drew a deep breath and began: "Max, you have become more than just an employee to us. You are more like an associate."

"And a friend," Lee added.

Max was somewhat embarrassed as he acknowledged this.

Con continued, "That's why we wanted you to know now rather than later what is happening to Fairhavens.."

Max could see that this was not so much a conversation as an announcement. And so he remained quiet as Con revealed some very devastating news.

"Things have gotten so bad in regard to the Vermillian development. They are tearing up the valley and coming very close to

us. The disturbance their construction causes is more than we can
bear. It's not going to get any better. Consequently, the Board has
just about decided to sell! There is a buyer and we are considering
signing a 'buy-sell'."

Max could hardly believe what he was hearing. He didn't know
how to respond. "How soon?"

"That is part of what hasn't been worked out yet. The board is
due to meet within the week—as soon as we get word from the
realtor. Not everyone on the board is favorable to this; but it looks
like the majority are."

"How do you feel about it, Con?"

"I have mixed feelings, but I am leaning toward selling—even
though personally, and professionally I don't like it. Con turned to
his wife, "Lee?"

"I favor hanging on longer. It's just that this is such an ideal
location—or it was."

"If you sell—, what next? Would you find another location?"

"The board is of the opinion that another location isn't feasible. If we found a suitable place, the price would be prohibitive,
we are all quite sure. The way land values have skyrocketed in the
Valley. No. Lee and I would probably move back to the Chicago
area. And then decide what the next phase of our lives will be."

Max finally responded: "This all seems so unreal. Fairhavens
has become so much a part of my life—to take it away seems out of
the question!"

"You speak for us as well, Max!" Lee said sadly.

"In a sale of a non-profit like this, what happens to the assets?"
Max asked.

"It can't go to individuals. It has to go to some form of con-
tinuation of the original project. The Board would continue as the
trustees of the proceeds received for the property. It does not yet
have a plan; but the idea which seems to be most attractive is for
the Board to form a foundation investing the money and using the
income for scholarships to people seeking counseling, and grants
for educational events of some kind."

"You make it sound like a done deal!" Lee protested.

"For my own feeling of justification," Con confessed, "it helps to know that there will be some good to come of it."

"I suppose you're right. But, Wow! What a change that will mean for all of us!" Max exclaimed.

Con cautioned, "Hold on! It hasn't happened yet. You know—real estate matters aren't so until their signed! And, Max—keep all this strictly confidential, will you?"

Max nodded his assent. He understood this as cue to take his leave. Max, thanked his hosts for the dinner and thanked Con for his thoughtful sharing of what was going on. He departed for his cabin, there to work through his own thoughts.

When Max was gone Lee asked Con, "Do you have the New Zealand address for the Inn Max was involved with?"

"Yes, I think so."

"I'd like it, Con. I'm going to write Bronwyn!"

"What in the world for?"

"I have an idea," she said without revealing any details.

As Max returned to his cabin he found himself thinking about Lee's reference to Bronwyn, as well as about the future of Fairhavens. He resolved to write Bronwyn "one of these days."

Then he thought of Calvin Munson, troubling thoughts. Not just that Cal had lost his faith, as he said, but that he represented a vast segment of the population "out there." People who have reduced faith to a rational utilitarian support for their own human endeavors. Their god, he thought, is really themselves. In some ways the part that hurt Max most was the distinct impression that Cal felt that anyone who hung on to traditional faith was naive and behind the times.

Max felt he needed to get this into his journal, but after the kind of day this had been, he had no energy left. Maybe tomorrow. These thoughts would keep!

CHAPTER 23

She parked her second-hand "wee" red Toyota in the Bank of New Zealand car park between two large shiny new cars, one a Mitsubishi, the other a Ford. Grabbing her file folder she entered the bank and asked for Mr. Whitney. The young woman at the information desk directed her to a desk in the front corner of the main floor of the bank. A middle aged man in a dark pin stripe suit greeted her as she entered his cubicle: "Good morning. Mrs. MacKenzie, is it?"

"Good morning. It is 'Miss' or MS, if you want. You are Mr. Whitney?"

"Yes, please sit down; and we can get started. I was given the financial information on the Colac Bay Inn, which you submitted to the loan department last week. Very complete records, I might add."

"I was hoping that what I brought to the bank would be what was needed," Bronwyn said with a note of hopeful pleading in her voice.

"Yes—I've gone over everything and I think I can fairly well sum up your position, Miss MacKenzie. I have it here in a report, which I'll give you. But let me tell you what the report indicates."

"Good, I'm very anxious to have your professional opinion."

"I am sorry to say that the figures you have presented do not point to a viable business future. Your projected income does not provide for an adequate budget for necessary minimum overhead costs, such as maintenance and routine capital improvements."

Bronwyn offered: "It has not been easy since I returned to the Inn a month ago and began to operate it on my own. I suppose you are correct. Revenues and costs have been so close lately that I have found almost nothing available for maintenance, let alone improvements," she paused a moment and then asked, "What am I doing wrong? What might I do differently?"

Then Morris Whitney, professional banker though he was, made a remark unbecoming of a dignified financial advisor, and one which surprised both himself and Bronwyn MacKenzie. "What might you do? You really ought to get married!" He looked embarrassed as he heard himself saying this.

Bronwyn was both surprised and offended by this abrupt and seemingly inappropriate remark. "Really, Mr. Whitney—I've come for financial advice, not personal!"

"I am very sorry; but in fact that is financial advice—of a sort. Let me explain as briefly and directly as I can. You see, the Colac Bay operation is just a wee bit too big for one person to handle. You have indicated that you have had to close off two units, because you can't handle a full capacity house. Your volume of business; the extent of your property and buildings, and the nature of inn-keeper scheduling, makes this an operation requiring more than one person. But you are not a large enough operation to expand staff."

Bronwyn nodded in agreement. "I know. Sixteen hour days— seven days a week are more than a person should handle."

"Precisely. Now the simple answer would be to hire another full time person. I say full time, because the amount of work required to operate the Inn adequately adds up to two full positions, not something less, such as one and a half. But, and here is the catch: the income side of your ledger is just not strong enough to provide another full time employee. What you need is a spouse to share the load without requiring the full time wages a stranger would command. That is why I said what I did."

"I see what you are saying," Bronwyn said pensively. She remembered how good the finances had held up during the time Max was helping. Like a husband. she thought. Poor Max! it was "All work and no pay!" She turned to the banker and said, "Since marriage is not in the picture, what other options do you suggest?"

Whitney looked at Bronwyn for a moment, and then took a glass of water from the cadenza behind him and after a short drink, swallowed, and said point blank: "Needless to say, The Bank of New Zealand cannot in good conscience give you a loan. The only other option is for you to sell."

"Sell!" she repeated stunned. "I couldn't do that. The Inn has been in the family for generations."

"Speaking of family; might there be other family members who can help either financially or at the Inn?"

"No. I'm all that's left. Oh, there are some distant cousins up on the North Island. They don't know me; and I have never met them,"

"In that case, I repeat: your only option, then, is to sell the Inn. In fact I have prepared an analysis in the written report which gives you a range in which a fair price can be fixed. I have also included a listing of property agents whom we would recommend to handle this sort of small scale commercial property."

"How soon do you think I must sell—or marry?"

"As soon as possible! Our financial projections show that you are operating at a loss presently; and that if you stay open you will continue to show a loss. Sell within six months, I would advise."

"Well, Mr. Whitney, that's a bit soon for a wedding!" Bronwyn said, trying to lighten the mood of their conversation. But the dour Mr. Whitney did not apparently see the humor. Then, casting about for some other alternative, Bronwyn asked, "Why can't I just close the Inn and find a job for myself?"

"We considered such a possibility and found that the taxes and insurance as well as debt servicing due to capital improvements made over the last five years would add up to more than you could handle on any reasonable income you might be able to accrue," Mr. Whitney answered. With a note of warning, he continued. "No, Miss MacKenzie, your only option is to sell—and in the very near future."

Visibly shaken, Bronwyn thanked Mr. Whitney, put his report in her file folder and left his office and went out the door of the bank. She got in her car, which seemed to her even smaller and older now that the full impact of her financial standing had hit. She drove out of Invercargill bound for Colac Bay and the Inn—her home.

As she drove the familiar route 99 slowing down for Wallacetown and again through Riverton, she thought out loud, "Oh, Max, if only you were with me here to help me sort this out!"

When she arrived back at Colac Bay, she parked her car. She then made her way to "Max's unit" and sat down on his porch chair. After pondering her situation she came to a conclusion. She resolved to work even harder and longer hours. She would re-open the two closed units. She would spend some time each day on routine maintenance—painting, repairing, and other such tasks. What little free time she had previously given herself, would now be needed for Inn projects. This will be difficult, but selling would be far worse, she thought.

After having slept on her resolve, the next morning she awakened with a new and brighter attitude. Believing that she had chosen a viable option, she returned to her routine duties with renewed excitement and resolve. She would save Colac Bay Inn single-handedly! Despite The Bank of New Zealand's dire—and dour—predictions.

Six weeks later Bronwyn was pouring over her book-work. Her energy level had sunk so that even book work had become almost insurmountable. But she doggedly continued with it as she had for the many other tasks required of her on a daily basis. As she tallied the receipts for the month she found for the first time in months that the income had surpassed the expenses—not by much; but this represented the first sign of a financial turn-around. She decided to take this month's end statement sheet in to Mr. Whitney. But that was not to be.

Very early the next morning the guests in the Inn were awakened by the siren of the ambulance from Riverton as it pulled into the Inn parking area. Those who got to the their windows in time saw the E.M.T.'s wheel a gurney from the big house into the waiting ambulance. Soon the emergency vehicle wheeled around and was off down the road to Riverton, on its way to KEW Hospital in Invercargill.

By mid-afternoon Bronwyn regained consciousness while the attending physician was at her bed-side. Her look of question and confusion was answered by a gentle word from the doctor: "Ms MacKenzie. You are here in the hospital after a collapse which you experienced in your home this morning."

"Oh—" Bronwyn replied softly. And then after time to let this information sink in she asked, "How did I get here? I don't remember a thing."

"One of your neighbors found you lying on the floor and she rang up for an ambulance."

"What's my condition?

"We don't know yet. When you are able, we want to do some tests. But for now we are calling it physical exhaustion."

"Oh—" She said as she fell back into a deep sleep.

A nurse came in and covered Bronwyn with a white blanket and looked knowingly at the doctor as he left the bedside.

Nine days later three of her friends from church were assembled around Bronwyn's bed waiting to hear her dismissal recommendations which the doctor would give. Her friends had been summoned in place of family members.

The doctor entered, accompanied by a nurse. He addressed the little group:

Ms. MacKenzie has come through a very critical episode due to total exhaustion and will need to rest for at least three weeks. Above all she cannot under any circumstances return to her work at the Inn." Then turning to Bronwyn he said gravely. " In fact, it would be my recommendation for you to turn over to someone else the responsibility for the management of the Inn and for you to remain clear of it during the foreseeable future."

"I don't see how I can do that, Doctor."

"And I don't think you should do anything else but let go

totally. Is there some place where you can go to regain your strength—at some distance from the Inn?"

It was as this point that Patricia Gibbs, one of her church friends, offered: "Mervin and I would be glad to let you stay in our house at Wanaka for as long as you need to, Bronwyn!"

Before she could reply the Doctor cut in, "That is exactly what I believe you should do."

There was an audible release of tension in the room as this idea took shape. The wisdom of this plan was obvious. Lake Wanaka was well known to everyone in the room. No better spot for recuperation could be imagined.

Carved by glaciers many thousands of years ago Wanaka is one of the lakes set in the midst of a magnificent landscape dear to the heart of many a South Islander. But it has not been "discovered" by the usual procession of tourists, who regularly visited Queenstown on Lake Wakatipu only about seventy-five miles to the south. It is situated at the base of the untamed wilderness of Mt. Aspiring.

After her dismissal and a day to prepare for her respite Bronwyn was ready for Wanaka. The day was bright and cloudless. Lake Wanaka could not have glistened more beautifully in the afternoon sun, when Pat Gibbs drove Bronwyn to her prescribed retreat. Though not on the lake shore itself the Gibbs' summer place was a modest two story framed house nestled among the trees which isolated it from neighboring dwellings. The first floor consisted of a lounge with a fireplace and a kitchen dining room combination. Up a rather steep stairway were two small bedrooms and a bathroom.

After briefly introducing Bronwyn to the house and what it had to offer, Pat took her leave so that Bronwyn could be on her own and at ease during the weeks ahead. With pleasant anticipation Bronwyn settled her things and sought to make herself at home. She had resigned herself to this time away and was eager to get on with it.

Someone in the Gibbs household apparently had developed a passion for nineteenth century English novelists, for the bookcase next to the fireplace in the lounge was amply supplied with the novels of Thomas Hardy and Anthony Trollope. Bronwyn was delighted. These suited her taste as well. In the coming days she would find some of these to be quite engrossing.

She settled in to a routine of walking to the public park at the shore of the lake in the morning after fixing herself a simple breakfast. She usually took with her one of the books she had found. She spent most of her mornings reading near the water's edge.

In the days following her hospitalization she rarely spent much time thinking about the Inn, or about her future. When thoughts of the Inn popped up, she made a concerted effort not to concentrate upon them. She also suppressed thoughts of Max. His failure to write troubled her deeply. Instead, the stories she was reading were of an age gone by. The Victorian period pretty well occupied her mind with images and characters from imagined times and places. She began to feel at home in that earlier more quiet time, separated from her own anguish.

So far as her day-to-day contacts were concerned, these remained casual. She did not care to develop any relationships with the permanent residents of Wanaka. The tourists who frequented the lake were merely a passing parade of temporary faces.

However, it was a chance meeting of a tourist couple at Wanaka which would change the course of Bronwyn's life. She often took a bit of a lunch to eat while on the waterfront. One afternoon toward the end of her stay, while having her lunch at the lake shore, a tour bus rumbled into the car-park and emptied its eager sightseers into the park. Each passenger had been given a box lunch for a quick picnic before returning to the bus. A young man and woman came up to the picnic table where Bronwyn was seated and asked, "Might we sit here with our lunch? It is the only spot left."

She cordially invited them to join her, "Yes, of course. Do sit down."

"We are Stanley and Virginia Compton from Pahia," the man

said, awaiting Bronwyn's introduction. "That's on the North Island," Virginia Compton added.

"Good to meet you. I am Bronwyn MacKenzie from down around Riverton." She offered. It had been a long time since Bronwyn had mingled with tourists; and it was a familiar excitement for her to meet this couple from the North Island.

After they had gotten started on their box lunches Bronwyn offered opportunity for some conversation. "Is this your first trip to the South Island?"

"Yes it is, and we are enjoying your beautiful scenery." the young man replied. His wife added, "But we really are here on business, not just as tourists."

Bronwyn asked in surprise, "Oh, what business are you in?"

Virginia Compton continued: "We have a Bed & Breakfast on the North Island and would like to sell it and buy one down here. We want a place where there are fewer B. & B.'s."

"Yes, we are on the Bay of Islands and there are so many B & B's that some of us don't get the volume we need." her husband added. "We thought it might be better to find a spot in this region someplace where there wouldn't be so much competition."

What a coincidence! Bronwyn thought to herself. "Might you be finding something here then?" She asked.

Virginia sounded somewhat frustrated when she replied, "No, we've not found anything yet."

"We haven't seen much coast, and that's what we would really like. Some small out-of-the-way shoreline bay on the sea coast." Stanley said.

Bronwyn couldn't help but smile at his description. "That's Colac Bay, where I live!" she said.

"Any B. & B.'s in your town?" Stanley inquired, without any real hope.

"Oh yes!" Bronwyn said with a grin, "I have one!"

"You do now?" they both exclaimed. "You wouldn't be wanting to sell? Would you?" Virginia asked, her face lighting up.

After a moment of hesitation Bronwyn answered, "No,——but I should," she added under her breath.

Just then the driver of the tour bus gave a short honk of his horn to summon his people onto the bus for the next leg of their tour. Virginia gathered up their lunch boxes and said, "Stan, we'd better hurry. We almost missed the bus in Christchurch! Remember?"

"Yes, you are right, Gin!"

"Cheerio. Thanks for the table!'

With that they were on their way to the bus.

Arrangements had been made for personal mail to be forwarded to Bronwyn, but none of the Inn business mail. A few days before the end of her stay at Wanaka a letter from the U.S was forwarded. She did not recognize the name on the return address, but the address was familiar: L. Schneider, Box 98, Pray, Montana, 59065, U.S.A. She opened the letter with trembling hands, for she felt a foreboding. Standing by her window looking toward the lake she read:

> Dear Ms MacKenzie,
>
> I know that you do not know me, but I feel as if I know you since Max Ritter has spoken so often of you. My husband, Conrad Schneider and Max work together at Fairhavens and he has become a good friend of both of us.
>
> My reason for writing is to invite you to come to the US and to visit Fairhavens. From all that Max has told us of you, I know that you would enjoy seeing Fairhavens and participating in some its program. I know that such a visit would require a major expenditure. For that reason I would personally like to make available to you scholarship funds which Fairhavens has at its disposal. These are sufficient, I am sure, to make this trip possible.
>
> Bronwyn, two factors have prompted me to write this letter and to extend this invitation. First, there is a very real possibility that Fairhavens will be sold in the near future and its program disbanded. And secondly, I know how

badly Max feels about what he believes is the case—that you and he probably won't ever get to see one another again. It would make "night and day" difference to him if you were to come.

If you can accept, and I hope so dearly that you will, I think it would be great fun to work things out so that your coming would be a surprise to Max!

Please accept! And let me know by return mail!

Cordially yours,

Leona Schneider

After finishing the letter Bronwyn sat down, still holding it. She appeared to be in deep meditation. "Oh, Max, do you really want me? You've not written for a very long time." In her mind she heard Max question her: "Do you want to come? To see me?" Then it was her own voice which she heard. It startled her with a resounding, "YES!"

As her respite at Wanaka was drawing to a close Bronwyn's thoughts began to return to Colac Bay. Not only had the Gibbs's loaned her the use of their house in Wanaka, but others in the Riverton congregation had volunteered to fill in for Bronwyn at the Inn during her absence. This had permitted her to put the Inn out of her mind, which had been therapeutic. But, the best therapy had been the many hours she had spent on the lake-shore bathed in the softly enveloping beauty of the scenery. So often it had been a view of the distant Mt. Aspiring which had been the focus of her attention as she had looked up from her reading. These had been times of meditation as well, as Aspiring had lifted her spirit upward to the heavens. Though Wanaka had not been a place she and Max had visited, in some mysterious way after Lee Schneider's letter he had frequently seemed to be nearby.

Her final day on Wanaka arrived, for Mervin and Patricia were due to arrive in the early afternoon to take her back to Colac Bay. Bronwyn awakened early. After breakfast she tidied up the house in preparation for her leaving. She then took her last walk to the lake shore. It was another cloudless day. Mt. Aspiring made its final appearance—and Max as well!

On this morning she did not bring a book. She would spend her time in thought and meditatior. She lay back in the grass in an isolated part of the lake front park. Lost in reverie and in the half consciousness of meditation she seemed to hear a familiar voice:

"You've met a possible buyer for the inn, Bron? How do you feel about that? I know you have been advised to sell; but do you want to sell?" It was Max whom she was hearing in her trance-like reverie.

"I don't want to sell the Inn, Max. It has been my life as it was for my parents before me—and my father's people before him. How could I be the one to lose it? And yet, I now know I can't manage it alone. And, Oh Max, I know I'm told I must sell." She said aloud in anguish.

Her words were lost in the gentle breeze. There was silence broken only by the lapping of the water. Until she drifted into nascent sleep. Once again the voice of the one she loved: "What about selling part interest and retaining partial ownership with the right to make major decisions regarding the property? What if the couple you met were willing to buy out a third or a half, allowing you to remain as a silent partner. They would manage the business and derive a fair profit for their work. And you, Bronwyn, would get a lump sum and a small monthly income—at least when the Inn was making a profit."

Bronwyn laughed aloud, "Max, you sound like a banker!" When she heard those words she was brought up short and a bit embarrassed, hoping no one was rear enough to hear her talking to herself—or was she!

Before she left the lake shore there was one final word which she heard: "You'll need a lawyer to draw up such an agreement. But I think it just might work, Bron!"

Later that afternoon on the drive back Bronwyn was unusually quiet for most of the six hour trip. There was so much she was turning over in her mind. Between Lumsden and Invercargill she began thinking of the things she needed to do as soon as she returned home. She formed a list in her mind. Close to the top of her list was Leona Schneider. I need to write Mrs. Schneider to thank her for her kind invitation. She would have to write a "Thanks—but no thanks" letter, she thought—regretfully. While she wanted so much to see Max, she simply could not let a complete stranger pay her way. But if I could sell a portion of the Inn! As they drove through Riverton, Bronwyn suddenly found herself asking Mervin and Patricia, "Do you know a good solicitor? Perhaps someone here in Riverton?

A few days after returning to Colac Bay she found a letter from Max in her post-box. She could hardly contain herself, until she could find a quiet and private place in which to read his letter to her.

Dear Bronwyn,

I hardly know how to begin, because I feel so badly about not having written you since my return to the US. It's not that I have forgotten you. On the contrary, you have *often* been in my thoughts and prayers. But, I guess, there was something about leaving New Zealand which led me to believe that it would be wrong to "string you along." It just seemed so impossible that we could ever get together again; and that I ought to free you to re-start your own life after Duncan's death. So I didn't write. And I am sorry!

But the other night while having dinner with my boss and his wife, she made me see things differently. She pricked my conscience. I have felt since that conversation the need to write you. If possible to make amends!

Tears came to Bronwyn's eyes, so much so that it was difficult to read. She thought, Oh Max, it is just like you to think that way. But, you didn't know how much I wanted to hear from you! After wiping her eyes she read on:

My life has been more or less routine until this past week when some union troubles erupted at the Vermillian

job site. That's the outfit which has bought up land surrounding Fairhavens. They are putting in a "disneyland-
type" theme-park resort. And then at that same dinner with
the boss I referred to, he shared with me the devastating
news that most likely the board will sell Fairhavens because
of the intrusion of the Vermillian project. This leaves me
completely at a loss to know what I'll do next. Fairhavens
will not continue here or anywhere else, so I've got to make
a big change!

I can hear you saying, "Why not the ministry, Max?"
And my answer is that it still isn't for me. I have had a few
ministerial activities lately, and each time it is a major hurdle
for me. So, I don't know. As I write this I am becoming aware
of how much I would like to be talking with you face to
face. You would be a help to me, Bron. I know.

She paused and said to herself, "And I would like very
much to talk to you about this!"

Now, tell me about yourself? How has it been for you
back at Colac Bay? I mean personally as well as business-
wise! I've wondered about you so much, even though I had
never let you know that. So, if you are willing to, please
write me! And better yet, tell me that you are making plans
to come to the U.S.!
        With my love,
        Max

When Bronwyn finished reading Max's letter she carefully folded
it, smaller than it had been in the envelope, and she tucked it in
her blouse—near her heart! Where it would remain until she found
opportunity to write a proper letter. It would be over a week before she found time to respond to Max. But her reply would have
to be another "thanks—but no thanks." She would need to stay
close to the Inn for whatever changes or developments might fall
into place. Maybe someday, but not now.

CHAPTER 24

Connie Dexter had asked Max to conduct the service in the Mill Creek Community Church. She and Al had attended there a few times. Max had requested that the Mill Creek pastor be involved in the service. He had eagerly agreed and saw to it that a coffee reception would be provided after the committal service in the nearby cemetery.

The time came for the service and a small crowd gathered. In addition to Fairhavens workers and staff there were quite a number of workers from the project as well as a scattering of people from the valley who came to the funeral. The Dexter's hadn't been around long enough to have made a lot of friends and so this gathering of people would be a very real support to Connie. Max had been especially curious to see if Cody Vermillian would attend. He had not come; but a few minutes before the service Max noticed that Anna Vermillian had arrived. She took a seat in the back row.

It was a very sad service because Al had been so young and Connie and the baby were left so alone. In fact there were no other relatives in attendance, an absence which always seems to add to the poignancy of the bereavement. In their place Con and Lee Schneider sat with Connie, almost as surrogate parents.

Al Dexter had been put in Recovery. Finally he had been taken from Recovery to Intensive care. While in I.C.U. the CPR team had been called and he was resuscitated. The doctor at that point had reported his recovery to Mrs. Dexter. However only a few minutes later he had experienced a heart stoppage. The CPR team had been called again; but it had arrived too late to be of any assistance. When Max heard of this sequence of events he remem-bered hearing the calls for the CPR Team to ICU, while he had been with Connie and then again only minutes after he had left Connie. Fortunately he had gotten back to Connie in the waiting room before the hospital chaplain summoned her to the private conference room where he gave her the tragic news of Al's sudden death.

Max purposely kept the service brief, knowing how trying a lengthy service would be for Connie. Only one solo—"In the Garden"—sung by a woman of the Mill Creek congregation. It was during the solo that barely controlled weeping was to be heard throughout the little congregation.

After the interment in the Mill Creek Cemetery and the brief and somewhat awkward reception in the church basement, Max returned to Fairhavens feeling unusually distraught. When Conrad returned to his office after he and Lee had taken Connie and the baby home, Max stopped in to ask him for some time off. The funeral service for Al Dexter had been extremely difficult for Max. He didn't quite know why. He needed some time away.

The next morning he took off up to his "Colac Bay" retreat. He relaxed in his chair on the north-facing porch with sun in back of him and let himself drift into reverie.

Soon he was on Colac Bay facing south to the sea with the sun at his back. Bronwyn would be in the take-away nearby; and soon she would share morning tea with him. He needed to tell Bronwyn how he had felt while conducting the service for Al Dexter. Emotions were running high. Max had felt overwhelmed by what had been required of him. Facing Mrs. Dexter and the assembled congregation, he had imagined everyone's high and unrealistic expectation that he would somehow make it all right again by what he could say. He couldn't do that. No one could. He had felt so alone when he stood before the mourners. Had it not been for the Mill Creek pastor, he might not have made it. He had felt faint as he looked out over the congregation. Never since leaving Tipton had he been so fully immersed in the terrifying roll of pastor. In his brooding reverie, he felt the unnerving fear all over again as he walked himself through the funeral experience.

"Oh, dear Bronwyn," he said out loud. "If only you'd been with me. I needed your encouragement." Those were his only words, but he turned them over and over again in his mind and heart until he felt that he almost heard her voice, "I'll be with you again someday, Max Ritter!"

In the Lodge later that day he received a phone call, a woman's voice: "Pastor Ritter, this is Anna Vermillian, I need to see you."

"Some problem for you here at Fairhavens?"

"No, what I need is some pastoral counseling. Do you do that?"

"Really not, but I guess I'd be willing to have you meet me here in the Lodge this evening," he offered somewhat reluctantly.

In a small library off the lounge Anna told Max that she was Cody Vermillian's sister. She revealed to Max an account of Cody's alcohol problem. She concluded by saying, "A few days ago I was part of an intervention in which my other brother and I, as well as Cody's attorney from Billings, confronted him with the full implications of his problem and his behavior. As a result he has signed himself into the Rimrock Foundation in Billings for de-tox treatment and extended counseling. Yesterday his therapist met with me and told me that Cody ought not return to a life and work in which he is his own boss. When he is ready for release he needs to be employed under the constant supervision of a boss. In other words he can't be involved in this Emigrant project from here on. I need some help as I try to figure out what to do."

When Max heard this he immediately realized the precarious position this subject was putting him into. As an integral part of Fairhavens Max had an interest in seeing the collapse of the Vermillian project. Now as a pastoral counselor Anna Vermillian could very well be seeking his guidance regarding that project and its tenuous future. Max knew that he would soon need to divest himself of this counseling roll. However, he couldn't help but ask her to tell him more: "How are you involved in the project at this point?"

"The capital Cody is using is Vermillian family money. Our brother, Bennet, who accompanied me on the intervention, is a banker in Fresno. His bank is handling the family estate. Decisions are made jointly by Bennet, myself and Cody. In fact the reason I came here in the first place was out of family concern that Cody had fallen off the wagon; and that, we felt, would put the project in serious jeopardy."

"I see. What options have you and Bennet considered, now that Cody will need to be out of the picture."

"That's my problem. Bennet wants me to stay on and fill Cody's shoes."

Considering this for a moment Max asked further, "Is that something you feel you can, or want to do?"

"I thought so. But something about the funeral for Mr. Dexter has disturbed me very deeply. It makes me reluctant to take over the project."

"How was that? What was it about the funeral?"

"I don't really know. I guess it sort of brought me down to earth. I hadn't admitted it, but I felt there was something not right about this project. Most of it is Cody's brain-child. Being involved in forcing Cody to hit bottom; learning that an innocent man was shot and killed as a result of this project; and then something about Fairhavens. All this came together as I sat in that little church. I have to admit that I don't believe in the project anymore, as I did, when Cody was here doing it and talking the rest of us into it; and I was far removed from it in California."

This was getting too close for comfort for Max. "Ms Vermillian, I must tell you where I am in all this and why I can't let you go on."

"I don't know what you are saying," Anna asked, seeming disturbed by Max's response.

"What I'm saying is that it would be grossly unfair of me to pretend to be an objective listener, let alone your counselor—when my strong loyalties lie with Fairhavens. The fact is that most of us at Fairhavens have been upset by the Vermillian project. For me to advise you in any way would be a conflict of interest. I don't know whether or not you are aware, but in the beginning stages Fairhavens tried to stop your project."

"No, I really hadn't known anything about that. But if you see this as a conflict of interest, I guess I shouldn't press you any further with my problems," she said without any ill will toward Max, "I'm still left with my quandary, but what you say about Fairhavens' view of the project adds to my problem. I'll have to do some more thinking."

"I'm sure that's so," Max added, "and I'm glad you see the bind I would be in if I tried to counsel you. Meanwhile it is good to have you here as a guest. If there is anything I can do in that regard, please let me know."

Thus the counseling session was aborted. Anna left the library to go out onto the porch where she would sit a while, before retiring to her room for the night.

Needing some time alone after his session with Anna Vermillian, Max walked out into the night air. Away from the Lodge under the star-lit sky. He found a place where he could rest back upon a mound of earth and take in the grandeur of the dome of stars. He really didn't know much about the stars, except to identify the Big Dipper and Orion. He also knew that he would not see the Southern Cross!

Somewhere beyond the southern horizon would be the Southern Cross and under it the one person he truly loved! Would he ever see Bronwyn again? Or would circumstances keep them apart forever? Since leaving New Zealand the second time they hadn't written each other. He had not been entirely sure why not. Instead there had been the fleeting times of mysterious dream-like communication as he had experienced earlier in the day. It was only at such times that Max felt whole and complete! The rest of the time there was a nagging loneliness in his life

As he peered into the sparkling dome he tracked the tiny light of a satellite as it streaked from north to south across the sky. When it disappeared he wondered if perhaps in the next few moments Bronwyn would see it in her sky."No," he thought, "It's daylight where she is—afternoon tomorrow. But if I were to come out here at a time when it is still dark, and dark in New Zealand as well! Maybe one of these nights I'll do that!"

Max returned to his cabin, strangely warmed by the thought of seeing the same moving light as Bronwyn only a few minutes apart! "'tis a good omen, Max Ritter" she seemed to say! Who knows? he thought. The least I can do is to write Bronwyn." That night Max wrote Bronwyn, after having been so strangely silent since returning from New Zealand.

It was Conrad Schneider's custom to post announcements of the time and place of his next Fairhavens Orientation meeting. These were opportunities to introduce new guests to Fairhavens, its philosophy and what it had to offer both in the area of recreation and in the field of renewal therapy. Anyone was welcome to attend these.

A few days after her consultation with Max, Anna Vermillian took advantage of the open invitation to orientation and attended Dr. Schneider's presentation. His talks were not "canned" presentations, but always had a freshness to them borne out of whatever was going on in Paradise Valley and Fairhavens at the time.

During the orientation which Anna attended Conrad commented at length on the effect of the Vermillian development: "At the very core of the Fairhavens concept," she heard him say, "are the values of primal quiet in a natural setting, and isolation from all that is artificial and stressful in modern urban life. Currently both of these values are being seriously threatened. Those of you who have been around a week or so, will know what I mean when I allude to the fact that our quiet is being disturbed. The number of vehicles traveling past our front door has reached unacceptable levels. It is more difficult to experience isolation as more and more of the countryside nearby is being torn up for the purposes of a developer and those whose capital he is using. Our isolation is in jeopardy."

The next morning at breakfast Con came up to Max, "Before

you get involved in your work this morning I'd like for you to join me in my office. Anna Vermillian has asked to see us."

"When's that?"

"At nine,"

Max joined Con in his office at nine. Without acknowledging her consultation with Max, Anna Vermillian began: "Circumstances have changed dramatically in connection with the project my brother, Cody, has been directing. Because of an illness his doctors have made him remove himself from the project."

Con indicated surprise and started to say, "I'm sorry . . ." and then he changed the direction of his response to say, "I'm sorry your brother is ill, I mean."

"Thank you for your concern, Dr. Schneider." She continued, "At the urging of our older brother, Bennet, in Fresno, I will re-place Cody, at least for now." She hurried on, not wanting any courteous reaction to this news. "The reason I am telling you all this is that I have decided to change the direction of this project. And this change will involve Fairhavens."

"Oh?" responded Con. "How is that?"

"I am aware of some of the conflict in values between our plans and the Fairhavens philosophy. That concerns me. I'd like to see how we can lessen the potential conflict."

Max felt the need to join in the conversation. "What do you have in mind, Ms Vermillian?"

"I'm not prepared to say;" and turning to Conrad Schneider she continued, " but what I would like, is for your people and ours to meet to discuss the matter. Bennet is willing to fly in for such a meeting and both our attorney and our architect from Billings are ready to come over."

Max sensed in this request a significant break-through. Con responded enthusiastically, "Our next regularly scheduled Board meeting is a week from Saturday. That would be a time when most of our folk would be on hand anyway."

Anna considered this, looked into her date-book and said, "I think that would work out well for us."

"Then, let me issue you and your group an invitation to attend our next Fairhavens Board meeting. In fact I'll draft a letter to that effect which you can share with those whom you want to attend."

"Thank you, Dr. Schneider. I really think that it will be to our mutual advantage to meet. I'll be eager for the meeting."

After Anna left the office Con turned to Max and said, "I believe you should come to the next board meeting. I think you can be helpful as the two groups come together."

Max accepted the invitation.

Soon the day of the joint meeting arrived. The Fairhavens conference room is located in a building behind the Lodge and is more than adequate for the joint meeting of the Board and the Vermillian group. All of the Fairhavens board had arrived. Anna and her brother, Bennet, were joined by Todd Brown, the project architect, and Worth Benson, their attorney. After an hour and a half of general discussion of the Vermillian project and of the Fairhavens mission the two groups met separately for the balance of the morning. After a luncheon served by the Dining Room staff they re-joined. It was at this time that Bennet Vermillian gave the report which would put the two groups on a cooperative course in the coming months:

"The Vermillian group has re-examined its Paradise Resort development in the light of changes in our structure and personnel. In consideration of what we have come to know as the Fairhavens philosophy, we believe that it will be to our mutual benefit for us to integrate our project with the existing Fairhavens program as best as we can without jeopardizing the overall economic feasibility of the Paradise Resort. Therefore we have decided to limit our development in two significant ways. First, we have decided to abandon the historic mining town and casino phase of our project." Bennet declared somewhat pompously.

There was a noticeable hush in the room when this announcement was made.

"And second, we plan to re-design our overall site plan to

include a quarter-mile green space around seventy per cent of its perimeter. Specifically, we will include in our site plan this green belt on the north and east boundaries of the Fairhaven property. In this way we believe that we will be contributing to the preservation of the isolation factor which we understand is very important to the Fairhavens program. And, of course, we shall grant access to our lands so that your people may enter the National Forest conveniently."

Again the hushed awareness in the room was palpable.

"Beyond the green belt on the Paradise Resort site we plan one acre home sites for individual purchase and building. Finally in Emigrant Gulch where the re-constituted mining town was to have been built, we shall plan a small neighborhood street with town lots for individual purchase and development."

Bennet then drew his remarks to a conclusion saying, "In these ways, friends, we hope that the Paradise Resort will be a good neighbor to Fairhavens and that in time we will merit your respect. Thank you."

The applause from the Fairhavens board was instant and enthusiastic.

As the applause subsided Max realized that some response was needed and he wondered how Con would appropriately acknowledge the declaration made by Bennet Vermillian. As always, Con Schneider was able to present himself in a dignified manner: "Mr. Vermillian, Ms Vermillian, and associates: You have addressed the two areas which have concerned us most critically. Your proposed resolution of those concerns I believe our board will find most suitable. In fact, I believe the Board will receive your altered plan with deep appreciation! Thank you very much for your willingness to bend in the light of Fairhavens' program."

Once again there was instant applause. This time from both groups.

"Thank you, Dr. Schneider," Bennet replied, "And now, if you will excuse us, we need to attend to some further business today."

With that the Vermillian group got up to leave. The Fairhavens board, members out of courtesy arose, and shook hands with their guests as they retired.

After completing some routine items on the agenda, one of the members asked, "What have we heard from Prudential? Aren't we supposed to meet when we get a firm offer?"

"That's right," said Con.

"Another member said, "It seems to me that what we have heard from the Vermillian group should cancel out any further consideration of selling!"

There was general agreement on this point. There followed a motion: "That the Fairhavens Board communicate to its realtor that the property is now off the market and no sale is contemplated."

The motion was seconded and when the vote was called for, the motion passed almost unanimously. There was one negative vote, however. Clyde Blackwood apparently still favored the sale of the property. But then, the Chamber had been solidly behind the full Vermillian project from the beginning. The Board then adjourned. Blackwood was the first to leave.

Con hurried home to share the news with Lee. Max left for his cabin.

CHAPTER 25

"Yes, Ms MacKenzie, we can draw up a contract by which you retain a fifty-one percent ownership and so that your partner with forty-nine percent accepts full operational responsibilities." Her solicitor stated authoritatively.

"And, what then would be the monetary aspects of such an agreement?" Bronwyn MacKenzie asked.

"At this point we do not have dollar figures. That would be dependent upon the appraisal and, of course, the negotiations with a prospective buyer. However, the contract could be set up so that you are paid at the outset forty-nine percent of the agreed upon price. And then over the months following, you would be entitled to a certain percentage of the profits—not, however forty-nine percent since the buyer would be active in the operation of the business and you would not."

"What percentage would that be?"

"Not very high, considering that you would not be engaged on a day-to-day basis—maybe ten percent. But we'd have to negotiate that with the buyer."

"I see. That's less than I anticipated."

"I doubt if we could get a higher percent." the lawyer replied reluctantly. "Now, what about the buyer? Do you have such a person?"

"At this point, no." Bronwyn was flustered at this question. It made the matter so real! "I met a couple who might be interested, but the trouble is I don't have their name or address. It was just a casual conversation before I even had begun considering this possibility."

"Do you have any way of finding them?"

"All I know is that they operate a bed and breakfast on the Bay of Islands. They told me their names, but I have forgotten them."

"They wouldn't be too difficult to trace, would they?" He said as he began closing up the file he had referred to for his consultation with Bronwyn. "If you will let me know when you have a buyer, Ms Mackenzie, I will be very pleased to meet with you and the buyers to negotiate an agreement; and then to draw up the proper legal instrument." he said conclusively as he rose to show Bronwyn out.

"I will certainly let you know, Mr. Roberts." She replied as she prepared to leave his office.

"And, oh, one more item," Ned Roberts interjected, "I'd advise you to procure a real estate agent."

"Yes, I plan to." Bronwyn said, even though she had not thought of this.

"It would be to your advantage if you put your real estate agent in touch with me so that we can coordinate his arrangements with the contract agreement you desire."

"Yes, I'll be sure to do that."

Considering the engaging of a real estate agent as she drove home was not a pleasant thought at all. As she drove toward the shore line of the bay and turned west, the Inn came into view. She saw an image of a "For Sale" sign in front of it. In that moment she felt a lump in her throat. The Inn was like a child of her own; and to think of selling it, or even making a public notice of such an intention was a sorrowful realization for her. How could she ever do that? Her life and that of Colac Bay Inn seemed always to have been one and the same. Now the idea of letting go—of even a portion of it was too difficult to think about. All this seemed too much to handle alone. If only Max were here, she thought.

She parked her car and walked around to the front and entered the office. Just then a couple drove up and paused in front of the office. The man turned off his engine and after a brief conference with the woman in the passenger seat, he got out and came into the office to arrange for a room. Bronwyn was glad to be diverted from the strenuous thoughts which had been overwhelming her. It was so good to be back at the Inn. She was energized by so simple a task as checking in a tourist couple. How, in all the world could she give up the Inn, she thought.

After a light meal Bronwyn thought of the two letters she had received from the U.S. Before going to bed she wrote a reply to Leona Schneider, but found writing to Max—more than she could deal with just then. At another time, she told herself she would write.

In the days following she busied herself with the responsibilities of inn-keeper, and she was having a good time of it—until she got out the books to tally up the finances. The books had become a chore she dreaded; for the resulting balances were never good. But, somehow, she was still managing to squeak by. For how long? She was afraid to guess.

Once again Bronwyn's days had become routine. Up at six in order to have a good pot of porridge ready for early risers; and to prepare scones for morning tea. Some of the smaller tour buses frequently stopped to have a look at the bay, and to allow passengers to stop for tea. Of course there was the usual cleaning of the units and general maintenance around the grounds. In the evening she spent an hour or so in the take-away lounge offering casual conversation with any of the guests who cared for a chat before turning in. It was usually ten o'clock before she could safely curl up with a book in her own house.

Her continuing love for some of the Victorian novels led he to search out others of this genre in the public library in Invercargill. But she frequently returned to *Jane Eyre*. She identified with Jane's long and sad period of separation from Rochester. She was experiencing in her long distance relationship with Max some of the same feelings—longings of the heart, she thought. However, it would be days before she came to a decision as to what she would write to Max.

One evening Bronwyn felt constrained to walk out onto what she had come to call "Max's Point," the spot on the rocky cliff overlooking the sea which he so regularly occupied. There was only a crescent moon in a cloudless dark and star-filled sky as she picked her way along the pathway, a track which she knew so well. The comfortable lapping of the waves became louder and louder as she reached the spot. She settled into the natural rock seat Max had used. She let her consciousness slow down to a quiet calm. There was only a slight breeze coming from the lapping of the silvery black ocean as it rolled successively into the rocky shoreline wave by wave. She leaned back on the earthen breast behind the rock, letting the dome of stars provide her cover. She wished she had learned the stars as she picked out various configurations. But she did know the Southern Cross, which she identified in this night's sky. It was all so still. Whatever motion in the heavens would be so slow as to be imperceptible.

She felt her separation from Max even more poignantly as she pondered: He won't be seeing any of these stars. He is under a completely different sky—in another world—a universe apart! But, she thought, we are both under the heavenly love and protection of the same God! Before leaving this sacred spot she prayed out loud: "Oh God of love, I pray for Max. Together in your providence I feel close to him. I have come to love him so. Guide and protect him this night and in the days to come. Amen!"

After her prayer her eye caught a moving pin-point of light arching over head. It seemed to have come from over the Inn and was now heading out to sea. A satellite, she guessed.

As she crossed the road onto the Inn property she noticed a trickle of water flowing across the pavement and wondered what that was. It had not rained recently, she thought. Checking the take-away she could see nothing amiss, but she heard the pump for the well running, which seemed strange. Perhaps someone is showering—but all the units were dark. She went back outside to see where the trickle was coming from and found it to be bubbling out of the soil near second unit. Not enough to be concerned about tonight, she concluded; and went back to her house and to bed.

She was awakened the next morning at five-thirty with a knock at her door. It was the guest from Unit 2. "Excuse me, Ms MacKenzie, but we have no water this morning."

"Please let me give you some to hold you over until I see what the problem is." She gave him a large plastic water carrier and said, "Use the faucet on the outside of this building and take all you need. I'll be right over to see what I can do to remedy the problem."

She quickly dressed and went over to Unit 2. The trickle which had become a formidable stream of water was now gushing out of the ground. The ground around the unit had become saturated. She could hear the pump straining and went to the pump-house behind Unit 2 to shut off the pump. Fortunately Unit 3 was vacant. Bronwyn, on an intuitive impulse, unlocked number three and when she opened the door found that water had oozed up through the carpet and there was standing water in a number of areas throughout the unit. Built on a concrete slab, apparently the water had formed a lagoon under the cabin.

When the "Willard's Well and Pump" repair truck arrived, the repairman announced immediately, "Ah, yes! Your water line has burst. You will need to shut off your pump first thing! Then I'll have a look"

"I have done that already. The rest is up to you."

As the plumber returned from a survey of the situation he said, "From the smell of things, I would say you're pump was ready to burn itself out; and chances are a totally new line will be needed. I will need to have a backhoe brought in so that we can dig up the line. It looks like about a thirty meter line. But the worst of it is that the line runs under the building—Unit 3. If the break is under the building, our excavation will be difficult at best. And of course that would make the whole job more costly."

"How long will all this take?"

"By evening tomorrow, we should be able to have it all dug out. Another day should be enough time to put in a new pump and line. If you have enough garden hose we can hook it up temporarily to the units, and tap off of your house, if your house is on a separate pump and water supply."

"Yes it is; please do that for me, would you?" she replied, concluding that the matter was at least temporarily cared for. But, Bronwyn worried about the cost. Since returning from the hospital and Wanaka the finances had been breaking even—or almost. A major repair would require further indebtedness. But her banker had been unwilling to work with her any further.

Perhaps the time has come, she wondered hesitantly, to use Mum's nest-egg. Her mother had left her a small sum which she had wanted Bronwyn to save as a wedding gift, a hope-chest, she had called it. With Duncan gone it went un-used; but from time to time lately she had fantasized a wedding with Max as the bridegroom. Nothing very certain had ever been said; but there had been something in the air when they said their good byes at the air terminal. As Bronwyn thought about her hope-chest she felt that to use any of it would be to admit that there never would be a wedding for her, at least to Max. And to think of any other—was impossible. But if she could sell her half interest, then Mum's money could be kept inviolate!

Three days later the Willard's man came to the take-away and presented the bill, saying, "Everything is tight and running, now. As you could tell, we had to excavate under Unit 3; and in cases like this it is necessary to install a new holding tank in addition to the new pump and line. Those are the reasons the total is as large as you see it

Bronwyn took the statement and looking first at the total, she had to catch her breath—$5,782! Not wanting to respond, she took her time reading the itemized listing of costs and charges. Finally, she looked up and asked, "When is this due?"

"Thirty days, Ms McKenzie."

"Thank you for you assistance. I'll be sending a check." Clearly this was a higher figure than she had anticipated. More than Mum's hope chest, she said to herself sadly. And on top of that, she thought, there will be considerable expense to replace the carpet and to clean up Unit 3. She thought about letting number three remain vacant, but she could not afford to reduce any further her income potential. Reluctantly she concluded that selling was the only option remaining. If she could find a buyer willing to agree to her 49% contract proposal.

Bronwyn chose a real estate agent willing to take on her proposed agreement; and one who was able to do some sleuthing to look for the Pahia couple. She was assured of this when she rang her up a week after she had engaged Barbara Frances as agent for the Inn sale: "Ms MacKenzie! I have a wee bit of news."

"Oh, do you now?"

"Yes. I have found the couple with whom you spoke at Wanaka. They are Stanley and Virginia Porter. They have the Sea View Court B. & B. in Pahia."

"Ah yes! those are the names I had forgotten! Did they show interest?" Bronwyn asked hopefully.

"I couldn't determine that, because they were just about out their door on a holiday trip to Australia. But they promised to talk with me upon their return."

"How soon would that be? I'm quite up against a time urgency. I have major bills due in thirty days."

"They said they'd be over there a fortnight."

"That will be close, and then if they don't accept the offer, I'm in real trouble." Then she added this request to her agent: "Please do all you can to solicit interest in this property in the meantime. Perhaps there is a buyer nearby!"

"I'll certainly do that, Ms MacKenzie. You will be hearing from me."

However, in the coming days Bronwyn did not hear from her agent until Porters returned from their holiday in Australia. On their return they had contacted Barbara Frances immediately. The agent brought them down to see the Inn. As a result of this investigation the Porters indicated their interest to the real estate agent. Subsequently they signed the agreement as prepared by Bronwyn's lawyer. Thus, Bronwyn became a silent partner in the Inn. For all practical purposes she would soon be out of work!

The night on which the deal was closed Bronwyn returned to the take-away counter in the Inn at Colac Bay feeling depressed when she should have been elated. When Barbara Frances had handed over the check for the 49 % equity in the Inn she said flippantly, "Now you can take a trip to Disneyland!" The Porters grinned and Bronwyn had laughed dutifully, even though she felt anything but gaiety.

Porters had left for the Bay of Islands to tie up their business in Pahia, having sold the Sea View a few weeks earlier. They would be back the first of the month to take over the management of the Colac Bay Inn. They had leased a house near the Inn. Bronwyn was retaining ownership of her house. In five days time the changeover would be effected and she would be free of the day-to-day management—and the worries. This should be reason enough for celebration. But it was having the opposite effect. She would be losing her reason for being, it seemed. What should she do with her life now? And even more pressing was the question of what kind of employment she should take in order to survive. The percent of profit from the Inn would be minimal, if at all during the first months, perhaps for a year or more. She would need work. It would be fool-hardy to cut into the lump-sum payment she had been handed. That needed to be invested safely and immediately. An image of her father had loomed in her mind as she had held the check. This was his money from his family inheritance. It was sacred; and Bronwyn must use it in a way which carried on her father's legacy.

At 9:30 in the evening she closed up. It was already fully dark outside. She walked out to the Point of Rocks—Max's rock, to think, and to meditate—to share this day with Max in the secret chambers of her imagination. It was another clear night with the starlit dome ablaze. She leaned back in time to see the satellite orbit southward across the Pacific sky. She thought about the day, the signing of the contract in the solicitor's office; the two strangers who had appeared in her life to take from her the Inn; and the bubbling talk from Barbara Frances. "Disneyland!" she thought. How ridiculous. She had never had the least interest in going there. There were families in the church in Riverton who had gone with their children and had come back with enthusiastic accounts; but Bronwyn had not been tempted. Besides, that money was not hers to spend. it would be father's, if he were living. Another moving point of light arched across the heavenly dome, this time from south to north. In a few moments it would be streaking over Disneyland, or perhaps over Montana, over Fairhavens, over the place where Max would be! In the silence of the night the lapping of the sea, she felt she could hear a distant voice: "That light in the sky could be a flight bringing you here, Bronwyn MacKenzie! Everyday there are people coming here from New Zealand—it could be you, dear Bronwyn! You have the time now—and the funds!"—And then she heard only the lapping of the sea washing against the rocks beneath her.

The day came for the shift in the management of the Colac Bay Inn. After the Porters had arrived Bronwyn worked with them a few days to show them the ropes. The next morning, instead of going over to the Inn, as she had done for so long, she fixed break-fast for herself at home. Then she wondered what to do next. The days ahead would be critical for Bronwyn. Losing her direct in-volvement with the Inn, she would need something else to lend meaning to her lonely life.

She decided for the time being to accept a full-time job offer at the pauah shell factory in Riverton. She adopted a new work-a-day life-style driving into town early each day and returning to her home in the evenings. But the zest was missing—and she felt very much alone. Sorting shells all day and returning to an empty house at night would not last forever. She was beginning to feel less and less at home in Colac Bay. It belongs to someone else, she thought.

So it was that when the owners of Balmoral Lodge in Invercargill rang her up one evening not many weeks after she had been on her own, Bronwyn found herself saying that she was interested. "Ms

MacKenzie, might you be interested in working for us here at Balmoral Lodge?" they had inquired.

"What sort of work do you have in mind?"

"We have need of a desk clerk and evening manager five days weekly."

"Ah yes, I see. What would the hours be for such a post?" Bronwyn asked with a growing interest in such a possibility.

"We operate with three shifts in a twenty-four hour day. Evening manager is from four o'clock until mid-night, when a night manager takes over until eight in the morning. I am in hopes of your interest, for we are aware of your many years of experience with the Inn on Colac Bay."

"Yes, your offer does sound interesting to me. Where is Balmoral Lodge located? I think I would like to see it before committing myself.'

"Oh yes, of course. We are located at 265 Tay Street, just a bit east of Mary Street. A good location. We are on Highway 1 from Dunedin. And we certainly do want you to see Balmoral!"

Browyn took the job, leased a tiny house on Melbourne street between the Lodge and Queens Park, and moved from Colac Bay for the first time in her life. She would not return. Her vital connection with the Inn had been severed; and now she would no longer be living in her family home. A new life was developing, the first phase of which was to be in Invercargill.

While the work was much the same as what she had done formerly, her new location and life-style were very different. Most of her routine activities she could do on foot, only using her Toyota for an occasional drive on a day off from the lodge. During her mornings and early afternoons there was Queens Park with its Museum which afforded many hours of pleasant relaxation when her tiny house proved too confining. But always she was alone.

First Presbyterian Church was nearby, only three blocks on Tay Street toward the downtown area. Even at church she felt very much alone. It had been difficult to leave the close fellowship of the Riverton church for the unfamiliarity of the larger church in

Invercargill. However, her loneliness was soon to end, at least temporarily.

One Sunday morning during worship she was surprised to see a face in the choir which she vaguely recognized. She couldn't help but fix her eyes upon a man about her age in the back row of the choir. His blond hair and cheerful face reminded her of someone from former times in her life. Try as she might, she could not come up with a name or a connection. Throughout the following week her thoughts kept returning to the familiar but mysterious face.

The next Sunday before worship as she was walking toward the front door of the sanctuary, she fell in step with the man she'd thought she knew. He had left his car at the curb and was entering the building when she turned and caught his eye and was bold to ask:

"Forgive me for being so forward but, you look so familiar to me, but I just cannot place you! My name is Bronwyn MacKenzie. Do I know you?"

He stopped to listen to her question and looking at her at first with a blank expression. Then suddenly recognition dawned upon him and he replied: "Bronwyn MacKenzie! It's been years!"

"Yes, I guess so, but I still don't know who you are, or what the connection was."

"Sam Stewart! Remember? We were in first and second form together in Mrs. McCullough's room in the Riverton school!"

"Sam! Surely! Now it all comes back. We sat next to each other; and you often teased my friends and me in the school yard."

"That was me! We've got to catch up, Bronwyn. But I must hurry in to choir now. How about meeting me out here after church. Perhaps we can go somewhere for a cuppa and renew acquaintances. Would you like that?"

"Yes, Sam, I would. I'll wait for you." Bronwyn replied eagerly.

During worship Bronwyn's mind kept wandering. Little did she know what might develop from this chance recognition.

CHAPTER 26

As Bronwyn would later recall, she had barley been able to pay attention to what was going on in the service—excepting the choir's singing, so eager had she to talk further with Sam Stewart.

After the service they met outside the church building. Sam said,

"I know of a little place we can go for a cuppa. Do you have time?"

"Yes, let's"

When they found a table in a small café on Spey Street Sam began, "Tell me about yourself. Where have you been? What do you do here in the city?"

"Until a month or so ago I still lived in Colac Bay—"

"Where you lived as a child was it?" He interjected.

"Yes, the very same house. After my parents died I took over the Colac Bay Inn which they had owned and managed. Just recently I sold part interest in the Inn to a couple who manage it now. So I moved into town and I'm evening manager at the Balmoral Lodge just east of here on Tay Street."

"I know it well. I live in Glengarry near Surrey Park and so I pass the Balmoral regularly."

"What about you, Sam?" Bronwyn asked genuinely wanting to know more about him.

"I am an engineer at the Tiwai Point Aluminium smelter just east of here. I have been employed there ever since university. I have lived on Adamson Crescent for a number of years now. Church is about my only activity other than work. Except I have gone up to Winton now and again to sing with the Ionians. What do you do besides work?"

For Bronwyn this was an embarrassing question, because, she thought of how she really didn't do anything. "Just having shifted to Invercargill I haven't gotten into any activities yet." She wanted to know more about Sam's family but didn't know how to broach the subject. She noticed what looked like a wedding ring, but there seemed to be no evidence of a wife or children.

Sam was a bit more forthright in this regard. "You seem to be alone. Are you married? And do you have children?"

"No to both questions. But it is better to give you a more full answer. I was engaged to be married, but my fiancé fell ill and died before we had the chance to be married."

"Oh, I am sorry."

"You are married then?"

"My story is somewhat like yours. I was married to an Air New Zealand flight attendant. She was away so much of the time. We began to drift apart; and then she divorced me for an Australian she met on a flight from Sydney."

"Oh, how sad! I can't imagine what that must have been for you, Sam."

"Yes, it was a very bad time for me; but that is over now, and I have decided to get back a life again." He looked at his ring finger and added wistfully, "Perhaps it's time to put my ring in my dresser. It gives a misleading signal, doesn't it?"

"Not to someone who is willing to enquire further—as I did!"

They had finished their coffee and it was clearly time to leave. Sam offered to give Bronwyn a ride to her home. When he deposited her at her door he said, "I hope we will have further opportunity to chat."

Bronwyn replied cautiously, "I think that would be fine. Thank you for the coffee and the ride home, Sam."

"Quite all right. I'll look forward to seeing you next week in the congregation."

"Yes, I will be there."

That afternoon Bronwyn walked in the park and thought about what Sam had said about deciding "to get back a life again." She realized that she had not made such a decision; and that it was most likely time for her to do that as well. She had mourned Duncan long enough, she judged; Max was so far away; and the chance of seeing him again seemed minimal at best. What was the old proverb—"A bird in the hand is worth two in the bush" or something like that. At least for the moment her life need not be so lonely, she thought.

She didn't have to wait for the following Sunday. Wednesday evening Sam phoned, "Oh, Ms MacKenzie, might I take you to tea sometime?"

"That would be fine. But I work evenings. This just happened to be a night off for me. You work days, I assume. "

"Yes, that's correct. Not on Saturdays, however. We might take lunch somewhere on Saturday. What do you say?

"If I can work a switch in schedule, perhaps I can get a Saturday off. I'll let you know Sunday when I can be free." When Bronwyn worked out her schedule for the Saturday after next she was able to arrange for her regular evening off to come on Saturdays.

Thus they found themselves together almost every Saturday and enjoying each other's company increasingly. In addition they frequently spent part of Sunday afternoons in one of the parks or on drives in the countryside around Invercargill. Sometimes they took drives out of town They especially enjoyed trips up into the Catlins, a wooded area near the sea, north-east of Invercargill.

As their friendship deepened Bronwyn felt fearful that Sam might soon become serious and possibly even suggest marriage. She could not bring herself to think in such terms, even though she found their time together to be the high point of her new life. She tried to keep things light. However, he was such a relief to her loneliness that she could at times feel herself falling!

For some reason unknown to Bronwyn she had not wanted to go back to Colac Bay with Sam. As one of their holiday jaunts approached Sam phoned her:

"I have been thinking lately that we have not gone back to Riverton or Colac Bay, even though that's where we first knew each other. I propose that Saturday we pack a lunch and drive over that way. We can have a look at the old school. I'll show you the house we lived in when I was a child; and then we could go to Colac Bay; and if the weather is fine, we can eat our lunch somewhere at the seaside. You must know a good spot?"

This caught Browyn so by surprise that she could say nothing but,

"Yes, I suppose that would be nice."

They both thought the school looked the same as it did when they were pupils there. Sam then said as they drove away from the school yard, "Now we must see Colac Bay. I want to have a look at the Inn."

A feeling of fear swept through Bronwyn's consciousness as they approached the old familiar places. She couldn't place the origin of the feeling, but it made her pensive as they drove by the Inn. She noticed especially that Max's chair was still outside "his unit!"

"Do you want to stop in?" Sam asked.

"No, I'd rather not just now."

"Then let's find a spot by the sea for out lunch."

She led them to a place along the sea shore, taking care to stay away from Point of Rocks. She found a large flat rock which served as a table and they laid out their lunch.

After packing up the lunch things Sam suggested a walk. In the course of their walk along the rocks overlooking the ocean, they passed "Max's" spot. Bronwyn caught her breath and became quite silent as they walked along.

"Is something bothering you, Bronwyn?"

"Oh no! Why do you ask?"

"You seem so quiet and pensive."

"I'm sorry." She replied; and she began to force herself to make conversation.

Soon they came to a convenient place to sit, and after settling down Sam spoke with a degree of nervousness in his voice:

"Brownyn, we have had many good times together. We really have come to know each other quite well, I think . . ."

Brownyn looked startled as she heard Sam moving into a level of conversation quite new to them. She had a premonition of what was to come. Her level of anxiety rose as he continued.

". . . We both live alone and are, I believe, lonely. I know I am. What I am trying to say is—Will you marry me?"

Suddenly Bronwyn's thoughts were colliding and her feelings were in a state of panic. Ever since driving past the Inn her mind had been occupied with thoughts of Max. These thoughts had intensified out on the rocks where he had so often sat. And now Sam had exploded his bomb shell. How was she to answer."A bird in the hand . . .?"

Breaking the silence Sam interjected, "I know this has been sudden, a shock, perhaps, but . . ."

"Sam," Bronwyn broke in, "I just don't know what to say. This is a surprise to me, to say the least."

"Yes, I realize that now. I've been thinking about this for some-time, and I guess I forgot that you may not have been thinking in these terms as I have. But, Bronwyn, I love you, and I want us to belong to each other permanently!"

This brought tears to her eyes as she saw the depth of his feeling and the total honesty with which he spoke.

"I need time to sort this out." she said in a way that was pleading.

"Take some time. Pray about this. I've been praying. Let's talk some more about this—soon when we have another day like this, can we?"

"Yes."

With that they got up and returned to Sam's car.

As they drove back to Invercargill they talked of other things. But Bronwyn's mind could not get past the thoughts and questions which Sam had invoked. She couldn't wait to be alone and to lay all this out and to begin to sort through the muddle.

When Sam dropped Bronwyn off at her house, he asked: "When have you another day off. I'll arrange to take that off too, if you let me know."

"I'm not sure. I'll have to let you know Sunday."

As it turned out they did not see each other on the next Sunday. That was intentional on Bronwyn's part. She needed more time to think and so decided to find another church in which to worship the next week. She needed space. Time and space! To get away and to think. Early Sunday morning she drove northward out of the city to look for a church. Driving through Winton she thought it a bit too early for services, so she drove north beyond Winton and then west across the Oreti River. She turned left and driving south-west she came to a small crossroads parish church. Oreti was its name. Cars were on the grass outside the building and people were entering. She pulled her Toyota onto the grass and went in for the service.

After she settled into a pew toward the back, the minister and one of the elders emerged from the vestry, each taking a seat. The organist, playing a prelude on a reed pump organ, stopped. Bronwyn was startled when the minister began to speak. He sounded so much like Max. There was something about his appearance and manner which also "was Max" to her. It was obvious to her that he was an American, probably he was serving temporarily in this parish. Not an infrequent arrangement in Southland parishes. At the conclusion of the service Bronwyn was warmly welcomed by the regular worshipers. When the minister greeted her she asked him,"Where are you from, may I ask?"

"From the U.S.A.—Missouri."

"What seminary?"

"McCormick. Why do you ask?"

"I knew an American minister from McCormick. He was a tourist at the motel I managed on the coast."

"That's interesting. What was his name?"

"Max Ritter.

"I knew him! He was in my class. But I had lost track of him. Where was he from?" he asked.

"Montana." Bronwyn replied.

"That's quite a coincidence!" the minister responded.

There were others behind Bronwyn waiting to greet the minister; and so she hurried out and then rather quickly went to her car and drove off. Later on she checked the bulletin for the service to see if the minister was identified. Fortunately his name was printed on it—Peter Conner. She would be able to tell Max.

As she drove down the road toward the town of Drummond, she felt strangely moved. Twice in the last few days she had been very near Max. Once when she and Sam had been out at "Max's Point" and now when Peter Conner had led the service and spoken to her. All the more need to sort things out.

She thought about the many happy trips with Sam. He had been so considerate of her, and they had genuinely enjoyed each other's company. He represented security—a good paying job—a fine house—stability, security, no more financial problems. She wouldn't be forced to work, though she could if she wanted to. A "yes" to Sam would mean all that, and more. Yet something seemed to be missing. Difficult to identify, though.

Max—not much security. He was still trying to find himself vocationally. Choosing Max would mean a shift to the U.S. most likely. She would miss her home and her country. He would be the only person she would know at first. Then, suddenly she caught herself and said out loud, "And he hasn't even asked me to marry him! What am I doing thinking this way!" But, if she went to Sam, chances are she'd never see Max again.

Bronwyn's thought process became circular as these ideas seemed to revolve in her mind. The more she thought the less sure she was of anything. Her pondering was interrupted by hunger pangs as she returned to Invercargill by way of Wallacetown on No. 99. When she saw the Pizza Hut she drove into its car park without much thought. When she sat down, she realized she was at the very table she and Max had occupied on their first outing. This became a third experience of nearness to Max. She remembered again his delight as she had brought him here to remind him of the U. S. She thought of their walks in Queen's Park. But she had walked there with Sam as well. Strangely different though.

With Max during those times together she had felt a sort of energizing tingle—physically. But with Sam it wasn't that way—pleasant, though. As she thought more about the contrast, Sam appeared so mature and self-possessed. He seemed older than Max,
although she believed them to be about the same age. There was
something boyish, almost dependent, about Max. Bronwyn felt
more self-confident in Max's company and more the child with
Sam. Such feelings, however, had been comforting during this time
of upheaval in her life. She told herself that she shouldn't be com-
paring the two. That really wasn't fair to either man. The question
was, she reminded herself, "Do I want to marry Sam?" I really
should marry him, she thought.

"A bird in the hand—" She mused further, if Max had ever
really asked me, it might be different now, but he didn't. She left
the restaurant, for it was time to go to work.

It was busy at the lodge for a Sunday evening; and so there was
little time to think about Sam and his question. But it must have
been on her mind, for she slept only fitfully waking up Monday
with an uneasy feeling. She wished the whole thing would go away.

Mail arrived usually around noon. She rarely picked up anything very interesting from her mail box, but on this particular
day there was a letter of interest—great interest! It was from Max.

> Dear Bronwyn,
>
> I haven't heard from you since I last wrote you. I know
> I don't deserve it, since I've been so remiss in writing; but
> just the same I'm concerned to hear from you! I hope that
> you are ok. Things around here have bounced back and
> forth. For a while it looked as though Fairhavens would be
> sold. Now I am fairly certain that it will not. The develop-
> ment project nearby has changed its focus. It's a long story.
> And now it does not pose much of a threat to our program.
> So, I still have a job!
>
> The struggle with the ministry question still goes on. I
> confess to feeling like such a failure, that I can't see myself

ever taking it up again. And yet I feel pulled in that direction every so often. I was asked to conduct a memorial service for the husband of one of our kitchen staff. Hard as it was for me to do that, after it was all over I felt pretty good about it. I just don't know. I wish you were here to help me think this through!

That reminds me. The other night I was outside and the sky was clear. While looking up into the stars a satellite arched overhead coming from the north and heading south. I was fascinated by the realization that not long after I spotted it you would be able to see it! Wouldn't it be fun for us to set a certain night when we'd both see it? How about it? I suggest two weeks from the date of this letter—10 PM your time!

That will be in the middle of the night for me, but I'll gladly get up, knowing that your watching too! Let me know.

I still am anxious to hear how you are doing, Bron!

Please write.

With my love,

Max

P.S. By the way, Fairhavens is looking for a Lodge Manager. How about it, Bronwyn? There's nothing in this world I'd like better than for you to come to Montana and take that position! I'm not kidding! If you tell me you're coming, I'll pull some strings and make sure the job is waiting for you!! Love, Max

The letter stirred up mixed emotions in Bronwyn. She thought about the satellite date and checked her calendar. It was only two days before the satellite date Max had suggested. It would be Saturday. And to think that she too had seen a satellite and thought about its traveling over Max's sky as well as hers.

The day arrived and she saw it from Queens Park. A tiny light moving across the sky. Only minutes before it had been over

Montana! She was overcome with a feeling of Max's closeness, almost as if they were seeing it together. It was a magic moment. As she walked home after seeing the satellite, she felt a warmth in her she'd not experienced before. It was as if Max were walking beside her, holding her hand.

From that time on, her confusion was dispelled. She knew what she would do. The biggest decision of her life! It seemed to her that it was not so much that she was deciding, but that it was being determined for her. By fate or fortune? Or, just maybe, by divine direction from God!

When she returned to her home, she immediately wrote to Lee. She wished she could tell Sam in a letter, but it would be necessary instead to speak to him face to face. That would not be easy. He had been very good to her, loving, in fact. Through no fault of his, she would need to leave him for another!

CHAPTER 27

With Anna Vermillian in charge the development had moved ahead adhering to the limits which her people had been promised. It appeared that the project would present a minimal intrusion upon the Fairhavens program. Now some months after her take-over, building had taken place on a few of the projected home sites. In fact Con and Lee had purchased one of the sites and had built a modest two story residence done in the neo Victorian style which was so much in vogue.

Having recently moved in, they were enjoying, among other features, the new house smell amid the bright rooms with white walls and fresh new oak trim. Lee found this experience exhilarating as she constantly compared her newly built home with her established stately residence in River Forest, the house in which her daughter now lived.

Lee looked forward to visits from her children which would take place in a month. One spring morning as she was busy straightening and dusting she was planning for an open house for the staff the following Sunday evening. But at the moment her concern was to be ready for their first house guest who was due to arrive on the late evening flight. She found herself becoming ever more excited at the anticipation of this event In fact, she couldn't wait.

It was a little after eleven P.M. when Con and Lee turned off the frontage road to enter the terminal area of Gallatin Field. "Not many pick-ups from the late evening flight," Con remarked as he located a parking spot for the Explorer.

"No, it's too bad, I always think, to get in this late and miss the magnificence of the mountains."

"But it makes the next morning all the more spectacular!"

"Well, it's going to be spectacular. I get goose-pimples thinking about it!" Lee said excitedly.

"Yes—it'll be 'awesome' as the kids say these days."

They mounted the rustic stairway inside the terminal building, walking under the metal sculptured Canada geese hanging overhead. They found seats near the passenger exit door at the Delta gate. "Should be here in ten minutes or so." Con said.

"I hope it's on time."

Waiting never had been Conrad's favorite thing! He thought he'd divert their attention be bringing up a subject which had been on his mind. "Lee, do you miss River Forest—and the Chicago area?"

"Not exactly. Mainly because I like it so much here. But there are things . . ."

"Like what?"

"Some of the associations I used to have at church and at the Evanston Home. And, I guess, some of the cultural opportunities around the city."

"I'm not surprised. I remember some of those feelings when I first moved out here. But they've faded. You know, the funny thing is—what I continue to miss are the trees! Elm, Oak, and a lot of the tall trees in that area."

Lee thought for a moment and said, "I guess I do too, but I hadn't thought of that."

Just then the overhead speaker burst forth: "Delta, flight 2099 has just landed and will be arriving at Gate 2 momentarily."

"This is it!" Lee said, squeezing Con's hand.

"How will we recognize each other?"

"We will!" Lee assured him.

The stream of deplaning passengers began coming through the exit door, lugging their carry-ons and some with children in tow. Many of them quickly greeted waiting friends or hugged their loved ones.

"There she is! Lee said, "I just know it."

Bronwyn came through the door and immediately Lee went

up to her and said, "Bronwyn MacKenzie! I'm Lee Schneider." As the two women embraced, both had a faint trace of tears. When they disengaged their arms, Lee said, "And this is my husband, Conrad Schneider."

"Hello, Dr. Schneider. At that Con said, "So very good for you to have come." And he hugged Bronwyn. Then Con broke the silence that followed, "Let's go down stairs and get your baggage."

As they waited at the carousel they exchanged all the usual small talk about the flight and first impressions. There would be more time for getting acquainted—much more time; for Bronwyn was coming not so much for a visit as for an extended stay at Fairhavens.

In the car Lee sat in the back seat with Bronwyn, for the ride of about an hour and a quarter. As Con entered the interstate and headed east all three settled back in pleasant anticipation of what was to come. "Max does not have the slightest inkling," Lee said.

"Not at all?"

"No—not at all. But tomorrow morning at 9 he'll discover our surprise, Bronwyn!" Then Lee told her about the plan. Con would ask Max to come to his office at 9 o'clock, saying that he wanted him involved in a job interview with a person who had applied for the new manager's position. "Then when we are sure they are in the office," Lee went on, "I'll bring you to the office for the 'interview'! And we can only imagine the rest."

"But, you will come into the office with me, won't you, Lee?"

"If you want me to," Lee answered, having hoped that she could be on hand for the surprise of a lifetime for Max.

"Oh—I want you to. I'll be nervous, won't I though! And to have you with me will be a good thing, Lee."

They fell silent as they both thought about this—Lee with relish; Bronwyn with anxious anticipation—butterflies, in fact.

It was after 1 A.M. when Con pulled into the driveway of their new home, located east of the Lodge beyond the green-belt. He put down Bronwyn'w bags and looked at his watch when they entered the entry hall at the foot of the stairway leading to the three bedrooms. "Let's make that job interview at 10:30. Can you wait, Bronwyn?"

"Not really—but yes, after all this time. Better to be rested, wouldn't it be?" Bronwyn replied.

"Yes, I think so," Lee said, and then she announced, "You and I will have breakfast at 8:30. Con will need to be at the office at 8, so he can fend for himself, can't you, Con?"

"Yes, dear! And now, let's all get to bed."

The next morning after breakfast Bronwyn came downstairs dressed in a new mid-calf full blue denim skirt and a new pink sweat shirt with a small kiwi bird embroidered toward the top at the left. "This is the sort of outfit I had on when Max first saw me," she offered.

"How romantic!" Lee said as she stepped back to have a good look.

Bronwyn's light brown hair fell loosely to her shoulders. Wearing no make-up, she looked the picture of youthful freshness. Ready to be re-united with the one she truly loved. Lee took an almost motherly pride in what she saw.

About 10:15 they got in the car and drove toward the Lodge. When it came into full view, Lee turned to Bronwyn and said, "Welcome, Bronwyn MacKenzie, to a place called Fairhavens!" It was an emotional moment for both of them.

"Indeed, Lee, I am here at last."

At that moment Max was sitting in Con's office with his back to the door facing Con at his desk. They were discussing business matters. It was not unusual for the two men to have things to work out together in the course of a week's activity. A little unusual to be in on a job interview, Max thought. But that had been Con's wish.

Max was telling about a repair problem when the phone rang: "Hello, Dr. Schneider, speaking."

Max could hear the voice of the desk clerk: "Dr. Schneider, your wife is here with your job applicant."

"Send them in."

Max continued his description of the problem he had brought up when the door opened and Max saw Lee coming into the office. He could see out of the corner of his eye that she had another woman with her. He turned fully around to greet Lee. And at that he saw Bronwyn!

"BRONWYN MACKENZIE!"

"MAX RITTER!"

Their warm embrace was seemingly without end. And when it ended they were both in tears. And so was Lee. Con, somehow, was embarrassed, but most pleased. "Max," he announced, "meet the new manager of Fairhavens!"

Max could hardly believe his eyes, and now what he heard Conrad say surprised him even further: "What! You mean that Bronwyn is the new manager?"

"Yes, Max. That is exactly what I mean."

Max turned to Bronwyn.

"Yes, Max. Don't you remember telling me about the job and how you thought I might take it."

"Oh—! In the P.S. I wrote."

"You started me thinking; and with the sale of part interest in the Inn, I was able to come. And Lee had suggested my coming and surprising you. And that's what we planned!"

"And now you are here, Bron—as I had always hoped."

At that, Con said, "Why don't you two stay here in the office for a while. Lee and I have an errand in Livingston we need to attend to."

After the Schneider's left Max and Bronwyn fell into non-stop talk as they brought each other up to date; and as they began to think ahead to their delightful prospect of working together—

"At a place called Fairhavens," Bronwyn proclaimed.

"Yes, Bronwyn, at a place called Fairhavens!" Max intoned,

Bronwyn took a room in the Lodge before deciding where she wanted to live. She easily worked into her new job as manager, for it was much like a combination of her work at Balmoral Lodge and at Colac Bay.

The open house which Lee had planned came a few days after Bronwyn's arrival and provided an excellent opportunity to introduce her to the rest of the staff in a relaxed and celebrative atmosphere. Max was delighted to observe the easy way she had with the others. Even the therapists seemed to enjoy her company. Maybe it's her accent, Max quipped to himself.

As the days sped by she and Max spent most of their off hours together, eating their meals together in the Dining Room and relaxing often at Max's cabin. The intensity of the their happiness in one another's company soared and their love for each other deepened as the weeks flew by. No thought of the future entered their minds as they savored each moment of each day they were together.

Con suggested that when her work slacked off a bit, she should take some time to go with Max around the entire Fairhavens property and to see the surrounding areas. Max was eager to share "his turf" with Bronwyn and they spent the better part of a day doing just that. He was especially eager to bring her to his "Colac Bay Inn" beyond the northern fence line. Fortunately, the day was cloudy when they crossed the fence and mounted the rise from which Bronwyn would view the deserted building. "There is a very special place I want you to see, Bron. When you see it you'll know why." When they got to the crest of the rise he pointed, "It's there. See it?"

At first Bronwyn seemed perplexed; and then suddenly she said, "It's the Inn, isn't it, Max?"

Yes—Colac Bay Inn! Let's go closer, and you'll see the sign."

"I see it—COLAC BAY INN—and there's your chair!"

"Yes, and how often I've dreamed of you while sitting there," he said, "Come up on the porch and look out and you can almost feel as if you are looking at the sea."

"Oh, Max, yes. It gives me the shivers."

"I know."

It came as a complete surprise one day when Con summoned Max into his office to announce to him, "Max, I have decided that

my work here at Fairhavens is completed and that it is time to
retire."

Taken completely aback Max hardly knew what to say. He
stumbled on his words, "Con . . . I can't believe it . . . you're too
young . . . this place won't be the same . . ."

"No, Lee and I have thought and thought, and this is what we
want to do. We'd like to spend some remaining years in Lee's home
and surroundings, closer to her children, and grandchildren."

Max declared, "It will take some getting used to! Who in the
world could take your place?"

"I've thought a lot about that. It is up the Board, but they are
open to my suggestion."

"Do you have a suggestion, Con?"

"Yes—You!" " A double whammy! Max blurted out. "I don't
know . . ."

And then there was silence.

"You think about it. Talk it over with Bronwyn. But, keep all
this confidential. Will you, Max?"

"I certainly will. Give me some time to think . . ." Max asked,
"When do you plan to retire?"

"Not for at least another month." Con replied. "Yes, take some
time, and let me know what you are thinking."

Max left the office—shaken. On the way out of the Lodge he
dropped by Bronwyn's office and said, "Plan to come up to my
cabin after dinner. We gotta talk!"

"What about?" Bronwyn seemed worried. "Can't you tell me
now?"

"Just very briefly. Con's retiring. He wants to recommend me
to the Board to take his place——can you imagine such a thing?"

"Yes, Max, I can."

That was all they had time for until after dinner when Bronwyn
very firmly convinced Max to agree to Con's suggestion. It was
Bronwyn' reference to Max's spiritual question which helped him
to see the call of Christ in Con's desire to turn Fairhavens over to
him. "Max," she said, "Don't you see that with Fairhavens under

your leadership, you can be the instrument of God, bringing Christ's love, redemption and new life to people!"

"I guess I hadn't thought of it in those terms."

"And when you think of it, that would be the ministry you were called to, wouldn't it now?" and then she added, "God calling you to a new people!"

"Bron, once again, you're God's angel in my life!"

The time came for Conrad Schneider's retirement. The staff organized a retirement party and held it in the Lodge lounge on the Sunday evening before Con and Lee were scheduled to leave for Chicago. Conrad Schneider had earned the respect and admiration of the entire staff. After Leona had joined Con, she too enjoyed the high regard of the staff. Thus, it was a time of genuine and fond farewell.

This was an especially poignant time for Bronwyn, who had become fast friends with Lee, who in one sense had been the one to have brought Bronwyn to Fairhavens. At the end of the evening after most of the staff had left the Lodge Bronwyn joined Lee on one of the couches. "I shall miss you deeply, Lee. You have become family to me."

"I feel the same. Conrad and I hope that some day you and Max will visit us in Chicago!"

"I'd like to!" Bronwyn affirmed.

Then Lee became more serious and turned to Bronwyn with a suggestion: "Now—Con and I think that you and Max would be perfect for our house here! That is, if you two will just go ahead and get married!"

Bronwyn was doubly surprised. Max had never broached the subject of marriage; and the idea of living in their house was both overwhelming and intriguing. "That would be something, wouldn't it?" Bronwyn said, "But we could never afford such a place."

"Don't be too sure. It may be easier than you think," Lee encouraged. "Con wants to talk to Max about it before we leave. I think he has a way it could work out for you. That is—if you two——"

The next day Con cornered Max and spoke with him concerning the house. "Lee tells me that she mentioned the house to Bronwyn. Did she tell you?"

"No. What about the house?"

"Oh, well it was just that we thought it would be a great place for you and Bronwyn should you decide to marry!"

"You're probably right. But, we don't have any such plans."

Con continued nevertheless, "Well, our plan is to rent it for a year. It fits our tax situation better that way. And if by then you don't want it, we'd have to sell!"

"Even so, I can't see how we could swing it," Max said.

"Max, if you get to that point, let me know, and I'll make it possible for you!" Con offered.

"That's good of you, Con. I'll let you know—if!" That ended the conversation. Max did not share that with Bronwyn.

The time came for Schneider's departure, after which the matter did not come up again. Bronwyn had moved into one of the older houses along the gulch which Fairhavens had bought from the Vermillian group. Though it suited her needs, it was minimal at best. The thought of living in Schneider's new home with Max as her husband was indeed enticing. Bronwyn wanted to talk to Max about the house idea, but was reluctant.

Soon after Con and Lee left, the Fairhavens board elected Max to replace Con. Fortunately this action met with the approval of the staff members as well.

Fairhavens thrived under the leadership which both Max and Bronwyn brought to their jobs. They, in turn, settled in to their new responsibilities happily. The Board was pleased. There was a steady stream of guests year round, some for recreation and many others for renewal.

Often during the extended daylight of late Summer evenings Bronwyn and Max would sit together on the Lodge porch, both reading. Max with his mysteries. He especially enjoyed P.D. James.

For Bronwyn her pleasure continued to be English novels of the nineteenth century. Max thought this might be her way of keeping her U.K. identity alive; and P.D. James, he mused, helped him to adopt her British background.

On one particular evening in late August when it had become too late to read by natural light, Bronwyn closed her book and took Max's hand to draw him away from his mystery so that she could suggest a walk. They walked away from the lodge and past the horse corrals, toward the mauve streaks of a spent sunset over the distant Gallatin range.

Bronwyn took Max's hand while she said, "Max, so often during the final waning of the sun my mind goes to remembering things! Most of the time—good memories; and my heart is warmed by them."

"What sort of things, Bron?"

"Oh, people—experiences—feelings I've had. Sometimes things I've read—" Bronwyn seemed reluctant to say more. But ventured, "Like now."

"You mean that something you've read is putting you into such a mellow mood?"

"Yes, Max. It's a vignette from a Thomas Hardy novel I read once. I think it was wile Duncan was so sick."

"You have me curious."

"I'll try and relate it to you, as I remember it. This scene comes almost at the end of the novel—*The Well-Beloved*. The story tells of a man and a woman who were two old friends from childhood who have been rejoined in later life, and have become close companions. They live in separate houses in the small town where they had both grown up. Apparently their renewed friendship had become a topic of local interest. It comes to the attention of the couple that the neighbors are saying things like, "Those two old timers should get married. They're always together.'"

At this point in her re-telling of the story, Bronwyn paused while both she and Max walked in silence. Suddenly she said:

"It's you and I, isn't it?"

"Yes, it is, Bronwyn!"

"Do I dare tell you the rest of it? You can guess, surely!"

"Go ahead. After all it's fiction."

"Here's what happened: As it turned out such neighborhood talk did finally convince them that they might just as well go ahead and marry, especially since it would make better sense to have only one house to maintain. And so in response to the neighborhood desire to give the local love story a completed and happy ending, the two were married–and lived happily every after!"

Again Max and Bronwyn walked in silence.

"Shall we make it truth, rather than fiction, Bron?"

"Ah, Max, the truth it shall be!"

They continued their stroll beyond the buildings under the sky at dusk. With hands clasped, their minds flooding with poignant memories. In silence they walked under the canopy of stars in the night sky, as if to an unseen altar.

Just then a satellite could be seen orbiting its way southward. They stopped to watch, this time together.

"It's a sign, Bronwyn!"

"A sign of God's will. Isn't it?"

"Yes, finally, a sign to me!" Max said quietly, as he took Bronwyn in his arms.

"To me as well, Max Ritter!" she whispered looking up into his face.

EPILOGUE

In Southland on a Sunday morning in late August, baby lambs were cavorting in the green paddocks. Spring was in the air. An early morning rain had freshened the landscape; and now the northern sun was illuminating the distinctive blue of a New Zealand sky. Inside the church in Riverton the organist was playing her prelude for worshipers taking their seats in the pews. She had chosen a version of Bach's "Jesu, Joy of Man's Desiring."

A world away at that very moment an organist in the Mill Creek Church was playing "Jesu, Joy of Man's Desiring" for those who had gathered to witness the wedding vows of Maxwell Ritter and Bronwyn MacKenzie. Patches of yellow had begun to turn in the Cottonwoods along the Yellowstone.

A touch of autumn was in the air. The morning had been crisp, but now in mid-afternoon on a Saturday in late August, the sun was high in the brilliant blue sky over the Absaroka's.

The Fairhavens staff were seated in the sanctuary. Anna Vermillian had come and was sitting with Connie Dexter. Dale and Maude Kober had driven over from Tipton that morning. Most touching of all, Con and Lee had returned to "give Bronwyn away."

After the pastor's final words: ". . . both now and in the life everlasting—Amen," the newly married couple kissed and walked down the aisle to Purcell's "Trumpet Voluntary." Everette and Jackson ushered the people out of the church; and in front the air was filled with joyous celebration.

After a reception at Fairhavens Lodge, Max and Bronwyn drove up into Yellowstone Park to the Lake Hotel. That night with a full moon casting shimmering silver streaks across mottled reflections on the black waters of the Lake, Bronwyn and Max, one now in spirit, mind and body, slept in each other's arms.

A world away, the waters of the Pacific rolled gently into the bay reflecting orange and pink streaks from the sun descending behind the Inn, while guests were on their porches savoring the peacefulness of dusk on a Sunday evening at Colac Bay.

And at a place called Fairhavens the quiet repose of night had come. In one of its guest rooms Con and Lee Schneider, having seen that all was well, slept in each other's arms.

While overhead swung a tiny speck of light, traveling southward across the night sky.